"Ava's story is witty and charming."

BARBARA FREETHY #1 *NYT* BESTSELLING AUTHOR

"If you like Nora Roberts type books, this is a must-read."

READERS' FAVORITE

"If ever there was a contemporary romance that rated a 10 on a scale of 1 to 5 for me, this one is it!"

THE ROMANCE REVIEWS

"I could not stop flipping the pages. I can't wait to read the next book in this series."

FRESH FICTION

"I've read Susan Mallery and Debbie Macomber… but never have I been so moved as by the books Ava Miles writes."

BOOKTALK WITH EILEEN

"Ava Miles is fast becoming one of my favorite light contemporary romance writers."

TOME TENDER

"One word for Ava Miles is WOW."

MY BOOK CRAVINGS

"Her engaging story and characters kept me turning the pages."

BOOKFAN

"On par with Nicholas Sparks' love stories."

JENNIFER'S CORNER BLOG

"The constant love, and the tasteful sexual interludes, bring a sensual, dynamic tension to this appealing story."

PUBLISHER'S WEEKLY

"Miles' story savvy, sense of humor, respect for her readers and empathy for her characters shine through..."

USA TODAY

OTHER AVA TITLES TO BINGE

The Unexpected Prince Charming Series

Love with a kiss of the Irish...

Beside Golden Irish Fields

Beneath Pearly Irish Skies

Through Crimson Irish Light

After Indigo Irish Nights

Beyond Rosy Irish Twilight

Over Verdant Irish Hills

Against Ebony Irish Seas

The Merriams Series

Chock full of family and happily ever afters...

Wild Irish Rose

Love Among Lavender

Valley of Stars

Sunflower Alley

A Forever of Orange Blossoms

A Breath of Jasmine

The Love Letter Series

The Merriams grandparents' epic love affair...

Letters Across An Open Sea

Along Waters of Sunshine and Shadow

The Friends & Neighbors Novels

A feast for all the senses...

The House of Hope & Chocolate

The Dreamer's Flower Shoppe

The Dare River Series

Filled with down-home charm...

Country Heaven

The Chocolate Garden

Fireflies and Magnolias

The Promise of Rainbows

The Fountain Of Infinite Wishes

The Patchwork Quilt Of Happiness

Country Heaven Cookbook

The Chocolate Garden: A Magical Tale (Children's Book)

The Dare Valley Series

Awash in small town fabulousness...

Nora Roberts Land

French Roast

The Grand Opening

The Holiday Serenade

The Town Square

The Park of Sunset Dreams

The Perfect Ingredient

The Bridge to a Better Life

The Calendar of New Beginnings

Home Sweet Love

The Moonlight Serenade

The Sky of Endless Blue

Daring Brides

Daring Declarations

Dare Valley Meets Paris Billionaire Mini-Series

Small town charm meets big city romance...

The Billionaire's Gamble

The Billionaire's Secret

The Billionaire's Courtship

The Billionaire's Return

Dare Valley Meets Paris Compilation

The Once Upon a Dare Series

Falling in love is a contact sport...

The Gate to Everything

Non-Fiction

The Happiness Corner: Reflections So Far

The Post-Covid Wellness Playbook

Cookbooks

Home Baked Happiness Cookbook

Country Heaven Cookbook

The Lost Guides to Living Your Best Life Series

Reclaim Your Superpowers

Courage Is Your Superpower

Expression Is Your Superpower

Peace Is Your Superpower

Confidence Is Your Superpower

Happiness Is Your Superpower

Children's Books

The Chocolate Garden: A Magical Tale

OVER VERDANT IRISH HILLS

THE UNEXPECTED PRINCE CHARMING BOOK 6

AVA MILES

Copyright March 2023, Ava Miles.
ISBN: 978-1-949092-49-3

All rights reserved. No part of this book may be reproduced or transmitted in any form by any means—graphic, electronic or mechanical—without permission in writing from the author, except by a reviewer who may quote brief passages in a review.
This is a work of fiction. All of the characters, organizations, and events portrayed in this novel are either the products of the author's imagination or are used fictionally.

www.avamiles.com
Ava Miles

*To artists everywhere
like the ones in this story.*

ACKNOWLEDGMENTS

Living in Ireland for nearly two years gave me insights I'd never have gotten from regular research. I want to especially thank a friend who told me all about the man who inspired Malcolm Coveney. As I sat at his kitchen table, I have to admit to being rather shocked by the story. But then my author mind kicked in, and suddenly I had the kind of villain you could sink your teeth into.

And lastly, to Shane, for his "shower of dumb @#%!$" comment, which I couldn't use in the book. The corresponding tale of unimaginable ineptness was just as good as his language, which is one of the most visually descriptive and charming I've ever come across. Eoghan's use of "me olde flower" comes from Shane too, and every time he called me that, a part of me delighted at the poetry, something he doesn't even realize. The whimsy of the Irish language lives on through people like him, and I must say... I hope it will always be so.

A wise heart can recognize one's soulmate in the blink of an eye.
And when that monumental moment comes, two lives are forever changed.
Such love has ripples that spread like a sweet tide over a beach,
bringing new beginnings and more magic to the world.

Those who embrace the love embrace the magic.
And it's that magic that grows into the tree of life Ireland is so known for.
Because love is the greatest magic the world over,
lifting every heart, every circumstance.

Yet some fear the love and block the magic,
for reasons all their own.
Unlike the tide breaking, those who love must stand to preserve it,
or the world as we know it will be lost.

CHAPTER ONE

Sophie Giombetti had expected a welcoming party upon her arrival in Dublin.

She hadn't expected a gorgeous man to be among them.

Her excitement had skyrocketed as they flew in over the rolling Irish hills, shaded every color of green imaginable. She could all but feel her restlessness and dissatisfaction, both personally and professionally, fly away from her as the plane thundered down the runway to a stop. When she'd decided to come to Ireland to reach a new level of artistry in her glass work, she'd known it would have personal ripples for both her and her daughter.

Already, it was surprising her.

Her daughter, Greta, grabbed her hand as they approached the security barrier and the women shouting their names and waving enthusiastically just behind it. Although Sophie had never met Ellie Buchanan in person, she felt she knew her through her father, Linc—the very man who'd convinced her to accept a residency at the Sorcha Fitzgerald Center for the Arts. The other woman was Kathleen O'Connor, Ellie's closest friend and another artist at the center, whom she recognized from photographs on the center's social media accounts. While Ellie was a stained glass artist, Kathleen's medium was metal, and she'd designed an enormous metal pirate ship sculpture for the center.

They were known to her. They were *expected*. But not so the man who stood with them—the third in their small party. He was tall and had fathomless cobalt blue eyes that captivated Sophie's attention as she wheeled their luggage toward them. Although both Ellie and Kathleen were married, she'd seen photos of their husbands—he wasn't one of them.

She loved using blue glass in her installations to convey calm and endless peace, and she saw both qualities in this man with the unruly mop of brown hair. He drew her in with his warm gaze and casual stance, hands tucked into simple gray pants that worked nicely with his white button-down shirt.

An answering warmth spread languidly through her, and her heart unfurled like a flower in the sun. She almost stopped in place to savor the feeling. She had never felt such a strong and immediate attraction to a man, not even the man she'd divorced.

Was this love at first sight?

An artist knew herself and her emotions, and Sophie knew he could be important to her if she let him.

"Mama, who is that man with Mr. Buchanan's daughter?" Greta asked in her inside voice, pausing just as the baggage claim doors closed behind them.

"He's obviously a friend to Ellie and Kathleen," she said, bending at the waist to assure her incredibly shy daughter, "so he must be nice."

She watched as Kathleen gave the blue-eyed man a playful punch, making him break eye contact with her.

She'd heard stories about Ellie and Kathleen for some time from Ellie's father. They'd been best friends for years, and Kathleen had followed Ellie to Caisleán. Their story got even more charming—they'd recently married a pair of brothers. While they were about the same height, the women couldn't look more different. Ellie had long honey blond hair and a casual style while Kathleen had short black hair and looked like a badass in all black with matching canvas hightops. Their bond was a rarity between professional artists and women, and Sophie couldn't help but envy it.

Greta looked back at the group and crossed her arms, her brown eyes narrowing as she took her time assessing them. Sophie had cultivated her daughter's skill in sizing people up. It was an ability she'd learned the importance of early in life, as the daughter of two famous—and often infamous—artists.

"He looks nice, Mama," she finally declared.

High praise, Sophie thought, glancing over to see him still smiling warmly at them. "I like the look of him too. Let's go meet everyone, shall we?"

They navigated the cordoned-off space and people hugging enthusiastically in reunions. When they reached the group, Ellie thrust out a mixed bouquet of late summer flowers from behind her back, grinning. "Welcome to Ireland! We thought you'd like flowers since you're famous for your glass flowers. Gosh, it's so great to have you here, Ms. Giombetti."

"It's Sophie, please," she said, biting her lip to contain her smile. "I'm only a few years older than you."

"Not in the artist community," the younger woman

continued, bouncing on her heels. "You've been a legend since you hit the scene at twenty-one with your 'Secret Garden' installation. I about melted when I saw it!"

"*Ellie*," Kathleen warned.

"I know, but I've been a huge fan of Sophie's—yours—for years," she gushed. "I mean, everyone is saying you're the next Dale Chihuly—"

"Okay, enough fangirling," Kathleen said, elbowing her gently. "I mean, I'd like to have her autograph too. Big fan. But we're here to welcome you and Greta. Not make you fear spending the next three hours alone with us in a car." Then she hummed the *Twilight Zone* medley, making Sophie fight back a laugh.

"It was nice of you to offer us a ride to Caisleán."

"It was easier to secure a long-term car for you locally, and it's sitting in your new driveway," Ellie said. "The center is still working out the best way for insurance—"

"She doesn't need to hear about that snore topic, Ellie," Kathleen countered. "She just arrived, and you're already talking her ear off."

"Maybe Sophie and Greta will ride with me to escape you mad lunatics and your chatter," the mystery man said with a quiet smile. "I'm Jamie Fitzgerald. Greta's new teacher. We wanted to make Greta feel welcome at her new school."

Sophie's mouth parted at the news, and then her brow shot up as he sank to his haunches to be at Greta's level. His name was familiar, and it only took a moment for it to click into place. "You're also on the board of directors for the arts center, along with your brother, Carrick, who's married to—"

"Angie Newcastle, the painter, after his first wife,

Sorcha—ah—passed away," Ellie broke in. "Who the center is named for, among other things."

Kathleen shot her a look Sophie couldn't interpret before shifting her attention back to them. "Wait until you see Angie's work in person. It's absolutely terrific."

"I can't wait," she responded, clearing her throat as Jamie's quiet gaze held hers again. "You were the only member of the board without a photo on the website."

"He's such a shy baby," Kathleen teased, reaching up and playfully ruffling his curly mop of hair. "And modest. He's also in charge of our arts program for the kids."

"I remember." She smiled as Greta looked up at her. "I'm excited about that. I can't wait to hear more."

"They're building the shed as we speak," Ellie said, miming a hammer pounding. "The Irish *love* their sheds as you'll find out. Jamie's still working on a formal plan."

"Now's not the time for those details," he said, rolling his eyes playfully at the two women. "I'm meeting my new student. Hello, Greta. I hear you're six, eh?"

"Yes, and I like it a lot better than being five so far." Her daughter pulled her tiny hand free and held it out. "It's nice to meet you, Mr. Fitzgerald. Thank you for coming to welcome me."

Then Greta smiled fully, the kind of rare smile she reserved for people she knew she could trust. Sophie clutched the luggage handles for support as he gave a heart-stopping smile back, the kind that could end world conflict, she thought. Her mind captured the moment, and her artist's eye wanted to draw its tenderness. Greta usually hid behind her when new people came around, and she'd spent most of the plane ride with her little face buried against Sophie's side. But this man had won her over in a hot second because he'd made a point of including her from the start. Getting down to her level too. Clearly they had chosen the right person to plan the arts center's program for children.

"You must be an incredible teacher, Mr. Fitzgerald."

He raised those cobalt eyes to her. "Jamie, please. Or I'll have to call you Ms. Giombetti. It would be a pity since Sophie is such a pleasant name to say."

Her heart flipped when he gave a sexy wink. Well, at least she thought it was sexy. But it had been a while, so a man's sweet attention would seem sexy to her.

"Greta, a few of your classmates made you welcome cards," he said, withdrawing a few small envelopes from his pocket and holding them out to her daughter. "You'll get to meet them when school starts, but they wanted you to know you have friends here."

Her throat caught at the thoughtfulness as Greta took them and pressed them to her chest like she would a bunch of fresh-picked flowers. "Oh, thank you! Mama, can I open them the minute we get to the car?"

"Absolutely! What a wonderful gesture. You're very kind, Mr. Fitzgerald."

"Jamie," he repeated, rising, making her aware of how tall he was. She was five-seven. She gauged him at six-two. And while he was thin, she could see the definition of muscles under his shirt. His masculinity enthralled her, and she became aware of the strong angles of his face, the defined lines of his neck and shoulders, and the sturdiness of his legs. His sexuality was understated, as quiet as his demeanor, but she suddenly felt like she was swimming in it, like smooth waters lapping on her bare skin.

The warmth in her chest changed to pressure, and she could feel something inside her gathering, tightening, ready to be ushered forth. She took a breath and paused before saying his name. "Jamie." She knew she would remember her first utterance for a long time.

He nodded crisply and then gave another showstopper of a smile. "That's the way of it. Sophie."

She felt the sound of her name and his subsequent pause all the way to her toes. Yeah, she was going to remember this.

"Come," he said, "and we can discuss the driving arrangements. I drove on my own, knowing how these two like their girl time."

"We just don't get it as much as we used to," Ellie declared, "what with Brady and Declan being around. Which is great. I mean we married them, right? But girl time is sacred."

"Sacred, yes," Kathleen said, "but Jamie's right about us talking. You might be better off riding with him, especially since Ellie's a madwoman who has dreams about driving in the Indianapolis 500."

"Do not!" Ellie exclaimed.

"Even Linc is terrified of her driving," Kathleen continued, "and he's her father."

Sophie laughed, charmed by them. "That's saying something since nothing makes Linc's knees tremble."

"Except his woman," Ellie said with a grin, stepping out of the way as an eager passenger nearly lost control of their baggage cart. "Daddy said you knew there was something between him and Bets when they visited you in Provence."

They'd come to convince her to join the arts center—and she'd been of a mind to be convinced. There'd been an electric energy between Linc and the director of the arts center. She'd noticed it at once. Lifting a shoulder, she said, "I'm a pretty quick study of human nature, like most artists. Linc texted me that he's driving up to another town on the sea an hour-plus away to buy crabs for our welcome party this evening. That's just like him."

"Daddy loves a good crab boil, and Ireland has great crabs," Ellie said brightly. "And don't listen to Kathleen about my driving. She's from Boston and wouldn't know good driving if it bit her in the—"

"Ahem," Jamie interrupted, clearing his throat.

"Right." Ellie winced. "Sorry, Greta."

"You can say butt," her daughter replied shyly. "It's the A-word you can't say."

"A-word?" Ellie asked as Sophie fought laughter.

Kathleen rolled her eyes and whispered it in her ear.

"Oh, right! *That word*. Yeah, I definitely wouldn't say that."

Jamie gave a snort. "That's not what your husband tells me. Shall we go? People are going to start hugging us in welcome if we stand here any longer, but it's better than moss growing on our feet."

"It will?" Greta asked.

He smiled down at her. "Not really. It's only an Irish saying. We have a lot of them." He held his hand out to Greta, and Sophie's heart seized in her chest when she easily took it. When had Greta last taken to someone this quickly?

"My friend Eoghan taught me some," her daughter said, "when he came to visit Sandrine. I should have said it earlier. *Dia duit*, Mr. Fitzgerald."

"That's very good, Greta," Jamie replied. "One of the best ways to say hello and goodbye in Gaelic. You know, I met Sandrine a few days ago. She told me she's taken care of you since you were a baby. Your mother too."

Sandrine had left France ahead of them with Eoghan. It was one of life's beautiful miracles that Sandrine had fallen in love with the charming man and *wanted* to come to Ireland, because Sophie wasn't sure she could do without her.

"She's Eoghan's girlfriend, you know," Greta told him with a little laugh. "Mama says it's great they've found love at their age. I think she said that because they're so old."

She winced, but it was technically true. Eoghan was ninety-three and Sandrine was eighty-two. "How about we say seasoned? But it *is* an inspiration to see people at their age finding love and now talking marriage. Did you know they've moved in together? I'm glad Sandrine came early so she could settle in. She'd never seen his home."

"It wasn't so hard for us to do things by ourselves, was it?" Greta looked at her. "Even though we *do* count on Sandrine for everything. Of course Sandrine helped Mama pack up our shipment that's coming in a few weeks. But we managed the luggage. Right, Mama? Although it weighs a ton."

"Oh, my God," Ellie said, lurching for the handle of one of the bags. "We're totally going to help you."

"Thanks," she replied, wanting to wince again, but once was plenty. "Like you said, Jamie, Sandrine has been with me since I was a kid, and my parents worked and traveled a lot. We've been inseparable, but yes, Greta, we've been managing great. And will continue to do so even though Sandrine will be living with Eoghan."

"You look almost grown up enough to live on your own, Greta," Jamie said with a teasing smile, making her daughter grin back. "You'll be driving soon too. How about I take your mother's bag, and we'll start walking to the car park?"

"That's very kind," Sophie responded, as he gently

removed her hand with a smile, the touch igniting a trail of sensation.

She watched as Jamie and her daughter walked off hand in hand, trying to still the shock of his brief touch. Goodness! She could still feel the warmth on her skin. She felt like she'd won the lottery. A handsome man who was great with kids? Ireland must be as lucky a place as people said.

"He's a wiz with kids," Ellie said as if reading her mind. "And such a great friend."

She bit her lip at the endorsement. Had she made her attraction obvious?

"Declan told me some of the kids who have trouble with their parents ask if they can run away to his house," Kathleen added, patting her heart. "It's so sweet."

She shook herself, wishing she'd had that kind of teacher growing up. "Thanks again for coming all this way."

"Please! We *really* wanted to welcome you," Ellie said, bouncing again. "I told Daddy I couldn't believe he hadn't introduced us before, especially knowing what a fan I am. Gosh, I *do* sound like a fangirl. Sorry."

She chuckled. "It's okay. The attention is always a little weird, but you two will find out for yourselves soon enough. I've seen your work online. I can't wait to view it up close. Ellie, your stained glass captures the light as if you gather sunlight into your hands as you work. And Kathleen, your 'Heartbreak' series evokes in metal the very pain of loss and betrayal in relationships." Her divorce and the collapse of her marriage had taught her a new level of agony, one she was finished with.

"She just complimented us." Ellie slumped against her friend. "OMG! I'm going to expire right here."

Kathleen gave her a goose, making the woman squeal, which caused the newly reunited group beside them to glance over and grin. "Keep it together, Buchanan, or Sophie's going to go back to Provence."

She laughed as Ellie made a face at her friend.

"Your sisterhood makes me wish I had a sister," she told them.

"Ah... Now you're going to make me get mushy," Kathleen said. "I have seven older brothers. Ellie was my estrogen godsend!"

"Yeah, we love each other like crazy," Ellie said, wrapping an arm around Kathleen. "Now we're married to brothers and are technically related in a way we never imagined. Brady and Declan can't wait to meet you. Hell, the whole village can't wait."

"Speaking of," Kathleen said. "Jamie and Greta will be in the next county if we keep talking like this."

She didn't question the rightness of it. She reached out and hugged both women. "This is the best welcome ever."

"You'll have to tell us all about your last few years in Provence," Ellie said as they started walking toward the car park.

When they reached Jamie and Greta, he was on his haunches again, talking to her on her level in front of a black SUV. Greta was still clutching her cards, a bright smile on her face. When she sighted them, she waved and ran over. "Mama, did you know there's a pony farm in our village? Mr. Fitzgerald asked if I liked animals, and when I said yes, he told me our class is going to take a trip to visit it. Isn't that wonderful?"

"Beyond wonderful," she replied as her daughter raced back to her new friend.

Wonderful was a word she'd taught her daughter straight off. As a child, her famous artist parents had thought it too banal a word to describe reality. But if you couldn't find wonder in life, why bother? Artists didn't need to suffer to be better artists. She'd dealt with plenty of misery in her marriage, and it hadn't improved her art or her life.

Every day with Franz had been a mercurial minefield—as a piano maestro, he'd gone on tour frequently, and she'd found his absences a relief. Leaving him two years ago had been one of the best decisions of her life, even though Greta was still young. Franz had never planned to be a hands-on parent, which had made the decision easier. He rarely saw his daughter, and in many ways, that had given them both time to heal.

Having put her divorce behind her, now she wanted to find a supportive community where she could raise her daughter. The quaint town of Caisleán more than fit the bill, especially since her old friend Linc Buchanan had settled there too and was playing a crucial role at the arts center. It had seemed like a further sign that Sandrine had so quickly and thoroughly fallen for Eoghan.

Being in Ireland would also breathe renewed life into her work. Ellie was right. She'd been famous for her flower sculptures since she was barely out of the Pilchuck Glass School, but she was thirty-six now. She needed a new direction for her work, like glass needed fire to melt. And she knew she would find it among the verdant Irish hills in the countryside where she would live. Her glass would breathe and shimmer like Irish rainbows.

Her initial proposal for her first glass installation was the Celtic Tree of Life, a beautiful center point for the museum the arts center planned to build. Over the next month, she would fine-tune her design to make it sing. Being here was going to give her additional inspiration—she just knew it.

The sound of Greta giggling reached her, a sound as rare as one of Greta's favorite birds, the puffin. She looked over to where her daughter was standing, talking to her new teacher with none of her usual shyness.

Jamie.

His head turned a fraction, and their eyes met. He was still listening to Greta. That she knew. But when he smiled, she knew it was for her.

Her heart expanded again, until she was sure her lungs had no room for breath.

She wanted him.

The shock of it had receded. Now there was only surprise. After her divorce, she hadn't felt a ping for anyone. It had never dawned on her she might meet a man here. Certainly not one who made her heart and body react with the kind of epic swings so powerful only artists could capture them. But she knew this was a once-in-a-lifetime chance, the kind of attraction that could define one's life—like Elizabeth Barrett and Robert Browning or Dorothea Tanning and Max Ernst.

When he finally stood, studying her, his cobalt blue eyes seemed to darken. He liked her too. There was no mistaking the signs. The slight curve of his mouth hinted at his regard. Her gaze dipped to his ring finger, looking for a wedding band, and found none. As she'd thought.

She told herself to be smart. He was Greta's teacher. She was new in town. She had a daughter to see settled. A new community to learn. Her own art installation to create.

But those were excuses for a woman who didn't know herself. Didn't trust herself.

She could not pass up this chance or this man.

But she was wiser now. She would approach it in the beginning like she would her own work. *They* would be the glass heated to perfection and then shaped with passion and tenderness. And afterward, she would make sure that whatever happened between them cooled slowly—just like her sculptures—to prevent anything from cracking or shattering.

Their love affair was going to be a masterpiece.

She would make sure of it.

CHAPTER TWO

She was here at last.
Sophie.
Her name might still be new to lips, but his heart beat steadily when he thought of her, and he had since his former sister-in-law Sorcha—now the unofficial matchmaking ghost of Caisleán—had told him a few weeks ago that he and Sophie were soulmates.

He believed it without doubt. Before and even more so now, having seen her.

Sorcha's track record was true. One by one, his boyhood friends had all found their soulmates in the women Sorcha had named for them.

He'd volunteered to be part of the greeting party for Sophie and her daughter today, wanting to be one of the first people to welcome them to their new home. Some might say he was putting the cart before the horse, but ghosts were always right in Ireland. And, indeed, he'd felt something in his very being when he first met her—the kind of slow falling a star makes through the dark sky on a cold Irish night.

She was his.

He'd felt it all the way to his bones. Her catlike green eyes had looked into him, as if she could see his very soul, and her dark brown hair and lithesome body had his hands wishing to hold her and make her his own.

His whole life, romantic pursuits had been rare and fleeting. His first girlfriend had decided his profession was not pleasing enough. Others had agreed. He was a mere teacher of young children, and with his ever quiet demeanor, apparently not a catch.

After seeing his brother find a love for the ages, not just with one woman but now a second—with his deceased wife's help, mind you—he'd thought he might simply be a man for whom great love was not meant to be. He'd tried to make peace with the prospect of a life of quiet bachelorhood like a couple of other older male teachers he knew. He'd even done his part to broaden his horizons by agreeing to help with the Sorcha Fitzgerald Arts Center and its children's program.

But hope had bloomed in his heart with Sorcha's news, and he'd wanted to see the woman she spoke of the moment she stepped foot in Ireland.

She was everything he'd hoped she might be, and he *had* to know if she was of the same mind.

The way she'd looked at him as she stood there in her loose red sweater and wide-legged black pants over matching boots had given him his answer. She could not yet know of the bond Sorcha spoke of—but she felt something.

So he didn't mind as he listened to Ellie persuading Sophie to take a girls' only joyride to the village, saying Jamie wouldn't mind the peace of his own car. She even joked that she'd let Kathleen drive despite how much *longer* it would take to reach their destination, which had caused Greta to start giggling again.

"You sure you don't mind being alone on the way back, Jamie?" Sophie had asked, her inquisitive eyes boring into him.

"We can't very well split you in half, can we, or separate you from dear Greta," he said, pleased to see her smile at his riposte.

"You shouldn't have to drive all by yourself," the little girl said, still clutching the welcome cards in her hands. "You look a little sad."

She saw way too much. The trip suddenly wasn't as bright with their absence from him looming in front of him.

"I'll tide my sorrows over our parting in the Irish way," he told Greta with a playful wink.

"How's that?" she asked, curiosity in her big brown eyes.

"By singing loud and long. I'll see you soon enough at your new house, and maybe you can wave at me while we're on the road every once in a while. Perhaps when we get to Caisleán, you can tell me what magic you saw on the drive." He loved seeing things through children's eyes as much as they liked being asked for their opinions.

"I'll watch very closely, Mr. Fitzgerald," she told him in her very serious way.

She was a classic only child, the kind used to conversing with adults. To his teacher's mind, her vocabulary and mental comprehension were a few levels ahead of her age. He'd also noticed the way she'd tucked herself against his pant leg once they'd arrived at the car park as a passenger bustling past them bid them a good day. She was shy with strangers, though not with him. His Irish heart had warmed at how easily she'd taken to him.

He supposed it should be so, what with the bond Sorcha had proclaimed might grow between him and her mother.

He glanced at Sophie one last time. Her mouth formed a quick smile, but it faded as if she too was feeling their brief parting. They'd have plenty of time to get acquainted, he assured himself as he waved and headed to his own car.

They would take their steps. Slowly. He would make himself an ally and find ways to make her and Greta's life in Caisleán easier and happier, and when the time was right, he would ask her to dinner.

He was smiling at the wisdom of his thinking as he settled himself in the driver's seat. Bringing up his favorite playlist, he started singing as he began the long drive to Caisleán. Greta did indeed wave to him from time to time, as did her mother, he was pleased to see. Yes, this was how it should be. Win them over. Let them know they could trust him.

"You've got it all planned out, Jamie, me boy."

He jumped in his seat, hands clutching the wheel, and fought a shriek. "Jesus, Mary, and Joseph, Sorcha! I'm driving! *For pity's sake.*"

She stretched out her legs—or the mirage of them—tapping her feet in time to U2's "Song for Someone" as her familiar scent of oranges spiced the car. "I miss all the times we used to have a pint and sing our hearts out at the Brazen Donkey, but a ghost shouldn't run with nostalgia. I was only dropping in to tell you a few things as we near Caisleán. You aren't going to faint, are you?"

He glared at her. "Not anymore. You've been popping in with no warning and scaring the life out of me for weeks now. Your last 'boo' had me almost cutting my face off while I shaved. But I don't feel light-headed when I see you anymore. Who could have imagined such a boon?"

Her sense of amusement hadn't changed now that she was a ghost, nor had her teasing laughter. "You should thank me for it, as you've been afraid of ghosts since you were a child."

"For good reason..."

"You needed to stop fainting so we could get down to the business of your love life. Your quiet life and sense of routine weren't serving you anymore."

He shot her a look. "I know it better than you, and it was one of the reasons I agreed to be on the board of directors and head up the children's arts program—even before I knew about Sophie and her daughter coming."

"True, and it's to your credit. But you were meant to be with someone and make a true home. I've been waiting for you to find the right woman since Carrick and I first hooked up. I was worried about you, my boy, but no more."

She gave a hearty gale of a laugh, the kind that had made her a dear childhood friend and captured his brother's heart. Losing her in a tragic car accident had decimated all of them. Nothing, not his own Irish superstition, could have prepared him for her returning as a ghost to settle them all with their soulmates, a boon she'd wanted to give Carrick's friends for looking after him when she'd died.

He wasn't ready to say it, but he was rather glad to know she was watching out for all of them, himself included. But he knew her, warts and all, and the stubborn and determined woman she'd been had become a tenacious and bullheaded ghost, God help him.

"Sophie is beautiful," he told Sorcha, "more than any photo can capture, and her little girl is as dear as they come."

"You have the right of it," Sorcha said, "but knowing

you as I do, I expect you're thinking about taking this courtship as slow as a donkey cart. Don't."

Take his time he would, so he said nothing as he navigated the narrow streets through Foxford before turning onto the N26.

"You still drive like an old woman," Sorcha chimed in as rain started to patter on the window shield.

He hit the wipers and decided not to rise to the bait. "She will love me for the patient man I am."

Sorcha played with the folds of her white dress, the very one she'd died in. Seeing her in her ethereal form still made him seasick, he realized, when he looked at her whole. He jerked his gaze back to the road.

"Indeed she will, but there are surprises and challenging times coming, Jamie. She and Greta both will need you to stand up with them. To support them and protect them when needed. To listen to them."

"Those are traits I'm well known for."

She hummed in acquiescence before saying, "It's the romancing you'll need help with, and that's why starting off with the whole *let me be your friend* play isn't going to work here. Sophie is a woman with deep passions, and you've already awakened them. Or didn't you notice how she looked at you in the airport? The fairies couldn't have flown through the air it was so thick with desire."

"Don't be an eejit," he told Sorcha, though he couldn't help but feel gratified.

"Her heart was affected, and yours was pounding in your chest," she said in that knowing tone he knew all too well. "Jamie, you must make her know you want her. Straightaway. Otherwise, she might think you only want to be her friend. You'll confuse her if you look at her one way and then offer to pick up anything she needs at the SuperValu instead of asking her to dinner."

He scoffed. "It was Tesco I was thinking of, and I think you underestimate the power of friendship between a man and a woman. I hear you women say all the time how you want us to help around the house more and do the little things."

"But we also want you to take us out to dinner, kiss us passionately, reveal your very soul to us, and make love to us until dawn." She gestured to the air. "Why is this so difficult to comprehend, I ask myself! Women understand this."

"Well, men don't," he grumbled. "All you Irish women do is complain about how terrible we are. Hanging out at the pub too much with our friends and leaving our clutter around the house."

"Don't forget about dragging muck through the house with your boots," Sorcha added.

He took a breath. "My point exactly! So we try and do things to make you happy. Like the shopping. And then you go and dump cold soup on us. Or at least that's what you used to do with Carrick. Don't think I've forgotten."

"For not texting me that he didn't plan to be home for supper because he had a pint with you lot!" She gave a little shriek. "Oh, it's a shower of dumb eejits, the whole lot of you. But God knows, I love you to death. And beyond death, as you can see," she said, gesturing to her shimmering frame.

His stomach curdled. "You enjoy making my hair stand on end."

"I've teased you since you were a boy. Why would I stop now? So, let's circle back to your plan. You *will* ask Sophie out as soon as possible. That means days, Jamie, not weeks. You understand me?"

He could feel his back going up. "You sound like my mum."

"I love your mum. Tell her hello."

"I will not! I am not telling a soul about Sophie until things are further along. Otherwise, I'll have a shower of dumb eejits poking their noses into my affairs and giving me advice on romancing when I'm already getting plenty from you."

"But I know better," she said with a laugh. "All right. Be a donkey if you want. But keep your eyes open, Jamie. Things are about to get bumpy."

She disappeared, her orange scent lingering. He rolled his window down, which did nothing to disperse it. How she managed to have a scent from beyond the veil he would never know, but Irish folklore was filled with fantastic happenings.

He turned his mind to what she'd told him. She'd made some sensible points, but he still had to do it his own way with Sophie. He could all but feel himself growing tongue-tied at the thought of asking her out. She was so beautiful. He could look at her forever and never say a word.

But if he didn't speak to her, she definitely wouldn't go out with him. Maybe Sorcha was right.

When they crested into Caisleán a short while later, Kathleen slowed down, likely to show Sophie and Greta the sights. He knew them all well, from the Brazen Donkey to the butcher store, the Last Chop.

As a kid, he'd used books as a gateway to bigger cities and other worlds, ones he'd only dreamed about traveling to. He'd always thought he would leave Caisleán for someplace bigger—Dublin maybe or even London—but a teaching position had opened up, and so he'd stayed. Besides, he loved his family and his friends. His very nature was rooted here, and like getting out of his seat at the pub to approach a woman, he hadn't been able to rip himself away from his comfort.

He still read books for the worlds they opened to him. Sophie had *seen* that greater world, and he couldn't wait to hear about her travels. Then there was her art. It was like her: somehow both delicate and powerful. He was eager to learn more about her.

As the car with Sophie and company turned onto the drive leading to Linc's former home, which was to be theirs now that he'd moved in with Bets O'Hanlon, he noticed a large black lorry with a crane idling down the road with its hazards on. He wondered if it was having mechanical issues, so he continued straight and pulled up alongside it. There was a flatbed behind it. God, it was a monstrosity.

The driver rolled his window down after Jamie made the motion with his hands. "You having trouble?"

The older man pulled his brown cap down further on his forehead before responding, "No, we were just waiting for the people at that drive you just passed to arrive. We have business with them."

He didn't like the way the man wouldn't meet his eyes. He could hear a few other men in the back of the cab, but he couldn't see them. They weren't from around here. "I'm friends of theirs and can tell them—"

"I'll follow you in then," the driver responded and promptly rolled up his window.

Jamie took a moment before turning around. Surely he was overreacting. Linc was probably having something delivered for Sophie and Greta last minute. Knowing him, he'd probably been brainstorming ways he could make his former home more female-friendly.

The women were stretching beside the car when he

reached the house, a luxurious mobile home Linc had bought and had delivered—a brilliant solution to the housing shortage in Ireland, Jamie thought. Sophie's rental car was parked in front of it.

"Mr. Fitzgerald!" Greta ran over and took his hand. "Have you seen our house and our new car? And the pasture! It's green everywhere—so many shades Mama is in artistic heaven—but that's why Ireland is called the Emerald Isle, right?"

"What a marvelous memory you have. That's the way of it exactly." He smiled at her, watching surreptitiously as her mother began to walk toward them. Ellie and Kathleen headed directly for the door of the mobile home.

My, she was beautiful, with the golds and reds of her hair shining in a patch of sunlight from above. He could quite simply look at her forever. Suddenly, he was sick of being cautious. He couldn't wait for the right time to get her alone and ask her out. He could not do so in front of Greta.

"I wish we could have driven part of the way with you," Sophie said, her green eyes direct, "but Ellie and Kathleen really didn't stop talking. Not that I mind. I love their enthusiasm. They're making sure everything is perfect inside before we get a tour."

"They're like puppies," Greta said with a wide grin. "So eager."

"Do you like puppies?" Jamie asked, casting a surreptitious glance over his shoulder as the lorry drew nearer.

"I love them! They're so cute."

He tucked that detail away. His friend, Kade, who took children out on pony rides, had two dogs and would surely bring them over for Greta to play with.

"Yer man said he has business here," he told them as the driver killed the engine and swung out.

"*My man?*" Sophie responded, regarding him with wide-eyed shock. "I've never seen him before."

"It's an Irish saying." He recalled his sister-in-law from America complaining about it. "It means some guy. Not someone you know."

"Oh."

Greta crowded closer as the driver reached them, prompting Sophie to give her little head a comforting stroke. "Honey, why don't you go ask Ellie to show you your room?"

Her daughter didn't move, and Jamie stepped closer so she could also take cover behind him.

Sophie sent him a brief smile, and he had the urge to draw her closer as well.

"Are you the owner of this mobile home?" the driver called out, playing with his cap again.

"No, that would be Linc Buchanan," Sophie responded. "But I'll be living here. We just arrived today."

The man pulled out a thick stack of papers from his coat, walked closer, and thrust them out aggressively.

Jamie stepped in front of Sophie. "Watch yourself."

"I'm not the one in the wrong," the man answered tersely. "The owner doesn't have the right permits for this mobile home. I'm here to take it."

"*What?*" Sophie's outrage carried across the yard, prompting Ellie and Kathleen to hurry out of the front door.

"That's impossible," Jamie said calmly. "I know for certain Linc Buchanan secured the necessary permits." They'd had this kind of problem before, after all, and Linc was nothing if not thorough.

"See for yourself." The man thrust the documentation against Jamie's chest and whistled loudly.

Six men exited the lorry's cab, all moving swiftly toward

the house. Ellie and Kathleen skidded to a halt next to their group, and Sophie started filling them in. Jamie didn't bother scanning the pages, sensing something crooked. He flipped to the end, looking for a signature. There was a rat, and he would have his name.

"This has to be a giant misunderstanding," Ellie moaned. "Daddy always handles things."

He found the signature three pages from the back: Malcolm Coveney.

Shit. He recognized the notoriously powerful man's name, sure enough. He hadn't realized Linc had attracted the notice of the man who considered himself as good as one of the old kings of Ireland, his modern throne being in Watertown, where his tentacles wriggled in everything from shaping people's lives to developing big-money projects he could siphon from.

"What does it say?" Sophie asked.

He slapped the papers against his knees, fighting frustration. He could try and argue with them, but he wasn't going to win. He could also try and block the road, but he feared their response. There were women and children here, and these men were the kind who might escalate to violence if challenged. There was only one person who might have enough power to prevent this, and that was the owner.

"It's a play aimed at Linc. Call your father, Ellie, and bring him over here stat."

A drill sounded, and Jamie looked over. Three men were getting to work removing the front stairs, decks, and porch roofs while the others disconnected the utilities.

Jamie had rarely seen servicemen move so swiftly. "Ellie, if there's anything inside you want—"

Kathleen took the phone from her friend. "Go! I'll call Papa Linc."

She darted in through the door, a determined look on her face.

"Greta," Sophie said, dropping to her knee in front of her daughter, whose entire frame was tight with tension. "Will you do Mommy a favor and sit in the car with your headphones on?"

She gave her a decisive nod, and Sophie saw her safely to the car and then jogged back. Jamie listened as Kathleen talked to Linc, who was still on his way home from Westport after a delay. He thought about calling his brother, but what could be done? These men had been sitting on the road, waiting for them to arrive. They intended to do exactly what they'd been sent to do. Because they'd pay mightily if they failed.

"Linc said he'd be here as soon as possible." Kathleen gripped Sophie's arm. "We're going to figure it out."

"They don't seem to be interested in negotiating," Sophie said, her gaze following their every move. "How come they got here at exactly the same time we did? I'm so confused."

"Like I said, it's a jab directed at Linc. Not you." Jamie turned away in disgust as they removed the mobile home's skirt and released the underground ties, separating it into two parts for transportation. They would be on the road before Linc arrived.

"They certainly seem to know what they're doing, don't they?" Kathleen elbowed Jamie. "Smart of them to arrive late Friday afternoon, right as things close for the weekend. I'm going to tell Ellie she needs to wrap it up. They might haul it away with her in it."

That he could not let slide. Jamie called out, "Hey! There's a woman inside. Didn't you see her?"

"Then she needs to exit the premises, doesn't she?" one of the eejits shouted back.

He locked his jaw. "These are the moments that challenge my character as a peaceable man," he told Sophie, "but I don't think challenging them will do anything but escalate the situation. I wouldn't want any of you to be caught in that, least of all Greta."

"I appreciate that, especially as the daughter of a volatile artist," Sophie said tightly. "Violence isn't the answer. Jamie, I saw your face when you got to the back of those legal papers. Who did this? You know him, right?"

"Only by reputation." He was relieved to see Ellie leave the house with a few large shopping bags, Kathleen rushing to help her.

Sophie stepped closer to him, her skin flushed red. "I know people have tried to sabotage the arts center before. If it's directed at Linc, that's probably what this is about, right?"

He thought over the nature of his response before saying, "I suspect as much, yes."

She planted her feet, the first whisper of fierceness radiating from her. "Tell me about the man who did this. This is my fight now."

"He's a bigwig operator from Watertown, a town about an hour away, who's used to getting his way. We don't have kings in Ireland anymore, but if we did, he'd put a crown on his head. He makes people's careers if they please him. He builds things. Gives permits when no one else can get them—"

"So he's a corrupt wheeler and dealer with a God complex," Sophie finished, "and he wants something from

Linc. Well, it's not the first time. Linc has been a billionaire for two decades. He knows how to handle crap like this."

"But he shouldn't have to," Jamie bit off. "And neither should you."

Kathleen and Ellie were arranging the bags in the car and talking to Greta now. Jamie watched as the six men worked the crane and lifted the first part of the house onto the trailer.

"Where are we going to live now?" Sophie asked with a harsh sigh. "Linc said the housing market was near impossible here."

Jamie took her by the arms before he registered what he'd done. A tremor went through her body and then slammed into him, the power of it like horses thundering across the pasture. "You'll stay at my house."

"What?"

He realized everything inside him was calm now. "Well, I was planning on asking you out for dinner, but it seems you need a place to stay more."

Her mouth tipped up to the right before falling away. "I would have agreed to dinner, Jamie, but we can't stay with you."

"Dinner we'll do, but stay at my house you will. Only I will be staying with friends. You and Greta will have the run of the place, I promise."

Her face softened as she stepped closer. "You must like me an awful lot, Jamie, to put yourself out like that."

His tongue knotted in his mouth as her scent washed over him, something a little sweet, something a little spicy. He wanted to pull her to his chest but fought the instinct. Now was not the time. But the time would come soon, sooner than he'd planned, thank the heavens. He should have known Sorcha had the right of it.

"I do like you a lot." He caressed her arms briefly. "That you should know straightaway, but I would never do anything to jeopardize my role as Greta's teacher or your integration into this community."

She swallowed thickly, glancing off toward Greta, who was still talking with Ellie and Kathleen, before returning her gaze to him. "Thank you for that. It's been a long time since I've had a man put me or Greta first, her father included. Jamie, I'm still not sure—"

"I am," he said, his voice full of the certainty he felt. "Think of it this way. I won't get lost coming to pick you up for our first date."

A laugh shook her frame. "All right, I'll stay there. But only for a little while, and only because I like you."

"Good," he said. "That makes two of us."

They watched as the crane lifted the final piece on the flatbed trailer. The iron arm was an eyesore in the clear late August sky. The six men worked as fast as ditch diggers during a flash flood, securing the pieces and then scampering into the cab. The lorry's engine roared to life, the brakes hissing before it began to drive off.

"Well, it was nice while it lasted," Sophie said matter-of-factly. "Now, let's talk about how we're going to help Linc kick some corrupt politician's A-word."

They were already talking like a unit, he realized, as the scent of oranges surrounded them.

Jamie gave in to the urge and drew her to his side at last.

CHAPTER THREE

Linc sized up a good life by how many friends he had, how happy his daughter was, how well his business was going, and whether his current relationship was decent or in the shitter.

Until recently, his entanglements with women had been unfulfilling and problematic. Then he'd met Bets O'Hanlon, and after their friendship had turned into a love for the ages, he was proud as a rooster.

Everything was coming up roses for once.

And, sure, little gnat-buzzing problems did arise—like the fact that he and Bets had fifty people coming over tonight, and the crabs he'd arranged to pick up hadn't materialized due to a busted boat—but he was nothing if not adaptable, and he'd grabbed every steak in the butcher shop in Westport, buying up Irish beef like he was a day trader on Wall Street.

And then he'd gotten Ellie's call about the mobile home.

Some corrupt asshole messing with him wasn't of the gnat variety. This was a buzzard, sure as shooting, and he'd just authorized the removal of the home Linc had promised to Sophie and her daughter.

Fuck.

When he arrived on his newly acquired land, all that was left of the house he'd put on it were the steps, porch, unplugged wires, and a whole host of other bits and bobs, as the Irish said. He was glad to see Jamie Fitzgerald with the women. He wondered where Greta had gone, but then he spotted a small leg in yellow tights visible through the open car door of the Audi. They'd put her inside. Good decision. A kid should never see their home taken away, and for that alone, he vowed, heads would roll.

He swung out of his Range Rover as his daughter ran forward. "Daddy, they moved so fast! Jamie didn't think it was wise to try and stop them. There were six of them. Big guys. Plus, Greta—"

Putting his arm around her, he walked them toward the group. "No, you did right. Challenging six guys with a legal notice would be reckless, especially with a child around." He sure as shooting wouldn't mention that Jamie had done right by protecting the women. They might get their backs up.

"I don't know much about legal orders," Jamie said, inclining his chin, "but the signatory was enough to quell my urge to challenge them. They came at Malcolm Coveney's behest."

Double fuck. He'd heard of him, of course.

"I'll handle it." He glanced at Sophie and gave an encouraging smile. "Sophie, darlin', I'd prefer to say something like 'Welcome to your new home,' but instead I feel like I need to apologize. Hell, this wasn't how we intended your first day to go. Is Greta faring all right?"

"She's watching one of her videos," Sophie said, shaking

her head. "You know how sensitive she is. This scared her a little, but we'll manage. The bigger question is what we're going to do about this Malcom guy."

"I say we find him and threaten to light a creative fire under his nut sack," Kathleen said with her usual bloodthirsty humor.

"That's my girl," Linc said, patting her on the back. "But what we need right now is to take some time to regroup. I can't get the mobile home back today, I expect. Besides, we have a party planned. Sophie, please don't tell me this ruined you for a good Irish party."

She made a show of shaking her head. "Please. I'm always ready for a good time with friends."

"Terrific, because we're having steak with a whole lot of delicious sides made by Bets and her friends the Lucky Charms. You'll love them."

"I thought we were having a crab boil." Ellie made a show of stirring a pot. "I was ready to throw the little suckers in."

"The boat broke down," he replied with a laugh. "Jamie, why don't you help me with Sophie and Greta's luggage. You two can stay with me and Bets until we get things settled. There's plenty of room."

"Ah, no, Daddy." Ellie and Kathleen shared a look. "You're like on your honeymoon with Bets. No one comes around before ten, and even after, everyone knocks."

Sophie coughed out a laugh before saying, "Greta and I already have a place to stay. It's all worked out."

Everyone turned to look at her. Everyone but Jamie, who was standing right next to Sophie in what Linc realized was a downright protective stance. He scratched his chin. *Well, I'll be...*

Then he smelled oranges. Sorcha. That girl. She'd

helped him and Bets get together. Seems she had plans for these two. Best news all day.

"But we were going to offer for you to stay at Summercrest with us," Kathleen said.

"*I'm* going to stay at Summercrest, if that's all right," Jamie said, clearing his throat. "I thought Sophie and Greta could have my house and a little privacy."

"Of course!" Kathleen exclaimed. "Jamie, you're always welcome. But doesn't Summercrest give you the heebie—"

He shot her a look. "The last thing Sophie needs is to see one of the guys parading around shirtless."

"Actually..." Sophie chuckled and tapped his arm playfully. "That might make me reconsider. I'm kidding!"

Ellie and Kathleen fought smiles, and Linc had to bite his lip. He could almost hear that old song playing, "Love Is In The Air."

"Sounds like it's all settled then," Linc said, refusing to be sheepish about Ellie's comment. He was having the best sex of his life, and with the woman he adored to pieces. So shoot him! He didn't plan on stopping either.

"Why don't we let you get settled at my house?" Jamie turned to Sophie directly, and it was suddenly like no one else was present. "I can pack up some things and then take you over to the party."

She touched him again, the kind of touch that lingered like raindrops on a windowpane. He touched Bets like that whenever he could.

"I say we just start the party and get to it. Greta will have an easier time if we transition directly into it. Besides, Sandrine will be there, right?"

"Yeah, she's helping Bets and the others," Linc answered.

"We'll have a great time," she declared as if her home hadn't just been unplugged and hauled off.

"You always were resilient." Linc put his arms around Ellie and Kathleen. "Come on, girls. I need help grilling up the meat. You'll ride with me."

"Sophie, you can follow me in your new car," Jamie said, laying a hand on her arm. "I'll go slow so you can learn the roads."

"Thanks, Jamie." Sophie beamed at him and then looked over at the rest of them, smiling. "I'll see everyone there."

The two of them walked away shoulder to shoulder. Linc steered the girls to his SUV and put them in the back before they could change their minds.

He was halfway down the drive when Ellie broke the silence. "I think they really like each other."

"You just getting that?" Linc drawled.

"Those were some serious sparks, if you ask me," Kathleen said with a wolf whistle. "You don't think Sorcha's involved, do you?"

A woman in white appeared between them in the back. They both let out a scream piercing enough to make his ears ring, but it was likely for the best, since they muffled his own pathetic yawp.

"You're in the know now, girls," Sorcha said, her long brown hair falling over her shoulders. "I'm counting on your help."

"You have it," Kathleen managed.

"Anything, Sorcha!" Ellie exclaimed.

"Linc?" Sorcha drew out his name in the car as he turned onto the main road.

"You know you have my support, Sorcha," he replied in all seriousness. "For anything." After all, she'd found a happily ever after for him *and* his daughter. His debt would never be paid.

"That's good, because everyone in Caisleán is about to come under attack from one of the most coldhearted, money-grubbing Irishmen out there. And he's being fed information by someone even colder than himself."

Triple fuck. He needed to find out what the Gaelic word for fuck was stat. He was going to be using it a lot from the sound of things. The money grubber had to be Malcolm Coveney. They'd be facing someone even colder?

"Who are we talking about, Sorcha?"

"The one person who wants the arts center's doors to close forever more than anything, even her own life," Sorcha answered gravely. "Bets' nemesis."

"Mary Kincaid," he answered and cursed again.

CHAPTER FOUR

Puppies made everything better.

Sophie wasn't sure if it was a law of the universe, but there was no denying their healing power. She smiled as she watched her daughter play with an adorable Jack Russell named Lucky in the corner of Bets' parlor. Jamie had asked his friend Kade to bring the brown-and-white-spotted puppy to the party. Both the pup and Kade's sweet nine-year-old stepson had befriended Greta straightaway. Now the boy, Ollie, was sitting on the floor next to his new friend, encouraging Lucky to jump off his leg and then showing Greta how to mimic the action, which she and the puppy did amidst more childish giggles.

Her daughter's transition from fear to delight had helped soothe her after the scene on Linc's land. She leaned back against the wall, still processing what had happened. Seeing Sandrine had helped, too, of course, for both Sophie and her daughter. Eoghan had pulled her aside and offered them a place to stay, but after thanking him, she'd shared her plans.

"A better man in Caisleán you won't meet," Eoghan had

said, and then he and Sandrine had exchanged a knowing look.

Her old friend had always been able to read her like a book, and apparently Eoghan was wise to her too. Yeah, she was soft on Jamie Fitzgerald.

People mingled about—a whole slew of folks who'd be her new community. She'd met everyone. After years of practice at art shows, she was usually great with chitchat and remembering names, but she found herself needing a little space in this crowd of new faces and Irish accents. She looked for the one person who had been a place of peace for her from start to finish today. He was standing in a group of people with Ellie and Kathleen and their husbands and a few other friends, his brother included. She'd been introduced to all of them earlier.

He glanced over then and their eyes locked. His mouth lifted up on the right in a sexy smile, and then he was walking toward her with a glass of whiskey in his hand.

"I'm happy she's having a good time," he said, gesturing to Greta as he joined her. "When I was a boy, I sometimes found parties like this overwhelming."

She already knew the deep baritone of his voice, tempered with his Irish lilt, a combination she found downright charming. She enjoyed the way her heart sped up at the sight of him. He had a five-o'clock shadow darkening his strong jaw, deepening the richness of his cobalt eyes. She couldn't wait to feel his stubble against her fingertips. "For me too. You were more than sweet to ask them to bring Lucky."

"When Ollie and his mom, Megan, first came to Ireland, they had puppy visits to help them settle." He rested back against the wall, whiskey in hand, so close their shoulders touched. "You and Greta could have the same if you had a mind."

She glanced over at her daughter again, who was clapping as Ollie encouraged the puppy to jump in the air for something in his hand. "We'd love that. Thank you."

"It's no bother," he said softly.

She'd heard him utter that phrase before so she supposed it was colloquial. One of the parts of travel she loved best was learning the nuances of a new place—the richness of the people and culture. She'd lived in five countries after leaving Manhattan, where she'd mostly grown up, and visited more than twenty. Her art had brought her on so many adventures. While she still loved travel, she wanted to have a home base. Needed it, for herself as much as Greta. Staying here for the next couple of years for such a large installation, her biggest yet, would be just the thing. She only hoped today's shot across the bow, so to speak, from Malcolm Coveney, wouldn't mess up her plans.

"Bets was rightfully upset about the events today." She turned her body toward him, blocking out the crowd. "She said someone named Mary Kincaid was behind it. Who is she?"

Jamie sighed richly. "Bets' former sister-in-law. Even before Bruce O'Hanlon died, his older sister's jealousy of Bets was infamous due to their yearly competition at the agricultural fair over roses."

"I can't imagine roses causing such ill will. They're one of my favorite flowers to use in my work."

"If Bets had liked cake baking, Mary would have challenged her with three layers of something dark and devious. You understand me?"

She nodded, her eyes taking in the little details of his face. He had a spattering of freckles on his nose and the thickest black eyelashes. When his mouth tipped up, she found herself smiling. "What do you think she plans to do next?"

He sipped his whiskey, the notes of leather competing with his subtle pine scent. "Cause more trouble, of course. She's a mean and vindictive woman, the kind who will cut off her nose to spite her face, if you know my meaning. I'm sick of the lot of it. We all are. But now it seems she has a very powerful man working with her."

Pushing off the wall, he faced her, his blue eyes narrowing. She could feel the intensity pouring off him in waves.

"You're safe here, and so is your child. So is your work. This community is behind you, and everyone associated with the arts center. We have an emergency board meeting set for tomorrow."

"I appreciate your assurances, Jamie," she said softly. "They must be pretty intent on causing trouble. You don't take away someone's house unless you want to send a big message."

His mouth tightened. "You're right, of course, but we'll face down whatever they throw at us. I only wish for your sake that the feud had ended."

He glanced down at his feet as if contemplating his next words carefully.

She put a hand on his arm in comfort. "What?"

He looked up, his blue eyes filled with fierce light. "Are you sure you don't want to go back to France? I don't want you to. Not at all. Only it seems unfair not to ask you. I've seen trouble like this before—for other artists—and it hasn't been easy. You're a woman who craves peace, I think."

It startled her that he could read her so well. "I had a lot of volatility growing up. Sandrine helped me find my peace until I learned to do it myself." Of course, she'd made some missteps there. She'd thought she was getting peace with Franz. He'd seemed such a quiet man in the beginning, but he'd been temperamental and dramatic—as much a narcissist as the parents she'd been desperate to escape.

He nodded after a moment. "If you went... I'd—figure things out on my end."

She didn't know what that meant exactly, but her answer was a no-brainer. "I'm not leaving because some people are trying to stop something good from happening here. Trust me, this ain't my first rodeo, as Linc would say. My father is a controversial pop artist. Think Andy Warhol and then take it a little further. My mother paints in the post-modern school and had a very controversial nudes period, which showcased people having affairs, like my father, and women having orgasms on their own. Like it's a shock we women have and like orgasms."

His mouth pursed like he was fighting a smile, but his face flushed.

"Sorry. I didn't mean to embarrass you. What I'm trying to say is that I'm the kid of two very out-there artists, so I've faced this before. People have petitioned to have my parents' paintings removed for indecency. But the most fun was when protesters threw rotten eggs at their work as well as our family when we arrived for the gallery showing."

His mouth parted before slamming shut. "But that's atrocious!"

"Yes, and that's why I sculpt flowers," she joked.

"Except you aren't doing flowers this time, right, but the Celtic Tree of Life?" Jamie waved his hand suddenly. "Forget I asked. Maybe you don't want to talk about your work."

"I'm happy to. A tree from Irish mythology shouldn't

rub anyone the wrong way, but maybe I need to add roses. Bets' roses. That might make Mary Kincaid see red, right?"

Jamie laughed. "I like your fighting spirit. But the thing with the eggs couldn't have been easy as a child."

She glanced over at Greta. Ollie was teaching her how to encourage the puppy to jump, and her daughter's sweetheart face was scrunched in concentration. She was still so innocent, so small. "No, it wasn't. Which is why I get the heebie-jeebies when I think about exploring other themes with my art, even though I want to break out more."

"Like with what?" he asked softly.

Before now, she'd only spoken to Sandrine about this, but it felt natural to confess the truth to him. "The female form. In glass. I've always secretly been drawn to my mother's more sensational paintings. It would be fascinating to bring something like that to life in glass. I happen to think women's bodies are beautiful."

"You aren't wrong there," he answered after a moment.

She met his heated eyes before looking away. "But I don't want Greta to get egged because of my work, even though it outrages me that anyone would try to suppress artists. I feel like a hypocrite sometimes. Crap, how's this for honesty. I sometimes feel like saying to a reporter, 'Hi, I'm Sophie Giombetti, the nicest artist in the art world, who's totally scared of controversy.'"

Suddenly it struck her hard that she'd landed smack-dab in the center of one despite having done nothing to rock the boat. No, she'd played it safe like she always did.

And yet, she wasn't running. In fact, she'd known this arts center had faced some pushback from members of the local community. Had she decided in the back of her mind to face her fears at last? She felt a tremor go through her body.

Jamie didn't ask questions—he simply extended his whiskey to her. Their hands touched as she took it from him. His eyes held hers while she drank, aware that his lips had touched the very glass she was now touching herself. The intimacy made her belly tighten with desire, and it was as luxurious a feeling as when her glass started to turn liquid from the heat.

"How old were you when you were egged?" he asked.

She lifted her shoulder. "Ten. I want to be brave and say it doesn't bother me anymore, but the truth is I can still smell the rotten eggs. Feel them hitting me. I know it's a mind trick, but it's there. And I can still see that disgusting yellow-green gunk staining my favorite cherry-red dress. We had to throw it out, of course, and part of me wants to say, *Get out the little violin, Sophie. You could afford another dress. No biggie.*"

He closed his hand around hers. "Except it was a biggie, as you say."

His quiet certainty was as calming as his honest gaze. "Yes, it was. Tell me more about you and your interest in art. You clearly want the local children to have access to art classes or you wouldn't be heading up that project."

"Every child should have access to art if they want it." He smiled then.

"I couldn't agree more. I'd like to help if I can."

His chest lifted with a deep breath. "I'd like that very much."

They fell silent, doing nothing but staring at each other. Everyone else's voices faded to the background, and all she could see was his face, his cobalt eyes shining brightly. Her heart beat steadily in her chest and her belly turned liquid. She wanted to touch him. Have him touch her. She looked at his lips, noting how the one on the bottom was fuller, richer.

Then he shook himself like a dog coming in from the rain. "But I'm monopolizing you from everyone else. I'm—"

"I don't mind." Her voice turned shy. "I attend a lot of parties with work, but I prefer to be the one in the corner with someone I know or a new friend."

He took his glass back and drank. "I'm glad it's me tonight."

"Me too." She laid her hand tentatively on his chest. "Jamie, I'm really glad to be here."

His free hand tucked her hair behind her right ear. His touch was also tentative, but the simple caress still sizzled like party sparklers. "I feel compelled to say it. If you really want to expand your art, we're behind you. I would make a grand rotten egg shield, I think, but I would recommend an easier way. Checking people's bags before entry."

She'd always wondered why the gallery hadn't thought of that. Then again, maybe they'd been okay with the controversy right up until it damaged the art they were exhibiting. Controversy caused discussion. Discussion sparked disagreements, which newspaper articles loved to report on. Press helped increase a work of art's value.

Art played its own games.

"I want to expand," she admitted, "and I'd been planning to give it serious thought while making the Tree of Life. Now I wonder if it's too tame. I was going for something beyond my normal. Flowers. But it's not really outside the box, is it?"

"I'm sure you'll figure it out," Jamie said in that deep voice. "And if you want to talk it out with someone, I'm here for you. In any way you need, Sophie."

The last phrase had her imagination going haywire. Fire

licked its way up her thighs, and she was sure her face was heating. "Good to know. And thank you."

He pressed the glass into her hand. "No thanks necessary. I'll go find us another whiskey. I'm going to swing by to see if Greta needs anything, too, if that's all right with you."

Shock stuck in her throat before she said, "That would be great. I'll just stay here." She could use a moment to herself.

Nodding, he headed over to her daughter, who smiled up at him and showed him how Lucky could jump. His endearing grin got to her. My, she was already in deep waters with Jamie Fitzgerald.

Her gaze averted to Bets, who'd walked over briskly, as though she'd been waiting for an opening, and taken Jamie's place against the wall. "I see you and Jamie are getting along."

"He's been nothing but solid."

"That he is." She worried her lip. "Sophie, I'm so sorry about today. I have half a mind to beat on Malcolm Coveney's front door first thing tomorrow morning, but Linc told me we need to be smart and not go off half-cocked. Despite how ready I am for a fight."

The orange-haired woman rapped her fist into her other palm, looking fierce despite her petite frame of five-three. Sophie had liked her from the moment they'd met in Provence. It had been enough that Linc thought the world of Bets, but Greta had shot it to the moon when she'd taken to the mother of three grown boys like a candy wrapper to candy.

"I hate to admit Linc is right," she continued. "We've called an emergency board meeting to talk about strategy, and Linc's going to call Malcolm tomorrow and shake the bushes."

"Tell him to watch for the snakes falling out." Then she grimaced. "But Ireland doesn't have snakes, right?

"Only the two-legged kind," Bets said with a roll of her pale blue eyes. "I wanted to tell you not to worry, but who am I kidding? They took your home away. Are you sure you don't want to stay with us? I'd happily put you in one of the cottages, but Linc doesn't think you'd like the spiders."

She fought a full-body shudder. "He's right. Greta wouldn't— No, Jamie was kind enough to offer, and we shouldn't have to displace him for long."

"No." The older woman clanked the ice in her cocktail, something pink and fruity. "We'll have it sorted out shortly."

She didn't sound convinced. Truthfully, neither was Sophie.

"It's important to stay positive," she said in her best mommy voice.

"As my son, Liam, likes to say, 'a negative mindset only breeds more negativity.'"

"Like mold," Sophie offered lamely. God, they were both trying too hard.

Bets winced. "We Irish have plenty of mold from the damp. Anyway, I'm taking my positive mindset off to let you mingle. We're glad you and Jamie are fast friends already, and we're even more glad you and Greta are here."

"So are we."

She watched as Bets strode off with her usual determination. Fast friends, eh? Well, that was one way to describe it. With an over-the-top, out-of-the-ballpark attraction. Funny, she wasn't bothered that people were talking about them.

She needed some of that daring in her art. The very act of telling Jamie she'd been thinking about taking chances in her art felt like it had opened the door. Funny, the Celts believed trees themselves were doors, gateways.

Her palms started itching, wishing for her notebook so she might draw her Tree of Life. Look into its center, the gateway. See what was standing inside it—the new addition to her work that would take her to the next level she'd been craving.

A sudden peace came over her. It was past time for her to challenge herself—beyond what she'd been imagining—and let her work grow. These people would be behind her. No one was a fiercer proponent of the arts than Linc Buchanan, and this community would back her up. The same could not be said for every community. Some places caved due to public pressure. Some museums or art institutes caved because their grants were going to be pulled or donations would go down. That wasn't an issue here.

Why wouldn't she take this opportunity?

Jamie had gotten caught up talking to someone, she noted, and as she wandered over to play with Greta and her puppy, the thought spun in the back of her mind. Her daughter's ongoing giggles and new kinship with Ollie Donovan needed no interruption, so she mingled like she knew she should. Ellie and Kathleen were eager to include her as they rested against their handsome husbands. She met Liam O'Hanlon, Bets' son, and decided he could inspire a pirate portrait, what with the gold earring in his left ear. Jamie finally appeared, bringing her the whiskey like he'd promised, and then his brother and sister-in-law joined them. Within seconds, he was holding his new niece, Emeline, who cooed sleepily at him with her big blue eyes.

Blue eyes must run in the Fitzgerald family, although Jamie's brother, Carrick, had eyes that were more Payne's grey than cobalt. His wife, Angie—the American painter who'd been one of the arts center's first teachers—had an infectious sense of humor, and they spoke about her recent pregnancy and birth as well as her nudes. She made painting them sound so easy and fun—nothing like the angst that had driven her mother's painting. Then again, some of her mother's most famous nudes had been inspired by her volatile marriage with Sophie's father and a Ferris wheel of betrayals.

Suddenly the door opened in Sophie's mind and she could see what was in the center of a tree. A goddess. Happily pregnant with child. And she was nude.

Her mind started doing somersaults. Yes. What was more beautiful than a nude woman pregnant with child?

Sophie had always thought she'd been her most beautiful when carrying Greta. She used to embrace her round abdomen and send all her love to the baby inside her. Every child should be so loved from the start, and so often it was not the case. She hadn't been, she knew. Her mother had seen her as an interruption to her work and still told stories about how challenging it had been to paint with a large belly.

She mulled it over as she sipped her whiskey. Her art had always been about spreading beauty and magic and love. This would go further and say more. What could be more natural than a pregnant woman nude? In glass?

Excitement raced through her veins like quicksilver. This piece would say something she'd held inside her a long time and in her way.

"You're somewhere else."

Jamie.

She looked over to the right to find him watching her with a warm smile. "I had a flash of inspiration. I'll need to think it through. The dimensions. The angles. Heck, the colors. Oh, stop me! I'll talk your ear off."

"Talk away, but perhaps we should get you and Greta settled at my home. It's getting late and I wasn't sure if she needed a bath or..."

Right. His home. Yes, that's where she was going. "Good idea. Let's make our excuses." God, she was acting like they were a couple. "I'll meet you outside in fifteen."

He bit his lip like he was holding back laughter. "Or you can just start walking to the door. I'll follow."

"Oh." Was it that easy? Her ex had always insisted on setting a timeframe for such things. But then again, he was an exacting man, more anal than a red-butted baboon.

"But I doubt you'll be leaving in fifteen, Sophie." His grin was contagious. "We Irish like to linger."

Turned out he was right. Every time she stopped to say goodbye to people, they'd start to tell her a story, none funnier than Brady McGrath. Ellie was a lucky woman for sure. Then Sandrine had wanted to fuss over her, Eoghan fussing right along with her. When she finally started walking toward the door, hand in hand with Greta, the puppy managed to jump out of Ollie's arms and race over, barking in little pips. Jamie just scooped the puppy up and took him over to Kade, who clapped him on the back. He had a knowing grin on his face, almost like—

She turned back around. Everyone *was* watching them leave—together—wide smiles on their faces. She found herself smiling back, her cheeks flushing slightly.

The late August night air was cold, much cooler than it was in Provence at this time of year. As she and Greta followed Jamie down the narrow roads, she paid attention to driving on the left side. His house was only six minutes from Bets', and for that she was grateful. She was starting to feel the effects of the day.

The front porch light was on, and it showed a nice cottage painted white, like it seemed all the houses were painted in Ireland. One story, it boasted a single navy blue door and three big windows, two to the right and one to the left. There was a small garden, and she could smell the roses as they headed up the sidewalk.

"My mother's work," he said, gesturing to the plants.

"Maybe we can pick some roses for a vase tomorrow," Greta said, walking slowly as she took things in.

"My table would be the better for it," he said, opening the front door and turning on the lights. "I'll make sure to give you a key, although I never lock it. You might prefer to if it's your habit."

"It is," she said, smelling fresh laundry and a trace of pine as she stepped inside with Greta.

"I'll grab your suitcases," he told her.

"I can—"

"Make yourself at home."

Greta let go of her hand immediately and started to explore. Sophie couldn't deny she wanted to do the same. She was struck by the photos of him and his family and friends on the bookshelves to the right of the woodstove as well as the mountains of books, some paperbacks, some hardbacks, not in any order. She made out names she knew —Patterson, Silva, and Brown—and ones she didn't— Dunnett, Gillespie, and Johansen.

A jar of sea glass in red, blue, orange, and white made her smile, as did the painting on the wall of a man reading a book under a lone tree in a pasture dotted with sheep. Angie's work, she noted, seeing the signature in the corner. The subject could only be Jamie. Angie had captured the lines of his body and profile well, but it was the calm he radiated that identified him. He didn't seem isolated in the scene. He seemed one with the world.

"Can I pick it up?" Greta asked, wandering over to an adorable stuffed sheep resting on the plain blue couch.

"You can touch anything you want," Jamie said, appearing with their suitcases. "I keep that sheep here for my niece. Her name is January because that's when the first lambs are born for the year. You'll love the lambing season. Even though I'm an adult, I still smile when I see lambs leaping atop the green hills."

Greta picked up January and clutched her to her chest. "Oh, I can't wait to see. Mama, can I sleep with January?"

She glanced over at Jamie, the intimacy of being in his home stealing around her. Her heart drummed in her chest as they gazed at each other.

"If your mother approves, I'm all for it," he said after she nodded. "If she's like my mum, anything she says goes."

"Yeah, it's pretty much like that," Greta answered, making Sophie laugh.

"Come on, sleepyhead. We'll do a quick bath and then tuck you into bed."

"I thought the room I'd created for my niece would do." He pointed to the closed door behind her. "I figured Emeline might like a place to rest her head and keep some things when she visits her favorite uncle."

Her heart squeezed with the tenderness of the gesture.

He showed her the bath, a simple tub and toilet, and told her the other bathroom down the hall had a shower. Then he showed her a switch for the immersion heater, something she needed to turn on if she planned to take really long showers. That was new, but she nodded, wondering how *long* was defined. She vowed to take brief ones and never find out.

He showed her to another bedroom, one decorated with a simple white end table, lamp, and a white *full-sized* bed. Wow. She hadn't seen a bed that small in... Their eyes met and lingered before he excused himself. Her mind brought up a wild fantasy of them on the bed, his body moving deeply in her, and she wondered if he had a bigger bed than this one. Not that she would have sex with him around Greta.

Was she already seriously thinking about sex with him? This soon?

Yes, she was.

Epic for her. She'd always been careful in her love life. Her father had been divorced four times and her mother had carried on many tumultuous love affairs after her parents' divorce, so she knew firsthand the emotional cost of such things. She'd never gone to bed with a man as a reaction to life events or an inspiration for great art. And she'd waited long enough to make sure the man would stay around. Of course, that strategy hadn't worked out in her favor.

Wanting someone this soon and following through with it was new territory for sure, but it didn't feel wrong. She rubbed her belly. Yeah, it felt way too right.

She found Greta in her room, clutching her stuffed sheep next to a twin bed covered charmingly in flowers. "How about you grab your jammies while I say good night to Mr. Fitzgerald?"

"I want to say goodbye too," Greta told her.

"Okay," she said and followed her daughter down the hallway to the kitchen.

He was staring into the open refrigerator and looked up

guiltily. "There isn't much here. I'll drop some things by in the morning if you make me a list."

"We'll be fine," she assured him. "Sandrine probably had the fridge stocked at the mobile home. She'll—"

He only raised his brow and crossed to the counter to grab up a notepad and pen. Rather than insisting on doing the task himself, he gave them to her.

Something about the way he handled it made her agree. "All right."

"Thank you." He shut the refrigerator and showed her where the coffee was—instant—and the tea bags, something called Lyons. His cabinets were fairly bare—pasta, a jar of sauce, and O'Donnell's potato crisps—but then again, he was a bachelor. Whoa! Wait. She walked to the cabinet and pulled out the bag of crisps. She stared at the brand. The crisp maker's brand was a tree of life design. That was a little freaky, but maybe it was a sign. She believed in them.

When she finished jotting down a few staples they would need, she found Jamie in the parlor with Greta. He was down on one knee again, at her height. That made her smile.

"I hope you have a nice time with your friends, Mr. Fitzgerald," Greta said. "Thank you for letting us stay at your house."

"You're welcome. You and January are going to have sweet dreams tonight. Night, angel."

Sophie watched him, her heart expanding, and their eyes met as he slowly rose, one long line of masculinity. "I'll walk you out," she offered. "Greta, jammies."

"Yes, Mama." She waved a final goodbye as they stepped outside.

Sophie left the door cracked but turned to look at Jamie in the harsh porch light. He had rugged angles to his face, the kind the artist in her wanted to draw, the kind the woman wanted to trace with her fingertips.

"I really don't know how to thank you."

"I told you there's no need for thanks." He shifted to block the glare from hitting her in the face. "You'll stay as long as you need. As long as you want."

The last part seemed laden with emotion. She swallowed thickly. "And clever you for knowing where to pick me up for our first date. When were you thinking that would be?"

He took a step closer, and this time she could see his eyes. "I know you'll need someone to watch Greta."

"Sandrine will still be helping—"

"And then I got to wondering, with you two so newly arrived, if you were worried about being parted from her," he continued, his mouth a serious line now.

"For a few hours?" she asked in shock. "God, I hope not. Wait! Is that a trick question? Like a bad mother question?"

"Not at all." He shifted again, the light playing off his face. "I want to ask you out tomorrow night, but—"

"Perfect! You can pick me up at seven after Greta's bath. Sound okay?"

"Sounds grand." He took her hand, and she was struck how much bigger it was than her own. "Sophie, I'm— I'm really glad you're here."

The near stutter was downright romantic. She impulsively leaned up and kissed him on the cheek. "That's for everything so far. Good night, Jamie."

"Night," he said softly before wandering off into the night.

She waited until she was inside to wrap her arms around herself and close her eyes.

The last person she'd fallen for was Franz, and that was

so long ago it was like it had happened to someone else. Divorce did that to a person. It stripped away all the good memories unless you sifted through the rubble for them.

But that feeling was back and bigger than ever, like the sun as it rises over the ocean at dawn. She'd wondered since she was a kid why it looked so much larger in the morning, but that was how it felt in relationships. There was so much promise in the beginning. Everything seemed bigger and more beautiful.

She wanted it to stay that way.

CHAPTER FIVE

Luck was on his side.

No one was at Summercrest when he arrived, the old manor so dark and creepy, his arms broke out in gooseflesh. His friends were obviously still enjoying themselves at Bets' house, no notion of coming home yet. He reminded himself he would be staying at a place that had terrified him since childhood for a good cause. But as he neared the door, something white flashed in front of him out of nowhere and yelled, "Boo."

He staggered backward, stepping off the sidewalk and nearly losing his balance. He clutched the bag he'd packed to his chest as stars danced in his vision. "Dammit, Sorcha!"

"But you didn't faint," she said, laughing. "I think you're officially cured. Now, I'm here to show you there's nothing to be scared of here."

He glared at her as he set his feet. "Your sense of irony stinks."

"And I wanted to congratulate you on asking Sophie out as fast as a March hare." The front door suddenly opened unbidden. "Come inside."

How she'd managed that, he didn't want to know. He remembered that used to happen here when he was a kid—doors opening unbidden, the flickering of candlelight inside even though no one lived there, and the feeling of someone touching his shoulder as he stood terrified in the courtyard, waiting for his friends to return after he'd fled to what he'd hoped was safer ground. "You're not making this any easier, you know."

"Well, turn some lights on, silly," she chided. "*I* opened the door."

He almost walked back to his car. He could stay with Carrick and Angie, but that would be cowardly. He could do this. Sorcha was the only thing he could see inside the manor's pitch-dark hall before he flicked on the lights. "You could be an exhibit for a school showing. Why do you glow in the dark?"

She glanced down at herself. "I honestly don't know. The light I'm made of is different than you maybe. But we're losing focus. I'm proud of you for offering up your home. Everyone knows what a homebody you are, Jamie."

He fought a sigh. "It won't be for long."

"But school starts on Monday, and you'll be staying in a house with a bunch of night owls. How are you going to manage to go to bed at nine o'clock like your usual?"

He started for the stairs. "You're trying to get my goat, and I won't let you. Now why don't you pave the way to my room and let me go to bed?"

"Bed? Some would have gone back to the party, but not you." She floated up the stairs with him, no whisper coming from her feet. "I admire your dedication to your routine, but you're going to have to give a little. Growth is good for you, Jamie. Being a recluse isn't. You've been burrowed down in your little den like a fox. Shaking things up will make what you're facing easier."

He turned left at the top of the stairs. Before leaving the party, he'd asked Declan which bedroom to take. He'd been directed to the room all the way at the end—two doors down from Liam should he need to call for help, his friend had added with a nearly straight face.

His footsteps echoed down the hallway. He tried not to remember that the old manor used to have a dungeon, which Liam had converted into a meditation room after Declan bought it and set to remodeling. For a moment, he could have sworn he heard the rattling of chains. He swung his head to look at Sorcha.

She lifted her hands. "That's just your imagination."

He paused outside his bedroom door. "How did you know what I heard?"

"I can read minds now." She smiled grandly, enjoying herself. "There's no ghost but me here."

Pushing the heavy door open, he held his breath, but all he saw was a full bed, a wooden nightstand, and a nicked-up dresser. Simple enough. He threw his bag on the stone floor and faced Sorcha. "You can go now. I'm locking the door behind you."

"I can walk through doors, Jamie." She plopped down on the bed. "Tell me about your plan for the date."

"I thought maybe McAllister's Tavern."

She clapped. "Well done. Another haunted castle with a nice restaurant. And your plan for the children's arts program?"

He narrowed his eyes at the haunted comment, since surely she'd know, and then decided to ignore it. "I'm still researching. The shed will be finished—"

"Next week, should everything go as Liam hopes." She

crossed her legs. "It will. Jamie, you need to move fast with setting up the program."

A quiver ran through his belly. "There will be more problems?"

"After today, yes." She sighed and stood. "Ask Sophie for help. It's a nice way for you two to get to know each other better. Besides, you'll need to work together to defeat what's coming."

His insides rolled with those words. "You're just full of bright news, aren't you?"

She wandered over to him, her face grave. "Jamie, after what you witnessed today, how could you imagine otherwise? But you'll weather it. Sophie will find the daring she's repressed, and you'll find a louder strength. Although not as loud as Carrick, thank God."

They both chuckled at that.

"I'll let you settle in. I hope you brought earplugs."

"Why?" he asked as she blew him a kiss and disappeared.

He found out a few hours later when he awoke suddenly to a loud banging on his door. "Jamie! Are you asleep?"

Brady's voice mixed with the rumblings of a few others. Picking up his watch, he groaned at the hour. "It's after midnight. Of course I'm asleep!"

"Open the door!" Declan barked. "We want to ask about your new girlfriend."

In the past, his friends had both teased him and worried over his lack of a love life. Maybe he'd find their interest touching at another time, but he knew if he opened that door, they'd all be in his room for an hour like flies on horses. Brady probably even had a bottle of whiskey in hand. "I need my rest. I have a date tomorrow night."

A cheer went up outside, and then Brady said, "Let's have a drink to celebrate!"

He couldn't help but smile. "Not on your life. You eejits take yourselves off to bed. I'm going back to sleep."

Someone booed him like he'd missed a goal in a football game. "You're missing out," Ellie called sweetly.

"Sleep well, Jamie, boy," Declan said after banging the door once more for effect. "We told the ghosts to leave you alone."

"Don't say that to him," Liam responded. "You know how it creeps him out. Jamie, I cleared the negative energy from this place. You've nothing to fear."

"Except us if you don't come out for a drink," Brady called.

He stuffed a pillow over his head. Tomorrow he really would buy earplugs. It grew quiet as his friends' footsteps slapped against the stone and faded away along with their conversation, thank God. He slammed his eyes shut and willed himself back to sleep. His date with Sophie wasn't the only reason he needed to be well rested. Linc had told everyone to be ready for an emergency board meeting tomorrow, the time TBD, and he and Donal had a few calls to make beforehand.

When his alarm woke him at seven, he opened his eyes and experienced a moment of disorientation. Then it clicked. Summercrest. *Sophie.* He needed to buy her groceries. A smile broke over his face. He would see her and Greta this morning, even for only a moment. But it would be enough. The best way to start his day.

He slipped into the bathroom across the hall and showered quickly, shaving while he bemoaned the increasingly cold water. He'd have to ask where the immersion heater was located and plan better next time. Dressing quickly, he cleaned up after himself and picked up his bag. When he opened the bathroom door, Liam was standing casually in the hallway without a shirt on, wearing loose white pants, his feet bare.

"Glad you didn't feel you needed to dress up to greet me."

Liam laughed. "I was off to meditate but heard you opening the door. Thought I'd see how you fared on your first night at Summercrest."

"Besides you eejits waking me up at midnight? Fine. I'm buying earplugs today in case you decide to try again tonight after my date."

"We're all happy for you, Jamie." Liam put his hand to his heart. "Seriously."

He nodded. "It's only just begun, but she's here, and she's of the same mind. That's all that matters right now."

"Dare I ask if you've seen Sorcha?" Liam arched his brow. "Smelled oranges around Sophie?"

He gave Liam his best teacher look. "If I say either way, you eejits will be all over me. Even more than you already are. I just want to enjoy our next steps."

Liam patted him on the back. "Then enjoy them. And if you need anything, you know where to find me."

Was he offering dating advice? Out of all of them, no one had dated more than Liam. "I'll find my way, but thanks. Liam, I did want to ask about the shed for the kids. You're sure it will be finished on time?"

"That's the plan."

Jamie remembered Sorcha's words. If she said they needed to rush, then so they did. "If I ordered some furniture, would your guys be able to set it up?"

"Of course." Liam tilted his head to the side. "You in a hurry suddenly? That's not like you."

He cleared his throat. "I... We might want to move forward a little more quickly after what happened with Sophie's house."

Liam was quiet a moment. "More trouble is coming? Of course you won't say who told you, but I've felt something brewing. Was going to meditate on it this morning."

Jamie didn't fully understand what that meant, but he knew Liam knew uncanny things sometimes. "Hold good thoughts for us."

They held each other's gaze, decades of friendship palpable. "Always. I left something in your room, by the way, for when you might need it. I thought it would save you figuring it out for yourself. I'll see you later, Jamie."

"Ah, thanks... Mind yourself."

He watched as Liam padded down the hallway. Jamie strode into his room with curiosity. Scanning the room, he spotted a box of condoms on the nightstand. His heart gave a little lurch. It was *very* early to be thinking along those lines, but Liam had been thoughtful, knowing he'd have to drive over an hour away to slip into a pharmacy where he wasn't known. Being a teacher, he was careful of his reputation. Not that he bought condoms often. It had been...way too long ago.

He stared at the box. Was it too early to put some in his wallet? He rubbed the back of his neck, his thoughts widely scattered toward lust and being a gentleman. He was an eejit. He grabbed a few and tucked them away before hiding the box.

Cheeks a little flushed, he found his keys and headed out. The air was cool, and the dark clouds foretold rain. Summer was all but over, the weather was saying. Terrific. They'd barely had ten days of sun this month. The Yanks spoke about how hard it was to get used to the lack of sunlight. Even the Irish complained about the weather. He hoped it would improve for Sophie and Greta.

He located her grocery list, his fingers tracing her handwriting. She used cursive, its elegant form fitting for her. He was glad the Irish schools continued to teach it. Many American schools didn't, and he thought it a shame, valuing it not only for its beauty but for what it did for a child's brain development.

What kinds of art could they teach that would enhance a child's brain? Maybe this was the approach he needed to create a sound plan for their program. Bets had talked about mission statements and Linc about vision. While he'd done plenty of research of his own, he hadn't been happy with his scribblings. He'd been stuck on levels of minutiae like class size.

Details. He was good there.

When he'd talked to Angie about the arts programs she used to run as the director of an arts center in Baltimore, she'd told him a bit about programs focused on particular skills. Kids could hand build ceramics, for example. That would teach them to build shapes, but it would also foster hand-eye coordination, problem-solving, and creativity. The latter was the hardest to teach, if you asked him.

As he made his way into Caisleán and shopped for Sophie's list, he gathered together other ideas and questions about the children's program.

When he pulled into the driveway of his house, Greta waved to him from the front window in a long-sleeved red top lined with yellow flowers over navy corduroy pants. In her other hand, she was holding up January, the sheep, a sight that touched his soul. Sophie opened the front door as he exited the car and popped the boot for her groceries. He tried not to stare, but saints preserve him, she looked beautiful in a light green sweater and jeans that fit her long, slender legs.

"Morning," he called out as he walked toward her with the bag. "Hope you two settled in all right."

"Good morning. We did great, although the wind gave a howl last night that woke me out of a dead sleep."

"Mama said she couldn't believe I slept through it," Greta said, joining her mother at the front door. "I think January helped me. Good morning, Mr. Fitzgerald. The weather is crazy. Mama had to get out my warm clothes."

"Mine too, although more of them are coming with our shipment, thank God," Sophie said, pointing to her sweater. "What happened to summer?"

He laughed as he stopped in front of them. "That's Ireland for you. Although I hear from the Yanks that the light here makes the weather mostly worth it."

"Yeah, I watched the sun rise this morning," Sophie said, her eyes on him, "and I swear it changed at least four times in a way that made me want to draw."

"It was like diamonds covered the trees after it rained a little." Greta peeked into the bag he was carrying. "Oh, good, you brought some milk. I'm thirsty."

Sophie waved him in. "Come inside, Jamie. To your house." She cleared her throat. "That is, if you have the time."

He nodded. "It's my last free weekend. Once school starts on Monday, I'll be grading papers on Saturday mornings."

"I can't wait for school to start," Greta told him, running ahead as he and Sophie trailed behind her on the way to the kitchen. "Can I see Lucky soon, do you think? Ollie said to pop by, but we should probably check with his mom."

"We'll see Lucky soon enough," Sophie said as Jamie

put the grocery bag on the counter, and she peered inside. "You bought me bacon?"

"The best in Ireland, if you ask me. We call it rashers here."

She beamed. "Oh, you're a sweetheart. How did you know I loved it?"

"Me too!" Greta called.

Sorcha had whispered it to him as he'd passed the meat aisle. Thank God she hadn't appeared out of the blue. He would have jumped and gone green. The people shopping around him would have thought their local teacher was going mad and needed to be institutionalized. "Only a feeling. I also bought you honey for your tea. Same reason." Although this time he hadn't heard a whisper as he'd wandered down that aisle.

"You're two for two." Sophie's hand was suddenly covering his, her bright green eyes spellbinding. "I'm not sure anyone has ever guessed my likes like that."

He understood. There was something special about someone knowing you—your likes, your dislikes, what made you tick. He supposed that was what soulmates did. "Seems a new day has dawned."

"Yes, it does, doesn't it?" Her voice was soft, barely audible. "Greta, shall we ask Mr. Fitzgerald to stay for breakfast?"

"That's a great idea. January would like it too. You can sit by us."

The little girl hopped onto one of his kitchen chairs and put her elbows on the table after depositing January in another open chair. Suddenly the scene struck him—the little girl humming under her breath as she smiled at him, Sophie putting away the groceries.

This could be the rest of his life...

He was getting ahead of himself again. As he pulled a chair out, his phone vibrated. "Excuse me a moment," he said, grabbing it out of his pocket. "I only keep it on if Carrick needs me with the sheep." He picked up his brother's call. "You have some escapees this morning?"

"Yes, a couple found their way out through the south fence. Also, Linc called the board meeting for nine. Can you come by and help before we head to the arts center?"

"I'm on my way." He clicked off, disappointed. "We need to catch some sheep before the board meeting. I'm sorry, but I'll have to take a rain check on breakfast."

"That's too bad, but understandable," Sophie said, setting the carton of eggs down slowly on the kitchen counter. "We're still on for tonight?"

He thought of all the ways he wished he could answer. *I'm counting the hours. I can't wait to be with you. Alone. Hear the sound of your voice. Watch you as you tell me about the things that matter to you. See you smile at me for no reason at all.* "Of course."

"Mr. Fitzgerald," Greta said, hopping down and snagging January. "How do you catch a sheep?"

He couldn't help chuckling as they walked him to the door. "You run a lot and hope you can circle them or direct them where you want them to go. It's not very fun, that I can tell you."

"January," Greta said, holding up the fluffy sheep to her eye level. "You'd better not escape on me."

Sophie kissed the top of her head. "I think we're safe. Should I wish you luck?"

He wanted to touch her cheek but didn't dare do so in front of Greta. "Sure. We Irish will take luck wherever and whenever we can get it. I'll see you tonight."

When he drove up to the south fence of Carrick's property, his brother was standing beside his car. He parked on the road, then got out and lifted his chin in greeting. "Any leads on where they ran off to?"

Carrick came forward and put his hands on his shoulders, making Jamie's eyes narrow as he met his gaze. "I made it up. I figured it would be better to talk here alone than at Summercrest Manor."

Jamie thought about pushing away his hands, but he knew his brother's way of looking him in the eye for answers. "Is this about Sophie?"

"Yes, and you letting her stay at your house. Everyone saw the way you were looking at each other last night. Angie told me to leave things be, but I can't help myself. God knows how much I've worried about you and your love life. Jamie, has Sorcha visited you then?"

He might be able to evade Liam, but he couldn't do it to his own brother. Especially not concerning Sorcha. "Yes, but I'd like to keep that between us."

His brother wrapped him in a bear hug and practically lifted him off the ground. "Thank God! Jamie, I couldn't be happier for you."

He slapped Carrick on the back before edging away. "Let's not get ahead of ourselves. She's just arrived, and we only have our first date tonight—"

"*Tonight!*" His brother rocked back on his wellies. "That's way fast for you, Jamie. Did Sorcha light a fire under you?"

He all but rolled his eyes. "Knowing her and knowing me as you do, what do you think?"

Carrick's nod was positively punctilious, and Jamie might have laughed if they were on a different topic. Instead, he looked at his watch.

"You lunatic. Sophie invited me to stay for breakfast

after I dropped her groceries by this morning, but I left to help you. Now we have almost an hour before the board meeting starts. What in the hell am I supposed to do?"

Carrick had the grace to wince. "Help me with some loose fence posts?"

For that kind of work, he'd need to take off his coat as his body temperature climbed fast. "If I didn't love you..."

Carrick clapped him on the back. "Given your brotherly affection, can Angie, Emeline, and I expect you to do our shopping for us now that it's a service you offer?"

He only glared at his brother, who laughed loud enough to prompt a few nearby sheep to dart off at the sudden sound.

"Did you hear that Keegan O'Malley's decided to go into sheep in addition to cows?" his brother called out, and they launched into the idle chitchat that accompanied such daily labors.

By the time they rolled up to the arts center, Jamie's hands ached from pounding in the fence posts alongside Carrick. The parking lot was populated with cars, and as they made their way inside, they waved to a few townspeople preparing for the Saturday morning pottery class.

Normally they met in the kitchen area, but today everything was set up in Ellie's studio on the third floor. Bets was pacing in front of a table covered with coffee cups and a stainless steel coffee thermos while Nicola Donovan laid out pieces of some kind of dessert bread. He imagined Bets was happy to have one of her best friends, another of the famous Lucky Charms, on the board. Nicola was a sound businesswoman, besides. She ran the village's only bookstore, One More Chapter, which had always boasted a good stack of art books. He'd bought some for his own research.

Eoghan sat beside his son, sipping coffee as Donal

texted on his phone. Linc was reading the legal papers from yesterday, the ones the lorry driver had given him before hauling away the mobile home.

Jamie called out a greeting, echoed by his brother, and went over to grab himself a coffee and slice of bread—lemon, he discovered—and sat beside Eoghan, who leaned over and whispered, "My Sandrine tells me you're taking Sophie out on the town tonight. I couldn't be happier for you, my boy. Couldn't be happier."

Donal clicked his phone shut after muttering an expletive. "Malcolm wants us to come to him. Monday. Ten o'clock. Said he has a family engagement this weekend."

"Likely story," Eoghan muttered furiously. "So we're to drive an hour to see his majesty and kiss his rings. Who's going?"

"Let's take a minute," Linc said, slapping the papers onto the worktable. "I'm still fairly new to town, but this smells like the kind of power play I've encountered time and again in my window business. Anyone want to tell me I'm wrong?"

"If only we could dress this up and say differently," Nicola said, sitting down in one of her black suits she wore working at her bookshop, "but you can't put lipstick on a pig."

"You know, I once attended a fair where they tried that," Linc said with a half smile. "So tell me what I don't know about Malcolm Coveney."

"He's the kind who wears a Crombie coat all the time," Eoghan began. "If you understand me."

Linc scowled. "No, I'm not sure I do. Why is a man wearing a British gentleman's overcoat daily significant?"

Bets gave a sigh. "Wait for it."

"Most Irish men, myself included, would only wear that kind of coat to a funeral," Eoghan finished.

"So he buries people daily?" Linc drawled.

Jamie and a few others coughed out laughs before Donal said, "What my dad is trying to convey is that Malcolm thinks he's better than other people."

"He puts on airs," Nicola said, "and yes, he probably does bury people every day. I've heard business owners in his town only thrive on his say-so. If you don't go along with him or do what he wants, your business starts to experience problems, permits being one of them."

"Malcolm Coveney considers himself the informal Minister of Rural Development of Ireland," Carrick added.

"So he's like the man behind yer man," Linc said, tapping his fingers on the table.

"Exactly right," Jamie threw in. "He's also a big one for parish pump politics."

"What we'd call the local yokel kind of politics in the States, Linc," Bets said with a fake smile. "Where things are decided by handouts."

"So he wants a payoff?" Linc asked. "I looked him up last night, of course, after the party, and he doesn't have any interests that would directly compete with what we're doing. Not that that always matters in these cases."

"We flew up the tree, so to speak, with the new funding for the arts center." Donal sipped his coffee. "Before we were just a little arts center in tiny Caisleán. Now we're about to have a swanky museum designed by a world-renowned architect—"

"And a classy hotel, which he does build with serious investors." Carrick steepled his hands. "So, we're on the map in a big way. Is there a reason you didn't ask the nonvoting members of the board to this meeting, Linc?"

He bit off a piece of lemon bread. "What do you think? Bets and I talked about it, but now I'm wondering whether we can trust them. If Malcolm Coveney is a king maker, it's likely some of them may be working with him, right?"

"Perhaps," Eoghan said. "Most Irishmen like to hedge their bets. This isn't going to be an easy fight."

"Except we don't know what he wants yet," Donal said, looking around the room. "All we know is he didn't want Linc to keep his mobile home."

"Or he didn't want Sophie here," Linc answered, his round face suddenly tense. "With her status in the art community, she instantly became our poster child. She's raised our profile internationally. No offense to anyone, but she has the power to bring more renowned artists to the center. I'm this close to getting Hans Shumaker to agree to come next year to paint something for the new museum."

"And he's considered a modern Picasso with his giant canvases, I've read," Jamie said, having read up on the man Linc was courting.

Eoghan breathed out, "It *would* be a big coup. His work hangs in the Smithsonian. The Met. The MoMa."

Linc nodded crisply. "But the news isn't to be shared until it's a sure thing."

Jamie broke off a piece of his cake. "I wonder if the news will help or make things worse, should he agree."

Bets made a face. "I'm tired of worrying about making things worse. We've worked hard to get this arts center where it is. Now the jackals want to come out and eat. I'm sick of it."

Linc patted her hand. "Agreed. So how do you handle king makers like Malcolm Coveney in Ireland? And moreover, why is Mary Kincaid talking to him?"

Donal kicked out his feet and scratched his jaw. "You have it on good authority Mary's involved?"

Jamie wasn't sure whether he should add anything to this particular thread.

Linc glanced at Bets and then nodded. "The best. Sorcha told me."

Well, they were going to go there apparently. Jamie leaned forward. "We'll need to stand up with Sophie."

All eyes turned his way, and he fought to control the color rising in his face.

"She's just arrived and wants to expand her art," he said, looking around the room. "If Malcolm is trying to get her to leave, we'll need to work harder to protect her. She said she's willing to fight, if need be. Personally, I hope it won't come to that. It's not fair to put our artists on the front line— even if some of them are used to it."

The story she'd told about the rotten eggs came to his mind. He still couldn't wrap his head around that. How could anyone do such a thing? Especially to a child?

"We've had our artists come under fire before, and I hate it as much as the rest of you," Linc said, glowering. "But, honestly, this kind of friction will only make Hans want to join us more. Some artists like butting their heads against the man, so to speak."

"Maybe from now on we should consider that when deciding on artists," Nicola said, crossing her arms. "I don't like thinking that way, but we need to be realistic. Mary is going to continue with her wicked ways, and people like Malcolm will keep popping up. We need rough riders, to use your Yank phrase."

"So the quiet, sensitive artist types are out?" Bets asked, shaking her head. "It sounds ridiculous when you say it out loud."

"It does, and let's not get ahead of ourselves," Linc said, drumming the table with his fingers. "I think Donal and I should go and meet Malcolm on our own. I don't want to formally make this an arts center issue. Yet. I'll say I'm bringing Donal because he's a friend I turn to for advice from time to time given his past association with the county council."

Bets glared at him. "Like I told you last night before you started snoring, I think the entire council should go—"

"We'd have to invite the nonvoting members like I told you before I nodded off," he said with a wry look. "If we bring them, we might have to deal with them double-dealing behind our backs. I'm not eager for that."

"Neither am I," Donal said, holding up his hands. "Bets, I see your point. Go en masse and show him we're a solid unit. He already knows that. Besides, if you go, you'll be tweaking Mary Kincaid's nose, and God knows what she's been telling Malcolm."

"And we'd like to get my mobile home back so Sophie and Greta have a permanent place to live," Linc said, sitting back as if trying for calm. "Jamie can't stay at the haunted house forever."

"I don't mind," he said, sending Bets what he hoped was a reassuring smile.

"Jamie, you've been scared of that place since you were a boy." Bets tapped the notepad in front of her, on which she'd written no notes. "Don't kid a kidder."

"He'll be facing down his fears," Carrick said, nudging him in the side and making his head turn. "We'll have Sophie to thank for it, won't we, Jamie?"

And Sorcha, he thought, but he simply nodded before saying, "A man can't be afraid of a mere house his whole life, can he?"

"My father managed to fear the cemetery his mother was buried in his whole life," Eoghan put forward with a laugh. "You're a brave man, Jamie Fitzgerald. How did the grocery shopping go this morning, by the by?"

More puzzled looks had his ears heating up. "Fine." He glanced around, then clarified, "I...ah, offered to do a little shopping for Sophie and Greta, it being their first full day in town and them not yet knowing the way of things."

"Took the duties right unto himself like a saint," Eoghan said, "even though my dear Sandrine and I would have been happy to do the shopping again after that buzzard Malcolm took the first batch along with the house. Again, we have much to thank you for, Jamie Fitzgerald."

He hated the limelight and, even worse, talk of him being a saint. Didn't he have condoms in his wallet? He flushed redder. Best to change the subject. "If we're voting on the matter, I agree on the strategy of Linc and Donal going alone to start."

"Are we, Madam Chairman?" Linc asked, giving Bets his full attention.

She straightened in her seat, tightening her lips. "I don't think we need to be that official. But we *should* meet with our nonvoting members and feel them out. Soon."

"How about a few of us meet with them at the pub?" Eoghan asked. "That's the best place to see into a man's soul outside church."

Linc laughed. "I might have to write that one down, Eoghan. Well, we have the outline of our next steps. Shall I nail down Hans then?"

"I say we put it to a vote right now." Bets scratched something at the top of her notepad. "All for Hans receiving a formal offer?"

Everyone raised their hand.

"Motion passes." She made another note and looked up. "Any other business before we leave? Although I think we'll be meeting soon enough."

Jamie raised his hand. It felt a little weird, because he was accustomed to calling on students, not acting the part of one. She nodded for him to speak. "I'd like to buy the furniture for the children's art studio. I have a feeling we're going to want to solidify things quickly. I'm hoping to present a draft plan shortly." He had no idea when exactly, but he figured it would only take a week, right?

"Any objections to Jamie buying furniture?" Linc asked.

"We need a budget of the items in a spreadsheet, and then we'll execute a purchase order," Bets informed him.

"A budget?" He wanted to groan, his eyes crossing when he thought of the millions of little squares. "Fine. Although I'd prefer to use an abacus."

"That's a good one, Jamie," Eoghan said, eyes crinkling with humor. "When I was a schoolboy, we simply added up numbers on our slates. Well, I'd say we're still in the thick of things, but everything is progressing well. We have a lovely new artist in residence and another one we're locking up. Shall we put out a press release once Hans agrees, do you think?"

Bets wrote something on her notepad. "Absolutely. The sooner the better. We want to show Malcolm we're stocked up."

"Like the River Moy with trout," Donal said, wagging his finger. "But we need to watch our steps. Malcolm isn't one to just fade into the shadows. Neither is Mary."

Bets rubbed her temples. "Don't remind me. Linc, what about Tom Sarkesian? When can he present his final plans for the museum? Releasing his design might also bolster our efforts to keep Malcolm from bothering with us."

Jamie didn't think Bets believed a word of what she'd just said. No one did. But it did get him to thinking about the possibility of Sophie releasing her preliminary design to the public as well. He might mention it over dinner tonight. Only...

Should he talk about the arts center on their date?

He'd only ever been on dates with local women. Usually they'd gone to school together or he knew friends of hers. There were no surprising revelations. With Sophie, there were whole parts of her life swathed in mystery. Wasn't that what he was supposed to ask about? If he talked about work, did that make it less of a date somehow? He turned to look at Carrick. Maybe he should ask his brother after the meeting.

"I'll call Tom today," Linc told them, chuckling when Bets wrote it down. "That's *T-O-M*—"

"Oh, put a sock in it, cowboy," she said, but her lips twitched as she wrote her note and held it up for him to see.

"Nice spelling job," he said with another laugh. "I thought Tom might meet with the Irish construction company everyone says is the only company who can do the job we're looking for on time and to budget."

"We have one of those, do we?" Eoghan asked. "News to me. Usually contractors here—"

"Let's not talk about the state of the Irish construction field," Carrick said with a groan. "Trying to make an addition to our cottage is an ongoing nightmare. They were supposed to be finished by the time Emeline was born, and they only just started. I'm thinking I might need to build it myself in my spare time."

"What spare time?" Donal asked with a smile. "Five hundred sheep and a new baby not filling the hours?"

Carrick rubbed his eyes. "If I sleep standing up like my

sheep, it takes less time. Even so, I can meet at the pub with our nonvoting members. I want to do my part."

Donal waved him off. "Forget it, man. Go home to your wife. Linc and I have this one since Dad is home with his sweetheart."

"We're babysitting Greta tonight actually," Eoghan gleefully informed everyone.

Jamie wanted to crawl under the nearest table.

"Since our wonderful teacher and board member is taking Sophie out for dinner tonight," the older man finished with his usual mischief.

"I thought I saw the way of things last night," Donal said with a smile. "Good for you."

"That's enough of that," Jamie said, holding up a hand. "Are we through here?"

"No word on hiring an assistant, Bets?" Nicola asked. "I would offer up my lovely daughter but I need her at the bookshop."

"The candidates just aren't...what I want from our last run in the county papers, and it makes me dread some of the future hirings I know we'll need as we grow."

Linc started ticking items off his fingers. "Like public relations and more teachers for—"

"Stop or I'll start crying." Bets made another note and then scratched it out. "I think we'd get better candidates from posting the job in *The Irish Times*, but housing is part of the problem, and it's just gotten that much harder."

"Let's cross that bridge when we get to it, as the Yanks say," Carrick chipped in. "I say put it in the national paper and see what happens."

"Then it's decided." Linc kicked back with a smile. "Anything else on your list, Madam Chairman?"

"Wouldn't you like to know." She gave a simpering look.

"But no, we're good at the moment. Lots of balls in the air—"

"And corrupt jackals circling for a kill," Eoghan said, rubbing his hands together. "With me involved in my ninety-third year, having just moved in with my girlfriend. Isn't life a wonder?"

Jamie did his best to hold on to his wonder as the group congratulated him on his date and wished him well. Finally, they all started making their way out, but he stopped Carrick by the door with a hand to his arm.

His brother waved to Donal before turning to give him his full attention. "What's on your mind?"

If there was anything Jamie hated it was feeling unknowledgeable about a subject, but there was nothing for it. He needed help. "A question. I'm thinking about my date with Sophie tonight. I guess I'm...wondering... Would it send the wrong message to talk about the arts center and my ideas for the children's art curriculum?"

"Like she'd think it was a work date or something?"

Jamie nodded, heat rising in his face.

"Tricky. I can see both sides. Wait a sec. I have an idea."

He pulled out his phone, making Jamie lunge for it. "No, for the love of God, don't—"

Carrick turned his back and quickly made the call. "Angie," he said when his wife picked up on speakerphone. "Jamie wants to know if a woman might think he'd asked her out only to discuss work stuff if he asks her about said work stuff."

Jamie started to walk off, but his brother snagged his arm.

"Tell him to balance the conversation," his sister-in-law responded. "It's important for him to seem interested in her work. Only don't get too technical—"

"Got it. Thanks, Yank. I'll be home soon."

He clicked off and proceeded to dial another number. "Clear as mud. We need another point of view. From an expert, I'd be thinking."

Jamie was too dazed to try and stop him, and within seconds a man's voice answered on speaker. Liam's!

"Hiya, Carrick. What are you up to on this fine day?"

"Helping alleviate Jamie's dating nerves," he said with a snort. "Here's the question."

Jamie stared off into the distance as his brother relayed his conundrum, wishing a sheep would escape the far-off fencing so he could take off at a run and look like a hero and not the bumbling idiot he felt like.

"I see what we're talking about here," Liam replied. "I would start by asking her about herself. Let her do the talking. A woman will tell you what's important to her. All you have to do is sit back and listen. Jamie's good at that."

Carrick nudged him. "That he is. He's just nervous, you know. It's been ages since he's been on a date, making this a monumental occasion."

"For sure," Liam agreed, making Jamie wish the earth would open and swallow him whole.

"Mary Magowan was the last girl, wasn't she?" Carrick asked.

Jamie couldn't believe he remembered.

"Sorcha told all of us it was a bad idea, if I recall," Liam said with a laugh. "We should have listened. Another girl who didn't think he was good enough in the end, being a teacher."

His brother put his hand on his shoulder. "Sorcha always had a matchmaking sense, didn't she? Well, I'll let you go. Thanks, Liam."

"Yeah, thanks," Jamie muttered.

Carrick clicked off and stuffed the phone back in his pocket. "There you have it, Jamie, but here's my advice. Don't be overthinking it. I know when I was first with the Yank, all I wanted to do was listen to her speak in that sexy Yank accent, enjoy her droll sense of humor, and watch the sun play with the highlights in her hair. Sometimes I didn't even hear what she said the first time, and do you know what? If I missed it, she'd just smile at me like she knew why and say it again. Trust me, if Sorcha is on your side, you have nothing to worry about."

Jamie nudged his brother back. "You know, sometimes I'm really glad Mother didn't leave you in the forest for the fairies to raise."

Carrick barked out a laugh. "Speaking of babies, do you need me to buy you condoms? I could get away with buying some with a new baby in the house, and Angie would back me."

Jamie walked off, giving his brother the bird, which only made him laugh harder.

"Remember, I'm on speed dial for you if you need any more advice."

He left the building and got in his car to leave, yelping when Sorcha appeared in the passenger seat next to him.

"He really is a good man, isn't he?" she said with a trace of softness in her voice before disappearing as quickly as she'd arrived.

Yeah, he really was, and so were the rest of his friends, even Liam with the condoms.

There was nothing to be nervous about, right?

CHAPTER SIX

Why was she so nervous?

Sophie fussed with the apple green cashmere scarf she'd chosen to keep warm on her date, but she doubted it would do any good. Ireland's weather service had all but issued *a date warning*. Go out at your own risk. It was August the thirtieth, and it was eight degrees Celsius—forty-six degrees—and pouring cats and dogs outside!

Unfortunately, the weather didn't allow for a sexy date look. She surveyed her black cords and thick red cashmere sweater doubtfully. She was wearing cashmere over cashmere, a first. Heads would roll for this in Paris. But Sophie Giombetti wasn't in France anymore, was she?

God, all she'd wanted was to look beautiful on her date, for herself as much as Jamie. She pulled off the scarf and frowned at herself in his simple wooden-framed mirror.

"It doesn't look too bad," Sandrine mused in French from her perch in the bedroom doorway. "Maybe you wear longer earrings?"

"And have them blow like seesaws from my ears and whack me blue during my date?"

"All you have to do is walk to the car—"

"Run," she corrected. "And then run to the restaurant's front door. Like I'm in a steeple chase. On my first date. With *Jamie*. Oh, why couldn't the Irish weather gods be nice to me?"

She wasn't equipped for this. God knows she'd experienced extreme weather while traveling the world—that earthquake in San Francisco, that typhoon in Hong Kong, and even that hurricane in New Orleans. All hell on glass...

But the howling, *screaming* wind and rain flying sideways? Yes, sideways! She'd never seen anything like it. Add in the bone-chilling cold, and she'd been forced to forsake any thoughts of wearing the cute yellow summer dress with her sexy white ankle-strap platform-heeled sandals she'd picked out after Jamie had left them this morning, bacon still scenting the air.

"You might have to wear your wellingtons, after all, and not the boots," Sandrine said, fighting a smile. "There are rivers of water running across the yard."

She flung her hand toward the bay window. "I might as well go out in a trash bag. How does anyone go out in weather like this? I'm already freezing, and I'm wearing the silk underwear you made me bring. Thank you, by the way."

Her dear friend laughed. "Eoghan likes to talk about how bad the weather is in Ireland. Before I moved here, I thought he might be kissing that Blarney Stone they talk about here."

"It's called the gift of the gab. He does have it in spades, doesn't he?"

In the next room, Greta let out a giggle, followed by Eoghan's endearing laugh. Warmth surrounded her heart. "I'm being silly, aren't I?"

"I still remember how much you fussed with your outfit for your very first date when you were sixteen."

She groaned. "With Elias Shaw, the renowned piccolo player. God! What was I thinking?"

Sandrine came over and framed her face. "Like now, you were being a woman, one who wanted her first evening with her new man to be beautiful. But it will be, my love, because you will be with *Jamie*. Do you remember how poets speak about time stopping?"

She'd never had that feeling before. "I believe I've read a few of those."

"Well, perhaps in Ireland, the rain stops." Her friend kissed her on both cheeks. "Or you stop hearing it. Now, I think you put the green scarf back on and pull out the wellingtons. You can only do what you can do with your outfit. The rest is in your eyes, Sophie."

With a final smile, she left her alone. Sandrine was right. She needed to be practical because she wasn't about to call her date off over something so silly as the weather. Not that she was telling Greta she was going on a date. This was her first since her divorce, and while she expected Jamie to be important to her, she planned on letting things progress before she broached that topic with her daughter. They were only going out for fun to a cool restaurant, she'd told her daughter. And Greta had clapped and said it was *wonderful*, touching Sophie's heart. She'd always had a way of knowing things, so it wouldn't surprise Sophie if she'd guessed part of it—or at least knew that Jamie was to be a special kind of friend.

She heard a door open in the other room, and her heart quickened. Jamie had arrived promptly, which must be an anomaly in these parts because Eoghan laughed and said,

"You're not living on country time tonight, are you, my boy?"

Sophie heard him laugh and decided one of the benefits of the small cottage was hearing conversations in every room. Pulling on her wellies, she went to go see him, excitement surging through her. He was here, and that was all that mattered.

"Hi, Mr. Fitzgerald!" Greta called, to which he bandied back a reply as Sandrine added her greetings.

"I hope it's not bad luck to open another man's front door for him," Eoghan said.

She stopped in the doorway to the bedroom, watching Jamie as he stomped his feet on the dark rug and pulled off his dripping brown cap, still unaware of her. "If anyone would know, it would be you, Eoghan."

Then he lifted his head, swiped at the water dripping from his face, and grinned at her with so much joy she was sure her heart tilted like a windmill.

"Hi, Jamie," she said softly.

"Hiya," he answered in a silky voice that sent chills through her. "Nice night out, isn't it?"

She couldn't help but laugh at the absurdity of it all. "An Irish tourism brochure waiting to happen."

Greta ran over to the window. "It's terrible outside. Mama says she's never seen rain go sideways like that."

Jamie held her gaze as he replied, "We have a lot of Irish words for rain because we have so many kinds. You'll learn them in school, Greta. There's the kind of rain we're having tonight—*batharnach*—a downpour."

"I'd be calling it *clagairt*," Eoghan countered, scratching his chin. "Pelting rain is a better description for this mess. But Jamie's right. We have a slew of words since we have every kind of rain known to man. Or woman." He added the last with a glint in his pale blue eyes.

Greta ran over to Jamie. "What other kinds do you have?" she asked.

He tapped his mouth as if considering before saying, "There's the sprinkle of rain that barely makes you blink, and the drizzle of rain, which makes you wonder about its duration, but it's the misty rain that's my favorite."

When he sought Sophie's gaze, her heartbeat slowed. The cobalt of his eyes struck her even more tonight, and she remembered why it was so favored among artists like herself —it wasn't just the lightness or even its rarity of color.

It was extremely stable. Like the man himself.

"The misty rain makes all the magic in Ireland rise around you, since it's usually accompanied by the sun. Where there had been a normal tree only moments before, suddenly the great oak or the ash is covered in a million little crystals. The pastures turn from green to golden, and on the fence lines, tiny stars seem to dance in a chorus."

Sophie realized she was holding her breath. Goodness, he was poetic.

"Wow," Greta breathed out. "That sounds so beautiful, Mr. Fitzgerald."

"Oh, your Irish soul is showing, my boy," Eoghan said, his voice rough. "Makes me think of Steve Spurgin's song, 'A Walk in the Irish Rain' where he talks about the mist being like teardrops from angel wings. Do you know it, Jamie?"

He nodded, and when Eoghan began to sing, he joined in with a deep baritone. Greta sat on the floor and crossed her legs, her face enraptured as she watched and listened. Sophie understood. She couldn't look away. His voice seemed to wrap around her, the resonant chords of the love song conjuring visions of them walking in a misty rain in fields of gold.

Sandrine came over and put her arm around her waist as the two men started to harmonize the chorus. Sophie had heard a lot of musicians perform in her life. She'd been married to a famous one, but somehow the purity of their a cappella rendition touched her in a way no other performance had. Everything faded to the rich texture of Jamie's voice and the rare light of his eyes.

When they held the final note in concert, Jamie's voice dipping to bass as Eoghan's lifted to a sweet tenor, everything in the room seem to still.

When they finished, it was quiet for a moment before she and Greta and Sandrine all started to applaud. She even added a cab whistle as Greta stood up and started jumping and clapping, saying, "That was *so* wonderful!"

Jamie and Eoghan's cheeks were flushed red, both men looking down at their shoes. Sandrine gave her a gentle squeeze before crossing over to Eoghan and kissing him on the cheeks.

Jamie found her gaze again and lifted a shoulder. "We Irish like our songs."

She wanted to cross over to him and touch his face. Communicate how much his words and song had meant to her. How deeply touched she was.

The corner of his mouth lifted, and then Greta was asking him if he'd teach her the song he'd sung. When he declared he would, her heart gave a happy somersault. Already, she knew he was a man who kept his word, and that was even rarer than the cobalt of his eyes.

"Shall we go?" he finally asked.

She nodded slowly and finally found her feet, moving toward him in the confounded wellies.

He donned his sodden cap. "We might need to run for the car, what with you in that outfit. You won't be used to the rain like the rest of us. Do you have a raincoat and hat?"

Greta ran over to the couch. "I've got them for you, Mama. Me and Sandrine got them out. Have fun with Mr. Fitzgerald."

After tucking the cream waterproof slouchy hat on her head, she shrugged into her matching mid-thigh cream raincoat with Jamie's assistance and belted it. Then she leaned down and kissed her daughter. "Have fun with Eoghan and Sandrine. I'll kiss you good night when I get home and fill your room with starlight."

"Good," she said, leaning in for another kiss. "Bye, Mr. Fitzgerald. Thanks again for letting us stay in your house."

"It's my pleasure, Greta," he told her before putting his hand on the doorknob. "Ready?"

Joy beamed within her, suffusing her entire body. "Let's go."

When he opened the door, the wind rocked her back on her heels. He shielded her with his body as he muscled it closed and then urged her with him through the pelting rain as they raced to the car. She had to squint as it ravaged her face. Her wellies stuck a little in the mud as she ran, making squishy sounds in the puddles on the grass. Jamie kept her close, matching her pace. At the car, he led her to the passenger side and helped her inside before heading around to his own seat.

She was wet through her pant legs past the bottom of her raincoat, the water sliding into the thick socks of her wellies. Wind rocked the car as Jamie opened the driver's side door and slammed it shut.

He cupped her shoulder, his hands emitting a warmth she wanted to curl into, and she turned to him.

"Are you all right?" he asked.

"I'm soaked through," she said, brushing the water running down her face, fearing for her mascara. "This is crazy."

He reached for something, and then he was dabbing her face with a soft towel. "You look beautiful, Sophie. The rain looks good on you."

There were raindrops on his face, and she took the towel from him and dabbed at the line of his jaw up to the cheekbone, his blue eyes blazing heat now.

"We should go," he said, touching her face again, this time in a caress.

Her eyes wanted to close. She wanted him to explore her face, but the wind was still howling and rain pelted the car in an attack. Besides, Greta had to be in the window watching. "Yes, let's. I still can't believe you guys go out in this weather."

"If we stayed inside for weather, we'd never leave our cottages," he said with a laugh as he started the car. "But don't worry. The place we're going to will have a fire lit in the hearth. I called to ask for it specifically."

Even though she was soaked to the bone and growing cold, her heart was warm. By the time they rushed into the restaurant *at a historic castle*, she was certain she'd never dry out for the evening. The dark brick tavern was near full of people like them, rain-splattered with flattened hair. Sophie had a moment of relief as they walked to the corner table beside the fire-crackling hearth, Jamie waving to several people he seemed to know. The heat was glorious, as was the sweet scent of the wood.

After the server seated them, she leaned forward to whisper, "Most people are eating dessert. When do you normally eat here in Ireland?"

He bit his lip before saying, "This restaurant starts serving at five thirty and closes at eight."

She checked the time. "But it's seven thirty!"

"I think they seat the ghosts at eight," he told her with a smile. "Just kidding. Don't give it a thought. I called in a favor. My mother taught the owner. I said you were from France and not yet used to our early ways."

"That's—" She sat back against her chair. "We eat at eight or nine in Provence."

"I know. Eoghan and Donal mentioned it to me, saying I'd better have a snack or I wouldn't make it." The wide smile he gave her prompted her to study his face. She saw humor in the corners of his mouth, his eyes.

"Wait! Are you kidding me?"

"Yes." His shoulders were shaking slightly. "About all of it. You seem to bring out a playful side in me. Besides, I like hearing you laugh."

Goodness, how could she not be delighted by that? "I'm going to have to watch you, aren't I?"

He gave a devilish wink. "I certainly hope so. Shall we have wine? I'll let you pick. I'm... I wouldn't know what to select."

She looked around. There were some patrons having wine, but beer and whiskey were more abundant on the tables. "Do you want a beer? I can have a glass of wine."

He frowned then. "Do *you* like wine?"

"I adore wine. It's truly one of the best reasons to live in France."

"Then I'm having it too." He nudged the beverage menu toward her. "I want to try what you like."

Another shock, and who would have imagined anything would make a bigger impression than the fact that both of them were dripping wet on the restaurant floor. "That might be the sweetest thing anyone has ever said to me on a date."

His head lifted sharply. "Really?"

Oh, he was nervous. That was so endearing.

"Yeah." She reached across the table and touched his hand briefly, aware of the eyes watching them. It was a little like being at the zoo, only she and Jamie were the lions and the others were the popcorn-eating public.

She'd learned how to tune rubberneckers out in childhood, but that didn't mean she wasn't aware of them. Many of the people here seemed to know him, and she was the new artist in town. They were on a date. Why wouldn't others gawk? "Now, tell me what you like to eat here."

He cleared his throat. "I've...ah...never been here."

She narrowed her eyes. "Wait. Did you bring me here because you thought I needed something fancy? Jamie, I would have been happy at a pub."

This time, he reached out and touched the back of her hand. "I chose this place because I wanted to take you to the nicest restaurant we wouldn't have to drive an hour to get to. You'd want to be close for Greta if she needed you."

Again, he'd thought of her daughter. "Thank you for bringing me here. Shall we look at the menu and guess what's best then?"

She edged her chair closer to him, and he smiled and did the same. Suddenly their elbows were touching as she opened the menu and scanned the starters. "How do you feel about smoked eel?"

"I actually feel bad for the eel. One day he's swimming the Irish sea and the next he's being smoked like a fag."

Right. A fag was a cigarette in this country. Not a slur. "Isn't this a nonsmoking restaurant? How confusing of them. What about *textures* of beetroot? What does that even mean?"

His rich chuckle was like eating a warm slice of apple pie, she decided, but perhaps she was influenced by the dessert menu printed beneath the entrée selections. "It's the sheep's milk ice cream with nutty flavors that worries me," Jamie said with a grin. "In all my years, I've never seen a sheep eat a nut. Not once."

She gave him an answering grin. "False marketing. Unconscionable. Cabbage leaves bathed in a Guinness mustard sauce?"

"Minus the bathing part, it has solid possibilities."

He leaned a little closer, their heads practically touching. At this rate, the raindrops on her were going to fall onto him, a thought that sent a rush of heat through her.

"You're famous for your smoked salmon," she said, "so I'll give that a go, but I'm not sure about the trout caviar. Ever tried any?"

"New to me." He shook his head seriously. "But I'm going to have to pass. I wouldn't want to tell the kids when they arrive at school that I ate twenty unborn fish that could have swum in the River Moy."

She swatted him playfully. "That's terrible. Shall we look at the main course selections?"

And so they flirted and teased their way through the selections, from sweetbreads—Jamie shared a traumatic childhood memory of steamed Christmas brains—to the lamb rump, which Sophie thought an unfortunate name.

"I think our server is scared of us," she said finally, wiping tears and leaning against his shoulder. "Let's close the menu and see if she comes over. We haven't even ordered wine yet."

"Or gotten water." He touched his shirt. "Maybe she expects us to wring out our clothes and drink rainwater."

"That's so gross." She let her fingers drift over the muscles in his arms. How did a teacher have arms like that? Then she remembered the sheep. "Did you catch the escapees this morning?"

His face went blank. "What?"

"The sheep that escaped from your brother."

He leaned closer, the firelight falling nicely over the planes of his face. "Oh, it's a sad tale, that. They escaped my brother only to end up as the lamp rump special tonight."

Laughter bubbled out of her. "Oh, Jamie, I'm having such a wonderful time."

He covered her hand with his own. "Me too. Let me see if I can get our server's attention. You're probably starving."

Her tummy had given a few rumbles, mortifying first date sounds that she hoped he hadn't heard. "You're so much bigger than me. You must be ravenous."

"The thought of sweetbreads checked my hunger pangs. For the moment."

She turned her hand in his and caressed his palm. "Let me know if you need another distraction."

"You're doing plenty fine," he said with a grin. "Here she is at last."

They ordered and drank a fairly mediocre red wine. She would totally have to order one of her favorite bottles and have it shipped from France to share with him. She would cook for him, she decided. In his house. On another date. Because they were so doing this again.

While they feasted on their starter courses and then entrées, she talked about whatever came to mind—how she'd fallen in love with glassmaking as a kid on a tour of a trendy open artist studio, how excited she was to add the pregnant goddess to her Tree of Life design, how she'd ended up living in her grandparents' home in Provence after her divorce, and how Greta was the light of her life.

Jamie's entire presence seemed to absorb what she was saying, almost like his clothes had absorbed the rain. She felt listened to—deeply—on a level no other person had given her, save Sandrine.

When the server arrived and asked if they'd like dessert, Sophie decided to go for it. She didn't want their evening to end yet, even though there was only one other couple still in the restaurant. Sophie would bet they were on a date too, given how the man was leaning forward as though hanging on the woman's every word.

Rather like Jamie was with her.

Feeling hopeful and bubbly, she selected the champagne and raspberry posset while Jamie chose the bread and butter whiskey pudding.

After the server left, she picked up her wine and took a sip. "I've talked your ear off, Jamie. Now, tell me more about you."

"I'm usually the quiet one," he said with a shrug. "What do you want to know?"

"Everything," she blurted out.

His brow rose. "That much? Well, I was born in—"

She nudged him flirtatiously. "You know what I mean."

He gave a sigh. "Yeah. I do," he began hesitantly, his eyes on the white tablecloth.

She realized he wasn't used to talking about himself. In fact, he probably would have rather eaten those sweetbreads, but he braved on, telling her about his love of teaching—a career he'd followed his mother into, inspired in part by tutoring her students. She rested her elbow on the table with her head on her hand as she listened to him.

He liked helping kids understand things, and if he didn't know something, he'd look it up so he could help them learn it.

"It's all changed so much," he said. "Back in the day, if I wanted to know something, I had to go to the library, but now you only need your phone or tablet—if you know what sources are reliable, of course. Still, you can learn anything. It's like a whole new universe of learning has opened to us. That's wonderful, but nothing will ever transport me like books do. They connect us to things we might never see ourselves."

The part of her that had fallen for him that first day—instantly, inescapably—tumbled a little more, but this time, it was like tumbling through a cloud.

When he lifted his gaze and met her eyes, he made a face. "Was it terrible? Me telling you about myself? I fear I'm not very good at it."

Had past dates shamed him? She extended her hand to him. "I could listen to you talk all night. I have more questions. But right now, I just want to hold your hand as the fire sparks. Is that okay?"

"More than," he said, his voice a shade deeper. "Sophie, another time, I'd like to talk to you about the children's arts center. I just...didn't want you to think I asked you out for work."

Work? She wouldn't have considered it possible, given the sparks between them.

"I'd love to talk shop another time, but I agree with you. Let's stick to date stuff. You sure you don't want to try that smoked eel? They must be making another batch. I think I see smoke coming out of the kitchen."

He glanced over his shoulder. "That's my bread and butter pudding they're scorching."

It was so natural to smile around him, so impossible to help herself.

As they were leaving, she decided there was another item she wanted to sample with him: a first-date kiss.

She wanted one real bad.

Outside, the wind was still howling and the rain was coming down in sheets. There was no way they were going to do anything but run from the front door. No kiss there. She wasn't sure she wanted to be drenched to the skin the first time she kissed him. No kiss in the car.

So after he paid for the check, she took his hand and surveyed their surroundings. This was a castle, for heaven's sake, with a hotel attached. There was always a little hideaway for some kissing in a castle, right?

Would he think her too brazen?

She didn't think so.

As they passed the library on their way out, she slowed and looked inside. There was a nice fire in the hearth but no people. Perfect.

She paused. "Will you come into the library with me for a moment?"

Her nerves kicked up as he nodded and followed her into the room. She made sure to put them out of sight, tucked around the corner. "I'm a little embarrassed to ask this, but I really want to kiss you good night, and with the rain and everything—"

"This seems the perfect place," he finished for her, facing her now after taking his cap off. "I was trying to work it out in my head too. I'm glad you came up with a solution."

"Call me ingenious," she quipped and then cringed at her own jest.

"You're that and more," he whispered as he touched her face, pushing a lock of hair behind her ear.

She'd purposely kept her hat off, and she was glad she had, because he threaded his fingers through her hair and gave her heaven as he bent his head and touched his lips to hers. His mouth was soft and seeking at first, learning her shape. She moved closer until she was flush with him—his heat, his scent. She might have moaned, softly, and it was then that he cupped her nape and tilted her head, changing the angle of the kiss, taking it deeper.

Yes. Oh yes, oh yes.

She pressed into him, lifting her hand to his jaw as his tongue traced the seam of her mouth. She knew he was asking, and she answered him with a slow slide of her own tongue. A deep groan sounded, and then he was taking it deeper. Her eyes closed, and she inhaled pine and man, and then he was kissing her softly yet again before lifting his head.

His eyes were brilliant cobalt, the color so pure and light her breath caught.

"Libraries have always been my favorite places in all the world," he said, "but now I've found a completely new reason to appreciate them."

She wanted to throw her arms out in joy. She felt young again. "I had a wonderful time tonight, Jamie. Thank you."

"You stole my line," he said, kissing her softly once more and then taking her hand. "We should go."

She looked around with a little sadness. This moment would be over in a hot minute, never to be repeated. And that's why life was different than art. Life didn't last forever, but art did.

"The ghosts are probably preparing for brandy and cigars, right?" she joked.

He startled and looked around. "Did you see one?"

He seemed so concerned she couldn't joke back. "No. All right, into the rain we go."

Still, he took his time scanning the room before he led her out. She tucked her hat on firmly before they headed outside, then they ran to the car. Once again, their clothes were soaked through. The car heated up from the rain and their breath, fogging up the windows. When they arrived at his house, he insisted on running with her to the front door. He shielded her with his body as he gave her a final kiss, then muttered good night as he opened the door to his house and proceeded to shut her into its warmth.

She leaned against the door, her fingers tracing her mouth, and realized Sandrine had been right.

The rain and wind had stopped when he'd kissed her.

CHAPTER SEVEN

Bets O'Hanlon had met all manners of corrupt Irishmen over the years, from grifters, thugs, and baby-kissing slimeballs. How many times had good-for-nothing men shown up at her front door with laminated brochures and fake credentials under the auspices of helping some charity—a hospital, a school, a nursing center—asking for money they planned to pocket? She'd lost count.

Then there were the utility men or service workers who wanted an "extra bit" for fixing something that was their bloody job. Don't even get her started on the dangerous men who came to the local farms and stole scrap metal and equipment right out of the farmers' sheds, usually armed with a knife or gun.

But Malcolm Coveney was truly one of a kind. My God, he wore gold rings with diamonds on *every* finger.

She would later thank Linc for finally agreeing to let her come along with him and Donal so she could complete her education. From the news, she was well aware that global indices like Transparency International had the data to show why Ireland was still more corrupt than most of its northern European neighbors. This short, gray-haired man could have been the poster child for that report.

She bit the inside of her cheek as she hesitantly shook his bejeweled hand and said, "What an incredible view you have," to which he only responded with an arrogant smirk through thick jowls matching his girth.

At least he hadn't asked her to kiss his ring.

She tried not to stare at his hands as Linc and Donal exchanged bullshit greetings with him, the kind men volleyed when they were out to kick each other's behinds. Coveney's Rolex winked out of his tailored three-piece navy suit. His silk tie shone in the natural light coming in from the floor-to-ceiling windows showcasing what really was a killer view of Watertown's bay. Luxury boats bobbed next to fishing trawlers. A red flag blew in the gentle wind on the new golf course on the right inlet. Tourists strolled along the sidewalk framing the water, posing for selfies.

Progress through corruption. It hovered in the air, as thick as peat smoke coming out of a chimney. A sinking feeling settled in her stomach, making her glad she hadn't had breakfast.

She sank into one of the white leather chairs in front of the man's massive mahogany desk. The top was riddled with files, the kind of scene designed to make him seem like an important man. No, wait. The three cell phones lined up in a straight row on his desk conveyed that. One buzzed as Linc and Donal sat down on either side of her.

Donal put his hands on his knees, the kind of posture he used to convey he meant business. Linc, though, leaned back and crossed his ankle over his opposite knee, looking like he had all the time in the world and wasn't impressed with this joker one bit.

God, was it any wonder she loved him?

"Thanks again for meeting with us, Malcolm," Linc began.

Bullshit.

"I know I'm still new to town perhaps," he continued, "but I've had great legal advice on securing things like permits, so it came as a real surprise to discover you had my mobile home up and taken away."

Malcolm's blue eyes crinkled as he gave a Cheshire smile. "I imagine there's still a lot of things you're discovering about Ireland, Linc. Even with the guidance of people like Donal O'Dwyer and a few of the council members on the Sorcha Fitzgerald Arts Center's board. No offense, Donal."

"Whyever would I be offended?" Donal asked, smiling back with teeth. "I'm sure you're about to tell us whatever it is we missed, Malcolm."

She was so going to choke on the bullshit.

"Mr. Coveney," she decided to add, "it so happens that the mobile home removed on Friday was actually being leased to a young woman and her child. Sophie—"

"Giombetti," he interrupted, picking up a phone as a text pinged and scanning the message. "The glass artist. Incredible work. The kind that should be seen by more people. Our town is a huge draw for tourists, and we already have the hospitality sector in place. Your plans seem redundant when you think about it, don't you agree?"

Redundant?

He leaned forward and smiled with over-bleached white teeth. "I think you'd do best to relocate the center and everything associated with it to our town, including the new museum Tom Sarkesian is planning."

Bets' mind went blank in shock for a minute. Then a seed of rage took root.

He wanted them to relocate the Sorcha Fitzgerald Arts Center *to Watertown.*

Linc started to laugh, a dark, thunder-cracking chuckle she'd never heard from him. "That's one hell of an idea, Malcolm," he said, slapping his knee before letting the humor fall from his face. "But you see, Caisleán really loves this center, and Bets here and many others already have everything in hand."

She was going to pop this man if she didn't do something with her hands. Fisting them in her lap seemed a good idea.

Malcolm's smile didn't slip. "But you're still in the early phases, Linc. You haven't even broken ground on your museum or your hotel, although I hear Kathleen O'Connor is working hard on her groundbreaking metal sculpture. But so many things can go wrong. Donal, *you* know."

Wrong? The word made her ill.

"The beauty of me knowing what can go wrong, Malcolm," Donal answered in an easy voice Bets could only admire, "is that I and many others know how to head such problems off."

"And yet I discovered none of you had filled out the correct permit for this mobile home. Now poor Sophie Giombetti and her young daughter are living in the simple Irish cottage of Caisleán's schoolteacher, Jamie Fitzgerald."

Icy fingers touched her skin. Only Mary Kincaid could have shared that news with this asshole.

"Sophie's been around the art world a long time," Linc said, stretching out both feet now, as if making himself at home in Malcolm's office. "She's resilient. This little permit thing didn't ruffle anyone's feathers. We'd just like to fill out the correct permit today, along with any fee associated with the processing."

Shit. Here we go. Fee, smee. Why couldn't anyone call it a bribe?

Linc cleared his throat and continued. "I'm sure you're as anxious as we all are to show Sophie and the other internationally recognized artists associated with our center what we mean by Irish hospitality. Malcolm, you know better than anyone that tourists come to Ireland to travel around and see its sights. Watertown is barely an hour from Caisleán, and it's considered one of the most beautiful places in the west of Ireland. They're going to end up here, seeing your beautiful sights and playing golf on your new course. Don't you worry none."

Malcolm's mouth shifted, reminding Bets of a serial killer straight out of a horror movie. "But we'd like them to stay in Watertown longer. Driving all around Ireland can be so tedious, especially for people who aren't used to driving on the left side. We'd be cutting down on accidents along the Wild Atlantic Way."

Linc gave another dark chuckle. Bets held her breath.

"You know, Malcolm," he began in that folksy way of his, "that's downright humanitarian thinking, that is. I even admire it. God knows life is hard enough sometimes, and it's a real pleasure to meet with someone like yourself who's thinking along those lines."

Linc stood up and extended his hand across Malcolm's desk. They were leaving? Bets shot out of her seat in solidarity as Donal did the same.

Malcolm laid his hands on his desk and rose slowly, finally shaking the hand Linc offered, gold and diamonds glinting.

"Thanks again for the meeting," Linc said, nodding as

he dropped his hand to his side. "We'll just talk to your assistant on the way out about that pesky permit and square things away. You have a right fine day."

Linc put his hand on the small of her back, turning her toward the door as Malcolm swiveled his hand toward Donal. From her peripheral vision, she could see Donal took his sweet time before shaking it.

"Have a great day, Malcolm," she called over her shoulder.

God, what she really wanted to say was: *I hope your way-too-white teeth rot and fall out so when you ask for bribes in the future no one can make out your words.*

Yeah, she'd lived in Ireland long enough too.

Linc paused at the *gorgeous* bleached blond assistant's cluttered desk, murmuring about the permit while Donal followed them out.

"I'm afraid I don't have an application printed out right now," the young woman said with a fake smile with teeth as white as her boss'.

"Could you print one out for us, darlin'?" Linc asked in his thickest Southern drawl.

She shook her head, giving them an eerie clown-like smile. "I'm afraid we've run out of toner for the printer."

Linc slapped his forehead. "Well, bless your heart! If I'd only known. I could have bought one for you at the office supply store we passed on the way to your offices. How about we do it the modern way then? Can you email it to us, sugar?"

Uh-oh. Not the whole *bless your heart* thing. Bets wanted to storm over to the woman's desk, push her aside, and help herself to the computer. Only she had an inkling... There wasn't another permit application they needed to fill out. It had obviously been the right one all along.

Donal clapped Linc on the back and said, "I'll talk to a few of my old friends in Watertown and get this sorted out. Would you mind writing down the address of where Linc's mobile home is being stored? He has some possessions in there that mean the world to him."

Linc patted his heart. "Drawings from my baby girl when she was only so high."

"I'm sorry but I wasn't given the address," she said hesitantly. "That's with another contractor."

"And who's that, sugar?" Linc asked, tucking his hand on his hip as if he had all day.

His patience blew her mind. She was going to lose it in a second if they didn't leave.

"Again, I don't have that information," the woman said, clown smile firmly in place. "I only knew about the violation."

"Of course," Linc said, nodding his head. "Well, we'll get it all sorted out. I'd hate for my baby girl to hear I've temporarily lost her childhood artwork. You have a nice day, dear. I hope you get your printer fixed real soon."

They walked sedately to the gold-rimmed elevator and went down one floor to the equally glitzy lobby. She fought irritation at Linc and Donal's easy pace as they walked to Linc's Range Rover.

The minute the car doors closed, she let out a low shriek as Linc took her hand comfortingly.

"Yes," Donal said darkly from the back seat. "That."

"Did you see his rings?" She twisted in her seat. "Every finger! It was disgusting."

"Not as disgusting as how swollen his fingers were," Donal replied. "I can tell you one thing: they aren't swollen from him working."

"Oh, he's working all right," Bets said, her face heating as she fumed. "It's called a shakedown. Extortion—"

"Seems so," Linc said, starting the car and driving off. "Donal, I've been meaning to ask you how to say fuck in Gaelic. I figure I'm going to be using it a lot after meeting with Mr. Goldfinger in there, and I'd like to mix it up every once in a while."

"Oh, we have a ton of words, but you might like *dia ár sábháil!*"

"It means 'fucking hell,'" Bets told Linc. "I have three boys."

Linc pointed to the office supply shop as they drove by and muttered, "*Dia ár sábháil!*"

Bets repeated the phrase while a bloom of dark thoughts swirled in the car.

The arts center and all their plans were in real trouble.

CHAPTER EIGHT

The first day of school might be the biggest event of the year.

Give Sophie a birthday or a Christmas holiday with her daughter any day. She could throw a party and shower her daughter with affection and fun.

But leave her alone at a new school in a new country after kissing her sweet little unsure face?

That destroyed her.

Even with Jamie crouching beside her daughter, his hand on her little shoulder, introducing her to a trio of her new classmates. These girls, Jamie had told Greta, were some of the ones who'd made her welcome cards. Her daughter gave them a shy smile and thanked them all.

Sophie grabbed on to that smile like it was a life preserver. Greta was going to be fine, she told herself. Her shyness would melt as the days went on. Jamie would watch over her.

She gave him what she hoped was an encouraging smile, wishing she could return to the bliss she'd felt on their date Saturday night. But the bliss was gone, and this gut-wrenching mommy moment was one she was going to remember for a long time.

"Would you like to see your desk?" Jamie asked Greta.

Her nod was hesitant.

"Esme can show you, if you'd like," Jamie said, "as she's sitting right in front of you."

"Come on," Esme said, her brown ponytail bobbing as she took Greta's hand with the authority of an eldest child and started leading her away.

Greta glanced over her shoulder one last time. Sophie's heart clutched as she gave her daughter an encouraging smile and blew her a kiss. Her little girl's mouth lifted, and then she was keeping pace with the other student. Their classmates trailed in after them. She and Jamie stood alone.

"I know it's hard," he said, turning his head to meet her eyes. "But I'll look after her. I promise."

She wanted to lay her hand on his arm, but this wasn't the place. "I know you will, and I'm grateful. I should let you go. It's your first day of school too."

"It's chaos and heaven all at once," he said with a charming wink, "but we manage to have a little fun. A field trip helps. Good way to ease them back in and break up the day. Today we're going to Kade Donovan's pony therapy farm to learn more about why riding horses can be so good for you."

"Oh, Greta will love that." She played with her coat sleeve. "As will the other children."

"Are you going to introduce me to our new parent and Caisleán's newest artist?" called out a low female voice.

Sophie turned and felt her smile fade as she watched the older woman walk over, her carriage stiff, her brown eyes pinched. While Sophie had never met her, she knew instantly the woman didn't like her.

"Sophie, this is the school's principal, Margaret Doyle," Jamie said as the woman rigidly shook her hand.

"It's nice to meet you." She wondered how many parents felt a sense of dread as they met school administration. Or was she the only one who'd gotten such a reluctant greeting? "Greta is so happy to be here and have Jamie for a teacher."

Her eyes narrowed in a shrewd, pointed gaze. "Our school might not be what you attended but we're proud of it."

"I didn't say—"

"Jamie," she said, turning to him with her taut carriage. "Make sure to welcome the other parents like you have Ms. Giombetti."

He was frowning, but he nodded. "Of course. Today's a big day for everyone, what with them putting their children back into our care."

Her haughty headshake rubbed Sophie the wrong way, and she was relieved when the principal walked over to the parents she'd implied Jamie was ignoring because of her.

"That was a little odd," he said softly so only she could hear. "Maybe she was intimidated by you or something."

Or something...

"Well, have a great first day. And thanks again for the other night."

"I was going to call you and ask if you'd like to go out again, but I didn't have your cell, and I wanted to get it from you personally. Maybe you can write it down and pass it to me when you come to collect Greta?"

She suddenly was aware of the eyes on them. "Of course. See you, Jamie."

After stealing one more glance in Greta's direction, she made herself turn around. Her daughter was out of sight anyway, and she and Jamie needed a better place to talk about their next date.

Thinking about what they might do and where they might go lifted her spirits as she headed to the arts center for her first day. She'd wondered yesterday when he would ask. She and Greta had spent the day pleasantly, sightseeing with Sandrine and Eoghan to Downpatrick Head. The wind had rocked her as she'd beheld the stack of massive rocks sitting on the tempestuous sea racked by blue-green white-tipped waves. The roar of the ocean had echoed in her ears, daring her to ignore its power.

She'd opened her arms and embraced it. In that moment, she'd acknowledged to herself that she was already falling in love—with Jamie, with this place. She was going to make magic in glass here, and perhaps after her Celtic Tree installation, she would do something with the ocean. Its waves would work perfectly in glass.

The Sorcha Fitzgerald Arts Center rested on a breathtaking verdant Irish hill surrounded by pastures of sheep. Unfortunately, none had positive words written on their sides. Eoghan had shown them a new flock of sheep yesterday who had lovely words spray-painted on their sides, like *Love* and *Dreams*. He'd told them they were love poems to the farmer's new wife, the hairdresser in town, inspired by Carrick, who'd once spray-painted his deceased wife's poetry onto his sheep. Those kinds of stories made her happy to be in their new home.

And like Greta, today was her first day in her new world.

When she pulled to a stop in the parking lot, she checked her phone for messages and winced when she saw one from her mother.

Sophie, darling. How are you and Greta faring? The wilds of Ireland must be positively rustic compared to Provence. I'm working myself up for a visit but all that rain... Tell Linc he'd better take care of my family. And do send photos of your new studio. I want to see where you'll be creating all your magic, darling. Ciao.

Two *darlings* in one text and the threat of a visit. She pressed her forefinger to the bridge of her nose. Like hell she'd send her mother any photos. Nothing would be good enough. Certainly not the corrugated metal shed she'd be working in. She tucked her phone in her work bag and exited the car, scanning the property. A trio of sheds were arranged around the back side, one of them still being finished by a lean construction crew led by Liam O'Hanlon, who waved and called out a greeting.

That sent up a squeal from another shed, and Ellie Buchanan raced out of it.

The honey-blond-haired woman skidded to a halt in front of her on the squishy ground and grinned. "Welcome! Happy first day!"

She couldn't help chuckling. "Thanks. It's great to be here."

"Ellie was so excited she baked some kind of coffee cake," Kathleen said, appearing in the open doorway in all black with a welder's apron on. "No one's died trying it yet."

"Hey!" The eager woman punched her friend. "It's pretty good. You're welcome to have some. We have coffee. It's not French—"

"It's perfect," Sophie said, stopping her and wondering why people kept comparing things like coffee and schools. She wasn't her mother. She wasn't about to look down on something just because it was different.

"Wait until you try it," Kathleen drawled. "You might change your mind."

"Honestly," she said, taking Ellie's hand. "I'm really touched by the welcome. I would have made chocolate chip cookies as a thank you for having *me*, but we were out yesterday sightseeing, and I'm still a little shy in Jamie's kitchen."

The friends shared a look before Ellie nudged Kathleen, who sighed. "Don't kill me and don't answer if you don't want to," she said in a *don't shoot the messenger* tone.

"Okay..."

"Ellie wants me to ask if you were smiling as much as Jamie was after your date on Saturday."

"He was *humming* he was so happy," Ellie gushed. "The guys said they'd never seen him so—"

"*Oh...*" She hadn't expected hearing about his post-date mood from her new colleagues, but she went totally soft and had to wrestle for control of the silly smile taking hold of her mouth. "Yes. Yes, I was. Shall we have a little of that coffee cake? Then maybe you can give me a tour."

People were clearly taking an interest in her and Jamie. She liked these women, but she didn't want to spend her first morning at work dishing about her date. Growing up, her parents had always kept a distance between themselves and other artists. While she didn't want that, she wasn't comfortable with such intimacy so soon, and in her place of work. So she kept the discussion to the status of Kathleen's massive metal sculpture in her new warehouse-sized shed and met the other workers on Kathleen's team. Then, since she had asked to see her shed last, they toured the actual arts center.

Ellie bounced up and down in delight when Sophie praised her incredible stained glass window in the entry.

They passed Angie's classroom next, waving to her and her all-female painting class, and then visited the ceramics studio, warm from Megan's kiln. After touring Ellie's stained glass workspace, she finally headed out to look at her shed.

"I wasn't here too long, but I loved it," Kathleen told her as she shouldered open the heavy metal door and hit the overhead lights. "It's going to be cold since the weather turned, but your kiln should change that in no time."

"The kiln and I are about to become good friends," Sophie told them as they walked into the large, airy space.

Glass artists didn't work in luxurious spaces, another reason Sophie's mother had never understood why she'd picked that medium. But the nature of the work demanded functionality. The floor and her workbench had to be fireproof, and the shed had to have a strong ventilation system. Her mother's atelier in Paris had a purple couch and a wine chiller stocked with French champagne. Nothing wrong with that, but it wasn't Sophie's thing.

"I'm totally going to geek out and ask you to show me all of your tools," Ellie said with a hopeful smile. "I hope that's okay. I'll bake you more coffee cake for a demonstration once you're up and running."

"Shameless," Kathleen said with a laugh, giving her friend a noogie, which made her shriek.

Sophie sent them an indulgent smile, enjoying their easy friendship. "First I'll need to load batch into the tank and heat the furnace, or the melting kiln, as some call it. It will take about six days to heat it to the correct temperature."

"How hot are we talking?" Kathleen asked as they wandered closer, all business now.

"The furnace runs twenty-four seven and stays between

2000 and 2400 degrees Fahrenheit. If it ever goes out, I'm out of commission for a few weeks, which is why I asked for a state-of-the-art generator."

"With Irish weather, that's a good plan," Ellie said, her eyes roving. "Out of commission would suck."

"Yes. I had it happen once when I was doing a demo in New Orleans. I've insisted on a generator ever since."

"What kind of glass do you use?" Kathleen asked. "I'm a total novice there."

She pointed to the bags beside the furnace, excitement coursing through her at the sight. "I use spruce pine batch for clear 96, and all the color blowing glasses: Reichenbach, Zimmerman, and Gaffer Kugler."

"And the other kiln?" Ellie asked.

She looked over at her new baby. "That's the reheating kiln—"

"Because the glass cools quickly," Kathleen said. "Not as quickly as metal I think, but don't quote me."

"We could do an experiment sometime to see," Sophie said, waggling her brows. "For the kids in the new arts program."

Kathleen inhaled sharply. "That would be so— I'm reining myself in."

"And *you* were teasing *me*..." Ellie nudged her friend before pointing to the large workspace. "Tell me about your tools. I love sharp, pointy ones. I'll even show you my glass grinder."

"Oh, Ellie—" Kathleen groaned.

Sophie only laughed. "Tools are pretty standard. Blowpipes. Punties. Soffietas. Tweezers to pull the hot glass into shapes. Jacks are tweezer-like but have springy handles so you can insert them into the glass you're blowing and expand its shape. The tag is a square-shaped knife that shapes or sculpts hot glass. Then straight shears and diamond shears to cut the glass. I adore my diamond shears."

"What's the difference?" Kathleen asked, walking closer and peering over at them on the table.

"The straight shears leave a long, flat cut mark in the glass." She picked them up and showed them the flat surface, aware that the tool didn't yet feel like it was hers. Broken in, so to speak. "The diamond shears are named for the shape, not the material. See. They make a diamond shape when the blades are partially open. They're used to pull the glass together. I'm probably getting too technical. You both know there are layers of details and reasons for why we do what we do in our art."

"I'd be happy to blow your mind with the rhyme and reason for stained glass making anytime, Sophie," Ellie said with a grin. "You're welcome to any of my classes—"

"Like I said, shameless," Kathleen said with a grin. "Tell me about the blocks."

Sophie picked up the 6 block, which was the first block in the row. "They're used to shape glass into uniform shapes, usually early on in the glassblowing process. They're made of fruit tree wood like cherry, and they constantly live in buckets of water. Observe all my special water buckets, ladies."

They made the required oohs and aahs before she continued with a laugh. "Blocks come in different sizes starting at a 6 block through 8, 10, 12, 14 and up. Now for the really technical tool: the newspaper."

Ellie and Kathleen watched her cross to where she'd dropped her large purse on the worktable. She held up the last copy of *Le Monde* she'd collected before leaving France. "Wet, this baby becomes a glassblower's best friend. It gives you the chance to be reasonably close to your hot piece while you're shaping it."

"I've always found it ironic that my bare hands can never touch the metal I'm welding," Kathleen said. "I'm shaping it by proxy, and that makes it a little less tactile than stained glass."

"Yeah, but I have to watch myself every second or I get little scars and cuts." Ellie pointed to a few. "It's not like painting or ceramics where you can use your hands dead-on."

"Exactly!" Sophie paged through the newspaper, beyond psyched to get working again. "Every glassblower I've met has their own way of sizing and folding a newspaper. My secret is seven sheets, both because it's a good thickness and a lucky number."

"No wonder you and my dad get along," Ellie said with a fangirl sigh. "You know he called our ranch in Oklahoma the Lucky Seven."

She shook her head, wondering how his meeting with Malcolm Coveney was going. They would soon find out. "I didn't actually. How funny. So this thin wad of paper curls into my hand and helps me make the magic, girls. Some glassblowers prefer to use newspapers already broken in, but not me. I suppose I'll have to get a subscription to *The Irish Times* next. I like to use a local newspaper."

"Solidarity." Kathleen nodded. "Like me using Irish steel. I see that you use safety glasses with a #3 welding glass. Me too."

"Gotta protect my eyes from the UV and IR that come out of the furnace and glory hole. Plus, I can see more easily into the tank."

"Glory hole?" Kathleen snorted. "That probably doesn't mean what my brothers used to joke—"

"Oh, God!" Sophie cringed, well aware of the other reference. "No, it's the reheating furnace I mentioned earlier that has a temperature of over 1000 degrees Fahrenheit."

"Can't imagine anyone being able to perform sex acts of any kind in that heat," Kathleen said with a snort.

"What?" Ellie asked, confusion on her face.

"Ask Brady." Kathleen smirked. "Later."

Sophie bit her lip to keep from smiling. "Moving on... You use the long pipe with the start of your blown glass piece on the end and heat it in the glory hole before—"

"You blow it again, right?" Kathleen's shoulders were shaking.

"Funny," Sophie said, batting her eyes. "We glass-blowers *do* like to blow a lot."

"Oh, stop," Ellie said, covering her ears. "Kids on-site."

"Yeah, you're such a juvenile," Kathleen said, coming over and half hugging her friend. "So that last kiln in the corner?"

She turned and looked to where Kathleen was pointing. "It's the annealer. You put your blown glass in it to cool slowly so it won't crack, which takes at least twelve hours for standard pieces, but upward of twenty or more with my bigger ones."

"And this is going to be a pretty big installation," Ellie said, bouncing on her heels again.

Sophie wandered over to her stainless steel worktable. "Which is why I had a special marver table made. This is where I roll the glass while it's attached to a blowpipe or punty rod."

"Do you ever use molds?" Ellie asked.

Sophie shook her head. "Not anymore. Optic molds don't have the sense of flow I want in my work. There's something special about forming it with my own hands. As you know."

Kathleen flexed her fingers. "Speaking of, I'm about set to heat some metal and pound it with these hands. No better way to spend the day if you ask me. Before we get out of your hair—meaning I'm dragging Ellie out with me—do you need help with anything?"

Camaraderie and support. Yeah, she was going to be happy here. "Bets already volunteered Liam, but thanks."

"You're in great hands there." She snagged Ellie's arm playfully. "All right, cutie, let's leave this poor woman alone to get down to business."

"If you need anything at all," Ellie said, blinking her eyes playfully as her friend pretended to drag her out of the shed.

She waved and then took a moment to savor the silence. Her place. Her tools. She needed to make it all her own. Here she would make her mark with another mind-blowing installation. But first, she needed to hone her design. The pregnant goddess added extra challenges to both the composition and execution of the work.

But first she should start her furnace, and for that, she needed Liam to haul some batch for her. When Linc had asked if she'd need an assistant, she'd told him she wanted to wait and see. She knew they were short on lodging space, and while she'd used one on and off, she liked working alone. Call her a loner or an only child. But she was used to it. Having other people around all the time could be a distraction, and she wanted—needed—her focus and energy to be on creating.

She found Liam and three other workers in the children's shed, hanging industrial lights on ladders. The pirate-looking man seemed to sense her because he looked over his shoulder, called out a greeting, and then jumped down from his perch with the *savoir faire* of Errol Flynn in an old swashbuckler.

"Mum told me to be at the ready for whatever you need." He crossed to her with the kind of smile that made her feel like they were already friends. His sandy blond hair was pulled back into a small ponytail, which added to his pirate look. "You settling in well? Couldn't have been anything but a shock seeing your new home up and taken away."

"Greta and I are really lucky Jamie offered his home to us. Looks like the shed for the kids is coming along nicely."

"Not too bad. We're on schedule. We need to build and paint a few temporary, moveable walls to make it more kid-friendly, but we should be in good shape. So, what can I help you with?"

She cringed. "Hauling bags of glass to dump into my furnace. Hope that's okay."

"It's one of my favorite things to do," he said, putting her at ease with his incredibly open smile. "I like helping people have what they want. At least that's how I see being a handyman. It gives me a chance to see and understand people and bring their vision to fruition."

Her artist instincts kicked up. "You're an artist?"

He laughed. "Not like you're thinking. I construct and paint things. Houses. Walls. Fences. Sheds. But I'll admit I've been doing some murals lately. I'm practicing on some of the walls and floors at Summercrest Manor. With both tile and other mixed media. If it continues to develop, I might offer to do it for others."

"I'd love to see that sometime," she said as they started walking back to her shed, the ground still squishing under her feet from the recent heavy rain.

"You'll have to get Jamie to bring you over." He gave her a winning smile. "Happiest I've ever seen him."

First, Ellie and Kathleen and now Liam. Yeah, she liked hearing how happy Jamie had been. She only smiled in response.

"Now," he said after a pause, "where are these bags?"

After she fitted them both with safety goggles, a mask, and gloves, he lugged them like they weighed nothing. Fortunately, he'd worn work clothes, so she didn't have to have him don a smock. Tiny glass particles could be dangerous. She supervised the loading and thanked him after the bin was full.

"Care to do the honors?" she asked, pointing to the controls. "I can walk you through it."

He held up his hands. "No, I wouldn't dream of it. I'll let you get to it. We're all glad you're here, Sophie. You need anything else, let me know."

Alone again, she longed for a bottle of champagne to break across the bow of her furnace, so to speak. "I hereby christen you the Glory Maker," she said with a radiant smile. "We don't want our glory hole to be all alone in the fun, do we?"

The furnace roared to life, and she set the temperatures and controls to her desired settings. Glass would soon start melting, as viscous as river water. The power of heat. God, how she loved it!

Satisfied, she dug out the design she'd been working on since receiving Linc's first call in the spring. Her worktable was soon covered with drawings. To make the addition of the pregnant goddess inside of the tree trunk, she would need to widen the glass base of the sculpture. Her metal armature would also require further modification, and she would need to add more pieces to the limbs of the trees now that she was widening the trunk and tree. Making the pregnant goddess would be a challenge of assembling hand-blown shapes—cones, circles, spirals, spheres.

Right now, she was hoping to top out at a twelve-foot tree. Three years of work, she estimated, but she often finished early. She would see. The installation was going to be her most complex one yet. She was thinking she might be in the ballpark of about six hundred individual pieces of glass. Each would be fitted with a plastic tube for stability. From there, she would place it on the metal aperture and connect it securely with metal rods. Cables from the museum's ceiling would hold it in place.

"How's it going in here?" a Southern drawl sounded.

She set her pencil down with a smile and looked up as Linc and Bets entered the shed. "Hey! How'd the meeting go? Or should I ask?"

Bets looked a little gray, but her vibrant energy was intact as she practically stomped over in her ankle boots. "No beating around the bush. It sucked."

She winced. "I'm sorry."

Linc rested his weight on one leg. "Malcolm Coveney has big eyes and probably an even bigger stomach. He wants us to move our entire operation up his way—to make it easier for tourists."

"They have *everything* set up in Watertown," Bets added with bitterness. "Why would we want to build anything down here?"

"Because that's called development." Sophie studied Linc's poker face. "How much trouble is he planning?"

Linc's mouth worked before he answered, "A heap, I imagine. Bets, Donal, and I talked the whole way back, and we have our marching orders. Donal is going to look into getting your house back as well as hiring a compliance manager ASAP."

"To field things like new permit issues or surprise safety inspections," Bets added. "It's happened before."

"Terrific," she said with a sigh. "Don't these people have anything else to do?"

"Apparently not." Linc took out a piece of hard candy and crunched, offering her one, which she declined. "I plan to lock down Hans Shumaker today and send out a press release."

"That's awesome!" She'd been the one to connect them, so she was particularly glad it had worked out. "He's a great artist and a great person."

"We also hoped you might be willing to talk to your reporter friend at *The New York Times*," Bets said, "who wrote the piece in May about your decision to join the arts center."

"The one I've seen you laughing with huddled in a corner at one of the fancy art shindigs," Linc added with a smile. "Taylor McGowan impressed me as a no-bullshit kind of girl."

"Yeah. She got jaded early on like I did. Her parents were big patrons of the arts, so we ran in the same circles. We also went to the same prep school, although she was a couple grades behind. But we had a few art teachers in common, whom we both hated. They thought she was a lost cause as an artist so she turned to writing, her other love. I always thought they were wrong about her, but then again, they said I was hopeless as a painter."

"Which you might have secretly wanted them to say," Linc said knowingly. "Well, seems we have our girl. Hate to ask but you know how good press helps. You might even mention our plan for the children's program."

And lay the groundwork to make Malcolm look like a bad guy if he tried to hold things up. Smart.

"Done," she said. "Maybe Taylor will want to interview Jamie. I know he's still working on the program, but he'd be able to convey the general idea."

"Great thought," Bets said, tapping her thigh, her pent-up energy visible. "I'll call him after school is out. He might need some tips on talking to the press."

Her heart sped up a little at the thought of Jamie. "I can walk him through it if you'd like. You want to see the near final design for the sculpture? I've added an additional component to the Tree of Life. It represents a new level for me—a step I've been a little scared to take..."

They both studied her as she gestured with her hands, seeking the right words as her nerves flared to life.

"My parents always caused a lot of controversy with their art. When I became an artist myself, I stayed away from that kind of attention. And yet the minute I came to Ireland—"

"You found yourself smack-dab in the middle of one," Linc finished for her.

"I'm so sorry, Sophie," Bets said, crossing to her and putting a hand on her arm.

"No, it turns out this was good for me." She touched her heart. "Inside I've been wanting to break out, but I couldn't figure out how. *This* is how."

She led them to her drawings. Bets gasped and raised her hand slowly to her mouth.

"Well, I'll be damned," Linc mused, rubbing his jaw. "It's the best you've ever done, darlin', and this cowboy ain't blowing smoke up your dress."

Bets' fingers hovered over the image of the pregnant goddess. "She's so beautiful."

Her chest grew tight. "Yes, she is. Like how I think all pregnant women are. Goddesses. That's how I felt with Greta inside me. I was filled with more love than I'd imagined possible."

The orange-haired woman's hand settled over her belly. "I remember that feeling like it was yesterday—the flutters, the kicks, the movement—even though it was decades ago."

"That's exactly how I recall feeling," Linc quipped with a lopsided smile. "Oh, this is going to draw people in, all right. The love is tangible. I mean, the tree is beautiful, Sophie, but the heart of your sculpture will be the goddess woman and her unborn baby. Way to take it to the next level."

"Thank you." She blew out a long breath, knowing it was full of her trepidation. "The Celtic tradition has goddesses associated with the Tree of Life, so it fits. It's going to involve some modifications, of course, and more glass pieces to blow, but I figure you're not concerned about that."

"Not a lick," Linc said, giving her a congratulatory hug.

Bets was next in line for a hug. "Thanks. I needed some good news after meeting with that jerk. Can you draw up a final design so we can show the board, including our nonvoting members?"

Sophie nodded. She understood the purpose of nonvoting members. Political backers and power players who could give an artist or the institution CYA. Cover your ass. "I'll finalize it today and call Taylor. I think an exclusive might be just the thing."

"That's a terrific idea," Bets seconded.

"People would love to hear Eoghan's story," Sophie added. "He's one of my heroes already, taking up art at ninety-three. Like Grandma Moses. I've told him that I think he might be ready to show some of his ceramics and paintings at the gallery level."

"Perfect," Linc said, tapping the front of the newspaper. "All right, now I need to call my investigator to see what's really under Malcolm Coveney's dress, so to speak."

"I dare Mary Kincaid to show her face with him," Bets said, her blue eyes flashing. "The whole village will want to run her out of town for cozying up with that Watertown hustler with his ten gold rings and his Rolex."

"Ten!" Sophie exclaimed.

Linc rolled his eyes. "I've never seen anything like it, and that's saying something. That man has definitely been nicely paid. Well, we'll let you get back to work. I know you'll need to go pick up Greta before long."

She was already looking at her drawings. "If it wasn't her first day of school, I'd have Sandrine pick her up. But it was hard enough to leave her this morning, and I want to be there with open arms for my little girl."

Bets smiled. "She's lucky to have you, Sophie."

She gave a self-deprecating smile. "Liam seems to have turned out pretty well. The pirate look is hot. Your influence?"

That had Linc snorting out a laugh.

Bets shot him a look. "I don't know where he gets that from. But it's not like he tries, despite all his friends teasing him about being an extra in *Pirates of the Caribbean*. He just seems to embody those qualities."

"Adventure," Sophie added. "Freedom. Fearlessness. A zest for life. Something we all want deep down, I think."

"Well, hell," Linc drawled, "if we stand around anymore, God knows what you'll be saying about me, Sophie. We'll let you get on with it. And thanks."

"Yes, thanks," Bets said, her eyes bright. "It's good to have more allies."

"For me too."

She watched as they left the shed, and then she looked back at her drawing. Yes, you could feel the love.

She picked up her phone and called her friend at *The Times*.

CHAPTER NINE

He had to have his final outline for the arts program done by Friday.

Usually, Jamie wouldn't be intimidated by such a thing, but it was the first week of school. He'd called Bets up at lunch to tell her so after receiving her text. She'd been understanding, of course, but urgency was in the wind after their meeting with Malcolm Coveney. So Friday it was.

Worse. A reporter from *The New York Times* wanted to interview him!

Him. Jamie Fitzgerald.

What in the world was he to say to a hotshot reporter from Manhattan?

He wasn't a man of many words outside the schoolroom, and even then, he let the schoolwork speak for itself at times. A child needed to learn *how* to understand and solve things. He or she couldn't always be spoon-fed information.

But Sophie had sent a message to him after Bets, telling him to come over after school so she could help him with his outline and give him some pointers on speaking with the press. It was some silver lining. He'd prefer to have another date with her, but he'd spend time with her any way he could. Even if it was for work. Seeing her when she picked up her daughter wasn't enough.

As he drove, he told himself he had the skills to handle the interview. He would listen to and learn from Sophie. He would even ask for a practicum and have her ask him mock questions. All he could do was prepare as best he could. Even so, the pressure to help the arts center lodged a rare hard ball of stress in his sternum.

The sight of Sophie waving to him from his front window was welcome enough to temporarily banish his worries. Her brown hair was pulled back in a ponytail like she meant business, but the warm smile on her face as she stopped waving and touched her heart had everything going quiet inside him. His heart filled with the new, surprising sensation of fullness and warmth.

Greta opened the front door with her mother behind her, and he swore he could hear his steady footsteps as he walked on the path toward them. The rightness of it blew through him, and when he crossed the threshold, it was as if something had changed within him. Like he was truly coming home. His whole life had changed in only a few days, and yet his Irish heart knew love could be like that.

"Hello, Greta," he said, holding out his hand, which she took with a smile and a warm greeting. "It's been ages."

That had her giggling. "I just saw you, Mr. Fitzgerald."

"You're so right." Then he shifted his gaze to her mother, whose eyes were as bright as spring fields. "Hello, Sophie."

"Hi, Jamie." She gave him a dazzling smile. "Welcome back to your home."

"Yes, welcome back," Greta added, erupting into more

giggles. "I'm waiting to go over to Eoghan's house to be with him and Sandrine so you and Mama can work. You should see her drawings for her piece. They're *so* beautiful. I told her I think she has the perfect one to show Ms. McGowan, but she's still fussing. Maybe you can convince her."

"Greta's my best art critic," Sophie explained after a shrug.

"You're always telling me that you should never overthink art, Mama," her daughter told her with a maturity that set her apart from others her age.

"I should probably listen to myself then," Sophie said with a laugh, stroking her daughter's head. Shifting her gaze to Jamie, she said, "See what you think. I've been working on the final since Bets and Linc gave me the news about their meeting."

He hadn't been fully briefed yet, but he hadn't needed a long rundown. Malcolm Coveney and his kind were a dime a dozen. Greedy bastards. He couldn't stand the lot of them.

"I don't know too much about the workings of fine art," Jamie said as he shrugged out of his coat and hung it. "I figure only the artist knows when it's finished. But I'd love to take a look."

"The artist should, yes," Sophie said as she picked up a colored drawing and handed it to him. "Perfection and judgment are the death of creativity."

He tucked that bit of wisdom away and gazed at her drawing. His heart seemed to slow. The beauty of it was palpable, but it was the emotion coming from the pregnant woman cradling her large belly that touched him the most. "I couldn't begin to guess how you could improve on this. It's stunning, Sophie. Moving. Powerful. Breathtaking."

"I told you, Mama," Greta said, hugging her leg. "I'll bet Sandrine will agree with me."

When they dropped Greta off, they brought the drawing with them to show Sandrine, who did indeed love it, but it was Eoghan who sealed it with his tears. "Isn't art the most wonderful thing in the whole world?"

His question lingered in Jamie's mind after they left his cottage. That sentiment was what he needed to convey in the children's arts program.

"You said earlier perfection and judgment are the death of creativity. Well, I must be feeling it. I'm a little nervous about showing you my outline. Bets told me to just do my best, but I'm a teacher. I can't in good faith only do an outline. The curricula has to support the plan, and that's where the devil is in the details."

She touched his arm, her hand lingering in a soothing way. "Thanks for trusting me, Jamie."

He withdrew his plans from his satchel and handed them to her. "I'll make us a cup of tea."

Sinking onto his sofa, she was already reading the first page as he walked into the kitchen. Everything was tidy, he noted, and dishes were drying beside the sink. Another detail about her he liked. He filled the kettle and prepped the cups with Lyons, fighting off his nerves.

When he returned, she didn't look up until he set the tea service on the coffee table and sat down beside her.

"Your ideas about art and brain development are a great frame." She tapped the first page. "So many people pooh-pooh art for kids because it's framed as some elite, hoity-toity pursuit that has no real-world practicality. I mean, what can you do with a suncatcher besides hang it in your window? But when you tell parents that you're teaching shapes and critical thinking and motor skills? They're more inclined to listen."

"I thought so too," he admitted, nudging the sugar bowl

and milk toward her. "I wasn't sure parents would see the purpose. Some might, but we have a strong bias toward agricultural programs for kids in these parts. Not surprising."

"Art can be a product of one's environment, a reflection of it, and a gateway to another world. It can be anything you want it to be."

"Imagination," he said, stirring in some sugar after she passed. "It's hard to teach."

"It only needs encouragement." She paged through his papers before stopping toward the back. "I love the depth of your proposal...the way you suggest appropriate curricula for the different age ranges. Teaching teenagers the principles of color, styles of art, and perspective. Guiding younger children to put geometric shapes together to make art. I love it. I mean, it's a nature walk meets art with the sticks, stones, and pine cones."

"I like the idea of teaching them that art is everywhere." He winced, hoping he didn't sound lame. "When the Yanks first arrived, we used to joke how excited they got seeing a rainbow. We say only the tourists go crazy for them, but I got to thinking that we shouldn't be so numb to the beauty around us. There's an old saying in Ireland that's stuck. You can't eat a view."

An absent smile crossed her face. "Hard times can do that, but to me, beauty gives hope that all isn't lost."

"Exactly!" He leaned forward, the stirrings of a good discussion racing through him. "Angie and Megan kept talking about the light and the colors—"

"For good reason," she said with a compelling sigh. "It's so beautiful here, Jamie. Even though I'm freezing my butt off at the end of August."

He laughed, wondering if she was cold now. "Do you want me to show you how to use the woodstove?"

"Maybe after I finish telling you my thoughts. Using subjects kids love as drawing models—like Wonder Woman or baby Yoda—is brilliant. And I love the reference books you've selected. Greta adores *The History of Art for Children*. The program you've designed lives up to one of the tenets in your mission statement: to take children on a journey of self-expression."

The tension in his diaphragm eased. The whole exercise had stretched him, as he'd wanted, but he'd fretted over whether it was good enough. "Good to hear. What more can we do?"

Her face was radiant with excitement, like one of his students when discussing a favorite subject. "I was thinking about Greta and some of the things we've done. I've mostly tried to undo the strict arts training my parents arranged for me. The teachers and schooling were...harsh. Rigorous. The kind you'd give a savant, which my parents hoped I was with painting. I won't do that to any child."

He'd always been able to tell when someone needed to work something out of their system, so he remained quiet and let her talk.

She exhaled harshly after a moment. "Sorry. But no kid should be subjected to that kind of pressure. Art should be fun, although I didn't know that until I made my first flower at a glassblowing tutorial that I signed up for secretly."

Secretly? He couldn't have imagined a pressure so great she would resort to hiding her deepest passion. "You'll have to show me that flower sometime. I'll bet it was beautiful."

She rolled her eyes. "I must sound like an idiot. Secret art classes. Bone-crushing pressure. Ugh! But it *was* beautiful. The first piece of art I enjoyed creating."

He poured her more tea, which had her gazing softly at him. He could stare at her forever. "What flower was it?"

"It was a calendula." Her voice was so dreamy he found himself reevaluating flowers. Before meeting her, he could have taken them or left them. "So pure. So orange. Happy."

"What's the hardest flower you've ever made?" he asked.

Her laughter poured out like water from a bubbling spring. "The naked man orchid. It was a birthday present for my mother. She didn't know what to do with it."

They had such an orchid? He was tempted to look it up. "I don't think we have those in Ireland."

"Probably not, but that's why nature is so great. There are shapes and stories everywhere, and when you break down the elements, they can be easy to capture in art." She tapped her chin. "Maybe you can add a module on drawing simple but realistic images. Fruits. Landscapes. Again, simple shapes. People's faces are the same way, you know. A nose is really only an upside-down triangle."

She picked up her pen and doodled one on the corner of a notebook lying on the coffee table. He was amazed at her speed as much as her realism. It almost made him believe he could draw a nose too. The triangle concept made sense.

"Everything is much easier to figure out and understand once you make it simple," Jamie said, taking a sip. "Progress is easier when you have the building blocks. I'm not an artist, but you're right, I think I could draw one if I break it down into shapes. It wouldn't be like your pregnant woman, mind you. She's living and breathing on that very page. So is your tree. I could almost feel the wind blowing through the branches."

"Thanks." She scooted closer until her knee was touching his thigh. "I was technically proficient at painting, but I couldn't convey emotion in that medium. Maybe I didn't want to since I was being pushed into it. You can't fake emotion in a piece. When I drew this, all I had to do was remember how it felt when I was pregnant with Greta. I used to draw myself when I was pregnant. To chronicle my progress. But I was too chicken to share them with the world then."

"But you're not now," Jamie added, his entire gaze filled with her.

"Oh, I'm still a little scared, but I'm equally as excited and determined." She took a sip of her tea and swore. "Hot. Good one, Sophie."

"Angie, Megan, and Ellie are going to give me their notes by Wednesday, so I'll have a few days to include them. Would you—"

"Absolutely!" She blew on her tea. "It seems I'm done with my drawing. Whew! You're pretty close too. Jamie, this is really impressive."

He lifted a shoulder. "It's only researching and seeing what makes sense. Then following up with the experts on the individual art modules. The program we run for the fall will be smaller, of course—as kids are in school. But Bets figures we can run longer programs in the summer, like camps. I figured it's important to give the kids an introductory program to start, something to help them figure out what they might be interested in before they sign up for a specific medium."

"Nothing worse than being in an oil painting class based on the Renaissance masters and hating every minute of it." She mimed a horrified expression. "You were supposed to laugh."

He only gazed back at her. "Hard to laugh at something that upset you so badly."

She leaned into him. "That's what makes you wonderful. Jamie, I know you're going to be really busy this week, but all I've been thinking about since you arrived is how much I want to kiss you and have your arms around me. Now that we've stopped working, can we take a moment to relive the other night?"

Her green eyes rested on him with what he thought was hopeful vulnerability. "That's all I've been thinking about too. The other night was one of the best of my life. Come here, Sophie."

She eased slowly into his arms as they watched each other. Her body was supple as he drew her against him and leaned in to kiss her. Her breath rushed out, and then she was pressing her mouth to his, their movements soft and unhurried.

Her low murmur had his blood heating, and he stroked the long line of her back, drawing her still closer to him until their bodies brushed and held. She was soft and warm and pliant, and as their mouths danced together, all he could think of was how she tasted like woman and spice, how she sought his touch, and how she moaned, low and light in the quiet around them.

When they separated, she put her forehead on his shoulder. "I'm falling for you. So fast that it should make my head spin. But it doesn't. Every time I feel like I'm falling, it's like that first sweet dive into the warm sea. Everything goes still. Everything gets quiet. And I'm floating in another world, one I never want to leave."

He caressed the back of her neck, the power of her words filling his chest.

She pressed back and studied him. "You didn't say anything. Is that because I freaked you out?"

His mouth lifted. "Do I look concerned? I don't have words like you. Our Irish sea isn't warm, so I can't describe my feelings on entering it in this very moment. But I can tell you how I felt as I was walking toward my house, seeing you and Greta waiting for me. Like I was truly coming home—not only to where I live but to the women I already treasure."

She lifted her hand to his cheek, her face breaking into a smile so warm he was sure it could compete with the sun itself. "You're not so bad with words, Mr. Fitzgerald."

The praise had him kissing her cheek. "Perhaps we can go out to dinner again on Friday night once I'm finished with everything?"

"I'd love that." She kissed his jaw. "What shall we do until Sandrine drops Greta off?"

Heated visions came to mind—too soon for him to realize them. He supposed he should ask her for media tips. "About the interview..."

"Just be yourself," she said, touching his arm. "I know that sounds corny, but it's true. Taylor is a friend and a great reporter. She knows how to make the person she's interviewing comfortable. She'll probably ask you to tell her a story about teaching or something to soften you up. Just talk to her. Like you would someone you wanted to get to know better. That's what makes her special."

"Except she'll be the one asking the questions," he said, wondering what story he could possibly tell.

"Sure, but you can ask her some too, if you want. Only they won't be in the article," she said with a laugh. "Trust me, this is going to be great."

He was still going to look up some online tips about interviewing. "How about we have another cup of tea, and you can tell me more about your mischievous side? It's not every woman who gives her mother a naked monkey orchid for a gift."

"Right? But my mother is internationally known for her

nudes, especially the male ones. Women who draw naked men dip into the taboo, especially back then. I was tortured at school for being the daughter of a perv. Or a slut."

"But that's outrageous!"

She made a face. "Yep! That flower was my own kind of snarky statement, and she knew it. But it was also my way of telling her I was mostly over it. Still, in my mind, the male form was always linked to my mother's paintings and the controversy over them. Not exactly a healthy perspective for a young girl. But don't worry. I'm mostly over thinking about my mother when it comes to nude men."

He couldn't laugh, although he knew she was trying to joke. Instead, he hugged her close, soothing her with slow caresses to her spine. "This is a side of you I really want to hear more about. I'll bet you have some great stories, and you know us Irish love a good story."

"Which side?" she asked with a twinkle in her eyes. "The wacky side? Or the messed-up side? They're two sides of the same coin."

"It's the Sophie you don't share with just anyone," he told her quietly. "That's the one I want to hear more about."

Shock rained over her face before she pressed her heart against his chest. "That Sophie is very happy to have someone want to listen."

He smiled softly to himself, knowing he'd be happy to do that for the rest of his days.

CHAPTER TEN

Sophie had always believed good news came in threes.

Bets told her that made her part Irish as they watched Linc's mobile home being reconnected on Friday afternoon, one week after it had been hauled away. She'd already packed her things and Greta's, including January the sheep. Jamie had told her daughter that she'd been chosen by the sheep and they couldn't be parted—he'd get another one for his niece.

"I honestly thought it was going to take longer," the petite woman exclaimed, bundled up in a puffy aubergine winter coat.

"So did I, honestly," Linc replied, resting against his Rover in a long leather jacket that was reminiscent of the Old West. "But apparently Donal and I have the right people on speed dial now, although that seems like a small victory after all the hullaballoo Malcolm caused."

"I still say it's win number one," Sophie said, holding up a finger. "Two is Hans formally agreeing to join us next year. And three is the article coming out in *The New York Times* on Sunday."

She didn't include her date with Jamie tonight, although she could scarcely wait. They'd seen plenty of each other this week, and it had only made her more eager for some time alone with him. There'd been school pickups and drop-offs, of course, and he'd swung by midweek to get some more clothes and pick up her final comments on his arts program. On Thursday, she'd included him at the tail end of her interview with Taylor after deciding he'd be more comfortable with her present. He'd been visibly relieved by Taylor's laid-back attitude and friendliness.

And her friend had followed up in pure reporter fashion after the interview by texting, *Do I sense romance in the air?* To which Sophie had responded, *No comment* with a winky emoji.

Truthfully, her mind was full of Jamie. While she would have loved to have an earlier date, waiting until tonight had seemed wise. She'd wanted to be home for Greta after school, and truth be told, she'd balanced a lot of balls in the air this week, her first in a new country and at a new job.

Being alone with him tonight while Sandrine and Eoghan took care of Greta was going to be blissful. They could flirt and gaze at each other like soon-to-be lovers. Her body was alive with desire for him, and after so long a drought, the feelings were marvelous.

They'd be able to explore those feelings more readily now that he'd be returning to his cottage, and she to this home. When they were ready, they had the space now for what was next. Romance. Lovemaking. She was liquid as glass with the possibilities, and she wrapped her arms around herself, wanting to sway in the cold breeze.

"You want my gloves?" Linc asked her, frowning as he misinterpreted her movements. "They're in the back."

She tucked her hands behind her back, hoping she didn't look sheepish. Bad pun. "No, I'm good. I do wrap myself up when I'm thinking sometimes."

"I bake cookies," Bets said, pulling up her collar when the wind kicked up. "I've baked four dozen this week."

"We have cookies coming out of our ears," Linc replied. "For good reason. We might have arranged the return of this mobile home, but Malcolm Coveney isn't done with us. At least I have his number now."

Sophie peeled her gaze away from the crew reconnecting the porch. "Do tell."

"He's in hock," Linc replied with a scary little smile. "With his new resort. The golf course and trappings haven't gone exactly as he'd hoped. He needs more occupants in his hotel, to say the least."

"That's where we're supposed to come in," Bets said with a scowl. "Just up and move our arts center for him."

"I thought golf was a big draw in Ireland," she said, not being among the fanatics herself.

Linc nodded, keeping an eye on the crew. "He'd arranged for a retired American pro golfer to give high-priced lessons and hang around the place, making it a serious golf destination, but it fell through."

"Rather like having artists in residence," Sophie added with a laugh.

"You knew you're the prize bear in our circus?" Linc quipped with a grin.

"Stop that," Bets said, clucking her tongue.

He made a face back to her. "Seems this golfer who I can't name for confidential reasons didn't care much for Malcolm's ways and told him straight-out. Didn't go over well. Major bookings got canceled. Even a charity golf tournament that had been expected to bring in lots of high rollers and press for the resort."

"That explains his clothes and all those rings," Bets said, waggling her hands dramatically. "The Irish have some great expressions for that kind of front. *When you're broke, you have to have a flash.* But my favorite is *dress well when you're going bad.*"

"Oh, I love that." Sophie was still picking up Irish sayings, and she knew it would take a while for her to develop a good vernacular.

"Makes me think of skinny-dipping with snapping turtles," Linc said with a naughty chuckle.

"Linc Buchanan, you are terrible," Bets exclaimed, socking his arm.

"And you love it," he responded, wrapping an arm around her waist.

They shared a deeply connected look for a moment, one that was rife with heat. Sophie looked away, thinking that she couldn't wait for that kind of look from Jamie tonight.

"We're done here," the head guy called. He was the same man who'd disconnected the trailer last week, and he didn't look the least bit chagrined about his behavior.

"Great!" Linc patted Bets one more time for good measure. "Would you mind texting Liam now, sugar, while I send them off? Sophie, I'll take your luggage inside."

Sometimes he was too much. "I've got it, Linc."

He shot her a look, so she stayed where she was after rolling her eyes, which had him chuckling.

"Let him do the guy thing," Bets said as she pulled out her phone and shot off a text. "It makes him happy. Anything else we can do to make you more comfortable?"

"Not a thing." She pointed to the sky. "Okay, maybe some sun and warmer weather. It's the beginning of

September, for heaven's sake. I knew about the Irish weather but this is—"

"Typical." Bets' sigh sounded downright depressed. "Even after all these years, the weather still gives me fits. I know it's last minute, but I wondered if you and Greta would like to come over for dinner tonight?"

"I'd love to, but I already have plans. Rain check?"

The older woman gave her a knowing smile. "Jamie?"

"I'm in new territory here, so I'm not sure if I should simply say *no comment* like I did to my reporter friend." She pointed to the band of men alighting in the truck. "They're finally leaving. Good riddance."

"Nice evasion," Bets added with a little elbow nudge to Sophie's side. "All right, we'll get out of your hair so you can settle in. And get ready for your secret plans."

With that, she headed off toward Linc as he took her bags out of the trunk. They spoke for a quick moment before Linc crossed the yard and deposited her luggage in the front foyer.

"I'll take it the rest of the way," she said, kissing his cheek and then turning to Bets, whom she hugged.

"Liam is going to check the connections to the house just to be sure everything is fine." Linc took Bets' hand. "We'll let you get ready for your date."

Busted. She shot him a frown to maintain appearances.

"Especially if you have to wash your hair," he said with a chuckle. "Women always seem to do that for dates early on. Hey, Bets, when was the last time you washed yours, by the way?"

"When was the last time you asked me out, cowboy?" she bandied back. "Bye, Sophie. Holler if you need anything."

She waved as they left and then shut the door, wheeling

their luggage through the house to the bedrooms. The mobile home was designed for luxury, what with its cherry hardwood floors and plush furniture—the polar opposite of Jamie's comfortable cottage.

Another world, she thought, as she stopped in the master suite, eyeing the marble floors visible in the bathroom. Jamie had simple cream tile floors throughout his house. There had been something special about knowing she was walking where he had. Longing had her wrapping her arms around herself. This place didn't smell like him, and for a moment she missed it. *Him.*

But as she fixed her gaze on the large king bed, she gave in to a little wiggle of happiness. So too when she sighted the jacuzzi tub in the bathroom. She could take a short but luxurious bath before picking up Greta from school.

When she turned on the taps, no water came out. "Not good." Crossing to the sink, she turned the silver tap. Nothing. "Great. I guess Liam has some work to do, after all."

She went back into the main suite and decided to unpack. There was a cedar walk-in closet to the right with double doors, which would be perfect for the shipment they had arriving next week. She flicked on the light switch. It remained dark. Suspicion rooted in her mind. No water. And now no lights.

Detouring to the kitchen, she eyed the gas stove and turned it on. No flame. She walked to the refrigerator, bracing herself for rotten food, but it was empty. The light was off in there as well.

Talk about sabotage.

When she heard the purr of a motorcycle outside, she headed to the front door. Liam killed the engine and swung off the bike, dressed in all black. He waved before taking off his helmet.

"Hiya. Happy to be back at your own place?"

"I was." She came forward, shaking her head. "I don't seem to have any water, gas, or electricity."

"Those bastards!" Liam's green eyes narrowed. "Good thing we thought to check the connections. I'll see to it."

"Thanks, Liam," she said, heading back inside.

Her phone beeped, signaling a text. Her mother, she discovered.

Darling, I just heard that Hans is headed to Ireland too! It's an art migration. Makes me reconsider my opinion a little. Perhaps I was being hasty, disregarding it. Linc wouldn't be involved if it weren't interesting. But seriously... How are the accommodations? You know I can't create unless I'm comfortable. You still haven't sent me a photo of your studio. Call me.

If her stomach wasn't so tense, she might have laughed. Her mother was *reconsidering*? No, she was feeling left out. Her mother would hate the rustic countryside. Her image of rustic was a villa in Provence, Tuscany, or Andalusia.

Sophie threw her phone on the couch. She didn't want her mother to have anything to do with the center. Keeping her career separate from her parents' had been important to her.

"Sophie?" Liam called. "Can you come out here a minute?"

She turned to see him outside the window. He gestured to the front with his thumb before disappearing. When she reached him, he was standing with his hands on his hips and a scowl on his face that put her in mind of a pirate who'd been repelled from taking a port.

"There's no easy way to say it. They shut off your utilities. As a precaution, they insisted. Total bollocks! Each service company said they couldn't send anyone out here until Monday at the earliest as they're closing for the weekend and are short-staffed for emergencies, which apparently ours does not qualify for. I'm sorry. We're dealing with prize fuckers here."

She started laughing. The whole thing was ridiculous! "Prize fuckers, huh? Gosh, and here I thought good news came in threes."

"You're lucky until you aren't, but this isn't about luck, it's about greed." He gestured to the house. "Can I get your luggage and help you settle back into Jamie's?"

"I should probably call him to ask—"

"No need," Liam interrupted with a wave of his hand. "He'd want you to have water and power and heat."

"Right," she said dryly.

Liam set his scowl aside and grinned. "Besides, he's finding new ways to stop us from sneaking up on him as he works in his room, which is pretty much what he's done all week, what with school and his proposal for the children's arts program."

This sounded good. "What did he do?"

Rubbing his hands together as if preparing for a good story, Liam waggled his brows. "Well, last night, he covered the rug in front of his door with glue traps for mice. When Brady and Declan got stuck, they howled so much with laughter, they fell on their bums."

"You're kidding!" She couldn't imagine quiet Jamie coming up with a prank like that.

"It gets better," he said, his green eyes bright. "The night before last, he rigged up a glass of water over his door. I got good and thoroughly drenched."

She couldn't help but laugh. "Sounds fun actually."

"It is. We're reliving our childhoods but good, the four of us. Honestly, I was sad to see Jamie go home today, mostly because I wanted to discover what he'd come up with next. It's like he's channeling *Home Alone*."

"I love that movie," she said, her heart lifting as the sun came out. "When I was a kid, it was my greatest wish to be left alone, but my parents were always dragging me off to some art show."

He grew quiet, reminding her a little of Jamie. "So you were like Kevin in wishing your family would disappear?"

She bit her lip. "Would you think badly of me if I said yes?"

"Not at all." He held up his hands. "I don't judge. Well, I'll just help you move your stuff back to your car. Then I'll follow you."

"You don't have to do that, Liam."

"I do and I will. I'll just be a minute. Enjoy the sun while she's out."

He headed inside, and she closed her eyes. Before she'd taken the sun for granted. Never again, she promised herself.

He was true enough to his word, stowing her luggage, following her over, and then hauling it back into Jamie's cottage. She decided she might need to delay the delivery of her shipment another week to be safe.

As he picked up his bike helmet, he tilted his head to the side. "You've been in touch with an old friend from America. Someone who writes. In New York?"

A shiver went through her. "Yes, a reporter. Did Jamie tell you?"

"He's not one for sharing anyone's business, if you understand me."

"Then he didn't mention being interviewed himself?"

"*Interviewed?*" Liam shook his head ruefully. "Not a thing, but that's no shock. We usually have to pull things out of him."

That fit with her Jamie, but it led to another question. "Then how did you *know*?"

He lifted a shoulder. "We Irish know things sometimes." He paused, studying her. "Was she in Paris before?"

More shock rolled through her. "Yes. Whoa! Hold the phone. She just left. Said it didn't feel like where she wanted to be anymore. Of course, being back in Manhattan hasn't cured the itch. She's still trying to figure out what's next. I mean, she can write from anywhere. Besides, she travels a lot for work because she writes for the arts and cultural section."

His face broke out into a brilliant smile. "Of course! Now I have the— Never mind. I'm about to creep you out a little more, but I must know. Is her name Taylor?"

She had to close her gaping mouth. "Okay, you're *really* psychic. Yeah, it's Taylor. How do you *know* all of this?"

"I heard it while I was meditating." He looked off and put his finger to his mouth, a portrait in silhouette, before turning back to her. "If you happen to speak with her again soon, tell her not to worry. It's all going to become clear. I'll be off now."

"Wait! I have questions." Hundreds of them. Maybe thousands.

He slipped on his helmet and gave her a thumbs-up—*a thumbs-up*—before throwing his leg over the bike and turning on the engine. With another wave, he was off, the Triumph thundering down the road.

She stood there, the sun washing over her face. She couldn't imagine having a gift like that. Would she even want to? She dug out her phone. She had to text Taylor.

Don't think this too weird, but a gorgeous Irishman who's obviously crazy psychic just told me to tell you that everything will soon become clear.

Her phone beeped with a reply.

How gorgeous? I'm on deadline. I need a jolt.

She laughed before replying.

Sandy blond hair. Leafy green eyes. Tanned. Nice body. Nice smile. Not that I'm looking. Rakish gold earring in his left ear, making him look like a pirate. Drives a Triumph motorcycle.

Taylor's reply was immediate.

He's not at the helm of Queen Anne's Revenge? Disappointing but still hot. I'm smoking my fake cigarette now. Send a picture if you can. And tell him... Thanks for the message? Are you sure he wasn't funning you?

She couldn't believe she was texting about Blackbeard's old pirate ship with her friend after delivering a psychic message. She replied:

I'll try and send a pic. And no, he's solid.

Taylor sent back a thumbs-up—a little eerie as Liam had just given her one before he left—and then typed a message.

Well, the Irish have a rep for being close to the veil. Whatever that means. I'm diving back into my article. Look for it in the Sunday edition. It's going to rock.

She sent back a thumbs-up and stowed her phone. Well, her job was done. She'd already sent her friend her finished design so she could run it with the article. Now all she had to do was pick up Greta and get ready for her date.

As she entered Jamie's house, she could have sworn she smelled oranges. Funny. The scent was so fresh, it was almost like the house was welcoming her back.

After what Liam had told her, she was almost inclined to believe it.

CHAPTER ELEVEN

She was back at his home.

Malcolm Coveney had something to do with the utilities issue. Of that, there was no doubt. Linc and Donal were already burning up the phones about it, Jamie knew, since he'd called Bets to let her know he'd sent her the proposal for the children's program to distribute to everyone for tomorrow's board meeting.

It was a formality. Given the input he'd had from the other artists, they didn't expect any changes. On Monday, Bets would put out a press release, along with the curriculum, and announce the upcoming fall term would start at the beginning of October. They'd be off to the races.

If only Malcolm Coveney would leave them alone. Hopefully their media blitz, as Linc called it, would counter the man's nefarious plans. All Jamie wanted was to think about his date tonight.

When he arrived at Summercrest, he was happy to find himself alone. Everyone was at work, it seemed. He dragged his suitcase back upstairs to his room. He'd stripped off the bedding this morning, so he'd have to find fresh sheets.

When he turned around to head to the linen closet, he let out a shriek.

Sorcha stood in the doorway, her white dress billowing from an invisible breeze. "You just can't escape the haunted things, Jamie. Me or this house."

He narrowed his eyes. "I thought you said it wasn't haunted. Never mind. I have things to do before my date, so you'd best tell me why you're here."

Strolling forward, her bare feet hovering over the stone floor, she said, "I'm here to congratulate you on how nicely things are progressing with Sophie. She's completely fallen for you. Now it's time to take her hand and face what's next. Have fun tonight, Jamie."

She disappeared with a quicksilver smile.

He threw his hands up. "Face what's next? Have fun? Why don't you simply spell out *DOOM* on the wall?"

Her orange scent surrounded him. Ignoring her, or doing his best imitation of it, he stalked down to the kitchen. If he was going to stay here, he needed another booby trap for his room. Otherwise, he'd be overrun with people asking him what was up and whether he needed help getting ready for his date.

God help him, Ellie had even volunteered to do his hair this morning as he'd grabbed a quick bowl of porridge, which had made Kathleen chortle with laughter before offering to pick out his clothes. Declan had followed up with an offer to pick up bubble bath so he could make himself squeaky clean.

They were eejits. All of them. But the ongoing shenanigans were making his stay at Summercrest enjoyable. When he opened the pantry, he pulled out the bicarbonate soda and grabbed an empty bucket and some wire from the closet before heading back upstairs.

After placing yet another *Do Not Disturb* note on his bedroom door, he rigged his trap and settled down to grade papers. He'd read enough comparative education studies in Europe to know that the seven-hour-a-week average most Irish children spent on homework was high. He'd done his best to incorporate in-school practicums for them to learn to reduce it to around five a week, but this being the first week, he'd been kind. He'd mapped their homework at around four.

When he came to Greta's worksheet, where she'd had to color and label simple fractions in the corresponding shapes, he wasn't surprised to give her a perfect score. She was quiet in class but extremely attentive.

He would need to challenge her, he knew. Mostly, though, he hoped she would enjoy coming to school. So far he couldn't tell. She was all smiles when she saw him at the cottage, but she was more reserved in the classroom, still finding her way with the other kids. But it was early yet.

Scraping in the hallway had him turning his head quickly toward the door. Did he have an intruder, or was Sorcha playing tricks on him?

He watched as the doorknob turned and sat back to wait. Then the door was flung open. A shower of bicarbonate exploded. He heard coughing and laughing before Ellie and Kathleen peered into the room.

"We got you this time!" Ellie said, clutching her belly. "We triggered your trap without getting caught."

"We're onto you, Fitzgerald." Kathleen pointed two fingers at her own eyes and then poked them in his direction, chortling herself.

He regarded them as he would truant children, by raising his eyebrow. "I'm glad you're amused. And here I thought you'd arrived to see what I was going to wear tonight."

They both stepped forward in their eagerness and hit the wire he'd stretched across the threshold. The bucket of water tipped, drenching them. Their outraged shrieks filled his chamber.

He couldn't help it. He started to laugh.

Sputtering, Ellie pushed soggy locks of hair out of her face. "You tricked us!"

Kathleen only wiped the water from her skin. "Crafty, Jamie. Very crafty. You're going to have to pay for that."

He jolted as she started to rush him. Oh, hell. He shot to his feet, using his chair as a shield and edging back against the stone wall. "Now, girls..."

"You forget I have seven older brothers," Kathleen called out, crouching in a menacing way. "Do you know what a wedgie is? Jamie Fitzgerald, I'm about to give you one. Block the door, Ellie. This is war."

He almost shrieked as she darted toward him, making him hold up the chair like he was a lion tamer. "You're the one trespassing!"

"Have you finally outraged the women, Jamie?" Liam asked, appearing behind Ellie.

"I had a *Do Not Disturb* up." He eyed Kathleen, who was now crouched, waiting to see which way he would run. "Liam, tell them to stop this."

"I'm just an impartial observer." Liam was biting his lip to keep from laughing. "Water *and* bicarbonate, Jamie?"

"He soaked us!" Ellie accused again with a finger pointed in his direction.

"Now he's going down," Kathleen said before rushing him at full speed.

He threw aside the chair, not wanting to hurt her, and

then she was grabbing him in a wet bear hug. She was a tall and strong woman, and he couldn't in good conscience break her grip by virtue of his superior strength.

"Give him the wedgie, Ellie," Kathleen called.

And that's when all bets were off. He picked her up off her toes and deposited her on the bed before running like mad for the doorway. Ellie, bless her, tried to block his way, but he knew she was ticklish, so he waggled his fingers against her side, making her shriek. He was in the hallway a moment later, running as fast as he could down the stairs.

His only thought was to find somewhere to hide—somewhere they'd never imagine he'd go—so he flew down the basement stairs and ended up in Liam's meditation room.

The former dungeon he would not call it, lest he go mad.

He wedged himself in the corner beside a bookshelf filled with self-help books and an odd trio of singing bowls. It wasn't so bad really.

Then he heard an unnatural laugh. An agonizing moan. And chains being dragged.

Sorcha!

Good God, he hoped it was her. He stood there, trembling in fright for who knew how long. Lifting his wrist, he saw his watch had stopped working. Didn't watches stop working during supernatural events? His stomach heaved.

"Jamie," Liam called. "I know you're down here. I'm coming in to meditate—alone. Don't jump me. I even brought your date outfit. Sweet of you to lay it out on the bed."

He didn't dare peer out. "The girls aren't with you?"

"No, they're cleaning up and changing. That was low, going for the two-step booby trap. Reminds me of when you put a firecracker inside the Christmas candle at school. Your mother shrieked like a banshee."

"I wrote sentences until my hand almost fell off," he said, slowly emerging but still watchful.

"Do you remember when you and Brady put holes in all the soda bottles at the St. Stephens party? You used to pull pranks all the time. I always wondered why you'd stopped."

He shrugged. "I grew up. Teachers aren't supposed to pull pranks. They're supposed to stop them."

"No, it would seem teachers grade homework and stay home a lot." Liam sat on a navy blue mat and smiled. "Looks like your inner child needed some expressing. It's hard to be serious all the time. After Sorcha died, I know your grief was compounded by Carrick's."

He lowered his gaze to the stone floor. "We were all struggling, Carrick most of all. I'm glad those days are behind us."

"Me too." Liam rested his hands on his knees. "I imagine this playful energy is good for your dating life. Why don't you hang out down here until you have to go? I'll help sneak you out of the house. I heard Kathleen talk about heading to Mr. Price to see if she and Ellie could find soaker-hose water guns."

Wincing, he rubbed the back of his neck. "I'm in for it then."

"Women don't like to get their hair wet—except perhaps from the rain. Plus, they aren't Irish."

"No, they aren't." Neither was Sophie. He would make sure to keep her hair as dry as possible.

"Brady and Declan are going to laugh until they're blue," Liam said, chuckling himself. "But not in front of their wives. Kills the bedroom fun, you know."

He hoped he would know soon. Having Sophie in that

way was something he could only imagine—and, indeed, *had* imagined—but he knew the reality would be a million times better. "I'll just be quiet and let you meditate."

"You can do whatever you want." Liam closed his eyes. "There's nothing that can bother me after today."

Jamie narrowed his eyes. He didn't want to interrupt Liam, but how could he resist? "What happened?"

Liam only smiled.

When he didn't respond, Jamie busied himself with checking his dress shirt for wrinkles and other silly things to pass the time. He was grateful Liam's watch face was visible in the position his hands rested in that mantra thing he did. When it grew close to time for his date, he excused himself into an unfinished closet and changed.

When he emerged, Liam was waiting for him, his entire being as calm as the sea after a storm. Jamie gestured to himself. "Will I do?"

"You look fine as fine can be." Liam started toward the stairs. "I can't guarantee they won't be waiting for you, but I'll draw their fire as best I can."

At the top of the steps, Jamie scanned the large hall. There wasn't a sound. The parlor was dark, the perfect hiding place. Jamie looked at Liam.

"I'd best run for it."

Liam nodded and together they took off. At the line of the parlor, he saw an orange flash and the line of a woman's body. He sprinted for the door as the first slap of high-powered water struck his back. He shrieked. Liam grunted. His friend turned around and held out his hands as Jamie opened the door, taking a steady spray to the chest.

"Have fun," Liam called as Jamie disappeared through the door and ran for his car.

He had his car keys out and was inside before the two

women emerged from the house, pummeling his car with their water guns. Backing up, he found himself laughing all the way to his house.

By the time Greta opened the door, he was feeling downright exuberant. "Hello there, young Greta. Would you mind if I picked you up and swung you around?"

"If you want to, Mr. Fitzgerald," she said, holding up her arms.

He carefully swept her up and around, making her laugh as Sandrine smiled and Eoghan clapped his hands. "Have the fairies taken you over, man?"

Setting her carefully back on her feet, he turned to see Sophie covering her mouth with her hand, amusement in her green eyes. How it enlivened him to see her.

"After today, I might believe in fairies," she said. "You look...wet, Jamie."

"On your front and back side but not that mop of curls you call hair," Eoghan said, circling him. "A strange rain it was then?"

He laughed. "From a water gun, courtesy of the Yanks after I played a little prank and drenched them to the skin."

Eoghan hooted with laughter as the other women started chuckling.

Greta snuck behind him and exclaimed, "They really got you, didn't they, Mr. Fitzgerald?"

"You could change into something else." Sophie's mouth danced with humor. "I mean, you live here, after all."

He waved a hand grandly. "It's no bother. Come. Let us go into the night and hope to see no more water guns."

She was grinning as she walked over to him and put a hand on his damp coat. "You're in great form. I can't wait to see how tonight goes."

The moment they arrived at the lively Irish tavern he'd

chosen, the teasing began. Everyone he knew asked about the lines of water across his front and back. He introduced Sophie as the new artist at the center, aware of the speculation, and told the story about the water guns, which led to questions about how he'd ended up staying at Summercrest Manor in the first place.

Sophie stepped in and grandly told the story about how he'd become her and Greta's unexpected Prince Charming by offering up his home. More speculation rained down on them as he guided her to the table with a gentle hand on her back.

"Whew!" She pushed a lock of hair behind her ear. "The Irish really do like stories, don't they?"

"They were hoping for a few more details, I think." He fingered his coat. "Maybe I should have changed, after all."

"People seemed positively shocked to hear about your water battle with Kathleen and Ellie." She thanked the server, who'd brought them menus. "Are you known for being so serious?"

He pursed his lip before saying, "Liam was just talking to me about that. I used to play pranks when I was a child, but you grow up. I'm a teacher now."

She made a humming sound. "And you're supposed to set a good example, right? God, we're a pair. You're the quiet, serious type while I'm the really nice artist. You want to shake things up a little?"

Now, *that* he hadn't expected. He leaned closer. "What do you have in mind?"

"If I were in my twenties, I'd say tequila shots followed by a cab home."

He laughed. "You can't easily get a cab out here, Sophie, and I hate tequila. What's your second option?"

She slid her hand onto the table. "How about we hold

hands? Because I'm telling you right now that I like you very much and want to make a habit out of being seen in public with you. If that's okay."

Taking her hand, he caressed the back of it with his thumb. "That's grand, actually, as I feel exactly the same way. But why don't you have that tequila shot anyway? If you're looking to shake things up..."

She tilted her head toward the band playing in the corner. "Maybe I can sing a little loudly too. Oh, Jamie, I feel so happy. Forget about those morons not hooking up my utilities or me having to delay my shipment. I mean, I'm here with you. In Ireland. My mother would think my studio's rustic, but I love it. I'm taking my art to a new level with my design, and on Sunday, the whole world is going to know it."

His stomach trembled as he thought about his inclusion in the article. "Let's forget about the whole world reading my name in the paper. All that matters is the children's arts program."

"You're too modest, but that's one of the things I like about you." She picked up her menu, obscuring her face, before she peeked around it. "I should probably tell you something else while I'm shaking things up."

"Yes?"

"Part of me was disappointed to be back at your house because I thought being in separate houses would give us an opportunity to take things to the next level. God, I'm talking like I would about my art. Let me be clear. I'm talking about sex. With you."

A flash of heat powered through him, stealing his breath. Suddenly, he could smell her subtle perfume, and all he could look at was the line of her slender neck where her pulse beat. "Good to be clear about such things. I've been thinking about having sex with you as well."

She gripped his hand, her green eyes intent. "What are we going to do about that?"

"I'm prepared, if that's what you're asking," he said, wanting to assure her.

Her face went blank before she started laughing. "Oh, you mean birth control. Right. That's easy enough. Condoms work until I can get back on the pill."

He cleared his throat. "I have them."

"Great!" She put her hand over her mouth, looking embarrassed. "I should probably lower my voice. What I meant was, what are we going to do about the logistics? I'm not a fan of having sex in a car. It wasn't as fun as I thought it would be."

He bit the inside of his cheek. "That's a shame. Maybe you were with the wrong person."

"Likely." She laughed, the sound rich with irony. "I was with my ex in the back of a limo. God, I really need tequila. Does it bother you that I was married before and have a kid? Whoops, did I just ask that?"

"If it's been on your mind, I'm glad you did." He scooted his chair closer so he could rest their joined hands against his heart. "No, it doesn't. Who you are today is the sum of who you were and the experiences you've had. Besides, if you hadn't been with your ex, you wouldn't have Greta, and she's an absolute angel."

She touched his jaw with her other hand, enclosing them in a new intimacy. "Oh, Jamie. I barely know you. We just met a week ago, and yet I feel like I've known you forever."

Those words had him stepping ahead a little. "Soulmates perhaps."

Her smile softened, and she leaned in and kissed his cheek, resting her lips there with an intimacy that wove through him. "Yes, I like that."

The server darted forward with her notepad and pencil, and they separated to order. And their dinner went much like it had the week before. They flirted their way through their cocktails as an Irish band played a classic reel.

"I really love it here," Sophie said as she dug into her potato wedges while he sampled the chicken wings. "I liked the castle, but this place fits my image of Ireland more. Of course, we should go to the Brazen Donkey next."

They would be clobbered by everyone in town. "Do you think we're ready for that? After the nosiness of the people we met tonight?"

She picked up the tequila shot she had indeed ordered and downed it. "I'm game if you are. Besides, I'm having trouble keeping my hands off you in public. If we put it out there with everyone in town, then I won't have to check myself. Although I still won't kiss you on the mouth when I drop Greta off at school, of course."

He fought a smile. "That's a shame, but I should probably try and set that good example I'm known for."

She blew out a raspberry. "Probably, but it's not as fun. But you can swing by my studio any time and kiss me. I'm all alone in there."

He laughed. "I'll have to do that sometime. You want to tell me how it's coming along?"

She grinned and launched into telling him about her furnace and how it was close to the temperature she wanted. Talking with her hands, she shot out details like cannon fire in her excitement. He didn't completely follow everything she said. What in the world was a *soffietta*? Had she named something she used after herself? He would have to research glassblowing this weekend to ground himself in the basics. She was so animated and vibrant, he couldn't bear to interrupt her with technical questions.

By the time they finished their ice cream sundaes, she was playing with the cuff of his shirt, making him very aware of her. He paid for the check and held her hand as they left the restaurant.

He wasn't ready for their evening to end, but he recalled what she'd said about being intimate in a car. He didn't want that for them. "Would you like to go to a beach for a little walk? It's not too far, and with the waning summer light and rising moon, we should be fine despite the cold. The tide will be in, but we can hug the shoreline."

She stopped in the parking lot and put her arms around him. "I couldn't think of a better idea."

When they arrived at the beach, he was glad to see no other cars. Only locals knew about this cove, but with the weather turning, they might have chosen to stay inside. But the wind wasn't strong, only a gentle stirring around them as they walked down the sandy path through the two pastures where cows were munching loudly on grass.

"They might have the best view of any cow in the world," Sophie said, throwing out her arms as they reached the beach. "Look at this, Jamie, it's gorgeous. The water is almost black in the waning light. It makes me wonder if we'll see a mermaid."

He touched her face, feeling the power of the sea course through his bones. "It was one of my fondest wishes when I was Greta's age. As boys, we used to chase seagulls, and we had crab fights on the sand."

She nestled closer to his body. "Like real crabs?"

"Yes," he said with an easy laugh. "Sometimes I'd even

bring them back home and let them race around in the parlor. My mum used to love that."

"I can imagine. Who ended up catching them after you finished playing?"

"My dad. He'd grab his cleaver and make us crab legs for dinner."

Her horrified look was priceless. "His cleaver?"

"He's a butcher. Or was. Declan took over his place, the Last Chop."

"That's a very graphic name but apt." She grabbed his arm as they wandered onto the beach, the sand giving under their feet. "It seems we're all alone. You don't think it's warm enough to go skinny-dipping, do you?"

He laughed. "If I were a jokester, I'd tell you to go for it. I mean, I'd love to see you slip out of your clothes and slide into the sea. But it's freezing, *mo chroí*. Maybe next time I can bring some wood, and we'll make a fire."

Her breath seemed to ebb into her like a wave before it rushed back out. "Jamie, I want to make love out here. With you. As the waves sound against the rocks. As the stars shimmer overhead. As the moon rises."

He cupped her cheek, his heart filling his whole being. "Then here we'll make love...when we've a fire. Until then, come and kiss me."

She leaned into him, and he brought her flush against him, their lips seeking the other's in heated passes that had him wanting to lower her onto the sand and cover her with his body.

But soon he pressed back, aware of the chill on her face. Their eyes met and held, and he could have sworn he saw a star fall into the endless sea behind her.

Words of love rose up inside him, ones he'd hoped for, longed for, for so long. He wanted to tell her how much he treasured her sweet, vibrant spirit. How he never wanted to be parted from her ever again. How he would lay down his life to be with her for the rest of his days if need be.

The sound of the sea slapping against the rocks seemed to grow to a roar in his ears. He could feel the urgency around them, the sand and sea changing as the tide ebbed and flowed in its eternal dance under the moon. And he sought words that would not be too soon but were still filled with truth.

"You're more beautiful than the sea and all the stars above," he whispered in the silence of the beach.

She laid her head against his chest and they watched the moon rise together, no words needed anymore.

Then he took her back to his home, knowing it was where she belonged.

CHAPTER TWELVE

Linc laid a stack of Sunday's *The New York Times* at the end of the bar as cheers erupted.

He had called an impromptu celebration at the Brazen Donkey after reading the article online when it went live. Taylor McGowan had hit a home run with the article on Sophie's expanded glass installation and Jamie's plans for the children's arts center.

"Take a copy for yourselves and have another drink—on me," he called out as he made his way over to the guest of honor. She was sitting in the corner with Bets and a slew of other folks from the arts center, who were holding court at a bunch of connected tables.

Sophie gave him a tremulous smile as Greta curled against her. Jamie sat close by, a reassuring hand on the little girl's back.

Bets had an empty chair waiting for him, across from the others, and he gave her a smacker and then sat, gesturing to Sophie. "Your phone still blowing up?"

She ducked her chin. "It's a little embarrassing how

many people have reached out to congratulate me on the design."

"Why wouldn't they?" Ellie shook her head incredulously, nudging Kathleen, who sat beside Declan on the opposite side. "It's *gorgeous*."

"A new level for you and your art, as the article said," Kathleen added, lifting her glass in a toast.

"Who doesn't like a pregnant goddess?" Angie patted Emeline's tiny back farther down the patchwork of tables. "It almost makes me long to do it again. Almost."

"We'll let this little one start walking before we talk about the next one, eh, Yank?" Carrick grinned beside her. "I loved the way Taylor tied in the mother in Sophie's design to our children's program."

"She's a master of weaving," Sophie said with a gentle caress to the back of Greta's head. "She's also an incredibly good artist, but her art teachers disagreed and gave her harsh critiques. Something we're not going to have at the children's program, are we, Jamie?"

"Only positive feedback and support," he agreed as he sipped his whiskey.

"Which you conveyed grandly in the article, Jamie," his brother said. "*Sláinte!*"

"I had a good coach," Jamie responded with a loaded glance in Sophie's direction, the kind Linc knew he gave Bets.

The usually reserved man had nothing but smiles for the woman sitting knee to knee with him. They glowed like newlyweds, if you asked Linc, and he couldn't have been happier for them both.

"What has your mother said about all of this?" Linc asked Sophie because he couldn't help himself.

"Yes, what *did* Brigitte say?" Bets owlishly blinked her eyes at him, making him chuckle.

He'd had a romp in the sheets with Sophie's mother ages ago, and Bets had teased him unmercifully about it after meeting Brigitte in Provence. Not only did the woman still want to tangle with him, but she'd also asked if he wanted to be a live model for one of her nudes. He'd taken it as a compliment, what with being in his sixties.

"Mother loves the design, actually," Sophie said with a conspiratorial glance at Greta, who grinned in response. "Of course she thought I could add a little more detail to the goddess' body."

Linc didn't want to know. Brigitte's male and female forms had rocked the art world for their *detail*. Her work evoked emotion and reaction in a very different way than her daughter's did, but Linc supposed that was the way of things. Ellie conducted her art with incredible precision and passion in a quiet studio while he'd always enjoyed walking the noisy floors of his window factories and talking to people.

"Any chance your mother will want to do a painting for the museum?" Angie asked. "I remember trying to get tickets to see one of her shows, but it was impossible. I can't even imagine selling tickets for one of mine."

Sophie's face tensed. "You're on your way, Angie. And I haven't asked Mother about coming here since that's up to Linc, Bets, and the board. Although Mother is happier in... sunnier locations."

"She doesn't like the rain much," Greta said softly, "and she's not sure about us living here yet. I told her not to worry."

Sophie's wince was priceless. "Let's talk about something else."

Bets tapped her glass on the table. "I have some good news. I checked my email just a moment ago and discovered a slew of inquiries from people about sending their child to our summer program next year. One was from as far away as Australia."

"Wow!" Ellie gasped. "It would be like summer camp. I know we'd hoped for a blend of local Irish kids and students from abroad."

"We're going to have more interest than spots, I think," Bets said with a grin. "Although I don't know where we'll house the kids. Maybe Linc can procure some mobile camp cabins like they had at the summer camp I attended along the Chesapeake."

"We'll think of something," Linc assured her, deciding to consider an expanded summer camp later. There'd be other details to sort out, from securing the correct permits to hiring teachers and camp counselors. "Jamie, it looks like you'll have your hands full come October. You sure you're up for teaching on Saturdays for three-week blocks during the regular school year?"

"It'll only be for an hour each week before the other artists do their intro practicums," he said, waving a hand dismissively.

"And I'm up the first week." Ellie shimmied in her seat. "Teaching suncatchers for two hours. That's where my love of stained glass began."

"Then Megan's up with ceramics and hand building in week two," Bets said, ticking the time off with her fingers. "Angie with basic drawing in week three before we wrap up week four on finishing projects and student feedback on what art most interested them. Soon we'll be bringing in other art teachers."

Linc rubbed her back. "Parents aren't the only ones

getting in touch. She's already got a list of art teachers who have volunteered to come for the children's program. We're going to need our hotel stat."

"Yes, we are." Bets met his gaze, the corners of her lips lifting. "Damn the torpedoes and full steam ahead, right, cowboy?"

He leaned in and kissed her cheek. They both knew it wasn't going to be that easy, what with the Watertown asshole, but they would forge ahead. "Exactly. Donal's been talking so much to the right people he's lost his voice."

"I wondered where he was tonight," Declan said. "Eoghan's been telling tall tales all night with Fergus."

"Eoghan told me he's missed seeing his cousin lately," Sophie said with a smile. "He hasn't been spending as much time in the pub now that he's living with Sandrine."

Neither was Linc, truth be told. "Love does that to a man."

"Or a woman," Bets added, tapping his chest. "The Lucky Charms and I haven't danced to Bon Jovi in forever. Perhaps tonight is the night to change that."

"Except you're down a few members," Linc said, "what with Carrick and Jamie's parents taking off to Portugal with Brady and Declan's folks."

"We can manage without Siobhan and Brigid, can't we, girls?" Bets rose from her chair. "Sophie, would you care to join us?"

She looked down at Greta. "Sweetheart, would you be okay staying here with Linc and Jamie while Mama goes and dances with these ladies?"

Greta nodded, moving closer to Jamie, who boosted her up onto his lap. "We'll be fine, won't we, Greta?"

Bets linked her arm through Sophie's as they left the

table, joined by Angie, Ellie, and Kathleen. "You don't happen to have a favorite Bon Jovi song, do you?"

"Are you kidding?" she answered. "Of course! 'It's My Life' has been my self-help motto since my divorce."

"Women really love that song," Linc said with a laugh. "Can't say I ever truly appreciated it until I hooked up with Bets."

Declan settled back in his chair, watching his wife retreat with a half smile. "Kathleen dancing to it does make it more appealing."

"I figure they'll keep it clean with the kids present, right?" Carrick gave his daughter a kiss on her round cheek.

Jamie laughed. "The dancing's not bad in and of itself. For me, it was seeing Mum sashaying around with a feather boa."

"My grandmama has a black feather boa," Greta suddenly said in a shy voice. "They get everywhere and tickle your nose when she tries to kiss you."

Linc knew a lot more about the merits of feather boas after living with Bets. He chuckled. "They should be outlawed," he teased the little girl. "How's school coming along?"

"I really like it." Greta turned a little and pointed up at Jamie. "Mr. Fitzgerald is a really nice teacher."

"If you have any trouble with him," Carrick joked, "come and see me. I'm his older brother, you know."

"Don't listen to him, Greta," Jamie said with a snort. "He keeps company with sheep most of the day."

"I like sheep, especially my stuffed sheep named January. Jamie gave her to me," she said as the music sounded over the speaker.

Linc couldn't help but smile as he watched the woman in his life and his daughter dance their pants off, albeit in different styles. Bets loved to sway and swish her hips, but Ellie started doing the robot at one point—a skill he hadn't known she possessed—inciting Kathleen to copy her movements in the style of a street mime. Sophie caught on and began to improvise her own robot moves, and soon, the dance was completely out of hand. Bets and Angie joined in, making Linc harken back to the moves the Tin Man had done with sweet ol' Dorothy in *The Wizard of Oz*.

"In all my days, I never would have imagined *this*," Declan said, scratching his head.

"Is that like some odd form of breakdancing?" Carrick asked.

"I like it," Greta said, tapping her hands on her knees. "It's funny. What do you think, Mr. Fitzgerald?"

"So long as it makes your mother and the other women happy, that's all that matters," Jamie replied. "But I can't imagine doing it myself."

Carrick kicked his chair leg gently. "Oh, give it a go, Jamie, me boy."

The brothers exchanged a pointed look as Declan hooted. Linc bit the inside of his cheek. "Wonder what Jon Bon Jovi would say if he saw this spectacle."

"We should have taken a video and posted it on that TikTok thing." Declan chortled. "They'd never live it down."

"The song *is* called 'It's My Life,' after all, and they're just expressing it." Jamie was all smiles again as he made his own version of robot hands, earning a laugh from Greta.

Linc was willing to do a lot to make kids laugh, but he was drawing the line on this one. His phone vibrated in his pocket, and because Donal had been in touch constantly, he pulled it out to check.

The text was from an unfamiliar number, but the first

lines had Linc opening it straightaway. *Nice article in The New York Times. Malcolm.*

Linc's mouth twisted. His cell phone number wasn't listed, so someone must have given it to Malcolm. He held out his phone to Carrick and then Jamie before tucking it away.

"What do you think it means?" Jamie asked.

"I have a feeling we're about to find out."

CHAPTER THIRTEEN

Sometimes her mother surprised her.

Sophie was shocked to find tears on her face as she finished the article in *Le Monde's* Thursday edition about her mother's upcoming gallery showing in Paris. Taylor had texted her this morning with a simple *WTF* and the link, saying she would have titled the piece, "Controversial Painter Has Heart After All."

Intrigued, she'd opened the article on her tablet and almost dropped it in several fits and starts. Her mother had actually praised her work! True, it had started with the usual vague sound-bite praise: *My daughter and her art have captivated the art world for good reason, and her new installation in Ireland at the Sorcha Fitzgerald Arts Center promises to be yet another expression of the senses and her unique creativity with glass.*

Then the article's writer had described a funny byplay between him and her mother. He'd asked: *Has your daughter ever worked with nude compositions before in glass?*

Her mother had reportedly smiled mysteriously before

responding: *She once gifted me a beautiful glass flower of the famous naked monkey orchid for my birthday. The workmanship was exquisite and the composition so alive—it was like the naked monkeys that give the flower its name were dancing in the glass. I keep it on my bedside table to remind myself of my daughter's affection. It wasn't easy for her to grow up with a mother who painted nudes, you know.*

Then she'd proceeded to show it to the reporter, who had taken a photograph and included it in the article.

Sophie hadn't known her mother had even kept the piece, let alone somewhere so accessible. Many of her mother's things were scattered around her various houses, so to think she'd kept this gift so close, on her bedside table...

Picking up the phone, she rang her mother. God, she was trembling.

"Sophie! It's good to finally talk to you. How are you and Greta faring?"

"We're wonderful, Mother," she replied a little formally, not wanting to go into too much detail—like the fact that they were staying at Jamie's cottage still because of the problems. Or the bond she had with Jamie, which had led to the offer in the first place.

"That's reassuring, darling," her mother answered in the same formal tone.

They'd expected to return to the mobile home by now, but the electricity company still hadn't shown up to reconnect their services. That was supposed to happen tomorrow, but she wasn't in a rush. She looked around the quiet little cottage. It *did* satisfy her to have this connection to Jamie. They'd seen each other every day, of course, at school, and he'd dropped by a couple of times to give them some time together. Then there was the spontaneous trip to Kade Donovan's pony farm, where Greta had ended up having a pony ride with Ollie as a host of cute little Jack Russell terriers followed in their wake.

He'd stayed for dinner at her invitation afterward, and it hadn't felt odd for him to be there, part of their weekday routine. If anything, it had felt odd when he'd left. Not that she was telling her mother any of that.

She glanced at her tablet. "I was just reading *Le Monde*'s article on your show."

"It's going to be a long evening tomorrow, but you know how it is, *cherie*. Endless questions about what was in your mind as you were creating. But the worst ones are the ones who actually *tell* you what was in your mind. Even after all these years, I can't abide the conceit."

Now this was the mother she knew. She was suddenly afraid to ask if there was more to the woman who had given birth to her and raised her. "Mom. Do you really have the naked monkey sculpture on your bedside table? Why haven't I seen it before?"

"Because I tuck it away when you visit. That sculpture was for me and me alone. You may have had your reasons for doing it. Some of them might even have been a little droll. But it was the only piece of your art you ever gave me, and it truly is flawless, you know."

Her throat thickened. "I never knew."

"Sophie, you know I express my feelings better in my work than I do in my life. Now, tell me more about your time there. Sandrine has been completely unhelpful as usual when it comes to informing me about you and your well-being."

She traced the smile on her lips. Her mother always poked around about her personal life. "Sandrine has always kept my secrets, Mother."

"What secrets?" She gave a husky laugh. "You are an

open book. The nicest artist to hit the art world since I don't know when. In fact, I wouldn't be surprised if some reporter mentioned how incredible it is that I can be such a dragon when you are such a dolphin, or some atrocious art metaphor."

"I like dolphins," she said with a laugh. "But I like dragons too."

"Hmm… I suppose we should talk about when I can come and visit you and Greta in the wilds of the Irish countryside."

"Oh, it's not so bad, Mother." She glanced out the window as a misty rain fell, making her think about Jamie's description before their first date. "The light truly is incredible. It might even be better than in Provence."

"*Sacrilege*! But I suppose I must see for myself. Tell Linc hello for me."

"He's with Bets now, Mother."

"I know, *cherie*. It doesn't mean I can't have a little fun needling him."

Controversy. Trouble. Her mother thrived on it. "Have a good show, Mother."

"Always. We'll talk soon."

She hung up, her heart aching a little. They never used words of love. Like her mother had said, she painted her feelings. Uttering them was gauche to her mind. And yet, she'd kept the birthday gift beside her.

Hugging herself, she glanced outside as the sun came out, making the raindrops on the trees turn to diamonds. Maybe that was what happened when you looked deeper. One minute life looked like something you thought you knew, and then in the next, it turned into something you'd never seen before, something beautiful.

The sound of tires crunching had her rising from the

couch. Sandrine was coming over to do a little laundry for her. Sophie had come home after taking Greta to school to start a *pot au feu* in Jamie's crockpot before going to the arts center, hoping she could entice him to come over for dinner again tonight. She'd wanted to make dinner herself. They were set for official date number three on Saturday night, but they both were too eager to spend time together to stay apart, as evidenced by the past three days. They'd seen each other in some manner every single evening.

She opened the door to greet Sandrine and stopped short. Two older unsmiling women stood on the sidewalk, a pair of contrasts. One was short and round with short graying curls while the other was tall and rail-thin with silver hair. Dressed somberly, they would have been great dour female models for the old Dutch Masters. "May I help you?"

"Are you Sophie Giombetti, the new artist at the arts center?" asked the shorter of the two.

Maybe she was suspicious by nature. Certainly, she was new to Ireland and had been told people just showed up and often walked into your home without knocking or being invited inside. But these women had tight mouths and hard eyes that radiated dislike. "Who's asking?"

"Concerned citizens," the tall one replied before the other woman could say anything. "You're living in Jamie Fitzgerald's cottage with your daughter. He's a member of this community, the village teacher, and a good man. We wanted to make sure you're not taking advantage of him."

Her mouth parted in shock. "I beg your pardon. Jamie offered his home to my daughter and me when my own place became unavailable."

"And yet it's back on Linc Buchanan's land again," the

round woman said with an arched brow, "while *you're* still here."

What the hell?

The stranger's accusing tone had Sophie trembling with anger. She gave herself a moment, reaching for a polite response, knowing a crisp retort wouldn't be useful with women like these. "Indeed. You've very observant. Again, how can I help you?"

"You can go back to where you came from with your art and your liberal ideas and leave a good man alone," the rail-thin woman said with her nose in the air. "We don't want your kind of woman around here."

"A *hoor*," the round one spat out.

She vibrated with shock followed by anger. She'd heard those words before—but they'd been directed by protesters at her mother. Never her. "I'd like you to leave."

"Well, that's too bad, as we don't care about what you want." The thin woman drew herself up and traded a nasty look with the other woman. "If you're smart, you'll take yourself and your child away from Caisleán."

Shaking, she closed the door and leaned against it, listening as the car drove off. Someone had come to where she was living and threatened her. Called her a whore. She realized she wasn't breathing.

"Oh, God."

She took a shallow breath. Thank God, Greta hadn't been home. But she needed to call Linc and Bets and inform them. And Jamie...

Was she hurting his reputation by living in his house?

Anger spurted up inside her again. They thought, what, that she was giving him some sort of favors in exchange for staying in his house? How could anyone think that of them? He was just being kind. But they seemed to know that, didn't they? Like they knew she was an artist. Who, to their minds, had liberal ideas! Like they knew the first thing about her or her beliefs.

She let out an aggrieved shriek. What was wrong with people anyway?

She called Linc and told him to put Bets on the phone. After relaying the incident, Bets said, "I think I know who would do this, but can you describe these women?"

Their images were so detailed in her mind, she could have described the round woman's worn brown coat down to the fact that it was missing a button at the bottom. She kept to salient details, marveling at how similar it was to filling out a police report. She hadn't done that since she and her parents had been pelted with rotten eggs.

"Dammit!" Bets exclaimed the moment she'd finished. "The rail-thin one is Orla MacKenna and the round one is Mary Kincaid."

She well remembered Mary's name. "Your nemesis and the woman trying to close the arts center."

"Orla is the wife of the former head of the council who caused us a heap load of trouble," Linc told her. "Sophie, we're on our way over. Lock the door, will you?"

Her knees grew weak. "They're gone now. I'm...not fine. But you don't need to come over. I was going to head to my studio shortly."

"Indulge a worrywart like me, will you, sugar?"

"They were trying to scare me off." She shook herself. "I've dealt with women like them before." The image of Jamie's principal rose in her mind. They hadn't spoken since that first day, but she always felt the woman's disapproving eyes watching her when she arrived at school.

Linc made a clucking sound. "You think they're done?

Malcolm and the rest of them are launching their next strike."

They didn't have to wait long. Thursday's edition of a major national newspaper published an article titled, "Daughter of Pornographic Painter to Follow in Mother's Tracks with Nude Sculpture in Mayo."

Jamie had shown up at her door early in the morning with a grim look and a copy of the paper. He'd wanted to be the one to break the news to her, and indeed, it had helped. A little. She finished the article and pushed the paper aside, feeling ill, and he picked it up and waved it around. "It's bollocks!" he hissed, keeping the volume low since Greta was still in bed. "The worst kind of vitriol."

"Yes, it is," she whispered. "It's full of twisted lies and innuendos. I mean, they intimated that I'm a deviant because I made my mother that naked monkey orchid for her birthday."

He pulled her into his arms. "It's totally out of context."

She gripped him tight. "The way that reporter implied that I'm a user and a whore because I'm living in your home with my child after just arriving—and you a schoolteacher. Jamie, I don't—"

"Like I told you when Mary and Orla spewed their venom at you... No one who knows me and the situation would think any differently of either of us. You're shaking, *mo chroí*. Come sit down."

"You need to get to school to prepare for the day."

He clutched her harder. "Don't bother about that now. I expect you'll have others here at your door soon enough. I was fortunate Carrick called me after rising early with Emeline and reading the paper."

Her fingers dug into the coat he hadn't bothered to remove yet "I'm glad you came. Jamie, I just can't believe this. I know reporters write crap all the time, but this is vicious. The kind of stuff my parents had to contend with decades ago. They called my design 'pornographic.'" Her voice broke. "They didn't even include a picture so people could decide on their own."

"People *will* decide. We'll see to it. Sophie, don't let these lies twist you up inside. You'll talk to Linc and Bets today and figure out a plan."

"Maybe Greta and I can move back into the mobile home even if the electrical company doesn't reinstate our account today."

He framed her face. "Don't be silly now. You'll stay here as long as you have a need. This will blow over. It's only some gobshite from Dublin making noise."

Linc called the newspaper and complained to their editor, who apologized and promised to look into the issue.

But it didn't blow over. Another paper out of Galway published an article the next day claiming the center's new children's program would be using books with pornographic images in them, meaning one of their nonvoting members had likely leaked it and was in Malcolm's pocket.

Jamie threw the paper on his kitchen table. He'd come over early Friday morning and brought it with him, knowing she'd want to see it straightaway. "The book they name is certified by numerous art associations for children. They're paintings! Masterpieces! Some of them hang in churches, for heaven's sake. And it's not like we're using that book to teach young children. It's for the teenagers."

She rubbed her temples. "You know I used to hover in the doorway as my parents tossed aside newspapers like this and railed at the injustice of it all. Jamie, it makes me sad to see them call Botticelli's *Birth of Venus* and Michelangelo's paintings in the Sistine Chapel 'pornographic.' I know they caused controversy in their day, but most of the world is past that."

"Clearly not the people we're dealing with." He pressed her gently into a chair. "Let me make you tea, *mo chroí*. Then we'll call Bets and Linc."

A raw vulnerability rose within her as she watched him fill the kettle. "You called me that Irish phrase before. What does it mean?"

He looked over his shoulder, a smile breaking across his face. "My heart. Do you want to cancel our date tomorrow night and stay home?"

"No!" She held up her hands. "Sorry, that was loud. No, I do not want to cancel our night out."

"People might not have read the article in the national paper, but they will likely have seen this one as it's closer to home. News like this travels fast as a fox in lambing season."

"I'm not going to hide and pretend we've done anything wrong." She rose and crossed to him, putting her hand on his chest. "Unless you want to keep away."

He took her hands. "Not from you. Never from you. I was only trying to protect you. Sophie, I'm on a kind of ice I've never skated before. I want to be a help to you."

"And you!" She squeezed his hands. "Jamie, they're bashing you too. I can't believe they told that story about you being in a water-gun fight, acting like a child in public. And what they said about you living with other artists at Summercrest Manor. They might as well have implied you were a bunch of hippies up to no good."

Jamie's eyes roved over her face. "And shame on them for implying any of it. If others find those images—or your design, for that matter—sexual or provocative, that's their issue. I personally don't find them arousing or threatening. They're art!"

"Exactly!"

"And as for using approved art books in our children's arts programs," he continued, his blue eyes ablaze, "we're introducing children of a certain age to important masterpieces that happen to have the human body as a subject. If you ask me, I think children who are brought up to see the human body as a beautiful and natural thing will have healthier attitudes toward human sexuality. And that's exactly what I plan to tell any parent or concerned citizen who asks me about it."

"Oh, Jamie, you are *the* best!" She threw her arms around him, feeling him grunt in response. "This is the worst firestorm I've ever been in professionally, and here you are, making me tea and snapping off comebacks. I can't think of anyone better to go through this with."

She leaned her forehead against his chest. "Let's have that tea and then I need to get Greta up. You both have school today."

"We do." He cupped the back of her head. "I wish we could all stay home and forget about this for a while."

"But life doesn't work that way," she said, raising her face. "I hid as a kid. I won't do that anymore. It's too important not to make a stand, Jamie. And what they're doing is wrong."

"They want to make *us* look wrong." He lifted the back of her hand and kissed it. "But we won't let them. Will we?"

"No, we sure as hell won't." She traced his jaw. "Will you do me a favor?"

"Anything."

"Bring wood for a fire on the beach tomorrow night, will you?"

He smiled slowly. "If it doesn't rain. Otherwise, we'll figure out something else."

"Jamie, I don't want all this crap to stop us from being together."

"It won't." He put her hand over his heart. "You have my word. We'll weather this. The truth always wins out, *mo chroí*."

She desperately wanted to believe it.

The stone in her stomach told a different story.

CHAPTER FOURTEEN

Things were getting out of hand.

Jamie wanted to crumple the letter he'd just opened and throw it against the wall. He was known for being a bottomless well of patience, but the letter he'd just received from the Irish Censorship of Publications Board was the last straw. Someone had issued a complaint of indecency and obscenity about two of the children's art books he'd chosen for the Sorcha Fitzgerald Arts Center. Given his role as an educator, they requested he send a list of every book he was currently using in school.

His stomach rolled like he had the flu. How could they! They were calling his very character in question, as a person and an educator.

Only yesterday, he'd told Sophie the truth would win out. Today, the burden on his shoulders felt like a yoke.

He picked up the phone and called Bets.

"Jamie! Sophie told me you gave an impassioned speech yesterday and made her feel better. Can you give me one? I've been inundated with people wanting to talk about

Sophie and her sculpture. Linc said this kind of blitz is normal, but I'm exhausted."

"It's understandable with people spewing this kind of filth." He took a breath. "I wish I could give you the kind of speech you're looking for, Bets, but my mouth went dry when I received a letter from the Irish Board of Censorship in the post."

She swore. "How bad?"

"I'm new to this kind of thing," he said, sipping the tea he'd brought up to his room. "They had a complaint about two of the books I selected for the children's arts program." He proceeded to fill her in.

"Those ninnies! All this nonsense makes me want to pull my hair out."

He could all but see her tugging at the ends of her curly orange hair. "I'll need guidance on how to defend this. Only... Bets, they also want a list of all the books I'm using at the school."

Her intake of breath echoed over the line. "But that's outrageous! Your books have been approved by the powers that be. It's a witch hunt! Malcolm Coveney must have a hand in this! Hang on. Let me get Linc. He's been on the phone nonstop too."

He heard something crash and then footsteps. A door creaked. Linc must be holed up in another part of the house. There was a murmur of voices, as if she had cupped the phone with her hand. Then he heard Linc swear loudly.

"You must be shaken by the letter," Linc said, his drawl clipped. "It's ridiculous, and we'll fight it. Malcolm's going for the jugular. He's got reporters in his pockets and apparently knows how to bring in the censors. Jamie, I've lined up specialized counsel for just this kind of issue. They're the best lawyers in Dublin. Can you take a picture of the letter and text it to us? I'll forward it to them today and get them started on a reply. For the arts center and for your work at the school."

"I'll send it the moment we sign off." He rubbed the back of his neck, trying to feel relieved they had expert assistance. "I'll need to inform my superiors at school though—if they haven't already received a letter independently."

"I want to say it's horseshit, Jamie, and to not take it to heart," Bets said tersely. "But it's got to be a kick in the gut. You just remember what a great teacher you are and that this community is behind you."

"And you asked me to give *you* an impassioned speech earlier. Thanks, Bets."

"You're welcome! Now go find Liam and meditate or something. No one knows how to offer sound advice in a situation like this better than my boy."

"And have a whiskey," Linc suggested dryly. "We'll talk soon."

He hung up the phone and texted them a photo of the letter. Rising, he picked up his tea and carried it back to the kitchen. Saturday mornings were usually quiet. The newly married couples didn't rise until nearly noon. As it should be. He detoured to the dungeon to find Liam. He was sitting on his blue mat—cross-legged in loose white pants, shirt off, and eyes closed.

"Need something, Jamie?"

He leaned against the doorway. "How did you know it was me?"

"Footsteps. Energy. The early hour." His friend opened his eyes. "What's wrong?"

"The vultures are circling." He brought him up to date on everything. "I'm not the kind to worry normally. All my life, I've used reason to work out any problems I've encountered, especially since Carrick's hot temperament usually only escalates situations. But maybe nothing truly bad has happened to me before. Maybe I've been naïve."

"If that's naïveté, we all need more of it," Liam said, gesturing for Jamie to join him on his mat. "I won't give you the New Age Hallmark card sentiment of 'What doesn't kill you makes you stronger.' I figure we can find our strength without going that far. But this has to make you angry, and that's not your usual mood."

He shook his head as he sat down. "I've lived a mostly quiet life. I've played by the rules. I've tried to do what's right. To have all that questioned now..."

"This censorship board and that arsehole who wrote the article taking shots at you...we're talking a few people who are going at you. Do they have power? Yes. But no one can question your character. Our lives are the sum total of a million choices, and yours are all on the balance sheet of damned decent and good. That truth will win out, Jamie."

"I told Sophie that yesterday," he said, tilting his head back. "It's a bit harder to swallow today."

"Of course it is." Liam leaned over and gripped his shoulder. "You've been kicked but good. Doesn't make it less true though. You call my mom and Linc about this?"

He nodded. "Yeah. She told me to come find you. Said you were one for sound advice in moments like this."

"I'm glad you listened to her. I know how private you are. This kind of public airing can't be comfortable."

"It isn't." He shifted on the mat, wondering how in the world Liam managed to sit in that position for so long without discomfort. "I don't like what they're trying to say about me—and Sophie, for that matter."

"She's had a lot on her plate, for sure. And yet... I sense

her relationship with her mother hasn't been easy, and Ellie told me about her mother's article in *Le Monde*. That's the kind of gem we can find in situations like this."

"I'm waiting for my gem. Maybe I need to buy a pickaxe."

Liam laughed and pushed off the floor in one easy motion, extending his hand to Jamie. "Maybe this moment was one of the gems."

Jamie snorted. "No offense, but I was hoping for something grander. Like a colossal emerald from the Amazon."

Liam made a show of clutching his heart. "Ouch, Jamie. And here I thought we were lifelong friends."

"You're an eejit. I'm going to start calling you Yoda like Declan if you don't watch out."

His friend clapped him on the back as they ascended the stairs. "You know. I believe you've already found your gem, Jamie. Her name is Sophie. I'll see you later."

Liam headed toward the stairs to the second floor, leaving Jamie alone in the main hallway. The pleasing scent of oranges surrounded him, and he turned his head slowly. Sorcha was standing under one of the metal sculptures Kathleen had designed for the house—a boxer in mid-punch, modeled after Declan, of course.

She gave a little wave. "I figured you had enough excitement today so I wouldn't frighten you."

"Thank you," he said grandly. "Are you here to tell me what to do about it all?"

"I figure you already know." She made a fist and pressed it into her other hand. "You must do what does not come naturally to you. Both of you. This fight isn't going to just go away. You'll need to stand up for yourselves and trust others to do the same. Hold fast to each other, Jamie. Liam was right when he said the truth would win. But do you know what else will?"

He shook his head. "What?"

Her smile softened the angles of her face. "Love. And that, my boy, you and Sophie have in spades. It will see you through."

With that, she disappeared as if she'd never been. He exhaled harshly, the sound echoing in the empty hall.

He needed to tell Sophie about the letter, and he didn't want to do it on their date tonight. She'd all but told him she wanted to make love with him. He'd been eyeing the weather nonstop, and while it would be cold, no rain was in the forecast. Not that the eejit weathermen were prescient. But he hoped they would be right. God, did he hope.

Deciding it best to tell Sophie about the new development now, before they went out, he located his wallet and keys. Tugging on a coat, he headed for his car.

Carrick was strolling up the drive pushing Emeline in a baby carriage. "Bets sent the censorship inquiry letter to all of the center's direct board members now that we know Malcolm has a nonvoting member in his pocket. Were you planning on calling and telling me?"

"I only just got it this morning." Jamie trotted down the drive, ducking under the rim of the carriage to smile at his bundled-up niece. "Our new postman was nice enough to deliver it to me here since he knows I'm not staying at my house right now. You'll tell Angie for me, won't you?"

"Already did." Carrick rocked the baby carriage. "I haven't heard her swear like that in forever. She invited you over for dinner tonight, but I told her you probably had plans. It's date night with Sophie, isn't it? Eoghan told me at the Brazen Donkey the other night how much he loves babysitting Greta. He and Sandrine are so vital at their age, we might even take them up on minding Emeline."

"Yes, I'll be with Sophie tonight." He squinted as the sun broke through the haze of clouds overhead. "She's the only grace in all of this. Not that she isn't getting kicked blue herself."

Carrick gripped his shoulder, his eyes intent. "I wonder if she's a little more used to it than you are. Do I need to worry about you, brother?"

He rocked back at the question. "That's not a question I expected from you."

"And yet, I'm asking it. Mum will want to know if she and Dad should return from their holiday early."

"For the love of God, no." He leaned under the carriage rim again to make sure to smile at Emeline after that utterance. "Linc has lawyers to help handle it, but I'm sure I'm going to have plenty of people asking me about the situation even if they think it's bollocks."

Carrick continued the easy motion with the baby carriage. "Eoghan will be outraged, and there's no better place to express outrage than in the Brazen Donkey, which I'm sure he'll be visiting this afternoon. Let him do his work, Jamie. He's good at rousing people's tempers. Because if this censorship board can go after you, they can go after anyone. My wife included."

He hadn't thought that far ahead yet. "Is she worried then?"

Carrick set his weight, like he was preparing to take on the world. "She says she's not, but I know my Yank. Her brow knit before she picked up the baby and turned away from me. The media attacked Sophie for a seemingly tasteful nude of a pregnant woman that lacks the kind of detail that's in my wife's oil paintings. Well, I imagine we'll know more soon enough. Malcolm Coveney is the kind of person who'll do everything he can to crush us into the ground if he can't have his way."

"So is Mary Kincaid and her coven," Jamie said darkly.

"If I wasn't a father, I'd be cursing for sure." He gestured to Jamie's keys. "I'm keeping you. Where were you off to?"

"To tell Sophie the news well before our date. I don't want anything to spoil it."

"Sound thinking. Kiss your niece goodbye, and then I'll be going."

The sweet smell of his niece and her drooling little face gave him a moment of solace. "You want a ride home?"

"No. We need to enjoy the days when it isn't pouring. Lately, I've come home so wet and mucky I have to wait to kiss my own wife and daughter. I'll see you later, Jamie."

His brother turned the stroller around and started down the driveway. Jamie tipped his head up and studied the sky. Carrick was better than any weatherman, in tune with the land as he was. If he said it wasn't going to rain, it wasn't going to rain. A shaft of hope opened up in Jamie's chest at the thought.

Tonight, he and Sophie would have their date on the beach and let love guide their way.

CHAPTER FIFTEEN

The fun times just kept rolling, like the Irish hills outside Jamie's cottage.

Sophie retied her scarf for the third time. Nothing was going right today. She'd stubbed her toe on the door as Jamie left this morning, having told her about the letter from the Irish Censorship Board. The pain had allowed her to howl how she was feeling on the inside.

They were going after a good man. It wasn't fair!

After he'd left, she'd called Sandrine and asked if she could watch Greta a little earlier, needing some time to clear her head. She'd headed to her studio, her sanctuary, and blew glass—just for the heck of it.

While she hadn't started with a shape in mind, the glass had slowly morphed into a tower of flames after she'd rolled it on the marver. Dipping the rounded glass in crushed orange and blue glass now that she knew what she wanted, she blew shape into it and finished the piece with her tongs, pulling the flames up into slivers. Upon finishing the piece, she placed it in the annealing oven to cool.

Breathing hard, she surveyed the final product. Fire.

The expression of her inner desire. Her anger. She wanted to burn them all down for the attacks on her and Jamie.

He'd been so brave this morning, even though his heart was obviously hurting. She'd been so upset she'd smudged her mascara. Wetting the end of a tissue, she cleaned up her eyes. You could always see someone's emotional state in their eyes. Hers right now were angry, spiked with the fire she'd brought forth in her art. Jamie's had been as sad as a basset hound, and his reasoning had brought tears to her eyes earlier. He hadn't wanted to tell her over their date.

He hadn't wanted to spoil their first time together.

She eyed her outfit. Silk underwear, fleece-lined jean tights, and her red cashmere sweater. Thank God she'd listened to Sandrine's suggestion and brought some warm clothes ahead of their shipment. Her socks were a bulky wool that barely fit under boots. How in the world were they going to have sex on a beach with this many clothes on? In this kind of weather? Sure, it wasn't raining, but the wind was so crisp, she'd seen lambs hunched and shivering against the lee of an ash tree on the way home from the studio.

"Greta would like to stay over at our house tonight," Sandrine said in French from the door. "Eoghan told her about the beauty of an Irish breakfast. She expressed excitement, which prompted an invitation to his—our—house. Is that all right?"

You read my mind, but then again, you always do. "That would be wonderful. I confess I've read about a full Irish, but I've never had one."

"Perhaps someone might make you one tomorrow morning," Sandrine responded with an innocent smile as Eoghan's and her daughter's laughter reached them.

"I'll bet the chances are pretty good," she answered, slicking lip gloss over her lips. "You're an angel, Sandrine."

"My wings are in the offing." She came over and embraced Sophie warmly. "You two could use a break from the ugliness. Have you decided what you want to tell Greta?"

"She's only six." Sophie flung out her arm. "How am I supposed to explain to her that some people have decided my sculpture is indecent and pornographic before I've even made it? Oh, I'd better not start. Jamie purposefully told me about this new development with the censorship board earlier so I could try and shake it off."

"Then you made a flame at the studio," Sandrine finished. "Bring that fire to your date and channel it into passion. You've waited a long time for a man like him."

Their eyes met. "Yes, I have."

"We're going now to give you some moments to yourself. I'll send Greta in to say good night."

"Do I need to pack her a bag?" She laughed at Sandrine's expression. "Sorry. I forgot who I was dealing with for a moment. Thank you, Sandrine. For this. For everything."

Sandrine folded her arms over her belly. "You know, when you were about Greta's age, your mother also struggled with what to tell you about the controversy she and your father caused. Do you remember what I finally told you when you came home from school crying?"

She had come home crying on so many occasions after the cruel taunts she'd heard from classmates. "I don't remember. It's a blur."

"I told you that your mother and father painted things that other people didn't see as beautiful. That those people couldn't see what your parents were trying to create as art. I told you it was like people not liking a particular color, which you couldn't understand—"

"Because I liked all the colors." She sat down on the bed. "I wanted to protect Greta from all this. Maybe I was wrong to add the pregnant goddess."

"Do you really believe that?" Sandrine asked softly.

Gripping her knees, she shook her head. "No. But I'm starting to wonder if that sculpture is going to be worth all this trouble."

"Your mother asked herself that too in difficult moments."

"She did?"

"Of course," she said emphatically. "She was at her lowest after they threw rotten eggs all over you. She was prepared to face the opposition, but she said you didn't deserve it. Hearing you cry that night tore at her. She and your father fought about bringing you to their art shows after that. Your mother wanted to keep you home, but your father said you needed to learn how to handle it. Life couldn't all be sweetness and light."

That summed up her father in a nutshell, which was another reason they hadn't reconciled before his death five years ago. "Daddy must be laughing from his grave then, because I'm right in the thick of it now. Are you going to tell me that controversy is the direct result of great art?"

Sandrine gave another of her soft smiles. "The only thing that matters in the end is what you think. I'll send Greta in."

Her daughter skipped into her room moments later and played with the end of her scarf. "You look pretty, Mama. Did Sandrine tell you? Eoghan is going to make me a full

Irish breakfast tomorrow. He said it's going to stuff me to the gills like on a prize trout. Isn't that funny?"

"So long as you don't turn into a trout." She made a fish face, sending her daughter into giggles. "I like my Greta exactly as she is. You have fun tonight, okay?"

"Eoghan said we're going to stay up late and sing Irish songs." She was already swaying from the music in her mind, Sophie knew, a habit she'd inherited from Franz.

"You'll have to sing them to me tomorrow. Now, come give me a kiss."

Her daughter leaned over sweetly. "You won't be scared to be here alone, will you? I'm going to leave January with you just in case."

Her heart melted with love. "That's a sweet offer, but you take January. What happens if she wakes up missing you tonight?"

"Okay, I'll bring her. Bye, Mama."

She hugged her tightly. "Bye, baby."

Eoghan called out a goodbye and then the cottage went silent. She rose and walked into the parlor to wait for Jamie. Picking up her phone, she noted a few texts. She opened the one from Taylor first.

Someone sent me the article in that Irish newspaper! You got hosed. Pornographic, my eye! Journalists like that make me so sick I'm considering a new story on artistic censorship. Care to be interviewed?

She typed an emphatic YES, and then opened the next text from her mother.

A friend sent me the article from that horrible Irish newspaper. I would have thought you would have sent it to me.

I hope you don't take any of it to heart, but knowing you, I'm sure you will. I'm not ashamed of my work, and neither should you be. My friends are outraged! Your 'pornographic' goddess is brilliant, and if they can't see that, then you know what they can do...

This kind of support was unheard of. She could all but hear her mother swearing in French as she wrote it. She read it again, feeling the warmth of the sentiments, as the crunch of tires sounded in the driveway.

Rising, she crossed to the window to make sure it was Jamie. He emerged from the car, his mop of brown curls wild from the wind. As he strode to the house, she rushed over to meet him at the door. He stepped inside quickly and closed it to keep the heat inside.

"There's no rain, but it's cold enough to freeze your very bones," he said, kissing her cheek. "I have the firewood, but I fear our plans might be better for another night."

She linked her arms around his neck. "Sandrine and Eoghan are our guardian angels of sorts. They've taken Greta to stay with them tonight."

His eyes widened, then seemed to light from within. "Angels for sure they are." He dropped a kiss on her mouth.

"So how about this?" She caressed the freshly shaved line of his jaw, savoring the scent of his forestry aftershave. "Since I've been thinking about it all day, let's still go and have a fire on the beach after dinner and hear the roar of the sea. Then come back here and make love."

He cradled her hips between his strong hands. "I like the way you're thinking."

After they left the quiet restaurant he'd chosen, they drove to the private cove they'd walked before.

The sea was churning, white with froth, the waves

crashing against the rocks. The air was alive with wind and sea spray, making her laugh as their boots sunk into the sand. Bird footprints were visible moments before the tide erased them. She hugged her arms around her as Jamie worked quickly to arrange stones in a circle and light the wood.

"I wasn't sure if you could get the fire to start in this weather," she said, grabbing the plaid wool blanket he'd brought along.

"You have to be a bit more canny, is all." He fanned the flames with a newspaper before tossing it into the fire.

She watched the pages crinkle and burn. "I hope that was the national newspaper that hosed me."

"And the local paper as well," he said with a wink. "I thought your artistic soul would appreciate the significance. I also brought the letter from the censorship board seeing as how I have an electronic copy."

She applauded as he extracted it from his pocket and tossed it into the flames.

"When I got to my studio this morning, I made a glass sculpture of a flame to clear my head." She watched the fire burn, imagining it was burning away the hate and the filth. "But we're not talking about that, are we? How are you tonight, Mr. Fitzgerald?"

"As fine as an Irish summer day." He dropped down next to her and wrapped the other side of the blanket around himself, enclosing them in its warmth. "And how are you, *mo chroí*?"

God, she loved it when he called her that. "I've been up and down all day, but being here with you... Jamie, I'm starting to feel calm and happy again. Like everything is far away."

"That's grand then." He tugged the bag he'd brought

through the sand until it was in front of them. "I brought some hot wine. My mother makes it for Christmas. I figured it might work for tonight."

"I love *vin chaud*!"

She leaned against his shoulder as he pulled out the thermos and filled two tea mugs. The smell of cinnamon and cloves warmed her as much as the wine, and she tilted her head back as she saw the first few stars appear. The ocean continued its thundering assault on the beach, but rather than being intimidated by its force, she embraced its power. The sea wasn't afraid of anything, she thought. She needed to be more like the sea.

"It's the kind of place where words aren't needed, isn't it?" Jamie turned his head to look at her. "I thought you'd understand that."

The fire flickered over his face, illuminating all the angles she knew and loved. "Yes."

They sat and drank their wine, and when the wind began to gust, Jamie pulled her to her feet. "We should go. The weather is turning, I think."

In the waning light—the colors of indigo and black merging on the horizon—she watched him put out the fire. When he extended his hand to her, she grasped it firmly, knowing what was next, wanting it as much as the sea needed the rocks to crest against.

When they entered his cottage, words didn't seem necessary here either. Hand in hand, they walked to his bedroom, a room she'd passed before with curiosity and hope. Undressing each other slowly—at first with amusement given all their outer clothes—and then with rising longing.

Their mouths met as his hands eased her clothes away, his kisses coming in heated passes over her lips. She caressed the strong line of his shoulders and chest as she helped him out of his shirt, and then her hands drifted lower to explore him as he undid his pants. He was hard and beautiful, and as she touched him for the first time and heard his groan, she knew she had never wanted anyone or anything more than him and this moment.

When their bodies were bare, he brought her against him, warming the last bit of chill in her bones from their time at the sea.

"I know it might be too soon," he said, his voice low and resonant, "but I need to say it now. I love you, Sophie."

Joy shot through her, and she closed her eyes as the words filled her mind, her heart, her very soul. "I love you too," she answered when she opened her eyes, gazing into the cobalt heat awaiting her. "It doesn't feel too soon, does it? It's like we've known each other forever."

"It is," he said, kissing the soft line of her neck. "Come and let me know you more, *mo chroí*."

He laid a trail of fire over her skin, and like the glass she used in her art, she melted from their heat. His kisses made her body bare to him, first her mouth, and then her breasts, and then lower, to the place that ached for him.

His fingers searched for the curves that made her moan, and she soon was seeking out the places where her touch brought him that two-edged pleasure of foreplay. His groans became her joy, and when he finally put on the condom, laid her back, and slid inside her, his thrusts had her finding a bliss she'd never known.

When she came, she sought to link their hands, riding the wave of her pleasure as he joined her, their cries mingling in the quiet of the home he'd given to her. They floated on that ribbon of bliss, tucked around each other, until he finally raised his head, his eyes shining brightly in the soft light of the room.

Everything she could ever want lay in that single gaze, and as she brought his mouth down to her, she knew she was sealing something precious, something rare, something that would alter the path of her life forever.

CHAPTER SIXTEEN

He shot straight out of bed, his heart beating madly.
Crying out, he beheld Sorcha standing beside the bed.

"There's someone outside," she said quietly. "Hurry. You might catch them."

He rolled out of bed quickly, rousing Sophie, and tugged on his jeans before racing to the parlor and jamming his feet into his wellies by the door.

"Jamie, what's the matter?" Sophie's voice was sharp with alarm.

"Stay where you are," he called back.

Footsteps scattered outside as he tore open the front door. In the dark night, he could make out two slim forms running down his driveway.

"Hey!"

Neither one turned around, and he watched as a car flipped its lights on. The doors opened, illuminating the interior, and for a moment, he could make out the backs of the two forms as they ducked inside. Male. Teenagers, from the slenderness of their frames. The tires squealed as they punched the gas, and he took off at a run to better see the license plate.

"Jamie!"

He was winded by the time the car disappeared from sight down the next bend. Sophie was rushing toward him, so he jogged back to her.

"I told you to stay inside."

"What happened? Did someone try to break in?"

Taking her arm, he found she was already shivering, likely from the cold as much as the encounter. "I don't know. One moment I was sleeping, and the next—" *My ghostly sister-in-law was beside the bed.* "Go back inside and let me check."

She stopped short and gasped sharply. "No need. Look."

The front porch light she'd turned on illuminated the crime.

Go Home Slut

The words were sprayed in a hateful scrawl of red on his front door. His front door!

"My God!" Jamie exclaimed, putting his arm around her. "Sophie— I'm so sorry."

"It's not your fault." She was shaking against him in nothing but a robe, he realized. "Okay, now I'm a little scared."

"We need to call the Garda." He stared at the offending graffiti as he tore open the door. "And Linc and Bets."

She stood in the center of the parlor. "I should probably get dressed. Jamie..."

He stopped reaching for his phone and crossed to her. "What, *mo chroí*?"

"If Greta had been here." Tears filled her eyes. "I'm starting to lose it a little bit."

Wrapping her in his arms, he held her tightly. "You go ahead and lose it, as you say. I might need a moment myself."

He looked up as Sorcha materialized in the hallway leading to the bedrooms. Her face was as somber as the day they'd buried her mother, he noted. Then she shook her head and vanished.

His heart was pounding in his ears. Had they planned to do more than write those hateful words on his front door? His car had been parked in the driveway, so there had been no mistaking his presence.

Who in the hell were those kids? He hadn't recognized them. It was dark, but his instincts told him they weren't from around Caisleán. He knew people's cars. The purchase of a new vehicle by anyone in town was big news and usually the kind to warrant a congratulatory pint at the pub.

"All right." She gave an audible sniff and wiped her nose as she eased back. "Go and make your calls. I'm going to call Sandrine...just to make sure Greta is okay. I know it's silly but—"

"It's not silly." He took her hands to his lips and kissed them. "We'll make this right."

He didn't know how right now, but he made the vow all the same. They would stop this. They had to. He'd never forget the look on her face when she first saw those words.

The call he made to the Garda was brief. He knew the man on the night watch and was glad to hear the officer they were sending was someone he respected. Not everyone at the station was of the same ilk.

When Bets answered after three rings, he was sorry to hear the fear in her voice. "Jamie? What's wrong?"

"We had some kids vandalize my house tonight. I just called the Garda."

"Summercrest?"

"No, I'm at my cottage." Best be direct about it as everyone would soon know the way of it. "With Sophie. Greta is having a night with Sandrine and Eoghan."

He heard Linc in the background. "We're on our way."

"Will you call my brother? He'll want to be here."

"Sure thing."

When they hung up, he went to find Sophie. She was standing in front of her open wardrobe. "I can't seem to pick anything."

Shock. "How about this?" he said, grabbing out a sweater. "It's warm and the color will look good on you."

"You should probably put on a shirt." She gave a rough laugh. "Not that it's not a good look. Jamie, everyone is going to know we were together."

"Good." He cupped her cheek. "Why wouldn't I be with the woman I love?"

"The people who sprayed *slut* on the front door might argue that." She shook out the sweater. "You know... Until this week, no one had ever called me that word. I was the daughter of a slut. And that stung. Boy, did it ever. It's a really horrible thing to say to someone, Jamie."

"The worst. Here, let me help you."

She took over and dressed herself as he hovered. Then he led her back to his bedroom and found his clothes. He eyed the bed. Only an hour before, they had finally fallen asleep in each other's arms.

"Sophie."

Her head turned, her eyes still foggy.

"This was the best night of my life. I won't let them ruin that."

She shook herself. "Neither will I. Let's make some tea."

"You're becoming more Irish by the minute. We should probably make enough for the others." It was going to be a long night, he imagined.

They were just pouring water over the teabags when he heard the first car arrive. Someone knocked, and Jamie realized he'd locked the door when he'd come inside as a precaution. Opening it, he faced his brother.

"I'm glad you had me called." He wrapped him in a hug. "What a horrible thing."

"The worst." He watched as another car turned into his driveway. "I probably should have guessed you and Bets and Linc would arrive before the Garda."

Carrick clapped him on the back. "Maybe they're searching for their notebooks so they can take extra-detailed notes."

He wanted to laugh but didn't have it in him.

"Shut the door, Jamie," Linc called as he and Bets walked toward them.

Even through the wood, he could hear Linc's Gaelic exclamation. "You're cursing in Gaelic?" he asked as they opened the door.

"When all this started, I asked Donal to teach me one." Linc's round face was pronounced with worry lines, the same as Bets. "I thought mixing it up would be good."

"Maybe you can teach it to me," Sophie said, coming out of the kitchen with a tray of tea.

"How are you holding up?" Linc asked, his jaw tight. "That's some nasty business on the door."

"I won't lie," she said, setting the tray down carefully. "My knees are still knocking a little."

Bets marched forward and stopped next to her. "Those

sons of bitches. Sophie, I'm so sorry. I have no idea what to say except that we're going to stop this."

Jamie wasn't so sure anyone could promise that. He turned as another car sounded in the driveway. "At last."

Only it wasn't the Garda. It was his friends from Summercrest.

"You called them?" he asked Carrick.

"Of course. They're our friends. Kade is coming too."

"So is Donal," Linc added. "I told Eoghan to stay with Sandrine and Greta. Part of me wants to take them to Bets' and lock them inside, but that just goes to show that even my knees are knocking."

The Summercrest contingent bustled into the parlor, the men clapping Jamie on the back and the women hugging Sophie. Kade arrived moments later, followed by Donal, whose face was grim.

"Bad news," he said as he closed the door. "I got a tip. The Garda is sending Denis Walsh as lead investigator. He showed up unannounced, saying he'd be taking the case."

Jamie's stomach twisted as Ellie blurted, "But he's the officer who did *nothing* when we called the Garda after that bullshit inspector showed up with bogus health and safety violations and closed the arts center last February."

"They have their *instructions* is all my source could say," Donal ground out.

"What does that mean?" Sophie asked, her voice laced with tension.

"It means they don't plan to do dick, that's what, and likely on someone's orders," Linc replied harshly. "Sorry for the language. Excuse me while I go outside and kick a tree."

By the time the yellow-and-blue-checkered Garda car finally appeared, everyone had a cup of tea. Denis took their statements and had his sidekick take photos of the graffiti, but it was all a rote exercise and everyone knew it. Sophie didn't bother to go into detail about the recent newspaper articles she'd been featured in, and neither did Jamie.

The only moment he almost lost his cool was when Denis looked Sophie over and asked what she'd been doing at Jamie's house in the first place. Her face blanked for a moment before she told him about the issues with the mobile home. But Denis didn't stop there, asking Jamie what he was doing at the cottage instead of Summercrest. He'd only answered, "We had gone out for the evening. When will you have a lead?"

"Hard to say," Denis said after giving them a knowing look that gave Jamie the uncharacteristic desire to deck him. "It sounds like kids from what you say. Just playing a prank."

"A prank!" Sophie cried out. "That wasn't—"

"I doubt we'll catch them given the lack of evidence," Denis continued. "You shouldn't hold out hope."

He nodded to them and left through the front door. Jamie and Sophie closed the profaned door after him. She wasn't trembling anymore. Her cheeks were flushed. Anger, he expected, the same emotion roiling through his veins.

When they turned back to face the crowded parlor, Jamie set his feet. "This is the third time we've had one of our artists intimidated, the first being Ellie with the inspector, the second being Mary Kincaid's son vandalizing Kathleen's shed. Now this nonsense has come to someone's home—mine—and I'm not going to swallow it anymore. A few of you have more experience dealing with this kind of situation than I do, but it's clear we can't count on the Garda for help. So what are we going to do?"

Sophie snorted. "One of the main actions artists are urged to take when they receive threats is call the police.

Guess we can cross that off the list. Groups like Artists at Risk Connection encourage artists to talk to stakeholders who can raise the visibility of the situation."

He turned to her. "So we go back to the media? They're part of the problem."

Suddenly she looked exhausted, her color fading to gray. "The media is always a mixed bag, but the right reporters and organizations can raise awareness. As we've discovered with Taylor and other positive press."

"But it doesn't keep you safe," Bets said, walking across the room and stopping in front of Sophie. "I have to ask you again. Do you want to just bag this and go back to Provence?"

Jamie's heart rate sped up as he waited for her to reply.

When she only pressed her fingers to her mouth, Bets laid her hand on her shoulder. "I hate to make a point of such a thing, but it would be unconscionable if I didn't. Greta wasn't here tonight and you weren't alone. You were lucky. We can't know they weren't planning more."

He thought of Sorcha again. If she hadn't woken him up...

"I've thought about leaving." Sophie stroked her neck. "I probably need to give it more thought, but I don't think me leaving solves the problem."

"It would for you, darlin'," Linc said gravely. "You could complete the statue in Provence—or forget the whole thing. No one would blame you."

She turned her head and met Jamie's eyes. His throat grew thick as they gazed at each other. He tried to smile, but it faded from his face all too quickly. He couldn't reassure her. What assurances could anyone give?

"I have discovered so many reasons to stay," she said, her voice breaking. "If I do, we'll have to figure out a more secure living situation. Maybe it's having lived in Provence, but I happened to like my gate, high walls, and sensor lights."

"We could have Jamie's house fenced in with a gate tomorrow, if you want to stay here," Liam offered. "The last utility company is still dragging its feet about your mobile home, as you know."

Jamie met her eyes again. "I would want to stay here with you and Greta."

She nodded. "I'd want that too." She bit her lip. "But I don't know if it's enough."

"We also could find you an excellent guard dog that's good with children," Kade added. "On our horse farm, we've had thieves scared off because of the dogs."

She gave an all-body shiver. "It's funny, the things you take for granted. For years, I didn't worry about these kinds of threats although my parents dealt with them all the time while I was growing up. Every time it happened, they stood their ground. While I understood that they should be able to paint anything they wanted without being hurt or threatened by other people, I still cringed every time I went to one of their gallery showings."

"You must have been a really brave kid," Kathleen said, making Sophie smile ruefully.

"I tried to do what they wanted. I was raised to believe in the importance of art, and I still believe in that. I smiled at the protesters as they shouted horrible things at us. I never shouted back. Blah, blah, blah. But right now... I want to send Sandrine back to our home in Provence with Greta so I can see if this will blow over. Because if it doesn't... I can't put her through that. I just can't."

He had to work up his spit to respond after hearing her voice break. "Then we'll talk to Sandrine in the morning."

"My father will want to go with them," Donal said after a moment. "I plan on visiting Denis' superiors. Hopefully they'll see reason. This is not good press for those who want serious law and order in this country."

"And you can bet we're going to blitz the hell out of this in the media." Linc made a fist. "You start threatening women and children like this, in their homes... The public is going to be outraged, and I'm going to sweeten the pot by offering a hefty reward for anyone with information leading to these goons' arrests."

"Let's hope that has the wolves turning on each other," Carrick said. "Kade, I'll be wanting one of the guard dogs you mentioned for my home. I take my sheep dog when I'm at the fields. I don't want Angie and the baby to be alone in the house right now without support."

"They can come and stay at our place," Bets said, gesturing to Linc. "Anyone can. It's not luxurious—"

"Neither is Summercrest," Declan added, "but all are welcome until we have a better grip on the situation."

"I'm going to fly in a couple of security officers from my former company for the arts center until I can hire permanent staff," Linc said. "Most of our board members are in this room. Any objections?"

Jamie shook his head along with everyone else, then said, "We also need to be proactive about the censorship issue."

"Bets and I are scheduled to meet with the Arts Council this week, time still TBD." Linc took a deep breath. "Anyone ever think they'd face this kind of shit when Bets first mentioned wanting to start a local arts center? Isn't life grand?"

"It's absolute shit sometimes," Kathleen said tersely. "My brother would kick those officers' teeth in for disgracing the uniform. He can't stand to see that kind of crap anywhere, whether it's in his own precinct or elsewhere. He's a cop in Boston, Sophie."

"He sounds like the kind of policeman who does his job," Sophie said. "Too bad we're not dealing with one of those here."

Linc rubbed his hands together. "If the Garda isn't going to do dick, maybe we need to have our own people look into the matter. Donal, what odds do you give us on Denis' superiors taking things seriously?"

He lifted his massive shoulders. "Thirty percent probably. Every Garda you talk to will cite stretched resources and jurisdiction issues. But we need to send a message even if it doesn't go anywhere."

"Then we'll send a message no one can ignore." Linc scanned the room. "I want to thank every person here who has put up with this shit. I wasn't present before Ellie arrived, obviously, but I know y'all have faced enormous obstacles. I can promise you this: I'm going to crucify these bastards, one way or another. We are going to make this arts center safe for everyone—children included—and when we're done, no one is going to be able to touch us."

"You really are starting to sound like an Irishman," Donal said, inclining his chin.

"Now I need to think like one." Linc tapped his noggin.

"Who would have put those kids up to this kind of vandalizing?" Ellie asked.

"Malcolm." Bets began to tick them off with her fingers. "Mary. Maybe even Tom MacKenna. What about that reporter who hosed you in the county paper, Jamie?"

"Hard to say." He rubbed the stubble on his jaw, suddenly sick of it all. "But he's in Galway and more the sort who'd use his pen for filth, I think."

"We'll investigate them all," Linc said. "Sophie, is any of this making you feel better?"

The sight of everyone crammed together in his parlor was a balm. Jamie put his hand on her low back as she unrolled her shoulders. "I'm not sure anything would ease my tension, but I really like the idea of offering a reward for information. I hate to be cynical, but the kind of people we're dealing with are motivated by hate and greed. I doubt they'll stop unless someone makes them. As for the media blitz, I'm already fending off inquiries after that article in the national paper. I hate taking away studio time, but it seems I'll be giving lots of interviews this week."

"Maybe we should call a press conference." Bets punched her fist into her other hand. "Send out international invitations to the press. Artistic intimidation, especially on women's issues, is a hot topic. So is censorship."

"I think a lot of people would show up for that," Ellie offered. "Maybe in the future we could even hold a conference on the topic. When we have a hotel..."

Reluctant chuckles sounded before Sophie said, "I know you're still looking for a publicist for the center. Why don't you let me call the woman my mother uses? She's French, of course, and a total pit bull. Nothing intimidates her. She's highly respected in art circles and has a lot of connections in both Europe and the U.S. If she invites people, they'll show up."

"Do it," Bets said after she and Linc shared a look. "And thanks, Sophie."

She blew out a long sigh. "I guess all those tools I learned from my parents are paying off. But I feel a little better now that we've got a plan."

"We've been reacting to events, and I'm tired of dancing to people's tune," Linc said. "Anyone else?"

"Time for us to play the music," Jamie agreed, taking Sophie's hand.

She glanced into his eyes, her gaze searching. "And Liam, if it's really no problem, I'd love having this place armored up tomorrow—with a dog, please, Kade. I'm starting to feel like this is home."

He traced her face, knowing what he was about to do would change things. "*You* are home, *mo shíogrhrá.*"

She might not know he'd just called her *my eternal one* but everyone else did.

He'd declared her as his own.

CHAPTER SEVENTEEN

Maybe she should never have started this.

"What are you mumbling about?" Linc asked as he undressed in their bedroom.

She wondered if he knew he'd been groaning as he got ready for bed for the second time that night. Bets eyed the clock. It was heading toward three. If it were any later, she would head out to her rose garden and pull weeds. How was she supposed to sleep after what happened tonight?

"I'm going to the kitchen to bake something." Bread maybe. She could punch that.

"Save your energy, sweetheart." He threw his shirt over her easy chair in the corner, a sign he was too tired to hang up his clothes like normal. "We're going to be going hard for the next few days."

Like they hadn't been all week?

"Christ, Bets, what a rough deal! I've lived a long time and seen a lot of things, but this takes the cake for me. I want to smash something."

She sank onto the bed, gripping her knees. "Linc, are we doing the right thing here? Should we just give up?"

He halted from unbuttoning his pants and strolled over until he stood in front of her. "Betsy O'Hanlon, you're hurting and you're tired like the rest of us. If you'd wanted to give up, you would have done it a long time ago. After the first punch."

She closed her eyes, the sting of rare tears burning hot. "Yeah. Probably. But dammit, Linc! They wrote *Go Home Slut* on her front door. Jamie's front door!"

He sat beside her and pulled her into his arms. "I know. Do you think I haven't thought about what might have happened if Jamie hadn't been there and woken up? You know how much I care about Sophie and her daughter. This is eating at me like battery acid, but she's right. Her leaving won't solve this. We have to think about other artists, Bets. The ones we have now and the ones we will have. If we don't make a stand for them, no artist worth his or her salt is going to come here and risk this kind of harassment and violence. Well, some will, but it limits our pool."

Pressing her face into his chest, she pounded the mattress with a fist. "You're right, dammit. I know you are."

"This is a watershed moment, darlin'. We'll have to rise to meet it or let it take us down. And you know I don't do no Alamos."

She lifted her head and touched his jawline, so familiar to her, so dear. "I still remember the bite in your voice when you told me that."

He rubbed the tense muscles in her shoulders. "Lots of other people feel like we do, Bets. We just need to take this wide and connect with them. I figure there've been a lot of bullying and beatdowns in the world by corrupt motherfuckers who want to see goodness fly out the window. I, for one, am fed up with it. Artists deserve to be safe to express."

"And women deserve to feel safe, and people need to

stop calling us sluts." She wanted to shriek. "I remember the first time I heard that word. I was fifteen and it was 1977. Some boy at school leered at me and said he wanted to take me for a ride in his car, and when I didn't answer him—because I was scared—he called me a slut. Loudly. Everyone opening their lockers stopped to listen. I was mortified. It was wrong then and it's wrong now."

"Now, we're getting up in arms about things that have sucked since the world began." He started to remove her sweater. "God knows we aren't going to solve it. We can only do our part. Now, we *need* to get some shut-eye. Oh, Bets, you put this on backward, honey."

She bit her lip to stop from crying. He was right. She was hurting and angry and feeling hopeless to boot. "Linc, do you really think we can turn this around? Because Sophie is about ready to send her daughter back to Provence, and I don't want them to be parted for no good reason."

"If I didn't think we could, I would have said so." He chucked her under the chin. "I won't sugarcoat it. It's not going to be easy. But we'll do it. Together."

Putting her arms around him, she settled into his strength. "I hope you're offering a huge reward and that I'm in the room when we find out who did what. I don't think Mary's behind this one. She's evil, but why bother paying young boys to spray an obscenity on Jamie's door when she already delivered her message in person?"

"My thinking too." He stroked her back. "No, this has Malcolm written all over it. If he can't have our arts center, he's going to crush it. Not that we'll let him. We need more allies. Big ones. I think we should form a wider advisory board ASAP. Remember how I mentioned courting Nobel Prize winners and other bigwigs in our long-term plans?"

"The ones with million-dollar-plus board seats?" The amount still shocked her. She'd always thought volunteering was about doing something from your heart. God, she'd been naïve.

"Yeah. That. Some early commitments to our international advisory board will help us short and long term. We should have a few important allies show up to our press conference if possible. I'll pull in a couple of my former executive secretaries who've retired to help put it together. I think we shoot for Friday. That way reporters can enjoy the weekend in this fine country as they write their copy for their Sunday papers. We'll probably have to throw a dinner. Something somber given the situation."

"I'll put up black crepe curtains and fill the room with funeral-themed peace lilies." She wanted to bang her head against the wall. "What about the publicist Sophie mentioned?"

"Brigitte would only have the best," Linc said, his hands continuing a slow and easy rhythm on her back. "I'll call her tomorrow morning after Sophie makes the intro. Heck, this morning. Christ, it's late. I feel old, and I hate that. Hate admitting to it as much as I hate the feeling itself."

"And I thought battle charges were supposed to make men feel young," she said, pulling away and continuing to undress.

"Only young people get a charge out of battle, Bets. Too stupid to know what's coming."

"I feel old too." She was sure her muscles were locked up tight as a drum. "Maybe there's a way for us both to feel a little younger."

His mouth turned up on the right. "I might have heard about it. It's a mighty powerful way to feel comfort too, and honestly Bets, I could use a healthy dose of that right about now."

She felt the burn of tears again and blinked them away. "Me too, cowboy."

Bets knew it was corny, but as he laid his lips on hers and helped the tension in her heart evaporate, she discovered love really was the most powerful force on earth.

CHAPTER EIGHTEEN

Sending Greta away was going to be the hardest thing she'd ever done.

As she knelt in front of her little girl, she prayed she was doing the right thing. All she'd done was rehash everything in bed as Jamie lay awake holding her. There weren't any good choices. To be separated from Greta—and her daughter from her—was horrible, and yet it seemed reckless to keep her here right now. She could give in and leave, but there were so many wonderful things for them in this community. To abandon it would feel wrong. To leave Jamie permanently would break her heart. And Sandrine would feel compelled to go with her—Eoghan as well—just when they were happily getting settled here and planting roots together.

"You know," she told her unsmiling daughter as she crouched down in front of her in Eoghan's front parlor, "Provence is going to be all warm and sunny. I'll bet you'll even be able to swim in the pool."

"That's what Eoghan said." Her big eyes were unblinking. "Mama, I know something's wrong. I'm not stupid.

Everybody has been whispering this morning. I saw Sandrine rubbing that spot between her eyes, and Eoghan's wrinkles looked deeper. Can't you tell me the real reason?"

The explanation she'd given her daughter was simple. Sandrine and Eoghan missed the sun, and they thought it would be fun for her to go with them for a little holiday while Sophie stayed behind. She hadn't wanted Greta to think she was too busy for her and didn't want her around. Now she was faced with a conundrum: lie to her daughter or scare her? And yet, from her own childhood, she knew it could be more frightening to be kept in the dark. "You know my pregnant goddess sculpture?"

Her daughter nodded slowly, clutching her stuffed sheep.

"Well, a few people don't like it, and they sprayed some bad words about it—like the graffiti you always point to when we're coming into the train station in Paris. I thought having you go back to our house in Provence might be happy for a little bit while everyone in Caisleán tries to find out what happened."

Greta was silent for a moment before saying, "But your design is so beautiful, Mama. What would anyone not like it?"

A question for the ages. "I don't know. Some people don't like art where people don't have their clothes on."

She tugged her sweater. "But we're all naked under our clothes, Mama. Our bodies are precious, like you always say. I don't understand why people would think it's bad."

"Neither do I, so we're going to talk about it with a lot of people this week and try to change things." She smoothed Greta's curls with a smile. "And you're going to send me tons of pictures of you with our flowers and swimming in the pool, okay? Maybe I'll even be able to dash off to see you. I miss wearing a dress and a skirt, don't you?"

The smile was slow to develop, but it was genuine. They were out of the woods. "The moment we get to our house I'm going to put on my blue dress with the sunflowers."

She was not going to cry. So she swallowed down the surge of emotion for the moment. "I love that one!"

Greta shuffled forward and toyed with the buttons on Sophie's cardigan. "Are you going to be okay, Mama? You look really sad."

Honest. She had to be honest. "I am sad, and a little angry too. I just wish people could see things the way I see them. Beautiful. But even if they don't, that we could agree to disagree without things turning ugly."

Her daughter nodded gravely. "Grandmama always says we should feel bad for people who can't see the beauty in life. People don't always like her paintings either, remember? Maybe you should talk to Grandmama about this."

While no one had shown Greta Brigitte's more controversial paintings, they'd explained that people didn't always like them because they included people without clothes on. In a million years, Sophie had never thought the same things would be said of her own work. Certainly not her character. "We've talked a little already, but you're right. I will."

She was understanding her mother on a whole new level, and it saddened her that it had taken something so awful to bring it about. But you truly couldn't understand what someone had gone through unless you walked in their shoes.

Sophie wanted to rip off these particular shoes and hurl them into the sea.

"I love you, Greta." She brought her in for a hug, trying not to hold her too fiercely. "I'll miss you, but we're going to FaceTime every day, so it's not like we're going to miss each other too much. Plus, Eoghan and Sandrine are going to be great company, aren't they?"

"We always have fun," Greta said, fingering the flower necklace Sophie had made for her. "Eoghan is so funny. But I'll miss you. Not just because you're my mama, but because I like you. Not every kid likes their mother. Did you know that? There are girls in school who don't like their mothers one bit."

She used to be a girl like that. Then she'd carried that feeling into adulthood. Of course, Brigitte wasn't an easy woman—never would be—but maybe it was time for Sophie to change her point of view and let the past go. "Well, I'm glad you like me. I like you too. Now, I'll bet everyone is freezing in the front yard, so we should get you going. Do you have everything?"

"Yep!" She held out January and then picked up her purple backpack. "We didn't have to pack much because I still have some clothes in Provence. Mama, I'm glad you're staying with Jamie. He makes you happy."

Her heart tore. Last night, she'd felt like she'd achieved the kind of heaven on earth she'd only dreamed about. She desperately wanted to get that feeling back, but the shadow of the vandalism and its ugliness loomed large. "I make him happy too. You might even say he's my boyfriend."

"Of course he is, Mama. You go on dates with him."

Her ever-practical daughter. "I'm glad you're okay with him being in our lives."

Greta's brown eyes sparkled. "I'll tell you a secret, Mama. I like him too."

She rose, giving in to the urge to pick Greta up and hug

her yet again as she carried her outside into the cold morning. "Oh, I'm going to miss you bunches."

Her daughter squeezed her with all her might and then pressed away. Sophie let her down and watched as she walked over to Jamie. He knelt on one knee, doing his best to smile. She leaned in and said something in his ear. He nodded, and then she kissed his cheek before running toward Eoghan and Sandrine.

Her eyes met Jamie's for a moment, her heart hurting in her chest, and then she made herself go over to the trio standing beside the car. Donal was taking them to Knock, where Linc's plane was waiting. He nodded to her from the driver's seat, the fatigue on his face evident.

She hugged Sandrine, her fingers gripping the older woman.

"We'll take good care of her," Sandrine whispered in French. "Like I did when you were that age. You be careful but you be strong too. You have it all in you."

God, she hoped so. She blinked back tears before turning to Eoghan. "You enjoy the pool and the whiskey and anything else. Including the studio. You use anything you want."

He touched her face gently, like she was precious. "But mostly I'll be enjoying the sun and your beautiful flowers. *Maireann croí éadrom a bhfad*, Sophie. It means *a light heart lives long*. If you'll take an old man's words to heart. Don't let others weigh down that beautiful heart of yours."

She rubbed her nose to hold back her rising emotion. "Thank you, Eoghan."

"Like every Irish storm, this will blow over." Then he picked up one of the stones in the driveway and held it out. "Even the wind and the sea have trouble moving the stone.

Be the stone. *Dia duit*. Come, Greta. It's time for our grand adventure."

She watched as her daughter took the older man's hand and gave her one last look before waving. Sandrine helped her into the back seat, and right before she alighted, their eyes met and held. Eoghan closed the door behind them and came around to the other side. The car doors slammed, a punctuation in the quiet front yard. Rocks crunched under the tires as Donal drove off. Sophie gripped the stone in her hand, the metaphor alive in her mind. Something might run over her. Push her deeper into the ground and make her cry out, but she would still hold.

Jamie's hands settled on her shoulders. "I can't imagine how tough it was to send her off."

She turned in his arms and laid her head on his chest. "I never want to go through anything like this again, Jamie. God, I hope I'm making the right decision."

"All we can do now is try to make things right." He made a rude noise. "Better. I don't know if 'right' is possible. Where do you want to work today?"

"You'll be helping with the improvements at your house, and I have a bunch of calls to make." She followed him to his car. "You'll be hammering, so I should probably go to Linc and Bets or Summercrest. Although part of me doesn't want to be parted from you. I feel all raw inside after sending Greta off and after last night. God, that's silly, right? I'm thirty-six years old, for heaven's sake."

He cupped her cheek. "I don't want to be away from you either, so I guess I'm silly too. But you might find it easier to make your calls way from the cottage today as you said. I'd also prefer you never see the words on that door again. I texted Liam when we left the cottage so he and the others could start on it right away."

The words might soon be gone on the door, but they were etched in her mind. "I hate to say it, but you should probably tell them to take a picture we can give to the press."

Jamie tucked his hands in his pants, narrowing his eyes. "I believe that's been taken care of. Horrible enough to see it on the door, so I suppose it wouldn't be much worse to see it in the papers."

"It's all worse at this point." She blew out a breath. "All right, I'm going to head over to Linc and Bets' and get going. Taylor is five hours behind in New York and still asleep, but my mother's publicist will be awake. I think I'll call my mother first. Greta, in all her wisdom, told me I should. Can you imagine?"

He opened the car door for her. "She's a sensitive and intuitive child. It doesn't surprise me at all. Put your seat belt on, *mo chroí*."

She loved it when he called her endearments in Gaelic. When he came around and settled into the driver's seat, she touched his arm. "You have any problem with me calling you something like babe or my love?"

His smile radiated joy—a first for him today. "You can call me anything you'd like. So off to Bets and Linc's then."

Linc was in full steam in the parlor when she arrived, already on the phone and pacing. He lifted a hand in her direction as Bets led her to a sunny room behind the kitchen.

"Make yourself at home," Bets said, clearing a few paperbacks off the low-slung engraved table. "I'm holed up in my office, but Linc needed space to prowl today, so he's taken over the parlor. He's already hired those temporary security officers he mentioned. They're from a company he used to tap when he was running his company. Who knew windows needed guarding? Bad joke. They'll be here tonight. He's still working on lining up an investigator, but he hopes to have that sorted out shortly."

She watched as Bets wrung her hands together. "That's great. Linc knows how to get things done."

"Donal has a meeting set with Denis Walsh's supervisors, likely in some pub. That's where the men like to do their business. Always drove me a little crazy. How are you doing this morning? Or should I even ask?"

She uncurled her hands from where she was clutching her purse and set both that and her workbag down on the table. "About as well as you would imagine. You don't look like you slept either."

"Not a wink. But I had three boys, and the habit of going hard without the Zs comes back easily to me, even after all these years." She made an attempt at a smile. "I want to tell you: I think what you're doing is brave. I don't know how I would have reacted if my boys were still little. I can't imagine a harder choice."

Her stomach was quivering again. She needed to start working and block things out for a while, or she'd be a wreck. "On that we agree. I'm going to reach out to the publicist after I call my mother. If she agrees to help us, and I think she will, given my mother is a long-standing client and friend, we'll have a whole lot of items rolling shortly. She's a whirlwind."

"Great! We need all the help we can get. I'll grab you some tea and let you make your calls."

Sure enough, Bets returned with a tray arranged with a teapot covered with a yellow cozy, a cup and saucer, and a plate of fresh-baked bread. Laughing, she set it down. "I needed to punch something this morning when Linc finally let me out of bed. Hah! I'll be in my office if you need anything, reviewing Linc's list of people to approach for spots on our advisory board. We're going after some big fish."

"Smart." She nodded. "It'll help to have some big names on the board. Thanks for the tea and bread, Bets."

Bets lurched forward and touched her arm in comfort before striding out, her tigerlike energy as palpable as Linc's. Sophie felt more like a bedraggled sparrow with feathers missing after a serious plucking. Wouldn't her mother love that analogy? If Sophie described the mental image to her mom, she'd probably encourage her to draw it. She'd always done that when Sophie was a kid—told her to draw her feelings. Right now, she felt like shit. Drawing *that* would probably be controversial. God, she was on her way to a pity party.

She dialed her mother, and after three rings, her mother came on the line. "Darling, how are you? This whole thing is absolutely nasty. I was so angered by being called a pornographic painter again that we displayed the headline on the wall in my gallery showing. People were absolutely outraged! *Le Monde* has an article about it in today's paper, did you see? Ghislaine wanted to rub those ignorant reporters' faces in their stupidity and highlight the ongoing problem we have with people with this mentality."

She couldn't have hoped for a better segue. "It's gotten worse, Mother, and I need Ghislaine's help," she said and proceeded to describe last night's incident in as steady a voice as possible.

When she finished, her mother was silent. Silent. A rarity. "Are you still there?" she asked.

"They painted *Go Home Slut* on the door to the house where you were sleeping! How is Greta—"

"She was staying with Sandrine and Eoghan, thank

God, and I'm sending her with them to Provence while we handle things."

"Handle what?" her mother practically croaked. "The *police* should be handling this!"

Here was the tricky part. "They aren't being very supportive, Mother."

"You mean they agree with the vandals?" She cursed fluidly in French. "Typical! I don't know why I'm surprised. The police told me I was asking for it with my art. They never said that about your father's paintings. Not once! I'll never forget when a police officer in New York City told me it might be better for everyone if I painted fruit. Fruit! They would never say that to a man."

Reeling as she was, shock still rolled over her. She couldn't imagine anyone telling her mother to paint fruit. Or what to paint for that matter. Why would someone think they had the right? It was insane. "I never knew that story, Mama."

"Of course not. You were eight at the time, but can you believe it? This ingrate was a decorated officer in New York City! The gallery was in Soho, and he was like, 'Lady, you're going out of your way to be provocative.' I was like, '*Monsieur*, I am only trying to paint what I see in my mind and feel in my soul.' But that's enough about me. You need Ghislaine, and Ghislaine you will have. I will call her the moment we hang up. Then I will take the TGV down to see my granddaughter. Unless you want me to come to Ireland to be with you."

She fumbled with her phone but caught it before it dropped. "You just had your showing, Mother. Greta will be fine, and so will I. Things are just unpleasant now."

"Are you taking precautions?"

"Linc has hired a few security officers and an investigator, and some people are making the house where I'm staying safer. I'm trying to stay optimistic."

"You mentioned Greta was with Sandrine last night. Does that mean you have a man in your life?"

She'd hoped that detail would slip past her mother, but her mother liked to joke that she could smell sex from a hundred yards away after all of her husband's infidelities. "Yes, I do. He's a wonderful man and a respected schoolteacher as well as the head of the children's arts program they're planning at the arts center."

Another pause. "Does Sandrine approve?"

"Yes."

"Good," her mother said softly. "She did not approve of Franz and neither did I."

She sat back in her chair. "You never said."

"Why would I? It's your life. The affairs of your heart—like anyone—are yours and yours alone. *Alors*, now I will call Ghislaine and rage at her on your behalf. Expect her to call you shortly."

Rage on her behalf?

"Thank you."

"And Sophie... You tell Linc to call me. For anything. I have a lot of experience dealing with this kind of thing. I'd... like to be helpful if I can."

Her throat thickened. Maybe the new understanding she had with her mother wasn't one-sided. "I'd like that too. *À tout à l'heure, Maman.*"

"Be well, *ma petite.*"

There had been a loving caress to her mother's voice, and she'd called Sophie her little one, something she hadn't done in ages. She reached for her tea to steady herself and waited for Ghislaine to call.

When the sun came out moments later, Sophie watched

as the green of Bets' yard brightened and the leaves on the surrounding trees became gold-edged. But that was what light did. It transformed everything it touched.

That was what they would have to do to turn things around.

CHAPTER NINETEEN

The sun was setting when they set the final wall in place.

Jamie was so tired he shifted his weight to his right leg, the ache in his back a fierce line of fire from the heavy labor. "It's a right fine wall."

Carrick clapped him on the back. "It is, at that."

"Do you want me to come by and add shattered glass or metal tacks to the top of them walls on the morrow?" Liam asked, dusting off his hands.

He frowned. "Even though I've seen many a wall such as that, I'm not sure I want to go that far. We'll hope my new dog will be as much of a deterrent as the motion lights we've installed."

Glancing over at Rex, the black-and-white Irish sheepdog Kade had delivered at noon, along with one for Carrick, he had to smile. He'd never wanted a dog, being how he was away so long at school. But things were different now. Sophie was here, and they would both take comfort from Rex and his canny patrols. The dog had sniffed every inch of his property after scenting all twenty-some men who'd shown up to help along with Kathleen and Ellie, who'd demanded to help alongside their husbands.

His friends and the village were behind them, and many had shown up at the site to express their outrage over the incident. He'd wished Sophie could see the support the community was offering, but she'd spent the day working with Ghislaine, Linc, and Bets on a rapid publicity press campaign. When he'd caught Sophie on the phone for a second earlier, the fatigue had been obvious in her voice. She needed a break.

They all did.

"Brady," he called to his friend, who was rubbing the small of his back with a pained look, "might I inquire if you'd be willing to open the Brazen Donkey so I can buy everyone a pint?" It still choked him up that Brady had closed the pub today to help.

"If you're buying, I'm opening." Brady grinned over the weariness on his face. "I'll see you all there."

"I just want to go home and take a bath after hauling those cinder blocks," Ellie moaned. "I don't know how anyone does this kind of work all day long."

"They have strong muscles and even stronger constitutions," Kade's father responded with a laugh. "You did pretty well for someone who's not used to working outdoors."

"I don't work outdoors," Declan said, putting his arm around Kathleen, "and I did just fine."

"But you're constantly at the boxing gym or lifting slabs of meat," Kathleen said, smacking him on the backside. "That qualifies. Who's going to tell Sophie, Linc, and Bets about our little meetup?"

"I will since I'm picking Sophie up," Jamie said, giving them all a smile. "You're a good bunch. The whole lot of you. I take back anything I ever said about you. See you at the pub."

Carrick squeezed his shoulder. "I'm going to pick up Angie and the baby. They were with Megan and Ollie at the farm, but I think they could use a little lift of the spirits. It's been a dark day."

"But lighter with friends, I'd be thinking." He watched those friends head to their cars, his heart full. "I had Ellie take some photos so Sophie can see how many people came to help."

"It's only the beginning. Have you heard from Sorcha?"

He glanced around to make sure they were far enough away from the others for this conversation. "She was the one who woke me in the night."

"That's fine." Carrick nodded once and then again. "It's good knowing she's looking after more than your romance. That seems to be taking root nicely. I'm glad for you, Jamie. We'll be seeing you soon."

He waved and headed over to where Liam was standing with a gadget in his hand. "I think we have it working right," their friend said with a devilish grin. "Abracadabra."

The newly installed gate for his driveway began to close, and Liam held the device out to Jamie.

He walked over and took it with a grateful smile. "You're the best."

"I'm handy, is all." Liam rubbed his brow. "Changes the view, doesn't it? Makes me rather sad. The need to put up walls is a tragic commentary on the state of affairs here in town. Let's hope this is only temporary."

"Right now, I can't even think that far ahead." He kicked at a broken piece of cinder block in his yard. "I only want Sophie to feel safe."

"Agreed. But you also needed to send a message. Not

everyone wants to be kind, and sometimes people can be downright nasty. You're saying you won't let them."

"No talk of forgiveness and turning the other cheek? We were raised on it, and all I can think now is that it's easy to talk about turning the other cheek when no one's beating on you."

"You know the old saying. *Every man is sociable until a cow invades his garden.*"

"Or a sheep." He turned to Liam, someone he knew he could share his inner turmoil with. "It makes me wonder how this will change me as a teacher. When a kid strikes another kid at school, we tell them not to hit back."

"But you're *not* hitting back, are you?" Liam faced him. "You're taking measures to keep yourself and those you love safe, and you're asking the law to hold people accountable for crimes. Crimes, Jamie. Ones that are as plain as day."

"Maybe we aren't taking schoolyard scuffles seriously enough." He sighed, suddenly tired. "That's where this all starts."

"My brothers and I fought when we were growing up." Liam nudged him gently. "So did you and Carrick. We didn't make a life out of it. We had fairness and kindness to balance it all out."

"Maybe." He didn't understand anything anymore.

"There aren't any easy answers. But it's despicable that someone put kids up to it. I'm guessing Malcolm figured they were less likely to be charged if caught. Hopefully Donal will make some progress with Denis' supervisors. All right, that's enough of that. I'll see you at the pub. This kind of self-reflection is good and natural. You're doing well, Jamie, for what's happened. If that's any comfort."

He clasped his friend's shoulder. "It is. Thank you for

everything, Liam. None of this would have come together as fast or as well without you."

"I was happy to share my gifts." He gave a jaunty wave and took off for his motorcycle.

Jamie locked the house—praising the saints that Ellie and Kathleen had borrowed heat guns from the arts center to ensure the paint on the front door dried quickly. Sophie was right. The words might be gone, but he could still see them. He imagined he would for a long time.

He picked up a couple more broken pieces of cinder block before petting Rex and telling him to stay. Closing the gate weighed on him as he left. His friends and neighbors would now have to ring him from a soulless box for entry. There would be no more flying visits or drop-overs for a spot of tea or whiskey.

That thought depressed him as he got into his car. Something precious had been stolen from him, and he hadn't even known how precious it was until today. The smell of oranges enveloped him, and this time there seemed to be a warmth attached to it, so much so his throat ached.

"You're down in the mouth, Jamie," Sorcha said, appearing in the passenger seat. "But you have good reason. What happened last night was vile, and there will be more tough days ahead, no doubt. Yet you've had them before, and you overcame them."

He glanced over to see her smiling softly. "Your passing was one of the darkest times I've ever faced."

"And yet all wasn't lost, was it?" She fiddled with the folds of her white dress. "So this will go, with everyone sticking together and standing up for what's right. Look at all the people who came around today. Even grumpy old Mr. O'Shea. It's like my mum always used to say. *Miracles love company.* Get ready for more, even as you begin to sift through the apple barrel for the rotten ones. Enjoy your evening tonight, my boy, and make sure to dance a jig for me."

With a saucy smile, she vanished. He almost chuckled. Sorcha knew he had no rhythm for the old dances, but he could manage a slow dance without too much shuffling. He wondered if Sophie liked to dance.

When he arrived at Bets' and Linc's, the lights out front were all turned on. The house was equally ablaze, but it was good precaution. They would all have higher electric bills, but if it meant feeling safer, it was a small price.

As he left the car, he thought perhaps he should have texted first. When Linc opened the door, he lifted his hand in greeting. "I got to thinking perhaps we should all text when we're coming for a visit, given the state of things."

"As an American, that's what I'm used to," Linc said, waving him inside. "I think it's a good plan for the moment. We should pass the word. How did the wall-raising go?"

The smell of a roast hung in the air as they walked into the parlor. His stomach grumbled. The sandwich he'd eaten earlier was long since gone. "We got the job done and well, thanks to the mass of people who showed up to help. I had your daughter take pictures, hoping it would lift Sophie's spirit."

"They would lift mine and Bets' too." Linc walked over to the bar stand. "Whiskey?"

"We're all meeting at the pub for a drink." He opened his hands awkwardly. "I figured everyone could use a lift, myself included. I'm buying the first round. We were hoping you'd be coming along."

"We'd love to." Linc forewent the whiskey and poured some of that sparkling water Jamie had never taken a fancy too. The bubbles sprayed all over one's face.

"How was your day?" he asked, hoping to hear Sophie coming, but the hall behind him remained silent.

"Got a whole lot done. Hired Brigitte's publicist and three security people, one of whom is an investigator. Discussed our situation with our current advisory members from the county council. We have an uphill battle locally. One of the idiots had the gall to tell me that we're veering into a dangerous territory. *Art as morality*. It made me think he was the one who leaked your syllabus for the children's program. I wanted to strangle him."

"Art isn't morality," Sophie said from behind him. "It's a *personal* expression. This jerk is on your advisory board?"

Jamie turned around. She looked as pale as a lily in the moonlight.

"We'll be parting ways soon," Linc said savagely. "He's reconsidering his association with us now that we're dipping into feminism and 'girls' issues.' You don't want to know what else he said, trust me."

Sophie rubbed her forehead. "Are they crazy?"

"Completely!" Bets sailed into the parlor with a tray that boasted steaming dinner plates loaded with roast, potatoes, and carrots. His eyes tracked it as she set it down on the coffee table. "Nicola did some research in her own bookstore and found out that you couldn't even print the word *pregnant* in Ireland until 1960."

"Where did they think all the babies came from?" Sophie asked.

"The fairies," Bets said, making a face. "Come, have something to eat. Jamie, have you had any dinner?"

His stomach growled again. "Don't mind me."

She rolled her eyes. "Sophie, let me tell you about the Irish and having dinner at someone's house. They won't take anything. They'll even watch you eat, stomach growling, and refuse a bread roll. Old school Irish stuff. You never take food from someone's table. Probably comes from the famine days. But I persevered. I finally asked my friends if there was any way I could convince them to break tradition, and they told me, all blushing cheeks and ducked chins, that you have to ask like this. 'Jamie, will you have a little bit?'"

He did his best not to smile. "Yes, and thank you, Bets. She's right, you know. We don't do the dinner thing like you Yanks. Angie is still mad about that dinner party she invited us all to. Only Liam showed up for it."

"Because he's half-American and has heard me complain about this to high heaven. Tea is fine. Biscuits fine. Dinner? Not so fine. Am I babbling so I won't pull my hair out about that jerk on our board?"

Linc pulled her to him. "Good thing he was only an advisory member. Ah, hell, it's probably best we found out early so we can boot him. I expect we're going to be hearing a lot more of that drivel. Now, let's eat up and then take off for the Brazen Donkey. Seems we're having a little get-together to raise people's spirits and celebrate this community."

Sophie finally approached Jamie. "The wall-raising went well?"

"I have pictures to show you." He laid a gentle hand on her arm. "We had more help than shovels."

"I needed to hear that." She blew out a breath. "It's been an up-and-down kind of day."

"Then all the better to have a little meeting of friends," Jamie said, taking her over to her dinner. "Have a bite, *mo chroí*. You look spent."

"You're sunburned." She touched his face. "I'm glad your day went well."

"Tonight is going to be even better," he promised her.

And it was. The pub was packed when they arrived, and everyone cheered as they sighted them.

"First round is on me," Jamie called out, making the crowd cheer again.

They found the seats reserved for them and sat down amidst their friends. Angie handed him Emeline with a smile, saying, "You look like you could use a little baby love."

Kade put the new Jack Russell puppy, Lucky, in Sophie's lap. "Usually Brady makes you leave your dogs outside, but he made an exception for this little fella."

"Wait until you see the Irish sheepdog Kade found for us, Sophie," Jamie told her as Brady put pints in front of them. "His name is Rex, and he's as well-mannered and alert as they come."

"The one I found for Carrick and Angie is a king too," Kade said, rubbing the puppy behind the ears, making him squeak in delight. "You should know that the owner donated them after hearing what happened. He said his granddaughter plans to come to the children's arts program, Jamie. All the way from Castlebar."

"Glad to hear it," he replied, watching as Sophie cuddled the puppy close to her side. "She'll be most welcome."

Of course, they would have to sort out the censorship board query if there was to be a children's program. God, he couldn't think about that right now. Linc had said the lawyers were on it. He had to trust in them.

Just like he had to trust in the people around them. As he gazed at his friends, he could see the weariness in their faces, from their waning color to the slumped lines of their shoulders. He stood up, feeling a rare need to speak rise inside him.

"I'd like to make a toast," he said in a voice he used to gather the children back into the schoolroom.

The conversations quieted, and he shifted on his feet as he became the center of attention. "You know I'm not one for talking much, but I'd like to raise my glass to all of you tonight. The Irish here will know this saying. *A best friend is like a four-leaf clover. Hard to find and lucky to have.* I look out tonight and only see treasured friends, and for that, I am grateful. *Slainte.*"

People lifted their glasses, some with tears in their eyes, repeating the toast. Sophie leaned closer and whispered in his ear, "I love you, Jamie Fitzgerald."

He traced the delicate line of her cheekbone. "And I love you, *mo chroí*. Do you dance? I thought we might have a slow one. We Irish have another saying you might not know. *Dance as if no one were watching. Sing as if no one were listening. And live every day as if it were your last.*"

She stood with Lucky in her arms. "Then let's dance and dance and dance."

They danced with the sleepy puppy between them until Ellie interrupted with a knowing smile and asked if she could take the little fella. Jamie mouthed a thank you as Sophie settled against his body, swaying to the music Brady had turned up. Other couples had joined them, dancing between the tables, in the front, and beside the bar.

He noted that the laughter came easier as the evening went on, for himself and for his friends, and he was glad they had all convened in the pub to lift their spirits.

When they all said their goodbyes, he was aware that the embraces were a little stronger, more assuring. No one needed to say so out loud, but they would be there for one another. No matter what.

He told Sophie the same when they reached their

newly walled home. "Oh, Jamie, you've lost your gorgeous view of the surrounding pastures! I didn't think."

"It's all right, *mo chroí*. Better our safety than a view any day. Besides, I'm hoping it might only be temporary."

Rex barked as he opened the gate, another sign of the changes.

"Do you think so?" she asked softly as he parked the car.

"I had a friendly spirit tell me today that miracles love company." He wouldn't mention Sorcha yet; he'd rather tell the tale on a happier occasion. "I rather liked the sentiment."

"Who doesn't like miracles?" She gestured to the heavens. "Probably the same idiots we're dealing with. Jamie, I'm glad we had tonight. I needed some hope."

He cupped her face. "We all did. Now come inside and let me love you."

"That gives me hope too." She laid her forehead to his. "Our love. The love from our friends. Even the love I felt with my mother today. Maybe your friend is right. Miracles *do* love company."

He thought of it as he introduced her to Rex and as he locked the door of his own home, a still unfamiliar act.

Seeing her undress in the soft light of his bedroom was also unfamiliar, but it was welcome, and he marveled at how something could be both.

Then he laid her down on the bed and slowly loved her, his very own miracle come to life.

CHAPTER TWENTY

Her mother's publicist was a whirlwind.
Ghislaine blew into Bets' front parlor like an Irish gale in her black Chanel suit and matching Louboutin heels. "Sophie, *ma petite*!" She kissed her Parisian style, on both cheeks. "How are you? I can't begin to imagine. Your mother has skin like a pet iguana now after all the vitriol she's experienced, but not you. You're as sweet as one of those little lambs I saw in those Irish fields we passed on the way here."

Before Sophie could reply, Ghislaine was striding across the room to Linc and kissing his cheeks as well. "And Linc Buchanan, you were an angel to send your plane for me. Brigitte's told me all about you, of course. I know you're a man of action, which is exactly what we need right now."

Sophie shared a glance with the man of action in question, fighting a smile.

"And Bets!" More face kissing, which Bets didn't lean into. "May I call you Bets? I think what you're doing out here is absolutely marvelous. Now let's talk about what we can do to keep all that expanding, shall we?"

Sophie bit her cheek to keep from smiling. She was used to Ghislaine's indomitable energy and enthusiasm, but from Bets' shocked face, she'd been blown over. She cleared her throat. "Ah... Ghislaine? Can we get you some tea?"

"How about a café, darling?" She unlocked the gold clasp of her chic women's briefcase with aplomb and pulled out a black notebook and a Montblanc pen. "Let me tell you who I have RSVPs for already for the press conference on Friday. So many people in the art community who know you by reputation, Sophie, are completely shocked on your behalf. You're the least most controversial artist out there—not that there's anything wrong with that—and this story is sensational for that alone."

Linc pulled Bets down onto the gold sedan with him and kicked out his heels. "Everyone knows Sophie's one of the nicest people and artists you'll ever meet."

She wanted to crawl under a rock.

"Yes, but not *everyone* knows how nice she is, Linc." She shot him a clever glance. "But don't worry. After we get through, they will. I mean, her statue is of a pregnant woman. Yes, naked. But it's elegant. Refined. No nipples. No—"

"Yes, we know your meaning," Linc interrupted, clearing his throat. "Can I see your list, Ghislaine?"

She strode across the floor, her heels tapping on the rug, and handed the stapled pages to him. "Things are going to move fast, but from what I understand, you'll have no trouble keeping up with me. Now, Bets, you know the local scene. I'll need your help there. I know there are plenty of Irish reporters out there who report with fairness and humanity. And the local people who support Sophie and the center—I'll want to introduce them to some of the reporters coming into town. I've already dispatched one of my favorite reporters from *Le Monde* to meet with Eoghan O'Dwyer after Brigitte told me all about him. Imagine taking up art at the age of ninety-three. He's an inspiration unto himself. Not mentioning that he's won over our beloved Sandrine. Anyway, are there others like Mr. O'Dwyer in town?"

"His cousin, Fergus, is in his eighties and doing art too," Bets said, locking gazes with the woman. "You're very well informed, Ghislaine."

"It's my job, and I do it well." She smiled, yet remained composed. "Now, let me tell you what else I'm thinking. Then I want to hear from you."

"Can we take a quick break so I can make you that coffee?" Bets asked, rising. "It won't be up to Paris standards."

She laughed, her long blond hair trailing down her shoulders. "Nothing is, darling. Not even in Manhattan, which I adore for other reasons. Sure, let's take that quick break. Then we're going to get rolling."

They already were, Sophie thought, as a knock sounded on the front door. Bets gestured to Linc. "Go and answer while I make us tea and coffee. Tell whoever knocked that I like this new system of ours."

"What does she mean?" Ghislaine asked as Linc left the room.

"The Irish don't normally knock when they arrive at someone's home. They just walk in."

Her brows shot to her hairline. "Really? But that's incredible! Talk about trust. We need to mention that to the press. Focus on the trust broken in this tight-knit community."

Male voices sounded in the hall, and then Linc was

coming in with Donal, who pulled up short, stopping mid-sentence.

"Are you all right, Donal?" He looked thunderstruck. Sophie's heart started racing in near panic. "Is it bad news?"

He shook his head, his green eyes taking in Ghislaine. "Only...an update on our Garda problem. Hello. I'm Donal O'Dwyer."

Ghislaine's hand holding her notebook slid down her side. "Ghislaine Monet. No relation to the artist, I'm afraid."

Sophie had heard Ghislaine use that line a million times, and usually it made people laugh, but Donal only continued to stare. So did Ghislaine, for that matter.

Linc finally nudged him. "You were saying..."

"Right." He coughed a moment before continuing. "Denis' supervisors aren't going to step in. I have a feeling they're more afraid of what will happen if they do."

"Meaning Malcolm definitely played a hand in this," Linc said harshly. "Tom doesn't inspire that kind of fear."

Donal nodded. "I'm going to take it to the next level—the Garda Síochána Ombudsman Commission in Dublin—but that's going to take more time. I don't have contacts there."

"Let me help you," Ghislaine said, shooting him a beatific smile. "By the time we've told our story, they'll be calling *you* to set up a meeting. You said your last name was O'Dwyer. Any relation to Eoghan O'Dwyer?"

His hard jaw shifted into a broad smile. "He's my father."

Ghislaine rested her weight on her back heel and smiled back. "Everything is as it was billed and then some," she said mysteriously. "Good genes and taste run in your family then. Are you an artist as well?"

Linc crossed his arms as Donal ducked his head, his cheeks turning ruddy. "I dabble a bit. I've only just started. But you don't want to hear about that."

"You'd be surprised." Ghislaine sent Sophie a look. "I can see why you came to this town, not that Linc's referral and my other sources weren't sufficient."

Other sources being *her mother*?

"Good to see you, Donal," Bets said, arriving with a tray. "How did it go?"

Linc took the tray from her and gave a harsh sigh. "As expected. He's going to submit a complaint against the Garda to the national body."

"Meaning more bureaucracy," she replied with a groan. "I suppose lots of places suck, but nothing is easy in this country, least of all fighting corruption, which is endemic, and eejits, who are all too common. And yet I stay."

"You must love it," Ghislaine said, taking a cup of coffee from the tray Linc offered.

"There are a lot of positives," Bets said, picking up her tea, "but the negatives really bite my behind, if I can be that direct with you."

Sophie smiled as Linc offered her the tray. "Next up, a French maid's outfit."

"That will be the day," he responded all John Wayne like, making everyone laugh.

"Is that orange pekoe tea, Bets?" Ghislaine asked. "I confess, it smells heavenly."

Bets' face went blank, and she shared a look with Linc, whose mouth parted before slamming shut. "No, it's just plain old Irish tea."

Donal's teacup clattered. "I smell oranges too."

Sophie sniffed the air. She'd smelled oranges at Jamie's cottage upon her return, but today she didn't smell anything. Maybe there was some flower or bush outside that emitted an orange-scented fragrance that carried easily inside a home. "Not me."

Bets shot to her feet and pressed her hands to her cheeks, a huge grin on her face. "Oh, I'm just so happy all of a sudden."

"Me too," Linc drawled. "That orange scent is about the nicest thing I've ever smelled. Right, Donal?"

The older man's smile widened as he shared a look with his friend. "It's heaven-sent, if you ask me."

Now she was really confused. "The smell of oranges is supposed to improve one's mood and create an uplifting spirit."

"I adore the smell," Ghislaine said, her eyes watching Donal over the cup. "It's feminine, yet it has a certain strength to it."

"We had someone in our village who was famous for wearing it before she passed," Bets told Ghislaine. "The poet we named the arts center after."

Sophie felt more goose bumps break out across her arms.

"Sorcha Fitzgerald!" Her mouth curved. "So I've heard."

"You have?" Bets asked.

Ghislaine smiled slowly. "I'm well informed. I read the story of her passing and how the center was the home she'd wanted, built posthumously after her death by her husband before he donated it to the village for the new arts center. He's married to Angie Newcastle."

"Your mind is a marvel," Donal said, his gaze fixed on none other than her. "Welcome to Ireland, by the way. We're very glad to have you here."

They shared another long look, one Sophie was both

shocked and delighted to see was filled with banked heat. Goodness, they liked each other! How about that? Then she remembered Jamie telling her that miracles loved company. Wasn't this the proof?

"I happen to be very happy to be here," Ghislaine finally said, her voice more hushed now. "Linc, do you remember how I told you I wasn't sure if I could fit you in as a long-term client?"

"Sure do," he drawled.

"Well, I'll make room." She traced her coffee cup with a well-manicured fingernail. "I feel like my connection to this place is just beginning."

Sophie lifted her cup to conceal yet another shock. She knew Ghislaine's list *and* waiting list were full. "That's wonderful! There's no one better."

Ghislaine shot her a winning smile. "Wait until you see where we are come Friday."

The days couldn't have gone any faster. Ghislaine steamed ahead, guiding everyone along with her. Sophie refined her statement again and again until she could say it as fluidly as if she were telling Greta a bedtime story. Jamie patiently listened to her as they sat in the quiet cottage in the evening, sometimes after having dinner alone and other times after a drink at the Brazen Donkey with friends. Keeping busy didn't stop her from missing Greta, but it *did* help knowing her daughter was having a ball with Sandrine and Eoghan.

A few people called in with information about the vandalism, but the investigator didn't consider them solid leads. That concerned her more than she wanted to admit, and she knew her troubled sleep was from the awareness that the person or people who'd orchestrated the vandalism were still out there.

On Thursday morning, she'd just finished getting dressed when Jamie came up behind her and rubbed her tense shoulders. "Maybe you should stay in bed a little longer this morning. You look exhausted, *mo chroí*."

She almost purred from the magic he was working on her again. He'd already well satisfied her this morning. "You are too, and it's not because school has suddenly gotten harder to teach, I imagine."

He made a sound that had her turning around. "No, it's the censorship board matters. They weigh on me. I know the center's legal team has everything in hand, but I don't like that I was also asked to submit my school curriculum. Some parents have asked me about the issue. Someone talked out of school. Literally."

"Any ideas who?" she asked.

He hesitated for a moment. "My principal confessed to having some concerns about the letter. Nothing official, mind you. Part of me can't blame her. It's rare for the censorship board to get involved with a small school such as ours, and with her being the principal, she might worry it reflects on her leadership. She was aware of my book selections."

Sophie could still feel a chill when she thought of the woman's disapproving look. "And she didn't find anything wrong with any of them?"

"No, of course not. They're all widely approved books. Yet I'm still unsettled by it all."

"As you should be." She touched his jaw tenderly. "All of this 'looking over your shoulder' and 'judging your work' is designed to inspire fear and make you doubt yourself. I know. I've had those dark thoughts too, but neither one of us is in the wrong here, Jamie."

"I know that, but it wears on me." He exhaled sharply. "When I asked to take off Friday to be at the press conference, my principal was less than thrilled."

Sophie narrowed her eyes. "What did she say?"

He lifted his shoulder. "She said, 'If that's the way you want to go.' I didn't like her tone. I told her this was personally important to me and the village. I even reminded her about my role heading up the children's arts program, but I left feeling like I'd drunk sour milk."

Now she felt the same way. "This is why I knew I'd never do well with a boss. Jamie, I appreciate you taking the day off for the press conference, but if you feel you need to—"

"No, *mo chroí*!" He took her in his arms. "You're the most important person in my life. When you love someone, you're there for them. You can count on me, Sophie. For always."

She was starting to think in those terms more and more. Maybe it was time to raise it. "It's always for me too. When this is over, we should talk more about what that means for us. And Greta. She's one of the most important people in my life too."

"And she's one of mine." He grasped her hands and raised them to his lips. "So I make that vow to you *and* to her. Now, I'd better be off."

"We should probably take a nap after you get home from school." She waggled her brows. "The dinner with the four new advisory board members tonight is probably going to run late."

"Any news on Linc's efforts to get Bono to join the advisory board?" Jamie asked with a rare grin. "That would impress everyone in town. Not that it's not incredible that we have Ireland's most famous female Irish boxer on the board, but U2 would be another level."

She laughed and savored the feeling. "It would certainly impress me! And no, there's no definitive answer yet, but if anyone can do it, Linc's the man. I like that he's including highly respected Irish people on the board along with the regular folks. Ghislaine is very impressed, and not only with Linc."

He took her hand and led her to the kitchen. "I've heard the news about her and Donal, and I'm thrilled."

"Me too. Ghislaine has not been lucky in love. They're different in all the obvious ways, but they're both cut from the same cloth. Strong personalities who stand up for what's right and savvy wheelers and dealers. They try to unify people with a common goal. I can't wait to see how it's going to play out."

"Sometimes you just know—down to your bones—when you see someone." He caressed her arm, which had her going all soft, because she knew he meant them as well. "Donal is already talking about spending time in Paris and traveling to New York with her when she needs to go. He lived in the States ages ago and is eager to return."

There would inevitably be compromises between the couple, growing up differently as they had. But she and Jamie were no different, she thought, wincing as he spooned in instant coffee to his to-go mug. He said it was good in a pinch on workdays when he needed a jolt. She, on the other hand, had gone ahead and ordered a mini espresso maker for herself because she'd needed to delay her shipment yet again. Her taste buds would revolt over instant after all her time with freshly brewed coffee.

"I know what you're thinking," he said after the kettle

whistled. "Be glad I'm not knocking back a Red Bull like so many I know."

She winced. "Miracles love company. I've thought about that a lot since you said it."

He kissed her softly. "They do, indeed. I'll see you later, and then you can get me excited about this dinner. I'm still not sure whether I'm going to enjoy it."

"Trust me. You'll enjoy it. Linc did not bring in any boring people."

"I do. That's why we all voted to let him make the choices in our emergency meeting Monday night. Everyone looks impressive, sure, but they live in another world."

She pointed to the changing light outside the window as the mist fell, sunlight breaking through the light rain. "So do you, Jamie. We all live in our own worlds. My favorite thing is when we can combine them or overlap for a while and realize how much we have in common."

"I have to kiss you again after that sentiment."

He laid his lips over hers and made her sigh. She nuzzled into his arms, her heart beating madly in her chest. "I wish you didn't have to go. But you do. So go. Before I throw myself all over you."

Laughing, he picked her up off her feet. "That's a possibility? Save it for later then. You can throw yourself at me when we meet for that nap you mentioned earlier."

With a final quick kiss, he headed out of the kitchen. "Lock the door behind me," he called.

She heard Rex bark as he left the cottage. The black-and-white dog was sweet, yet very serious. He liked to herd people to their cars and the front door. It was rather amusing.

As she turned the deadbolt, her mood dropped. The

quiet was still a little unnerving, and a pang of longing for Greta rocketed through her.

Her daughter would be awake. She crossed to her phone and saw a text from Ghislaine asking for a call. She could ring the woman afterward.

Sandrine picked up her FaceTime call right away.

"I thought you were going to call this morning," the older woman said with a smile. "A little someone is drawing flowers in the kitchen as Eoghan makes her a full Irish. I've never seen Greta eat so much. Every morning she eats one. She must be going through a growth spurt. Of course, he's complaining about our boudin not being a substitute for black pudding. I told him boudin is better, of course, but he'll hear nothing of it."

Would Greta be taller by the time she came back to Ireland? Sophie was desperate for their separation to end, but without any progress in finding the vandals, she wasn't sure yet when she'd feel comfortable bringing her daughter home. Tomorrow was the press conference. Another step. Donal and Linc thought it would help the Garda ombudsman address their complaint sooner, although no one could guess at the outcome.

When her daughter appeared onscreen, she found it easy to smile. Her blond hair had a blue butterfly barrette in it to match the butterflies on her white summer dress, and her brown eyes were shining with happiness. "I've been drawing flowers, Mama—the kind you like to draw. Everything is still blooming here because it's still so hot. Not like Ireland *at all*. Eoghan says his bones are finally starting to warm up. Isn't that funny?"

She touched the screen, wishing she could touch her daughter's sweet face. "I hear you've been eating a full Irish breakfast every morning."

"Eoghan says it makes you grow up strong and happy. Mama, I have something to tell you. There's been a giant heron landing in our front yard."

The small wonders of a child. God, how she treasured them. "Really? Where did he come from?"

Her daughter shrugged her little shoulders. "We don't know. But it's so still, and it moves so slowly. Even slower than Eoghan when his back is aching."

Clearly, the older man was entertaining her daughter with his gift of the gab. "You'll have to take a picture for me."

"We've been trying to leave it alone so it will know it's welcome here."

Eoghan again, she imagined. "Feeling welcome is important. Maybe you can put out some milk and cookies."

"It's not Santa, Mama," she said with a giggle.

"Are you sure?" She waved as Eoghan came into view. "I heard you have a visitor."

His wrinkles shifted as he grinned. "Our heron is a gift from the heavens. You know what it means, don't you?"

She frowned. "No, I don't actually."

"Oh, if you could watch it move, it would be as plain as day. Every step is taken with great patience and care, and there's a certainty about its pace that leaves you in awe. Even me. I'd go crazy taking each step that slowly, but the heron doesn't seem at all concerned."

Their eyes met, and in them, she swore she could see the old soul he'd likely always been. "The heron seems very wise."

"Greta and I thought so, didn't we?" He tickled her daughter's side, making her scream with laughter. "Like me, for example. Here I thought I was going on a holiday with my two favorite girls, only to end up meeting with a fine reporter from *Le Monde* and talking about my art and our beautiful center. One never knows what might happen. Isn't that right?"

She tried to smile, but her heart was too full to sustain it. "Yes, it is."

"Rather like my son informing me only this week that he's met his soulmate, a woman who'd already impressed me with her grace, beauty, and determination when we spoke." He slapped his forehead and uttered a cry. "And her smelling of beautiful oranges, a special symbol to some of us in Caisleán. Have you smelled the scent yet, Sophie?"

So it was a *symbol*? That strange moment in Bets' salon came to mind, as well as the actual fragrance she'd smelled when she'd returned to Jamie's home. Her arms were covered in gooseflesh again. "Bets said Sorcha Fitzgerald used to wear it," she said carefully, aware that Greta was listening.

He waggled his brows playfully. "She did indeed, and it's lovely to know she watches out for us in Caisleán. Do you believe people who've passed on can look out for others?"

Art and literature were filled with such stories, but she'd never had a personal experience herself. "I find it comforting to think so," she said truthfully.

"Then be well comforted," he said with another knowing smile. "All right, I'll get back to stirring the porridge."

With a final smile, he patted her daughter on the head and walked away.

"I'm coming, Eoghan," Greta called. "Don't let the fairies eat my share!"

Fairies. Herons. Ghosts even? She looked outside to see

if a rainbow had appeared. Not yet. But it was early. "If you see a unicorn, Greta, you call me right away."

Her daughter nodded emphatically. "Gosh, wouldn't that be wonderful? Tell Jamie I miss him. Okay, I've gotta go, Mama. The fairies really love oatmeal."

She blew her a kiss. "Not as much as I love you."

"Me too," her daughter yelled and ran off.

"She's happy," Sandrine said when she appeared back on the screen. "If that's any comfort."

She swallowed thickly. "It is."

"Good luck with the press conference tomorrow. I expect Ghislaine has outdone herself like usual."

"And then some," she said, cracking her neck. "But you know the pace."

"You should catch a few hours in your studio if you can." She tilted her head to the side, studying Sophie. "If only to make something simple. Your heart will feel better."

She was right. When her eyes alighted on the glass sculpture of flames she'd made the previous week, her heart lifted. "I do need my brain and mouth to rest. I've been thinking and talking nonstop."

"Your voice does sound stretched. Lemon and honey in hot water. *A bientôt, ma cherie.*"

See you soon. God, she hoped so. She put her hand over her aching heart. "*A bientôt.*"

When she ended the call, she didn't give herself a moment to think. She called Ghislaine right away.

"Good morning, Sophie. Isn't it a beautiful day? I swear, all this sweet Irish air and the endless green hills are better than any spa. Yesterday, Donal had me putting on wellies and walking through sheep pastures. I had no idea how heavenly it could be. Of course, having a new man in one's life helps too. But *you* know…"

She could all but hear the wink. "I'm glad you're enjoying yourself."

"Anyway, I was reaching out to tell you what I told your mother. You can feel free to disagree. She asked me what I thought about her coming tomorrow to the press conference. Either alone or with a whole bunch of other artists who are up in arms over what's happened to you. The bottom line is that she wanted to be here to support you."

Support you... Miracles did love company, she thought as emotion clogged her throat. "That's very nice of her."

"Yes," she said crisply, "but I told her no. Let me tell you why. This press conference is about you and the arts center. Your story. Your art. The current situation. And, of course, what the center has planned for the future, although that's not our present focus. Hence why I'm not having Jamie speak about the children's program and the censorship issue. One volatile topic is enough. We'll tease the rest out afterward... But if your mother came, people would want to talk about *her*, and that's off topic."

She'd been around long enough to know Ghislaine was right. "How did my mother take the news?"

"She might have huffed a little, but she's used me for decades as her publicist. Enough said. Are you angry?"

"Not at all." She thought of the heron. "We have a plan. We take our steps and don't rush things."

"Exactly!" Ghislaine continued with her usual enthusiasm. "Do you need anything else for tomorrow? Another run-through?"

"We did that yesterday, and I need to rest." She rubbed the back of her neck. "But you could send me the hologram you created of my statue."

Ghislaine knew sometimes bigger was better, so she'd created a life-size hologram of the sculpture based on a digital image to wow the audience tomorrow. "The moment we end the call."

"Thanks, Ghislaine. I'm glad you're here."

"Me too, Sophie. I just love surprises sometimes, don't you? See you and Jamie tonight."

Surprises, huh? Sophie had always thought surprises, like changes, were what you made out of them.

They were taking their recent curveballs and hitting for the fences.

Tomorrow, they needed a home run.

Her future and Greta's depended on it.

CHAPTER TWENTY-ONE

Linc had never much cared for hoopla.

People might call press conferences a circus, but he'd rather be watching clowns and a lion tamer than pressing the flesh with a bunch of reporters. He had nothing against reporting as a profession. News was an important service. But reporters who twisted people's words and information ought to be fired. It would be like one of his window makers substituting plastic or another inferior product for glass and still calling it a window.

Ghislaine had only issued invites to so-called credible journalists, but even so, they were a competitive lot, always looking to scoop one another. He was ready to step in if anyone asked a salty question of Sophie. Of course, she could stand on her feet. But if they went too far...

"You ready to go, cowboy?" Bets asked, coming out of the bathroom.

He whistled as he beheld her crisp navy pantsuit. "Business executive looks sexy on you."

"Would we call that a misogynistic comment?" she asked, shooting him a look.

Gesturing to his gray suit and tie, he modeled for her. "Don't I look sexy too?"

"You do." She picked up the new earrings he'd given her—ones he hadn't told her were diamonds although she'd probably guessed. "I'm doing my best to keep riding high after our kick-ass dinner with the new advisory board members last night, but my tummy is starting to get tight. This press conference is the biggest thing I've ever been a part of. Certainly, it's the biggest we've done for the center."

"All you need to do is smile when you're introduced and make your statement welcoming everyone." He crossed to her and rubbed her sides briskly. "Just tell your story. Why you started this place. It struck me right in the heart the first time I heard it. Others will feel the same, and if they don't, then you know what they can do."

She smiled. "Shove it where the sun don't shine?"

"Yes, ma'am." He extended his arm. "Let's get going."

His phone beeped, signaling a text. When he read it, he swore. "It's Ghislaine. She got to the center just now, and she said there are protesters outside. All women, likely from some kind of local women's association. They arrived in three buses and are blocking the driveway. Ghislaine has our security people trying to move them off the public road and is checking their permits, but our friend from the Garda is there with them."

Bets fisted her hands at her sides. "Of course he is! Denis couldn't have picked a better revenge. In Ireland, the Garda are supposed to help people keep it peaceful, but they *can* protest on public roads."

"Terrific. As the saying goes, 'the press is going to have a field day.'"

"I suppose we should have expected it," Bets said with a hard edge to her voice. "But most of them won't be from our village. We have support here. Still, twenty bucks says Mary Kincaid and Orla MacKenna are there with bells on, leading the charge."

Mary and Orla had more than bells on, Linc noted as they arrived. They had megaphones and were shouting something to the dozens of women standing shoulder to shoulder behind the now cordoned-off section of the road beside the driveway. Denis waved at them with a sneer, standing beside his police cruiser blocking one lane. *Asshole*.

"I've never been at a protest." Bets gripped her seat belt. "You?"

"Not my style. But from what I've seen on TV, the signs are about what I'd expect."

Not In Our Village one placard read in black while three others screamed in loud red *Nudes Are Sinful, Remove Your Filth,* and *No Sex Here.* That last sign had him chuckling —that was probably the sanctimonious woman's problem—before his eyes landed on a sign reading *Protect Our Children.* His humor died, and he continued to scan the messages.

The carefully stenciled sign with the words *Go Home, Slut* had Linc tightening his grip on the steering wheel. It couldn't be a coincidence, could it? "The same words the vandals painted on Jamie's front door are on that sign to our right. Do you recognize the woman holding it?"

"No." Bets turned to face him, looking away from the women shouting at the car. "And I don't want to. I feel ill. Mary and Orla looked at me like they'd like to beat me with a stick and drive me out of town. This is really ugly, Linc. Worse than anything we've faced before with the center."

"Yes, so I'll have security take pictures of the crowd just in case." His list had just gotten a little longer. "Identify who's here. Maybe we'll get lucky and the woman holding that sign will turn out to be the mother of a teenager who might be one of our hoodlums. Jesus, this is going to be fun. But don't fret none. We're in good hands."

Ghislaine more than proved his point when she met them in the entryway of the arts center, Donal standing at her side with an impressive glower. "Welcome to the party! I had a little inkling we might have protesters. It's like someone's been tickling me behind my ear. After all these years, I can smell them from a mile away. I shared my suspicions with Donal, and we came a little earlier than planned to check."

Linc inclined his chin toward his friend.

"It's nice having a man listen to you, isn't it, Bets?" Ghislaine continued. "Anyway, I've sent out mass texts warning everybody about the protesters. We've already cordoned them off. Of course, your dear little policeman out there said the protesters had everything in order, and he was going to close one side of the road for them. Nice fellow. I could hear Donal grinding his teeth as we chatted under your daughter's beautiful window. When I asked him why he hadn't notified us, given the public safety concern and this being private property, he said he'd followed procedure."

"I'll bet," Bets said, radiating frustration.

"I know it's never fun to see that kind of hate in person, but don't worry." Ghislaine laid a hand on Bets' forearm for a moment in comfort. "This is a good thing. Now the press will have a personal view of what's been happening. Photos too."

"I told Ghislaine there are only two women I recognize out there," Donal said in a grim tone.

"Yeah, we saw Mary and Orla." Linc tucked his hands

into his pockets. "All right, Ghislaine. What do you want us to do until this circus officially begins?"

She gave a dazzling smile. "Do what you do best. Greet people. Make them feel welcome. After people run the gauntlet of a protest, they tend to have plenty on their minds."

"I should have baked some cookies," Bets mumbled.

"We have a full buffet prepared," Ghislaine said, misunderstanding her. "Sophie should be arriving shortly, as will the first members of our esteemed press. Get ready, folks. It's showtime."

She wandered off, her heels a brisk rapping on the floors. Donal's eyes followed her like they had from the moment she'd arrived.

"Isn't she incredible?" he murmured. "I tell you...the moment I saw her, I was thunderstruck. And I never want it to end."

Linc sent Bets a smile. "I haven't known you as long as Bets, but even with all this hoopla going on, you should check the gooey expression on your face. People might think you're addled."

Donal turned his head to look him dead in the eye. "Gooey?"

"Sweet." Linc mimed the face. "Lovey-dovey. You know..."

His friend arched a brow in his direction. "I'll do my best not to look either addled or gooey, but trust me, it's the same look you've been wearing every time you're with Bets."

"Shh— Sophie's here." Bets strode forward and met the pale woman at the door, grateful to see she was hand in hand with Jamie. "I'm sorry you had to see that."

"At least they didn't have rotten eggs," she joked badly.

"It's not my first time, but I've never had the signs directed at me." She patted Jamie's shoulder. "He's more upset. Maybe. I'm pretty upset too."

"No need to measure it," Jamie said, shrugging out of his coat like he was burning with anger. "Did you see the placard that said *Keep Your Hands Off Our Kids*?"

Donal put a reassuring hand on the man. "Other than Mary and Orla, was there anyone else you recognized?"

His mouth twisted. "Besides Denis? Not a soul."

"These women aren't from our community," Donal said with a firm shake of his head. "Take comfort in that, man."

"It's Sophie we're here for." Jamie took her hand again. "What can we do for you, *mo chroí*?"

She straightened her shoulders. "Show me to Ghislaine. She'll keep me busy until showtime."

"Follow me," Donal said, jerking his head in the direction she'd gone. "I've never seen a more prepared person."

"Do you want me to go with you or let you be?" Jamie asked Sophie.

"I'm happy for the company," she said, kissing his cheek. "Did anyone bring any playing cards?"

No one had, and as they walked off, Linc patted his suit pocket. "Why didn't I think of cards? Oh, look, here's our first reporter." A woman in a slick black suit screaming city walked in through the door.

"How can you tell?" Bets asked.

"The newsroom gleam in their eyes," he said with an audible snort. "Come on, sugar, let's work our magic."

Linc had learned a long time ago that the success of any event was predicated on people being happy to be there. Sure, the presentation had to be worth it. But good conversation, good food, and even better coffee helped. They were lucky—Ghislaine knew that, and she'd also put together a very nice thank-you bag for every attendee using high-quality Irish goods. *Nice touch, that*, he thought.

By the time everyone had taken their seats, Linc was ready to do his official part. Striding to the podium, he gave the crowd his best aw-shucks smile and then froze. Malcolm Coveney was sitting in the last chair in the last row, his leg out in an insolent pose. Bastard must have slipped in. Linc made himself smile again as Malcolm waved his big gold-ringed hand, knowing he'd been sighted.

"Welcome to the Sorcha Fitzgerald Arts Center," he began with authority, shutting the man out. "I'm Linc Buchanan, new to these parts, as I'm sure most of you know. I've been in and around the arts for a long time, starting from the first day my beautiful young daughter took her crayons out and started drawing on one of my window samples from my business. She's now a rising stained glass artist here at this very arts center. You walked under her gorgeous stained glass window in the entryway, which, as a father, makes me tear up every time."

It wasn't hard to beam with pride as he talked about his baby girl, and he could see it was resonating with people. "It was Ellie who had me visiting this wonderful place and community, but it was Betsy O'Hanlon, the original founder of the arts center, who has me staying. Her vision is a special one, as is her story. Ladies and gentlemen, Betsy O'Hanlon."

He met her at the halfway mark and sent her a smile as he whispered, "Keep looking at the front of the crowd. Malcolm slipped in somehow, but you ignore him, okay?"

Her cheeks flushed. "But how did—"

"Not now, Bets," he said, nudging her toward the podium.

She nodded crisply and increased her stride as he returned to his seat so he could listen to her presentation.

He'd heard her story many times, and even after the shock of seeing Malcolm, she delivered it like a pro. He never tired of it. By now, he could read between the lines. She'd wanted more for herself and this community. She'd wanted to bring in new people with new ideas and to help people like Eoghan and others discover new aspects of themselves, which she'd accomplished and then some. She'd helped him do the same, and for that, he was a lucky man. Yes, a truly lucky man.

Her voice rang strong throughout her introduction, and by the time she finished, he could see a shift in the crowd's body language. They were eager for their story. Ghislaine's chef's kiss, to Linc's mind, was the short video message she played after Bets was finished. *Take that, you bastard*, he thought as he took her hand and gave it a reassuring squeeze.

Moments later, Eoghan's face appeared on the giant screen, his wrinkles as much a map of happiness as his smile. The older man talked about taking to art, and how it had transformed his life. Growing up in the wilds of Ireland, he said, so far from the big city of Dublin, no one had really talked about art much. In school, they'd learned practical things, no more and no less.

"But to dream..." Eoghan said with a grand sigh. "Well, that's in our Irish souls. Our dreams are as beautiful as our rainbows and disappear just as fast. Yet they don't have to. Art helps us capture such things, beautiful things, things we have inside us to express. We Irish have a saying: *May the road rise up to meet you.*

May the wind be always at your back.

May the sun shine warm upon your face,

The rains fall soft upon your fields,
And, until we meet again,
May God hold you in the palm of His hand.

I now think whoever penned that verse, as it's not known, must have been a painter, and a painter of landscapes at that."

Linc watched as smiles covered the faces of many in the crowd, Malcolm not among them, which only made Linc smile more broadly.

"Our center is very special to our village for the reasons I've given and so many more," Eoghan continued, "but there are a few who have no love for dreams or for beauty, and who have no respect for another's desire to express. I'll confess, that makes me very sad. I'm nearing my end, and I want to see a better world than the one I entered. Sophie Giombetti makes the world a better place, and I'm proud to introduce her to tell you her story."

With that, Sophie rose from her chair. Linc was glad she didn't know Malcolm on sight, but he was relieved Donal had taken up a sentinel position directly behind the man's chair, poised to stop him should he pull something.

He turned his gaze back to the podium. Sophie looked strong and beautiful and confident, like he'd raised his Ellie to be. He was proud of her, and one look at Jamie told him that he felt the same way.

"As Eoghan said, I'm Sophie Giombetti, and it's truly an honor to be at the Sorcha Fitzgerald Arts Center, especially to be introduced by someone as special as Eoghan O'Dwyer. Beginning art at ninety-three! And Eoghan gave me permission to share some exciting news he only received yesterday. He's having his first gallery show in Paris in a few months! Isn't that incredible?"

As everyone started to applaud, Linc turned to Bets, grinning. "Did you know?"

She was beaming too. "No, but how wonderful!"

"I'll have to admit," Sophie said as the room quieted, "I needed a spot of good news this week after a number of unidentified men vandalized the home where I'm staying with the words *Go Home Slut* after my newest glass installation design went public."

Linc let his gaze slide to Malcolm then. He locked his jaw when he noticed the man was smirking.

Then the hologram of Sophie's sculpture appeared, and many in the crowd exclaimed in awe. Linc turned his attention back to her presentation.

"I wanted to create something in keeping with Celtic tradition, which I've always had a fondness for, and I started with the Tree of Life, the symbol of rebirth and enduring strength. But I wanted a greater challenge, something to take my skills and vision as an artist to the next level."

The hologram shifted, showing a closeup of the woman in the installation.

"This pregnant goddess represents everything I think is good in the world. She is the messenger of birth herself, of love herself, and as a woman who has been fortunate to have a child. I've never felt more beautiful or powerful than when I was pregnant, and sharing that experience in this installation is precious to me. I've also never had as much love for anything as I do for my child. Every child should be so loved. That is why having my art so misunderstood and attacked has been shocking."

Linc watched as reporters leaned forward, some of them poised with their pens. Malcolm only kicked back more in his chair with his enormous girth, smirking.

"Controversy in art isn't a new concept, and while I

have watched other artists experience it—my parents included—it's never happened to me. Even though I see this pregnant woman as beautiful, to others she is indecent because she is nude. Now it's not my mandate as a human being or an artist to tell someone else what to think. My art is an expression. Not a moral or political statement of any kind."

The hologram shifted again, showing what the full installation might look like in the upcoming museum. Linc knew they had a long way to go, but seeing it visually made his heart swell. Yes, they were going to build it, and Sophie, Ellie, Kathleen, Angie, and Megan were all going to display pieces there along with their future artists. What a wonderful legacy! Fuck Malcolm Coveney.

"Artistic freedom is as important to me as freedom of expression is to the protesters outside these very doors," Sophie said, gesturing to the windows. "But violence and intimidation is another matter. It's a crime, and when it happens to artists—and it does, in many places around the world—we need the local police and other stakeholders to hold those people accountable. They are not simply expressing. They are violating the law."

Linc knew what was coming next. He'd had their legal team clear it. He watched as Malcolm sat up, his smirk disappearing.

"The arts center has lodged a formal complaint against our local police in Caisleán. They're called the Garda here. I don't have to tell you how serious the situation has become to warrant such an action. But it's important for people in every community to draw a stark line between dissenting opinions and crime. I stand for artistic expression as much as for people's freedom of expression. And I look forward to unveiling my sculpture at the opening of the museum the center has planned, which is being designed by the incredible architect, Tom Sarkesian. Thank you."

People applauded, and Linc shot Bets an encouraging smile as she unclenched her fists from her knees. He watched as Malcolm rose from his chair and brushed past Donal, ostensibly heading for the front. *Good riddance*, he thought, as reporters started to raise their hands.

"Do you still feel safe here, Sophie?" the first one asked.

Linc was glad that Malcolm hadn't stuck around to hear how his intimidation was working. Bullies fed on that kind of power trip.

Sophie blew out a breath before answering. "I have to admit I'll be a little on edge until the perpetrators are captured."

"Your daughter is six years old, correct?" another reporter asked. "What have you done for her safety?"

She went tight immediately. "It was a really hard decision, but I sent her back to our home in Provence with our longtime friend for a little holiday. I'm hoping she will be able to return soon. As a mother, I can't tell you how difficult that decision was."

"Your parents' art was protested and hotly debated for much of your childhood," someone called out. "Has this brought back bad memories?"

Nodding, she said, "Absolutely. I was telling someone recently how I can still remember the smell of the rotten eggs they threw at us and how it ruined my favorite dress. I was ten then. No child should have to go through that."

"What do you say to people who consider your design indecent and immoral?" another reporter asked.

"Like I said, they're entitled to their opinion, but they don't have the right to stop me from expressing my art.

When I'm not comfortable with something, I don't go near it."

"Can you give us an example, Ms. Giombetti?" someone called out.

"Sure thing. *Silence of the Lambs*. While I usually watch Oscar winners, I couldn't do it. I was too freaked out by the subject matter. But I'd never presume to tell Sir Anthony Hopkins or Jodie Foster they didn't have the right to make the movie."

A number of people laughed, and Ghislaine took her cue to stride on stage and join her. "Sophie is happy to continue the conversation as we mingle. Thank you, everyone, for coming."

The older woman put an arm around Sophie and led her back to where Linc and the others were sitting to the right of the podium. "Didn't she do incredible? You all did! Congratulate her, but don't take too long. There are reporters waiting for one-on-ones."

Jamie rose with the rest of them and pulled Sophie close. "You were magnificent, *mo chroí*. I was inspired and not only because I love you so."

She touched his face tenderly. Then she took his hand and turned to them as Donal joined their group, forcing a smile. They shared a look before Linc shifted his attention back to Sophie and said, "You nailed it like a pro. Not that anyone here is surprised."

"Personally, I think Eoghan stole the show," she said sweetly.

"He'll be delighted to hear you say that," Donal said with an easier smile. "But not as delighted as he is by the news about his gallery show. A gallery in Paris saw some of his art in the *Le Monde* article and contacted him. I'm still stunned."

Bets socked him. "Why didn't you tell us earlier?"

"Dad made me swear, and then Ghislaine followed up with one of her scary-sweet threats." He laughed. "Besides, this way I could do what Dad asked. He wanted me to video your faces when you heard the news. It was priceless. I did it from the back so I could get all of you in one shot."

Linc made himself laugh, knowing he was covering. None of them wanted to ruin this moment for Sophie. "I'll bet. When I next see your dad, I'm buying him a round."

"The whole village will," Bets exclaimed. "Donal, I'm so glad you decided to leave your cushy seat with us and video it from the back."

Yeah, they were all glad about that.

"I can't wait to see it," Sophie cried out, oblivious to the undercurrent of their conversation.

"Come see this!" Ghislaine cried out, running toward them in her heels. "It's incredible. In all my years as a publicist, this is one of the best things I've ever witnessed."

Maybe Malcolm had fallen into the muck and was rolling around like the animal he was. They all started hurrying toward the large front windows in the foyer as others started to stride over too.

"I'd know that sound anywhere," Donal said, shaking his head.

"Me too!" Bets cried out. "Did you do it?"

"Not me," he said, holding up his hands.

Linc didn't understand until he reached the window.

A herd of sheep was running up the road beside the protesters, their bodies covered in words. He squinted to make them out. *Love. Tolerance. Freedom. Compassion. Kindness. Safety.*

Malcolm Coveney was nowhere in sight, Linc was happy to see.

"Keegan O'Malley's new herd of sheep," Jamie said, an odd light in his eyes. "I take back everything I ever said about it."

"What?" Sophie asked, a crooked smile on her face. "But it's wonderful!"

"Carrick looks to be agreeing," he said, pointing toward his brother, who stood at the window with Angie and his baby daughter, grinning at the display. "Oh, but it's a grand gesture, it is. Keegan met his now-wife in ceramics class here, you know. Right at the center."

Sophie took his arm. "I remember Eoghan telling me. We'll have to mention it to Ghislaine. Come on, Jamie."

Linc watched as the sheep surrounded the protesters, their hateful signs falling from the blue sky.

Score one for the sheep.

CHAPTER TWENTY-TWO

Sophie had posed for a lot of photos in her time, but the one of her standing next to a sheep with *Freedom* painted across its body might become her favorite.

Reporters clustered together to take a few more photos while she smiled as the sheep sniffed her pocket for food. Then they asked her to take one with the sheep's owner, Keegan O'Malley, whom Denis from the Garda had called to secure his sheep, showing his true colors by threatening to fine him for the disturbance.

Carrick, Donal, and a slew of locals had laughed until they were wiping tears over that threat. Jamie, watching nearby, did not join in the hilarity.

"Maybe the sheep didn't know they needed an escape permit," Donal called out as Denis finally stomped off.

"Maybe they wanted to protest all this nonsense," Fergus shouted.

Sophie had to firm up her smile when Denis snarled back, "You're the ones causing the nonsense."

"And you say you're an impartial arbiter of the law," Donal bandied back as reporters recorded the incident. "I won't say whose pocket you're in, but he left not too long ago."

She jolted. Had Malcolm Coveney been at the press conference?

"Go home, slut," one of the female protesters shouted, "and take your filthy mind with you."

Her stomach trembled at the hate filling the air behind her. She wouldn't turn around. She didn't want to give them the satisfaction.

"Enough of that, Mary Kincaid," Donal called out. "You're allowed to protest but not to harass anyone."

Except she'd shown up and done it at Sophie's door.

"Like you'd know what was right or decent anymore, Donal O'Dwyer," the vicious woman shot back.

"Shacking up with Betsy O'Hanlon ruined you, Donal," another woman called out. "And now this new artist is ruining—"

"Stop it, Orla!" Donal interrupted harshly. "For the love of God, keep your hate-filled opinions to yourself."

"If we're all done," Sophie said to the eagerly listening reporters, keeping her back to the protesters, "I'm headed back to the arts center for some tea if you have any more questions. Again, thanks so much for coming."

Jamie took her hand as she started walking, her entire body gripped with malaise. "You did grand, *mo chroí*."

"I really need to work on not taking things personally," she told him, squeezing his hand. "I feel covered in slime."

"If you weren't bothered by people's cruelty, you wouldn't be who you are," Jamie told her. "They had no cause to call things out. Their signs were bad enough."

Yeah, she thought. They were. "Was Malcolm Coveney at our press conference?"

His face fell before he nodded. "Yes, Linc told me he

saw him inside. He must have borrowed a local reporter's press badge, as people had to show them at the door. He meant to intimidate, I imagine, but he left after you announced we'd filed the police complaint. You did good. Made him tuck his tail, I'd be hoping."

She fought a chill. "Yeah, I'll be hoping too."

Ghislaine materialized at her side after wrapping up her conversation with another reporter. "Ignore those spiteful women and focus on the positives. The sheep were an unscripted delight. And that idiot policeman doesn't seem to understand he's now been videoed misusing his power by trying to fine that sheep farmer."

"Or he doesn't think he can do any wrong given who's protecting him," Jamie muttered with a frown.

Her diaphragm tightened. God, she hadn't thought of that. Then again, Malcolm had shown up under false pretenses.

"That's not my department, Jamie," Ghislaine responded, although her mouth tightened. "We've exceeded all my goals, and we've got a three-dimensional human interest story with terrific pictures. The photos and videos of the sheep milling with the protesters are already going viral. This is going to be big!"

Sophie wanted to feel a sense of elation. Would she ever? "My best news was hearing from Eoghan this morning about his gallery showing."

"And all because the gallery owner saw the article in *Le Monde*." Ghislaine put her arm around Sophie. "Publicity at its best. I have a few more people I want to check on before they take off. Expect good things to come of this, Sophie."

"Miracles love company," she repeated out loud, trying to keep upbeat.

"Exactly." Jamie opened the front door of the arts center for her and ushered her back inside, where it was mostly quiet. "Let's grab you a cup of tea."

"You looked pretty good out there, surrounded by sheep," Bets cried out as she hurried over to them.

Linc took his time sauntering over. "They might have stolen the show in the best way possible. Now that's the kind of village support we're talking about. Even the sheep are behind you."

She smiled ruefully. "It was nice of Keegan to do it. Now, I need some tea and some time to gather myself. That was exhausting."

"Being 'on' has that effect on some people," Linc commented. "But the reporters seem to have what they need and are starting to take off. Why don't you two go on and head out? We'll take care of the rest here with Ghislaine."

"Are you sure?" She imagined they were as tired as she was.

"You bet," he said, kissing her cheek. "Turn your phone off for a while. Both of you. We'll talk later."

Bets gave her a quick hug. "Yes, go and unplug! And thank you, Sophie."

She waited until they were on their way to the car after Jamie had made his goodbyes, before commenting, "Imagine...them thanking me."

"There's plenty enough to thank you for," Jamie said, opening the car door for her. "Now, what can we do for the rest of the day that would help put an easy smile on your face? I'm without plans, as you know."

"How about a late lunch somewhere where no one will know us?"

He nodded. "Done. Buckle yourself in, *mo chroí*, and put yourself in my hands."

As they left the parking lot and turned onto the one-lane road, she struggled with whether to avert her face from the remaining protesters or stare them down, especially Mary and Orla. She chose the former. What good would come from a staring match anyway?

Jamie waved at a few of their friends milling about with Keegan, who were taking their time helping him with the sheep. Denis stepped into the road as they were leaving, blocking the way. Jamie paused the car. There was a momentary standoff before he finally let them past. The look on his face could have been painted with snake venom for all the malice it bore.

"He's scary, isn't he?" Sophie tried to take a breath, but her seat belt felt too tight. "I'll bet Malcolm Coveney is even scarier, right?"

"We've got you," Jamie said without answering, turning on the stereo and selecting U2's "Where the Streets Have No Name."

As Bono's iconic voice filled the car, she leaned back and closed her eyes. "I hope he really does join the board. I've always loved this song, but never as much as in this moment. I get wanting to run and tear things down, but I also want to go to that street so badly right now I can taste it."

"And with me, you'll go," Jamie said, putting his hand on her knee and caressing it.

She turned her head, his beautiful face in profile. "We'll go together."

They rode up the coast for about an hour, the landscape shifting from green hills and valleys to majestic, soaring mountains dotted with ancient rocks and brush in earthy tones. She smiled as she watched horned sheep climbing the tough terrain or bumbling down with gravity.

"I might have fallen in love with sheep today," she told Jamie as he rounded a vast black lake.

"Make sure to share that at the Brazen Donkey next time we go," he said, pulling into a sparsely filled parking lot in front of a green tavern with red trim. "You'll make everyone's day, my brother's included. Welcome to one of my favorite places in all of Ireland. The Lost Valley of Uggool. Come inside, *mo chroí*, and rest a spell."

She got out and heard the water lapping against the rock wall lining the parking lot. "It's so quiet and peaceful here, Jamie. I might never want to leave."

"We'll stay as long as you'd like, and then when you're ready, I'll take you home and love you as the day turns to night."

Lacing her fingers around the back of his neck, she met those cobalt blue eyes of his. "I'd love that."

She nourished herself on a hearty beef and Guinness stew served on mashed potatoes with thickly sliced soda bread slathered with Irish butter. Their table awarded them with an incredible view, and she found herself slowly unwinding. Jamie knew she needed quiet, and perhaps he did as well.

"I wish I could find a way to make you laugh right now," he said as he pushed around his mashed potatoes with a fork. "For once I wish I had Eoghan's gift of the gab."

Reaching across the table, she placed her hand on his arm. "You don't have to make me laugh or even smile, Jamie. Right now, all I want is solace and to be here with you. I've talked myself out these last few days."

"I know what you mean. So let's just sit here together."

"And maybe have some bread pudding for dessert," she

said, able to smile at last. "That's good comfort food, and I know it's a favorite of yours."

His mouth lifted. "Since childhood. My mum makes a good recipe. When they come back from Portugal, I'd like you to meet them. Both you and Greta, if that's all right."

She laced their fingers together, like their lives were beginning to do. "That would be great. I suppose you should meet my mother soon. Before, I might have dreaded it. But not now. We seem to be having a renaissance in our relationship. I think she's going to be quite nice to you."

That had him chuckling softly. "I find myself relieved to hear that. Family is important to me, and while I'd respect her regardless of whether we get along, I'd prefer to get along."

"Just don't get all nervous if she asks if you'd like to pose nude for her, okay?" She winced. "It's as much a compliment as a way of testing your mettle."

"Then I'll think on how to answer well and still keep my clothes on." He made a show of touching his shirt buttons.

She laughed, a glorious sound after everything. "She's asked me before, and I've always told her that being immortalized is overrated. She, of course, can't imagine where I learned that from."

Leaning closer, he said softly, "Next time, tell her it was the fairies who whispered it to you."

Inside her chest, her heart was starting to feel warm again. "That's a good one. I can't wait to see the look on her face. Jamie, let's eat our dessert fast. I want to go home with you."

His eyes brightened as he signaled the server. "We're of the same mind."

The bread pudding was laced with a whiskey caramel

sauce, and her enjoyment of it was another sign she was coming back to herself. She'd always withdrawn to someplace inside herself when dealing with conflict and criticism, but the ice had melted faster and easier in Jamie's company.

As they were leaving, she swung his hand, watching as seagulls crested on the wind over the dark lake. "You know, you really do match me. In every way I seem to need. I'm grateful, Jamie."

He stopped and framed her face between his hands. "Me too, *mo chroí*. More than you could ever know. Let's hope the fairies hasten our trip home. I can't wait to love you."

Raising on her toes, she laid her mouth gently on his, feeling her pulse quicken. "I like all the uses these fairies have. You'll have to tell me more stories about them as we travel home."

"I will," he said, caressing her cheek. "And we're going to take a different way home. There's more of the country I'd like you to see."

So they got in the car, and he regaled her with tales about the raised Irish hills called fairy forts and superstitions about leaving a pub with one's jacket turned inside out to thwart a *pooka*, a fairy known for its mischief making. The views on the way back were different but equally breathtaking. The mountains tore into the cold, gray sky, sometimes with clouds dancing around the peaks. She watched for trails of water between the rugged stones and smiled as Jamie shared with her his delight about finding an old Roman coin in a fairy glen when he was a boy, which he showed to his class each year while teaching world history.

Their progress could be marked by the changing landscape. As they got closer to home, the roads grew less windy, and the mountains faded into lush valleys and then the rolling green hills she was becoming accustomed to. Her earlier tension edged its way back inside her, like a foot inserting itself in a door one wished closed.

She shut her eyes and focused on Jamie's voice, breathing deeply. When he slowed and Rex's bark sounded, she knew they were home. The gate to the cottage slid open, and she had to admit she was relieved to see it close behind them. In France, she'd never given her gate a second thought. Homes had them for privacy more than security. But here in Ireland, she was starting to see them in a new light, and as she left the car, she saw a flash in her mind: a door made out of glass separating two people, one angry and the other afraid.

She'd never truly expressed her own personal experience in her art until now—nothing like her parents had, that was for sure. It was as if a wheel had turned inside her, ushering her into the greater level of her art she'd been craving.

Oh, what an installation it would be!

After her current one, of course, but that didn't mean she couldn't start initial planning. It was always good to have another installation design in the wings. The vision felt like another sign of miracles loving company, even amidst their current hardships.

"Jamie, I just had the most glorious idea for a sculpture," she said as they left the car.

"But that's wonderful," he said after she described it to him, "and powerful too. Sounds like we have something to celebrate."

When they arrived at the front door, a note from Ghislaine was taped to the freshly painted wood. *Your dog adores me. Turn on your phone! Support is rolling in.*

The news was welcome, of course, but her heart didn't blip with a happy response. She still wished none of this were happening. "She's relentless," Sophie said, pulling the note down. "But great at what she does."

He unlocked the door and waited for her to precede him before stepping inside and securing the deadbolt. "Good thing Rex knew her. Do you think she scaled the wall alone?"

"Donal probably gave her a leg up," she said, shaking her head.

"Indeed. Go on and see the news. I'll make some tea."

She stopped him with her hand. "It can wait. Come and make love with me."

He cradled her face tenderly, searching her eyes, his love shining brightly. "For all my days, Sophie. For all my days."

Leading her to their bedroom, he undressed her slowly after adjusting the heat. "You're always concerned with me being warm enough. It's sweet, Jamie."

"Can't have you covered in gooseflesh." He started unbuttoning his shirt after taking off his jacket. "Not that you wouldn't be beautiful with those bumps on your skin as well. Sophie, you're the most beautiful woman I've ever seen."

She took over, undoing the buttons slowly. "And you're the most wonderful, handsome man I've ever met."

He undid his belt and pants so she could pull his shirttails out. "Aren't you lucky then that I'm your soulmate?"

Laying a kiss over his heart, she caressed his chest, making him inhale sharply. "The luckiest. Maybe I really am Irish deep down."

He picked her up and walked the few steps to the bed.

"I'll have to investigate. I hear some people's freckles resemble shamrocks, and I know just where I want to look."

She was laughing as he settled her onto her stomach, stripping out of his remaining clothes before pressing an agonizing kiss to the bottom of her spine. He gripped her hips in his hands, continuing to press kisses along her back.

"Funny, Jamie."

"I have you back to laughing, *mo chroí*," he said softly, sliding his hand over the round skin of her bottom. "I plan to continue it. Ah, look, I wonder if I need a magnifying glass for this particular freckle."

"Jamie Fitzgerald," she called with another laugh as he laid a kiss on her flesh. "Don't you dare zoom in on my butt."

His deep rumble had her grinning. "But it's such a fine arse, and imagine it peppered with shamrock-shaped freckles. Everyone in the Brazen Donkey will be delighted in the telling."

She flipped onto her back, pretending to study him suspiciously. "You don't want to be going there, boyo," she said in her best imitation of an Irish accent.

His mouth lifted before he smothered the smile. "What's this boyo thing?"

"Don't you Irish say that? I've heard it in all the movies."

"I've never heard it." He lay down beside her and pulled her flush against him. "Which one?"

Her mind took a moment longer to give her an answer since she was preoccupied with the way his body was rising to her own. "Ah... *The Untouchables*, I think. With the great and dreamy Sean Connery."

"But that was set in the 1930s or something, right? Eons

ago. It is a good movie, though. Up until Sean Connery dies."

She traced the ridge of muscles in his forearm. "I know. I cried at that part."

He waggled his brows as he rose over her. "How about you let me help you cry in an altogether different way?"

She was grinning as he lowered his mouth to hers. His kisses were magic, giving heated attention to her bottom lip before sucking on the top one with the kind of intensity that had her wanting to move things along. But when she tried to take him in hand, he captured her wrists and gently brought them over her head.

"Not yet," he whispered, his cobalt eyes on hers. "I have other plans for you."

And plans he had aplenty, kissing his way down her neck slowly before supping at her breasts. She bowed back under the pressure of his mouth and groaned, luxuriating in the sensation. As he continued, kissing her belly and then the valley between her thighs, she squeezed her eyes closed and felt her desire skyrocket.

"Don't stop," she whispered. "Please don't stop."

His mouth kept up a steady campaign of kisses, licks, and little nips. He continued to bring her higher and still higher until she fisted her hands in his hair finally to hold him in place and surrender to the greatest desire she'd ever known. That she could find it on this day was a boon but not a source of wonder. It had been a day of extremes, outside and inside, and her body was ready for its due.

When he put on a condom and slipped inside her, she moaned brokenly, needing more, wanting more. "Come into me harder, Jamie. I need you."

He adjusted her hips and thrust deep, making her cry out.

"All right, *mo chroí*?" he ground out.

She met his eyes, needing to see him, wanting him to understand. "God, yes. More, Jamie. God! Give me more."

Her plea seemed to unlock some part of him because he took her swiftly, deeply. She had no time to catch her breath. She needed to ride this wave and crash where she would. Locking her ankles around his waist, she brought him still deeper inside her and felt her body scream for mercy. She broke in a sea of pulses wrenched from her very soul. He followed her with a loud cry, as though torn from him.

She lay there panting, his body slick on her as he lowered himself to his elbows, breathing hard near her ear.

"Jesus, Sophie," he rasped out. "Jesus, Mary, and Joseph."

Laughter bubbled up as her body continued to pulse. "Thank God I'm not a Renaissance painter, or I'd be imagining painting the nativity scene right about now."

He laughed until he wheezed. "It's probably the biggest form of sacrilege, my saying that, but you're twisting my funny bone something fierce."

She was laughing too, the hilarity contagious. "I think people laugh like this when they reach their limit."

"Then we should reach our limit more often, *mo chroí*, because that was otherworldly."

Caressing his sweat-slicked back, she had to smile. "I have to agree. It's been really good between us—not that I'm a huge expert in this department—but that was a whole new level. Kind of like my art."

He lifted his head, his mop of brown curls a sexy tangled mess around his strong face. "I'm sure we can achieve more new levels if we put our mind to it. In the bedroom, or the kitchen or the parlor, for that matter. With the gate and wall, I'd feel more comfortable about loving you in the parlor—my own version of being positive about changes. It's a nice benefit that no one can pop by for a chat and spot us through the window."

"God help us! That would be mortifying. Oh, Jamie, I love you. For making me laugh. For making me come. And for being by my side when I really need support."

Kissing the top of her nose, he smiled broadly. "As you said, we're a grand pair, and I love you for all those things you said and more. Now, you really should turn your phone on. I wouldn't put it past Ghislaine to pop over again, would you?"

"You're right," Sophie said with a laugh, rising to find her phone. "I'll grab my phone and some water and be right back. I'm too hot for tea."

"You certainly are," he joked, "naked as you are and with the sheen of desire flushing your skin."

"Talk like that is going to limit my screen time," she called as she left the bedroom.

Balancing her phone under her arm, she brought back the water glasses only to find him lying blissfully naked with his eyes closed.

"If I did paint nudes professionally," she said, lying down beside him, "I would paint you like this."

He opened one eye. "As I know my brother enjoys it when Angie paints him nude, I just might let you. Of course with the understanding it would be between us."

"Doesn't Angie show the nudes she's done of Carrick?" she asked, intrigued.

Laughing, he blushed a little. "He's struggled mightily with it. They've settled on a couple of agreements. First, that she not make his likeness unmistakable, and second, that the nudes are only shown at galleries outside of Ireland where no one would know him. I told him anyone from Caisleán could go online and see the paintings, but he says it's not the same. He's a mad lunatic sometimes, my brother."

Chuckling at the logic, she turned her phone on. "I understand the conditions. Mostly. But Jamie, if I were to do a nude of you in my medium, I don't believe I'd have enough glass."

It took him a moment to snort at her joke. "It's a grand instrument, this, and only for you, *mo chroí*."

"I'm glad we agree on that. Now, let me start with the text from Ghislaine." There was one from her mother, too, which simply said *Bravo!*

She opened the Press Insights document Ghislaine had sent, something familiar to her from other campaigns. The first thing that struck her was the hashtag at the top of the page—*I Support Sophie*—and the impressions. One million plus so far!

"Holy—"

She pulled up Twitter first and started scanning the tweets. Some were from artists she knew—her mother included—as well as others in the community. But it was the surge of support from women that had her pressing her hand to her mouth.

"Jamie! Look at this."

They huddled together and started reading, but when she got to the first tweet with the hashtag #PregnancyIsBeautiful, tears started streaming from her eyes. Tweet after tweet from women who had taken photos of either their naked bellies or bodies. And she'd been tagged in past tweets from celebrities who'd posted nude pregnancy photos after Annie Leibowitz started the trend by photographing Demi Moore for the *Vanity Fair* cover in

1991—Beyoncé, Rihanna, Serena Williams, Kim Kardashian, Christina Aguilera, and many others.

"OMG!" she whispered in shock.

"Holy mother—" Jamie breathed out before whistling. "Your situation seems to have sparked a powerful outcry."

Her head suddenly felt like lead. She'd never had this kind of publicity before. "No wonder Ghislaine left a note. She must be in publicity heaven."

"This is good, *mo chroí*," he said, tucking his arm around her. "Listen to this tweet from someone named Helen Marcozi. *Sophie Giombetti gifts the world with her glass sculptures, and her new design of a nude pregnant goddess is beautiful. Ireland is lucky to have her. I'll be visiting it when she finishes.* Well, that's a smart woman. We *are* lucky to have you, Sophie."

She touched the screen as her head went light. "You don't know who Helen Marcozi is, do you, Jamie?"

"Is she another artist then?"

Laughing, she brushed back the locks from his forehead. "She won the Best Actress Award last year."

His brow knit. "Like at those Oscars things?"

"Yes!"

"We don't get many movies out this way, *mo chroí*. The closest movie theater is—"

"Don't tell me," she joked with a watery laugh. "Oh, Jamie. This is big. I kinda can't believe it. I never imagined."

"This tweet says it all for me. *If someone thinks it's indecent or immoral to portray the beauty of a pregnant woman in glass, paint, or any other kind of medium, then they need their heads examined.* If I had the Twitter myself, I would do that retweet thing."

Jamie with a Twitter account. "Now that's a supportive partner."

"I'm the ideal soulmate," he shot back with a grin. "Now, I really think we should celebrate. There's a bottle of champagne in the fridge. Isn't that what you said the French would do?"

She hid a smile, not bothering to say the French had it daily, like they would a cheese plate. "Yes, I believe I am feeling in a celebratory mood. Let me check one more thing."

Clicking back to Ghislaine's report, she looked for local media and organizations. Her mouth parted. There were already three hundred messages of support for her from groups like the Irish Artists Forum and Irish Women and the Arts as well as some key media and TV and film celebrities. Ghislaine had included, verbatim, a top tweet by a national Irish politician.

Women in Ireland experience violence aplenty. It is wrong and something we need to fix. The recent case of American artist Sophie Giombetti is appalling, and the local Garda should be investigated for their complicity in not upholding the laws of the Republic. Ireland supports the arts. It is our history.

"Do you recognize his name, Jamie?"

"He's the head of one of Ireland's biggest political parties," Jamie said softly. "I wouldn't put my hat on it, but it's a good step in the right direction."

Her brain was fried. She set the phone down. "I want to start feeling really optimistic, but part of me is scared."

Jamie plucked her phone up. "Understandable. But this is going better than we could have imagined. Oh, look! Keegan O'Malley's sheep have their own hashtags."

She laughed as she read, "#SheepAreSmarterThanHaters and #SheepforSophie."

He pulled up a tweet. "Hey! This sheep farmer from

Scotland painted his sheep with #ISupportSophie. Wait! There are more sheep farmers joining in and spraying sheep with positive words and sayings. Carrick will love that, seeing how he started it. Isn't that wonderful, *mo chroí?*"

Oh, she was a mess. She wiped away more tears, her heart glowing, because if things continued on this way, Greta would be able to come home soon. "After this, Jamie, I might need to buy a few sheep. January might not be enough for me. It's turning into a love affair."

His face was a mass of comic angles. "Saints preserve us! I love you more than the stars above, but don't ask me to do sheep. They'll be eating our yard up and escaping like the crazy animals they are."

She kissed his bicep, trying not to laugh out loud at his exaggerated horror. "We can visit Carrick's sheep then."

"Oh, thank heavens!" He slumped back against the pillows with his hand over his forehead. "My life flashed before my eyes."

The laughter felt good. Cleansing even.

"How about I help you come back to earth?" she asked as she slid onto him.

He lifted his hand, as if shielding himself from the sun. "I'd be most grateful. My bones are still trembling from fear."

Taking him into her after they took precautions, she smiled as she started to move. There was a lot she still didn't understand about Ireland, sheep, and Jamie Fitzgerald, but she knew one thing.

She loved all three.

CHAPTER TWENTY-THREE

When Liam texted about needing his help putting up a curtain, Jamie knew something was wrong.

One, Liam was handy with a hammer on a ladder on his own.

Two, Brady and Declan lived with him, and he could easily ask them for assistance.

Three, it was Sunday morning, and usually a time of rest for everyone, himself included.

Still, he kissed Sophie softly, breaking her out of her social media trance, and told her that he needed to go to Summercrest Manor.

"I won't be long, *mo chroí*," he said, running his hand over her silky dark hair. "Respond to as much as you can online, because when I return, we're going for a drive and a spot of lunch."

Wincing, she tucked the phone to her chest. "I know I've been going nonstop, but there's so much to respond to. Ghislaine says big media requests are starting to roll in. American news programs like *Good Morning America* and a whole slew of others in Ireland, Britain, and Paris, of course. Some even want to interview Keegan O'Malley about the sheep."

"That's grand, Sophie. We need more feel-good stories like that."

She nodded. "Jamie, it would mean being away for a week probably. I'm still thinking about it. Especially since I want Greta to come home as soon as possible. Once I get on the roller coaster..."

"If it's good for you and the center—and to help raise awareness about this issue—then you should go. I'd come with you, but I don't feel right about taking more time away from school."

She worried her lip. "Maybe I can see if Ghislaine can get them to agree to a remote interview, but she'll argue in person is better. I'm really torn."

He drew her hand over her heart. "Listen to this. It's guided you well so far. I'll see you soon." Kissing her one last time, he headed for the door. "I'll lock it behind me so you—"

She was already typing on her phone. He loved that she wanted to thank as many people as possible for their kind posts, but there were so many it would be like picking up every grain of sand and thanking it for being part of the beach.

When he arrived at Summercrest, he frowned at the additional cars. Carrick's and Kade's. Letting himself inside, he heard heated voices and followed them into the kitchen.

"It's the vilest and lowest form of—"

Declan broke off mid-sentence when he spotted Jamie in the doorway. Everyone turned, their faces grim.

"Who's being buried?" he asked.

Carrick raised his hand and walked forward. "I'll be the one to tell him."

Ellie grabbed something from the counter and thrust it out as he passed her. He crumpled it fractionally in his hand.

Jamie's stomach turned sour. "That bad, is it?"

"Bad and then some," Carrick said. "Liam went out for milk this morning and found these flyers plastered around the village. And there are placards in the churchyards."

"Then there's the gossip," Brady broke in harshly.

"We'll get to that." Carrick held up the wrinkled flyer. "Mary and Orla's response."

The first words he saw were the all caps *THIS IS ART?* Two paintings were depicted under it. Nudes. He colored at the depictions and wanted to curse himself for doing so. One was of a woman watching from a doorway as a couple had sex, while the other depicted a woman pleasuring herself on a gold divan in the sunlight with her skirts raised.

Under the paintings, there were more bold all-caps words. *STOP THE DEVIL'S SPAWN FROM RUINING CAISLEAN.*

He took a moment, feeling his heart rate pick up. "The paintings are by Sophie's parents?"

"Conveniently left out, of course," Kathleen said with a fist to her hand. "The one with the woman watching the couple is her mother's. She painted it after catching her husband cheating, and it's one of three paintings about betrayal. I've always thought it was powerful, but then again, I did my own series on the subject in metal."

"The other is by Sophie's dad," Ellie said softly, "and I think it's both beautiful and tasteful. However, that's not what this is about. Mary and Orla are trying to say Sophie's going to start following in her parents' footsteps or some such crap. And that's not all that's being said. Tell him, Brady."

Jamie crumpled the flyer because it felt good and glanced over at his friend. "Let me guess. Pub talk."

Brady nodded. "No one in the pub was saying any of it from conviction. They think it's wrong, as wrong as it comes. But they passed it on to let me know which way the wind's blowing."

He braced his feet. "Just say it straight."

"They're saying you're going bad," Brady said, his mouth twisting. "Because of Sophie."

Nothing could have braced him for that. She was the best, the sweetest and kindest woman in the world. "That's horseshit! All the way."

"Oh, tell him the full of it," Declan ground out.

Brady gave a pleading look. "I can't say it."

His brother gave a nod, then speared Jamie with a brooding look. "I take no pleasure in it, but you should know what's being uttered. Jamie, they're saying you're 'cuntstruck.'"

His intake of breath echoed in the quiet kitchen.

"And those same vicious people are saying Sophie is the devil's spawn and a whore," Kathleen continued, anger lacing her voice. "That she sent her child away so she could have deviant sex with you this week."

He choked out a cough. "Deviant? But that's mad! She sent Greta away to protect her."

"Not according to their tale," Liam added. "We built the walls and gate for you both to cushion your ecstatic howls and protect the village from knowing about your wild orgy behavior."

He couldn't believe this. "I've lived in my village my whole life, *and people are saying this about me!*"

"Only a few." Carrick laid a hand on his shoulder. "Mary started this, I've no doubt. At the protest she called out something about Bets having ruined Donal, and now they're saying Sophie is doing the same to you. Jamie, these same people said you took off time from school for this."

He almost doubled over at that sucker punch. "They're questioning my loyalty to my students and my oath as a teacher?"

Everyone was silent before his brother nodded. "It's the worst sort of spite I've ever heard in my whole life."

Kade finally walked over and took him by the other shoulder. "Some people like to hurt others, and Mary and Orla know how to rile people up. Sex has always been a hot and predictable topic. Who's having it. Whether they should be and with whom. Are they married? What does it say about the woman? You know the undercurrent of that kind of talk."

He did. He'd just never been the target.

"It's not right," Kade said in that even tone of his, "but it's something you'll have to deal with. Both as a member of the community and one of its teachers. We decided to tell you first and then let you decide what to tell Sophie. Because it's all over the village, Jamie, whether we like it or not."

It felt like he'd been turned inside out. "She's been on cloud nine with all the support. This will crush her. Calling her those things and saying what they have about us..."

"She's stronger than she knows," Liam said, drawing his gaze. "And so are you. When someone lies about you, you set the record straight."

"But I shouldn't have to!" he finally exploded. "I've lived a good life. All my life. In this very village! And taken grand care of their children, for pity's sake!"

Kade gripped his shoulder. "We know, Jamie, and most

in Caisleán do too. This is vicious gossip from evil people. We need to raise our voices over them."

"Until their lies are drowned out by the truth," Declan finished.

He hung his head. "What am I supposed to do? Stand on a chair in the pub or the square and tell everyone I'm not having deviant sex with Sophie? That I love her with all my heart and want to marry her, and she isn't leading me to ruin? For all that's holy, now I feel like I need to delay asking her because these vipers will assume it's to cover up our deviant behavior. Jesus, Mary, and Joseph!" And he'd just started letting himself dream of buying a ring and asking for her hand...

"Maybe you should tell them the sex *is* pretty wild," Kathleen said, "because that's how it's supposed to be when you're in love. Stick it to them in the face."

Declan put his arm around her and kissed her. "That's not Jamie's way."

"I'm not speaking of my sex life," he said in a resounding voice. "It's our private business."

"Then you keep telling everyone how much you love Sophie," Liam said, "and we'll keep talking about how the walls and gate wouldn't be needed if Denis and others at the Garda did their job and caught those vandals."

"And your brother and friends will keep reminding people in the shops and at the bar and on the street that Jamie Fitzgerald is the same good man and teacher this village has known and not to listen to these gossips," Carrick said with more compassion than Jamie had ever seen from him.

He tried to hold on to the kindness of the words but felt overwhelmed. "I...thank ye. All of ye."

"Brady will be holding court in the pub with a bunch of

us today to talk about these matters," Liam said, "while Carrick and Kade are going to pay some calls. I imagine others will start to join us as they hear about what's papering the village. I'm headed to my mum's to tell her and Linc shortly."

"And I'm off to Donal," Carrick said, "where I believe Ghislaine will be, as they're inseparable and better for it. It's not going to an easy few days, Jamie, but we'll fight it with the truth just the same."

The ability to nod was beyond him. "Again, I thank ye. I should...go home and talk to Sophie."

Carrick pounded him on the back and then hugged him. "You should go for a drive. Let us handle the talk today while you find your feet."

How could he find his feet when they were mired in a quicksand of hateful lies? "We'd been planning to. I'll...see myself out."

He had to focus on putting one foot in front of the other. Driving home slowly, he tried to rehearse what he could say to Sophie. But how did you tell the woman you love she'd been branded a whore set on ruining him?

She was still working away as he let himself back inside. "Hi! Come see this! A Basque shepherd in Wyoming and some other ranch workers sprayed over two hundred sheep with positive words and took them through the center of town to encourage more kindness amongst the townspeople. He thanked Keegan for giving him a way to show his community how much they mean to him, having welcomed him with open arms. Oh, Jamie, I was in tears reading his post."

He shrugged out of his coat and hung it in the closet. She was so happy—

"What's wrong?" She shot out of her chair and rushed to his side. "Did something happen on the way home?"

Taking her in his arms, he looked down at her dear face. "I have something to tell you. Mary and Orla have responded, and it's ugly. As ugly as it gets."

Her face was like a map of her inner turmoil as he told her, going from ice to fire and then to brokenness. Afterward, he held her as she cried, his own eyes wet with tears.

"Everything was starting to turn around," she whispered, her fist pressing against his heart, where his own hurt throbbed. "I was feeling like we were closer to me bringing Greta home. Now..."

He'd guessed as much. "Maybe you should go visit her and do those news shows while the others and I address these vicious rumors."

She pressed back, swiping at her eyes. "The people saying them aren't going to change their minds. Jamie, I'm putting your reputation at risk."

"It will survive this, seeing as they're wrong." He took a breath. "It's vicious gossip, some of the worst this village has seen. But we'll keep reminding people about why we built that wall and gate out there, why we sent a child away to protect her, and get them to focus their energy on what really matters. Making sure everyone's safe in this town. As for the rest of it, we're going to remind people it's your art and not your parents' that is coming to Caisleán. I'm sure there are other points, but I can't remember them. We should go for a drive, *mo chroí*."

She laid her head against his chest again. "I just want to curl up in a corner and hide, and I hate that."

"So do I. But we're stronger than that."

"I don't feel very strong right now." She rubbed her nose. "It's really ironic, you know. I came to Ireland for a fresh start and to level up my art. I figured I'd found a quiet community for Greta to flourish in. I'm not so sure that's true anymore. But Jamie, you've been the most unexpected surprise of all. Whatever happens, I love you."

He didn't like how she was sounding. "And I love you. More than all the stars in the sky. This will blow over. No one in Caisleán will want to live in a place with this kind of hate. People will help us stop it."

She wrapped her arms around him. "I hope so, Jamie. I hope so with all my heart."

He did too, and as he held her, he promised himself he would keep believing that. For both of them.

But when he arrived at school the next morning and found Margaret waiting for him at his desk, sitting in *his* chair, he could feel his promise slipping from his grasp as he beheld her stiff and disapproving face.

"Jamie, I've decided to suspend you from school on the basis that you are not putting the children's welfare first, as well as on grounds of immorality."

His whole body rocked back in shock, and then a greasy and oppressive sickness wrapped around him like a burial shroud. "You have to be kidding! Those are vicious lies. I'm a good teacher, a respected one—"

"Not lately," she said, holding up a bound report and slapping it on the desk in front of her. "It only takes one slip to make a bad fall, as I've detailed in my report, which I am referring to the county Education Officer, per the rules. We will begin the formal process addressing your performance. You have ten days to respond through the regular procedures. Should you not be able to address our concerns, we will forgo the creation of an improvement plan and execute the firing process."

His ears were ringing as his rage peaked. "Fire me?"

"Jamie, I am deeply disappointed in you and your actions of late, and they leave me no choice." She crossed her hands over her chest and seemed to look down her nose at him. "You are to leave the premises now before the students appear, and you are advised not to speak to either them or their parents. I bid you good day."

He stood there as her icy demeanor filled the room. The set of her shoulders conveyed her determination to have him out. After three years of working together, Margaret Doyle intended to sack him, just like that. He'd never had a problem with her before now, but there had been warning signs. His mother had never gotten along with her. Indeed, she was one of the reasons his mom had been happy to retire a few years early from the school. "I wouldn't have thought you would be among the gossips."

"I wouldn't have thought you'd conduct yourself in such a manner," she said with a scoff. "But men are easily led where women are concerned, aren't they? As an educator, it's something I'm aware of. A man's nature. Now, again, I ask you to take my report and leave. Students will begin arriving soon."

He stalked over and picked up the report. "You will have my reply shortly."

She smiled tersely, rose, and turned her back on him. He stood in his classroom, hoping it wasn't the last time. His handwriting was on the chalkboard, and his spare raincoat hung on the back of the door. He walked over to it and plucked it from the hook, the shape capturing his attention. She might as well have buried that hook in him with all the accusations she'd laid at his door.

He left the room and walked down the hallway, his footsteps echoing against the walls as he departed.

When he reached his home, he couldn't find the energy

to leave his car. Rex barked beside his window. How was he to tell Sophie of this?

When she opened the front door and stepped out, her concern was etched in her face. He pushed himself out of the car and faced her.

"My principal has filed a report for my termination," he said, his voice like sandpaper.

Her face crumpled and she shuffled forward until she could touch his face. "Oh, Jamie, no!"

Then he folded into her, this time letting her hold him as his world fell to the ground and shattered.

CHAPTER TWENTY-FOUR

Bets' research into overcoming small-town gossip mocked her.

"You know, I've lived here for almost forty years, and this is the first time I've researched what to do about gossip even though I've been the subject of plenty, especially back in the day." She glanced over to where Linc rested in his new armchair with his eyes closed. "Do you think that means I'm stupid or just desperate?"

He gave an audible snort. "Probably a little of both. There've been plenty of people who've thought they knew my business well enough to spread it around. I used to write it off as a hallmark of success. Now I'm rethinking my position. Some people are cruel to the bone. Does your list have anything good on it?"

She shifted on the couch and studied the hastily scribbled notes in her hand. "One, ignore it. Which we can't do. Two, try and talk to the person about their behavior. Been there. Gotten nowhere. Three, educate and correct misinformation."

"Most everyone in town has been talking themselves

blue for the past couple of days defending Jamie and Sophie."

"Don't forget about Ghislaine's response to the flyers." She'd spread flyers of her own with the headline THIS IS THE ART COMING TO CAISLEAN, accompanied by Sophie's design. Not her parents' paintings.

"Mary and Orla knew what they were doing," Linc drawled. "They sure stirred the pot good. Sex always sells, or so they say. I never could figure out how to use it to sell windows."

She couldn't help but laugh. "Four, feed the gossips little details about your life to keep their small-minded brains and boring lives fulfilled—"

"Some expert really said that?" Linc chortled.

"Yes. It keeps getting better. Five, stop associating with the gossipers."

"I'll cancel Mary and Orla's invitation to our next BBQ."

"Right. How about this next one? *Just live your life and be happy.* Seriously?"

"It's not a bad thought—unless someone is gunning for you, which is our exhibit A, B, and C right now."

Yeah, it sure was. "Six is the most dire suggestion, if you ask me."

He sat up, frowning. "What is it?"

"*Move*," she said darkly, tossing her list onto the couch next to her.

"For some, it's a reasonable strategy. Bigger towns, more anonymity. Of course, it's not an option for us."

"But it might be for Sophie, and Greta's already left," Bets said, lying back and studying the ceiling. "And Jamie... what if he doesn't beat this, Linc?"

He rose and came over to her, rearranging her so her

head was cradled in his lap. "Come on now. We can't think that way. His mother is coming home from Portugal to show support and talk to other people in the school administration, here and county-wide. We've already got a win in our pocket. The censorship board has withdrawn their complaint against Jamie, given all the national exposure. I believe they said *additional information has been brought to light...*"

She'd read their letter with disgust. "It shouldn't have been started in the first place."

Stroking her hair, he said, "Let's focus on the upside. Our children's arts program is a go again."

"With our program head in very hot water." She squeezed her eyes shut. "I know he doesn't want to take the issue to the papers like we did with the Garda situation, but—"

"He's trying to protect Sophie," Linc growled. "With one of the charges being immorality, I can see why. It's a loaded accusation, and reporters *love* to ask questions about it. I mean, what are they going to ask him? Do you get out the whips and chains with the artist on rainy nights or maybe just on days ending in *Y*?"

"Good God! Is that what people think when they hear *immoral*? We should hide that crop you use on me the next time company comes."

He gave her a gentle squeeze and laughed at her joke. "Yeah, you know me. So deviant. Not that it's anyone's business what two consenting people do."

"I still think Ghislaine is right." God, she really liked that woman, and she couldn't be happier for Donal. "They should let her craft a press release about this mess. It can be simple and to the point—he's been a great teacher with terrific performance on record, and now he's being targeted for working with the center and being in a relationship with Sophie."

"Some men don't want to look weak, and that could be interpreted—"

"I don't care." She punched the sofa. "Say they've fallen in love and have a healthy and committed relationship. Make it a love story."

"I couldn't agree more." Ghislaine stood in the doorway, holding Donal's hand, both of them so radiant they were another example of a love story come to life. "I did knock, but since you already knew I was coming, I let us in. Donal was against it."

"I'm becoming un-Irish about opening people's doors without invitation," he said with a snort. "But we bring good news. Denis has been suspended indefinitely and without pay. The ombudsman has concluded their investigation, and they didn't like what they found. We'll be getting another officer from a different locality to take over in the meantime."

Bets shot out of Linc's lap as he let out a whoop. "That's a victory!"

"Yes, it sure is." Donal grinned. "Ghislaine didn't tell me until this morning, but she'd set up a camera outside the protesters' area, so we weren't limited to what the reporters picked up."

"The *Turn Here* sign, to be exact, and the footage ended up in the ombudsman's mailbox somehow," Ghislaine said, touching Donal's arm with a familiarity Bets was all too happy to see.

Thank you, Sorcha.

"The fairies, I'm sure," he said drolly. "The camera caught him telling Mary and Orla not to worry. He said he would 'take care of everything.' While it was a vague enough promise, it raised concerns. Didn't help that he tried to fine Keegan over the sheep. But what nailed his coffin was when the ombudsman discovered he hadn't followed up on the vandalism case and had ordered others to steer clear."

"You didn't happen to get video of Denis conspiring with Malcolm Coveney, did you?" Linc asked.

She shook her head. "Afraid not. But now that I know what he looks like—a train wreck—I'll keep an eye out and my phone handy."

So would Bets. "So, being positive, we hopefully have the Garda situation handled."

"But the vandals haven't been caught yet," Linc drawled, his mouth twisting. "I guess we'll have to wait and see what this new guy can do."

"Yeah, so all we have left is to contend with Jamie's disciplinary issue," Donal said, his mouth leveling into a savage frown.

"Yeah, only that," Bets said dryly.

"My dad is chomping at the bit to come back to Caisleán and help." Donal made a frustrated gesture in the air. "But he knows he's needed with Sandrine and Greta. It's been over a week now since Sophie and her daughter have seen each other."

Bets didn't know how Sophie was managing it, given everything. Probably staying busy like the rest of them. "That can't continue. They shouldn't be apart."

"I still think we need to use the media on this issue," Ghislaine said softly. "I know 'immorality' is a loaded topic, but so is calling someone a devil's spawn and a whore and saying she's ruined a good man. You don't want to know what Sophie's mother had to say about that, and trust me, she's heard it said about herself."

She could imagine. Bets gripped her knees, knowing there were other ugly phrases being tossed around about Jamie and Sophie and one started with a C. A deplorable word she'd raised her sons never to say. "Do you ever wonder why it's always the woman leading the man astray? Even when the man is sixty—like you two—and he starts dating a younger woman—"

"Like the twenty-three-year-old my ex dabbled with while we were married?" Ghislaine added, putting a hand on her hip and glowering.

Donal muttered about some men being bastards and caressed her back comfortingly.

Bets swore in sympathy. "Yes, like that. Even when the man has tons of life experience and the woman is fairly new to being an adult, she's still the one they say is leading a man astray."

"Donal, you know what I hate?" Linc lifted his chin. "How people think that just because we have a johnson—excuse me, ladies—that we're stupid enough to be led around by it all the damn time. Like we have no reason or self-control."

"It's horrible being a stereotype for sure," Donal replied, glancing at Ghislaine. "But apparently I like being a ruined man. Who knew?"

Ghislaine gave an indelicate snort before touching his chest. "If you're ruined, then the Easter Bunny is real. Now, who's going to talk to Jamie? The news cycle is fast. We need to move."

"I've known him the longest," Bets said. "I'll try to talk him around."

"I saw him helping Carrick put in some fenceposts on the west side of his pasture by the giant hawthorn tree," Donal said helpfully.

"Don't all the roads here have names?" Ghislaine asked.

Donal chuckled and kissed her cheek. "No. Takes the fun out of describing them. The Irish like things being hidden sometimes."

"I have a lot to learn," Ghislaine said, smiling at Donal. "Glad I have a great teacher. All right, we'll be going. I have to talk to a couple of TV shows about Sophie and Keegan doing remote interviews since neither of them are open to traveling at the moment. I had a great excuse with Keegan. He needs to take care of his cows and sheep."

"I would look after his sheep if it came to it," Donal said, making a show of his arm muscles. "I could still heft one if needed."

"Heft one?" Ghislaine asked in shock. *"A whole sheep?"*

"I hefted you last night, didn't I?" he said with a grin.

She leveled him with what could only be deemed a seductive glance. "And I let you... Shall we go, my love?"

Donal took her hand and gave them a last look before the couple turned for the door. Bets was smiling as she watched them walk out together. "Another victory. Donal found his soulmate."

Linc stroked her arm. "We have more victories than defeats. But I won't lie. It's been a rough campaign, and we're not through yet."

She kissed him softly. "No, we aren't. Wish me luck with Jamie. Any pointers?"

He rubbed his jaw, considering. "We're different men, but I'd say the same things matter to both of us. Our reputation. And protecting those we love. Sometimes we have to fight for them. Number one on your list isn't going to cut it this time."

She couldn't remember the order. "You have a better memory than me. What was number one?"

"*Ignore it*," he said harshly. "Ain't going to get it done here."

No, it wasn't, she thought, as she grabbed her things and drove over to Carrick's west pasture. She spotted them easily, one pounding in the post while the other knelt on the green pasture holding it. Sheep milled about in clusters, and her breath caught as the light suddenly shifted. The western sky seemed to split in two, half of it baby blue while the other half turned dark gray. Rain coming. She would need to talk fast. She'd forgotten her hat.

By the time she parked her Mini Cooper in the turnout and started walking briskly toward the gate to the pasture, the brothers were already walking swiftly in her direction. Carrick was taking out his phone, as if checking for disaster, so she gave them an easy wave as reassurance.

She thought about hopping the fence but didn't want to get muck on her pants. The gate creaked as she opened it, and knowing how canny sheep could be, she secured the lock.

"You have news?" Carrick called out.

She realized she did, actually. Might as well start with the good stuff. "The ombudsman has suspended Denis indefinitely, and a new officer is coming to us from another county to clean things up."

Carrick put his hands on his belt and rocked back. "That is good news! Isn't it, Jamie?"

The man nodded, but Bets thought his color was nearly as gray as the stormy sky.

"Well, I'll be grabbing a few more posts," Carrick said after an awkward pause. "Be right back."

Bets looked at the man she'd known since he was a boy and felt her heart thud. He was hurting. "I can't imagine how hard things must seem right now."

He tucked the collar of his jacket up around his ears even though the wind wasn't too cold. "Something on your mind, Bets?"

So he didn't want to talk. Well, she couldn't blame him. "Jamie, we think you should really consider—"

"Stop right now," he said, holding up a hand like a crosswalk guard. "I already know what you're going to say, and there's no point in rehashing it. My mind is made up."

She crossed her arms, trying to consider what to say next. Jamie was already looking off toward the pasture, his face a set of hard lines. "Will you at least talk to Liam?"

He turned his head and stared at her quietly, like a man who had more than made up his mind. This was Jamie Fitzgerald standing his ground.

"What about Sorcha?" she asked desperately.

"Matchmaking is her way—not this." He gave her arm a comforting pat as he walked off, likely to gentle his words. "I should help Carrick with those posts. Thanks for coming by."

She stood there as the sheep mingled about and longed for the scent of oranges.

CHAPTER TWENTY-FIVE

Ghislaine knew how to keep Sophie busy with interviews.

As she thanked yet another person on social media for their support, she had to admit that she was occupying herself pretty well on her own.

She was avoiding the unpleasantness and focusing on the positives to keep her going. But the bad things were out there, lurking in the shadows.

Her daughter was still away from her, and now that some of the villagers had turned against them, including Greta's principal, she wasn't sure when she could bring her back. Her stomach clenched as the bigger question arose. Did she *want* to bring her daughter back here? Most of the village supported them, but she wasn't sure if that was enough.

The school Greta attended was now part of the problem. Even if Jamie cleared the charges leveled at him, they would always be around, wouldn't they? Would that principal and others of her thinking malign Greta? If Sophie was a devil's spawn, and Greta her daughter, wouldn't some think she was as well?

Kids had called Sophie names because of her parents. It didn't take Aristotelian logic to imagine the possibility.

She leaned back against the couch, her heart pulsing with hurt. Rex barked, signaling Jamie's return. His brother had been keeping him busy with the sheep, which helped as a distraction and also kept him away from the village. Brady had said he'd love to have him hang out at the Brazen Donkey as barfly, but what good would that do when they were trying to quell talk of Jamie being 'ruined'? Declan had said he could butcher meat if it would help him feel better, but then he'd have to deal with shoppers, and who wanted that right now?

His steps were heavy as he came inside. The sound of him locking the door was loud to her ears. Before this, he'd never locked it. Before this, she'd never felt unsafe in her own home.

"How was your day, *mo chroí*?" he asked, kissing her on the top of her head after hanging his jacket on a chair.

He'd been focusing on the positives too—they'd agreed it was for the best. Their afternoons had fallen into a comfortable routine. They'd exchange heartening stories from Ghislaine, and he'd tell her about any funny things that had happened out with Carrick and the sheep. Yesterday, he'd even given her an azurite blue seashell he'd discovered while digging posts, knowing she'd appreciate its color and composition.

Then they'd huddle together on the couch and watch a movie before retiring and making love with as much comfort and tenderness as they could muster for each other.

But still there was a weight none of their actions could

dissipate, and it seemed today, the burden was too great for him.

"I was just missing Greta and thinking about things," she said, taking his hand as he sat on the couch beside her. "Jamie, have you thought about what comes after you win your job back?"

The skin on his face seemed to stretch tighter, as if she were stretching canvas over a frame. "You mean after I convince people who've known me my whole life that I'm not immoral, a deviant, and a bastard who doesn't care for the welfare of my students?"

Tears burned her eyes. "In some ways this is harder for you than it's been for me."

He tucked her against his side. "We don't need to be competing on that score."

"That's not what I meant," she said, smelling the fresh fields and sea air on his work clothes. "I mean, the people who have attacked me don't know me personally. But yours do. Even if it's a minority."

He scrubbed his face. "Yes, and that makes it the worst kind of betrayal. You ask if I've thought about what comes after, assuming I do beat these charges, which I'm still not sure of. I have thought of it all, the good, the bad, and the ugly, as they say. I wonder if my students and their parents will ever look at me the same and *trust me* as they did. Gossip tends to worm its way even into the best of brains."

She knew her tears were going to flow after hearing him force those words out. She let them sink into his shirt, hoping their love and compassion could heal the worst of his hurt.

"I wonder if I even want to work under a principal who would accuse me of such deplorable things, knowing she'll be watching for more. I wonder if I can even stomach what she might come up with in an improvement plan should I beat these charges. Then there are my students and their parents, looking to me to be a more serious model for a teacher than I've clearly been."

She straightened at that. "Except they're wrong, Jamie! You don't have to be more serious—"

"Word about the pranks at Summercrest hasn't helped my reputation, and perhaps I was hasty in them. I'm not a kid anymore but a grown man who's meant to set a good example."

God, they'd done a number on him. "You *do* set a good example. Jamie, this is shame talking."

"Let me finish. *Please.* Even with all those weights on my soul, mostly I think about you and Greta and what might be best for all of us."

She looked into his eyes for answers, to understand how he could say such things after all they'd shared. Love was shining brightly in them, but so was his agony.

"I wonder whether you and she should live in Provence," he began, "away from this place. I wouldn't have a word said against you if I could help it, but I can't seem to stop it or protect you, so—"

"And what about us?" she whispered, her heart tearing. "I love you. You're everything I could want in a man, a partner, a friend, and a lover. I know you'll be good for Greta as much as for me."

He framed her face. "I've agonized over this for days, *mo chroí*, and I have no easy answers. I love you too and will never find another. But I don't know how I can simply leave this place, the only one I've known. Even if my friends and family weren't here, I would hate the way it would look like if I left. Like I'd be tucking my tail between my legs. Like I'd done something wrong."

"But you haven't—"

"I can't ask you to bear that fight with me," he said harshly, "and I certainly can't ask it of a child, whom I already love. It's said you have to sacrifice for those you love. This is my sacrifice, *mo chroí*, the letting go of you."

She stilled under his hands. "You're going to make me a sacrifice? Jamie, I want to love you for this, but you're only making me mad. Why do you need to sacrifice anything? You've done nothing wrong, and neither have I. Yes, we have a lot of things to work out, and I've also been thinking about whether Greta will be able to thrive here—"

"See, you already know," he said sadly.

"But I don't agree that *you* have to stay here and suffer." She touched his chest, wanting to reach him. "I know your family and friends are here, and I know how much they mean to you. Maybe we should both go to Provence for a bit after you beat this. You can have the satisfaction of tendering your resignation to that horrible woman, because Jamie, I don't want you to have to keep looking over your shoulder either. You can teach somewhere else."

He laid his hands over hers, his calmness alarming her. "My teaching license is for Ireland, *mo chroí*. And while I could teach English in France as an EU passport holder, I don't want to."

So he'd looked it up already. "Then we'll go to New York. I grew up there, Jamie, and there are tons of Irish. Teachers too, I expect. We can start over there together."

"Such talk fills me with distress and anxiety." His harsh sigh seemed to punctuate it. "The truth is I'm a homebody, someone who's never traveled and likes his quiet, simple life. I can't imagine leaving, even for you, because I know you and Greta will be better off without me. You deserve someone stronger."

"That is complete bullshit," she said angrily. "So you want to just go back to your old routine and send me away. Jamie, I stayed and fought when push came to shove, and it terrified me. Now you're going to simply throw in the towel?"

The light in his eyes dimmed. "Do you think I don't feel guilty about this? But what kind of a man, what kind of a husband and father could I be after this? These charges have tarnished my character, and leaving here will only make me seem more culpable. I won't ask that of you."

She couldn't believe this. "That's ridiculous. Jamie, just because someone attacks your character doesn't mean it's tarnished. Take me. I've been called a devil's spawn lately, and I haven't checked my hairline to see if they're starting to sprout."

His mouth didn't even tip to a smile. "As you just said a moment ago, the people who called you that don't know you. The ones here know me. It's different."

"So this is about you taking on that shame, sacrificing me and Greta and all of our happiness, and living the rest of your life alone with this burden?" She touched the hard line of his jaw. "Dammit, Jamie, I knew the Irish had a reputation for putting up with bad situations because they think it's their lot, but this is ridiculous. I love you too much to accept this. I love you too much not to fight for you. For what we have."

When he tried to look away, his face a mask of agony, she held firm, feeling the power of love rising within her.

"If there's one thing my parents taught me—and look at me being grateful to them for it right now, after everything I went through as a kid—it's that we decide how we want our lives to be. We don't let others tell us who we are or what we can do. I'm not a whore or a devil's spawn—"

"Of course you aren't," Jamie said harshly, his eyes burning now.

"And you're not immoral or a bad teacher or any of the other things they said."

He took her hands, gripping them tightly. "But what then do we do?"

When his voice broke, she fought tears.

"Because I don't see a way through this," he continued. "Especially with us both wanting to keep Greta safe and happy."

In that moment, she knew what she must say. "Come to Provence with me for a few days. Finish your defense with your legal counsel for the Education Officer's review but do it from there. The yoke you've put around your neck is getting heavier every day, and I can't bear it anymore, Jamie."

She had to stop to wipe a stream of tears, but when he tenderly brushed them aside, she fought to keep her composure.

"You deserve better than this," she said hoarsely.

He caressed her cheek. "So do you."

When he rose, she let her hands fall to her lap. Reaching for him right now would be useless. The way he'd set his body was as finite as one of her glass sculptures.

"Go to Greta, *mo chroí*." He somehow found the energy to smile.

She could not answer it. "I don't want to leave you. If I do, I fear we'll never be together again."

A rare brightness shone in his eyes. "I do this for love of you and the child. Always remember that. Even when it hurts."

She didn't have the energy to denounce his words as utter bullshit again.

He grabbed his jacket and headed to the door. "I'll stay away to make things easier. Perhaps Ghislaine can stay with you until you leave so you won't be alone."

Their eyes met, sorrow pulsing in the quiet room.

"I love you." He paused, his throat working with emotion, and she wondered if it was the last time she'd hear him say it. "Lock the door behind me."

The snap of the door shutting was the final slice to her heart.

She laid her face against the couch and cried until she was spent.

CHAPTER TWENTY-SIX

Jamie wasn't surprised when Sorcha appeared in the passenger seat beside him.

He nearly pulled over and got out of the car, but she'd only pass through the metal and follow him. "I miss the old days when I would faint at the sight of you. It would save me from conversation."

She crossed her arms, glaring at him with her forest-green eyes. "I never thought I'd live to see the day when you'd turn as stupid and stubborn as your brother."

"You didn't live to see the day," he said, gesturing to her ephemeral form. "And I don't want to hear from you just now. I already know what you want to say."

Her muted shriek reminded him of days past, when he and Carrick would show up late for supper after a few whiskeys, arms around each other. "You're a mind reader now, are you? Jamie Fitzgerald, that Fitzgerald blood has finally risen up but good. And it doesn't look well on you."

He decided to pull off into a turnout, feeling his temper rising. "Stop your pecking. It will do you no good."

She swam in front of his face, making him cry out.

"Don't tell me to stop pecking at you. I did it with Carrick out of love, and I'll do the same with you. Do you not recall your own outrage at your brother for sacrificing the rest of his life out of guilt and misery after I died?"

He tightened his jaw. Dammit, he remembered it well.

"You're doing the same thing, giving up Sophie and your life together! And you're even stupider than Carrick here because Sophie is still alive. Oh, Jamie, have you learned nothing? When you find love, the kind that makes your heart sing, you love every day like it's your last. You don't throw it away. Not out of shame or fear and certainly not out of sacrifice. For pity's sake!"

He'd never seen her flushed red with anger as a ghost, and it made his stomach tremble. "I don't have to explain myself to you!"

"No, you don't. And you shouldn't have to with the school either! But Jamie, why would you fight that and not fight for a life with Sophie and Greta when you want it more than anything in the world?"

"I don't see a way," he cried out savagely. "Do you think I want to lose her and the child? You're right. Everything I've ever wanted was right there, and now it feels like a damn rainbow, here one minute and gone the next."

She uttered another shriek. "Jamie, your love *and* hers are still there. Hold your head up, man! Don't look at a year from now. Look at a few days from now, after you finish your review—"

"And then what?" he nearly shouted back. "Have her face the shame of me going back to work amongst the people who have pointed at me and called me immoral and unfit for children? I won't put that on her or Greta. I could never live with myself."

"There are other possibilities, Jamie, ones you're being

too thickheaded and stuck-in-the-mud to consider. You and your infernal routine! Other schools in this very county, not far from Caisleán, would be happy to have you for a teacher. Plenty of people know you're not immoral or deviant. The entire idea is ludicrous!"

"You and I and others know it, but—"

"Do you want to teach the children to let the bullies and biddies win?" She slashed her hand through the air so hard, he felt the wind of it. "If a boy is called a bad seed on the playground when he isn't, is he supposed to put a sign around his neck and wear it like a leper's bell? Is Sophie to wear *Whore* emblazoned on her shirt? You're not thinking, man!"

He pinched the bridge of his nose. "What would you have me do? I'd rather cut off my own arm than leave her, but I can't see a way for us to live after this."

She was silent, which made him turn his head to regard her. Composed she was, her temper behind her, all she emitted was compassion. "It's simple. You live together—"

"Where? I can't—"

"Stop thinking about the where and the how. Jamie, I love you with all the spirit I have left, but I tell you this truly. Decide to stay with her and the rest will fall into place."

"But I still don't see—"

"I know you don't," she said softly, her hand hovering over his arm in comfort. "It's the choice to love that must be made. The details must come after. With adjustments to be made, yes, which you will both make. No place is perfect, Jamie, even Caisleán, as you've learned. There are gossips and biddies the world over. Don't let them tell you how to live. You give them too much power when you do."

His heart thudded in his chest. Words failed him. The

talk would only die down if he went back to his old life and showed people he was the same man and teacher they knew. But he couldn't make himself say it. She might brand him a coward, only showing she didn't understand his sacrifice, and that would destroy him all the more.

"So that's it, then? I can't reach you all the way. Well, I'm not finished. I wasn't through with Carrick until he saw sense, and I'm not through with you. Wallow in your sacrifice, you may, but not until I've exhausted every avenue to help you and Sophie live as one. I will not fail in my duty as matchmaker, and I will not fail those I love. That, Jamie, my boy, is how you choose to love—no matter what."

With a flourish of white, she vanished. The scent of oranges came next, so strong he rolled the window down. But the smell only strengthened until he could taste it in the back of his throat.

He started the car and finished driving to his parents' house. They'd just returned from Portugal. Summercrest was out of the question. There would be too many friends to poke at him, albeit good-naturedly, and he could bear no more conversations.

When he arrived, his mother opened the front door. She was still sunburned from her time in Portugal, and he was sorry to see any respite she'd had from holiday turn to worry and sadness for him. His father appeared behind her, his arm at her back.

He braced himself as he left the car. "I need a place to stay for a night. Maybe more." He had no need to ask them if he could. They were his family.

His mother hurried toward him, her gray corkscrew curls bobbing. "You know the door is always open."

When she enfolded him in her arms, he rested his head

on her shoulder for a moment before lifting his gaze to his father's.

"Come inside." He gripped Jamie's arm, his blue Fitzgerald eyes filled with sorrow. "We'll have a whiskey and talk."

His throat clogged with everything he could not say. "I can't just now. I need—"

They stared at him helplessly. When he couldn't force the words out, he watched as they slowly reached for each other's hands, twining them together. The unity and comfort drove the final nail of pain into his heart.

He strode past them and headed back to his old room, stepping back into another old life.

On the bed, he put his face in his hands, hoping to banish the image of his parents.

He and Sophie could have been like that.

Now it was never to be.

CHAPTER TWENTY-SEVEN

She had never cried so much in her life.

With her face pressed against the couch, she felt hollow. Like her body was a husk. The love that had so revolutionized her life and given her joy and hope had turned into the most savage pain she'd ever felt. Worse than childbirth. Worse than any humiliation as a child. Worse than any betrayal during her marriage.

At one point, she'd thought she could hear her heart shatter like glass. It stole her breath and made her cry out louder, so much that Rex had started barking outside the window. She'd tried to gather herself after that, but it had cost her.

Was there any hope?

Was there any reason she should stay?

"Don't be afraid," a quiet voice said, then the scent of oranges came to her. "I'm here to help if I can."

She lifted her head sharply and gasped. *"Oh, my God!"*

A beautiful woman with long brown hair stood in front of her, wearing a white flowing dress Sophie couldn't imagine wearing in Ireland.

She gestured to it. "I admit, the day was warm when I last wore it."

Her inhale was stark in the room. *Last wore it...* She studied the woman more closely, her skin tingling with awareness. "Eoghan said you looked after Caisleán but this is... This is..."

"A happy surprise?" She gave a soft smile. "I'm Sorcha Fitzgerald, and yes, I look after Caisleán. I would shake your hand, but it doesn't quite work that way anymore. You might have questions so let me see if I can answer them. Yes, I'm a ghost, one who helps. And you, my dear, seem to need a great deal right now."

She started to curl into herself, her eyes taking in the way the woman's dress seemed to sway as if wind were playing with its edges. "I must need a ton of help if *you're* here..."

"You're funny, even amidst your pain." Another smile filled her heart-shaped face. "Are you sure you aren't Irish?"

She shook her head.

"Well, it's not unusual to have ghosts here in Ireland, but we exist pretty much everywhere. You know, I was in Boston a short time back, trying to help Kathleen and Declan. If I were one of those memes on social media, you would see me with a passport and the quote *This Ghost Will Travel.*"

The ghost's responding humor dulled Sophie's shock. "All right," she said, swallowing thickly. "Let's say I play along, being that this is Ireland and Eoghan mentioning you. Forgetting how I just cried my eyes out so hard I might be suffering from a mini stroke."

"You aren't, but do continue."

Sophie watched as the spectral woman walked over to

the armchair beside her couch and sat down. Her feet were bare. "Shall I make some tea?" she quipped.

"You do have a strong sense of humor, don't you? It serves you well, I expect. When you lose all hope, that goes as surely as the sun will set this eve. You'll remember I was Carrick Fitzgerald's wife before I died."

Sophie breathed out slowly. She was really and truly conversing with a ghost. "Yes, I remember hearing that."

"Well, to make the story short, here's the way of it. Carrick was very stubborn about finding love again, which is a Fitzgerald trait. The stubbornness. Not the other. They find love just fine. But Carrick took this stubbornness to epic proportions, being he's not a temperate man."

She hadn't seen that side of Carrick, but she nodded anyway so the ghost—*ghost!*—would continue.

"His friends went above and beyond to help him," she said with another soft smile, "as friends are wont to do. We helped him find love with Angie, which makes me happier than I can convey, but I felt I owed the men a debt for their help. And so I have stayed here, doing what I can to bring those men and their soulmates together. All the while helping Caisleán as well."

"That's very nice of you," she managed.

"Some have given me more trouble than others, although I'm not naming names. *They* certainly wouldn't call me nice."

Her chortle was almost enough to make Sophie smile. "People called me nice all the time. Trust me. It's not the greatest."

"Great or not, I'm nearly finished with my work here." She glanced over to the window, and Sophie's mouth parted as the light changed from gray to golden, the sun coming out in showstopping fashion. "I confess I will miss them. I might shout and curse a little at them, but I love them all dearly. None more than my former brother-in-law, Jamie Fitzgerald."

Sophie grabbed a throw pillow to her stomach, needing to clutch something. "I see."

"When I knew you were meant—by powers greater than me—I was so happy for Jamie. He's waited a long time for love, and he'd all but put those dreams away."

He'd put them away again, she feared, and her throat burned at the thought.

"Jamie certainly didn't want me around a few minutes ago, when I went at him for being such a complete and utter eejit." She tilted her head to the side, as if amused. "Not all of them appreciate my help when they need it the most, you see. Stupid and stubborn men they are. So I felt it was time for you and I to speak."

She had to take a giant breath, realizing she'd stopped breathing for a moment, captivated by the ghost's regard in the quiet parlor. "Being that I'm not as stupid or stubborn."

"Being nice has its advantages," she said, nodding encouragingly. "I don't have to ask if you love Jamie and want to be with him. Your tears still drench the sofa. What I do want to know is if you would be open to some help."

"Yes... I'd love some. I was hoping bawling my eyes out would help clear my head. I didn't expect help to come in the form of a ghost."

She chuckled softly. "That's how life goes, I suppose. You never know who might help or what might happen. That's why it's so important to keep an open heart. It's to your credit that you managed that after your divorce. That open heart is also why you didn't become reclusive and embittered after the ugliness you experienced with your parents due to some people's ignorance about their art."

Her mouth went dry from the compliment. "Thanks, I think. It's not really something you wish for."

"No, it's not. For every experience, we have the chance to respond. Jamie needs to be reminded of that. Because right now, he's retrenching toward reclusiveness, which is known and all too comfortable. Forget what he says about nobility and sacrifice."

She was really starting to like this ghost.

"He needs to answer those hateful charges against his character, yes, but doing so is not enough. He must be reminded to fight for love. For you. Because he *will* love you for the rest of his days. That I know."

A tear fell down Sophie's cheek, which she hastily brushed aside. "So do I. Like you said. Stupid and stubborn. I'm getting angry again."

"That's good." She stood. "His Fitzgerald blood is showing, and it's not a pleasing look on him, as I said to his very face. But like Carrick, that stubbornness is balanced by a courageous and loving heart. He would protect you and Greta and sacrifice himself."

"I don't want that," she said, her voice firm with a new resolve. "I know we have a lot to overcome, but I want to do it together."

Sorcha came over and stood beside her, reaching out her slender hand until it was inches from her face. "Call Eoghan and tell him we spoke. Ask for his thoughts about raising Greta in Caisleán should Jamie beat the charges against him. I imagine it's on your mind. I can also tell you that the forces that sent those vandals to your very door are orchestrating their fall as we speak—without them being on the line for ordering it."

She gasped. "Really? I know Linc and Donal were laying bets—"

"Even the wisest serpent knows when to return to its lair and Malcolm Coveney is that and more." Her mouth twisted. "Linc will be hearing the news soon, although I can't tell you the day. But even with this development, you will still have questions."

Nodding, she watched as the woman lowered her hand, her face a study in compassion.

"You must be sure, for yourself as much as for her. Jamie must be as well, to cure his recent thickheadedness. And ask Eoghan to do what he does best."

Her heart was beating fiercely in her chest now. "What is that?"

"Have him rally the town—for Jamie." Moving to the window, she looked out. "I hope this wall will come down at some point. As I told Jamie, no place is without flaws. The only choice we can make is whether we will love and walk with the ones who hold our heart. Good luck, Sophie."

With that, she vanished. Sophie slowly sat up and inched off the couch. She glanced around to make sure she was alone, and then she rubbed her eyes. No, she *had* seen the woman, the ghost. Oddly, she felt better for it.

Grabbing her phone, she dialed Eoghan straightaway.

His face was grave when he answered. "Sophie, me olde flower. How are you faring?"

Me olde flower? The endearment was out of a Robert Burns poem, she knew, but she'd never heard anyone use it before. "Eoghan, there's no easy way to say it, but Sorcha told me to call you."

His serious face shifted into a wide grin. "Has she at last? I've been waiting for something like this to break the dam of lies and deceptions we find ourselves in."

"That's an apt description. Let me start with the first question. You know Greta now. And me. And you've lived in Caisleán your whole life. Do you think she could flourish here after everything that's happened?"

"It's weighed on me like a stone, as I imagine it's weighed all the more on you." He gave a gusty sigh. "I've bandied it about with Sandrine, my love. Because I want Sandrine to be happy too."

"Her happiness is as important as ours."

"It is," he said, nodding. "I have lived with vipers like Mary Kincaid and Orla and Tom MacKenna and others like them, but I have never willingly associated with them. Of course, they have never sought to injure me as they have you and Jamie, and for that, I hope they get their just deserts and more."

Sophie had never been a vengeful person, but she was starting to really believe in things like karma.

"The number of people who agree with those vipers in our village is small. And yet their teeth are sharp. The school's principal has certainly shown hers, and I think a complaint should be taken up against her for her actions."

She raised her brow. "No one's thought of that."

"No one's *said* anything yet. Donal and I have been discussing it. We've been debating the timing. Whether it should come before Jamie's review or after."

"I don't know enough about that sort of thing, so I'm glad you and Donal are discussing it."

"It would be another first for our town." He combed a few stray hairs from his wrinkled forehead. "But if it helped us obtain justice with Denis Walsh, then I think we can take the same tack with Margaret Doyle. Report *her* for her actions to *her* supervisor. What parent wants that kind of woman running the school where their children go? If my grandchildren were still attending, we'd have had a fight, that's for sure."

She hadn't been thinking big enough. She'd only been reacting. "I'm really glad to call you a friend, Eoghan."

He put his hand to his heart. "Me as well, *a leanbh*. Now, tell me what else Sorcha said to you. Then I will go pluck Greta from the pool where she's happily splashing with Sandrine, wearing her new unicorn floatie, the one the fairies delivered."

The image lifted her spirits, as if the light inside her had changed from gray to golden. "Sorcha says to do what you do best."

He waggled his brows. "It's a compliment she's giving me. Along what lines?"

"Rally the town."

Mischief flashed in his pale blue eyes. "That I can do, and more. We'll only share our plans with a few among us for the biggest impact. I'll return, of course, as quick as a hare. But my, how me and my old bones will miss the Provençal sun."

She laughed for the first time in days.

"Now let me tell you what we need to do."

CHAPTER TWENTY-EIGHT

Sophie hadn't left.

Jamie's heart had thundered mightily when Carrick told him the news as they dug out rotted posts for replacing the following morning. "But why not?"

His brother speared the damp earth with his shovel, his anger evident. "She's not up for conversation just now. Same as you. Unless you want to tell me why you're staying with Mum and Dad now and not the woman you love?"

He locked his jaw. If he told Carrick the truth, his brother would be bashing him with the shovel. "Not particularly."

"Then let's keep digging, shall we?" his brother spat out. "And I'll tell the others to leave you be. For the moment."

The final words carried the whisper of a threat. They would all pounce soon enough. Likely after the Education Officer made her decision about the charges against him.

The next day, he and his lawyers, whom Linc had found for him, filed his defense well ahead of the ten-day window, but it gave him no relief. His shoulders and back ached from digging up posts, work Carrick must have seized upon to keep him busy, but he didn't complain. He and his parents were like ships passing in the night, what with them spending their nights defending him. Of his friends, he saw none. He spent the weekend alone, keeping the telly on for company, missing Sophie with all his heart.

He had the quiet he'd always thought he liked, but the silence scraped at his nerves now. Yes, his routine was different and he was living back in his parents' house, but being alone wasn't the same. There was no solace in it anymore—only agony.

Monday came, and with it more posts. When he asked Carrick again if he had news of Sophie, his brother ripped out the post roughly and threw it aside. "If you're ready to talk about your stupidness, then we'll talk. Otherwise, you'll need to seek your answers from someone other than me."

He knew the set of that chin, had known it since childhood. His brother was spoiling for a fight. And as angry and hurt as he was, Jamie still was not the kind of man to give it to him. "Never mind then."

Carrick ripped off his gloves and stalked off, calling over his shoulder, "I'm going home for lunch if you want to come along."

He sunk his shovel in the earth. While he'd love to see his niece, if he went, he would put himself in Angie's crosshairs. She could be just as fierce as Carrick. "No, I'll just keep digging."

"You do that!" Carrick shouted back.

He scowled and then jumped as Sorcha appeared on the fence in front of him, sitting on the post. He clutched his heart. "Jesus, Mary, and Joseph, you scared me."

"Did it knock some sense into you?" she asked with narrowed eyes.

"Why didn't Sophie leave?" he asked, unable to stop himself.

"I'd say that's her business, wouldn't you? You should ask her yourself. After you clean up, of course. And shave off that beard you're growing. You look like a grizzly."

He scrubbed his hand over his face, not wishing to tell her how much energy it took to simply get out of bed, forget shaving. "I'll grow a beard if I want to."

She rolled her eyes heavenward as she had in times past. "Glory! I see nothing is new with your mood. I'll leave you now, before I shriek so loud I scare the sheep."

When she disappeared, he exhaled in relief. She was as much a pain in his arse as his brother was becoming. Carrick grew angrier by the day, and like a pressure cooker, he was going to blow his top soon. Jamie scratched his beard. It itched, and it dripped water when it rained. He had planned to shave it until Sorcha had poked at him.

Then he stopped and rested his hand on his shovel. He *was* acting like an imbecile. He was evading his friends and the people who cared about him. He was also evading the one duty that hadn't been taken from him: starting the children's arts program at the center.

Of course, he didn't know if he could even continue with it given his current predicament. Wouldn't it bleed over? But maybe it was the first step in finding some clarity about his life. He could work behind the scenes to help, couldn't he? He decided to text Bets as opposed to calling her. That way he could be brief and to the point, no *how are you, Bets?* or *hasn't the weather been wet lately?*

Her response came immediately, and his knees went a little weak seeing it. *I was planning to call you after the school review. We have over a hundred children lined up for classes starting October 1. The media has been terrific for enrollment.*

He read the text again. One hundred students? He couldn't believe it! He started to write back *And the parents know I'm involved...* But he deleted it. If they'd asked for him to be removed, he didn't want to know. It would break him and the last shreds of his pride. He picked up his shovel and started digging again.

The next morning, when he arrived to help Carrick at the west pasture, he waved a hand to the rolling hills. "You moved the sheep without me?"

"You were in a snit, and so was I." He walked over and put his hand on Jamie's shoulder. "You know I love you. Even when you're digging your feet into the ground like you would a shovel. God knows, I've done the same. But, Jamie, I've never wanted to pound sense into you until now, and it tears at me to think about the trials you're facing. I just want you to know I love you, and Jesus, Mary, and Joseph, am I glad you shaved that beard off."

His mouth tipped up at that. He'd gone home after his call with Bets and summoned the energy to do that, at least. "Not a good look for me?"

"I was about ready to buy you the mug Angie showed me after all my blathering about it the other day. It said *Don't Hate Me Because I'm Beardiful.*"

He groaned at the pun, but his heart warmed from their interaction. If they could tease each other, they were back on solid ground. "I'm sorry I've been an arsehole and poor company."

"You put up with me and my bad moods aplenty when I had dark times," Carrick said, gripping his shoulder before letting his hand fall. "But I still think you're an eejit to be staying at our parents' when Sophie is sleeping at your home."

He bit the inside of his cheek to prevent himself from asking, but he couldn't refrain. Not this time. "Someone is with her?"

"Of course. We've got her, Jamie. She's still one of ours."

He had to turn away from his brother's knowing glance. "It's hard on me, being away from her. Knowing it has to be like this."

His brother snorted. "Don't start, or I'll forget my good mood and start wanting to bash you over the head again. Grab your shovel and let's get to work. Thanks for the help, by the way."

He glanced over as his brother broke earth. "It's not like I had anything else to do, and I appreciate the distraction." He was going to let Bets contact him for help. *After the school review...*

He hadn't heard an update from the Education Officer, and it grated at his skin like the barbwire fencing in front of him, the small slices deep and enduring.

A horn honked, and they looked over to see Kade Donovan's truck approaching. Carrick muttered something but kept digging. Jamie lifted his hand in a wave as Kade parked. He hadn't seen any of his friends in days, and he had to admit the sight of him eased his troubles.

"You're not riding your horse like usual," Jamie called out as their friend got out and walked toward them.

Kade lifted his hand, showing an envelope of sorts. When he arrived, he inclined his chin to Carrick, who grunted and speared the ground with his shovel.

"It was decided I was the best person to give this to you," Kade said, handing over the official-looking envelope. "Inside is a written complaint against the principal of our school, Margaret Doyle, regarding her improper use of power and authority regarding you and your teaching."

He blinked at Kade before turning to look at his brother. Carrick's calm demeanor suggested he'd known this was coming. "Let Kade tell you why you should do this in case it's not obvious to your thick skull," his brother said with a stern look.

Nodding, he watched as Kade slapped the envelope against his thigh, his tall form throwing a long shadow on the ground. "Everyone seems to think I might be even nicer than you, Jamie, and I one hundred percent think you should do this. What Principal Doyle did was wrong, and she needs to held accountable. For you as much as for the children and the school itself, and all served by it. File the report, Jamie."

He stared at the envelope. "All my life I've tried to make the peace, find another solution, or let things go."

"So have I, hoping to give a kind word and attention to change things, but you can't pony ride this problem into healing," Kade said, his brown eyes entreating. "This is about doing what's right and just, and what she's done—how she's used her power for her own agenda and opinions—is wrong."

Blowing out a long breath, he reached for the envelope. "Who's in favor of this?"

"Everyone close to you and the arts center," Carrick said, clapping him on the back. "Who do you think wrote it up? We're behind you, Jamie, but you have to do more than defend yourself. You have to try and hold the people who are assaulting you and your character responsible for their actions."

"There's no unringing this bell," Jamie said, feeling the

heavy stock paper with his fingertips, the weight of authority in it. "I could never work with her again."

Kade shifted his weight and regarded him. "Would you want to?"

Sophie's words echoed in his mind, about the yoke he'd put on his shoulders. Why did he think he needed to? What kind of twisted nobility was plaguing him?

"I know you don't want to hear it, but there are other teaching positions, Jamie, ones that could be happier." Carrick sighed heavily. "Angie came here because she lost a job she loved and look how that turned out. The truth is, if you aren't open to finding something better, you'll never have it, and that's not what any of us want for you. But you're the one who has to decide."

"Jamie," Kade said, putting a gentle hand on his shoulder, "none of us want to see you live out your days alone and miserable."

He knew that now. He *would* be alone and miserable in a way he'd never been before.

"I'd rather knock you on the head with this shovel," Carrick said half-jokingly as he picked it up.

He stared at the two men. They'd both faced tragedy and come through it well. He needed to find the courage to do the same. "I'll file the complaint."

"Good," Kade said with a smile, fishing into his pocket. "Here's a stamp. We had it addressed for you already."

He fixed the stamp on it with intention before saying, "So I see."

"I'll even drop it at the post for you in town," Kade said with a lopsided smile. "How's that for a friend?"

His throat grew tight. "Pretty fine, as they say."

"Now what are you going to do about Sophie being your soulmate?" Carrick asked, staring him down. "And you better have a sound answer this time because I can still use this shovel on your thick head."

He firmed his lips as emotion surged up inside him. "I need help with that too. To tell you the truth, I've hated every minute of being back in the quiet all by myself. And if this will help restore my reputation, I'll be glad and then some. I miss the warmth of her smile and the way we are together. Dammit, I don't want to live without her!"

"Of course you don't." Carrick put his arm around his shoulders. "You're not that thickheaded."

"Never," Kade agreed as they started walking.

"Where are we going?" he asked because Carrick's grip had purpose, like he was leading a sheep.

"We're headed into town, if you must know." Kade elbowed him gently in the side. "In fact, you can hold the envelope on the way. Don't take this wrong, Jamie, but I'm so glad you shaved your beard."

"That's what I told him!" Carrick said with a laugh.

"But how did you even see it?" Jamie touched his clean-shaven cheek.

"Your brother sent out photos to show how mired in the muck you've been," Kade said with a grimace. "Low tides, Jamie, but the sea always changes. Come ride in the truck with me. I imagine you and Carrick have had about enough of each other."

He shared a smile with his brother. "It's not been so bad."

"Speak for yourself," Carrick said with a laugh. "Go on. I'll be joining you shortly."

"Have fun," Kade called as they got into his truck.

Carrick lifted his middle finger in the air.

"What was that about?" he asked Kade as he handed him the envelope to post.

He started the car and took off. "You'll soon see, Jamie, me boy."

When they reached town, Kade made the turn toward the school. Jamie clutched the dashboard with one hand. "Ah...Kade."

"Have a little faith, Jamie."

When they turned into the parking lot, his senses leapt at the sight of rows of television trucks—even more so when he saw parents he recognized milling about with placards reading *Reinstate Jamie Fitzgerald* and *Mr. Fitzgerald for Teacher of the Year*. Another said *Jamie Deserves Better*.

He gripped his knees as he noted his friends standing at the front with the press and other people from the village. In the center of it all was Sophie. Her dark hair seemed almost haloed in the soft light of the sun. Their eyes met, and all he could feel was the heavy beating of his heart and his longing for her.

"It's a grand day for a protest with international press coverage, don't you think?" Kade said, reaching over and opening his car door. "Saints be praised, the other protesters have arrived on time."

Jamie heard the baying and thundering moments before he spotted Carrick herding sheep down the main road with Keegan O'Malley at his side. Some sheep had red words written on them. Keegan's, he knew. But the others had blue paint, and he recognized Carrick's prize sheep in the front, along with others he'd tended with his brother. *Justice* was sprayed on one, along with *Reinstate* and *Fairness*.

"But Carrick gave up the writing of words on his sheep," Jamie said, aghast.

"For Sorcha and for his new life with Angie," Kade said, nudging him out of the truck after unlocking his seat belt. "This is for you, Jamie."

The crowd started to applaud the moment he left the vehicle. The ground felt uncertain under his feet as he took his first steps.

"Jamie!" Eoghan called out, fairly dancing toward him on his old limbs. "Every parent in the school kept their children home today to protest Principal Doyle's treatment of you. Have you decided on filing a complaint against her?"

He realized the envelope was still tucked in his hand. "Yes, I will."

Eoghan exclaimed, "That's fine then! That's the right of it."

Kade took it from him and headed off. "I'm away to the post."

"Good," Eoghan called, putting his hand on Jamie and leading him forward.

People's faces swam in front of him as he walked to the front of the crowd with Eoghan. Cameras flashed and videoed his progress, but his attention was fixed on the woman in front of him. "You stay right here with this beautiful woman while I officially open this protest."

Beautiful she was, and he the eejit of the century. He brushed against Sophie, completely off-balance.

She only gave him a soft, encouraging smile. "It's good to see you, Jamie."

The urge to touch her rose up within him as the crowd continued to fade from his awareness. "And you, *mo chroí*. I've redefined thickheaded and martyrdom, I think."

"Your brother might have mentioned using a shovel on you," she said, a smile coming and going from her sweet face. "I'll admit to being tempted myself."

"Can we talk after?" he asked as Eoghan climbed onto a raised platform in front of them. "Or have I made a ruin of everything?"

Vulnerability shone in her green eyes at last. "Do you still love me and want to be with me?"

"With all my heart and for all my days," he answered as an air horn blasted.

Both he and Sophie winced at the sound, but she leaned in and said, "Then you've ruined nothing."

Relief poured through him like a waterfall, and he held out his hand. She took it without preamble, and with it joined them together again.

He turned as Eoghan took a megaphone from Donal. "We're here today to protest the unjust treatment of one of the finest teachers Caisleán has ever known. Jamie Fitzgerald."

Flushing as people burst into applause again, he waved at them to still their praise.

"Margaret Doyle!" Eoghan cried when the crowd went silent. "Come out and face us."

Jamie's nerves grew taut again. He hadn't seen her since the day she'd tried to ruin him. When she appeared in the doorway of the school, her face was as stiff and disapproving as ever, as if she'd been zipped up from the inside out.

"Say your piece, Eoghan O'Dwyer," she called back.

He bowed grandly. "The people behind me stand with Jamie Fitzgerald, both as a fine man and a wonderful teacher. Your charges against him are unjust and an abuse of your power. Your students' parents have made their wishes known by keeping their children out of school to protest these ridiculous charges and insist on them being dropped and Jamie reinstated immediately. And they'll keep their children out until you or the education authority accedes to those wishes."

She waved a hand of dismissal at them, her mouth tight.

"I also inform you that a complaint has been issued

against you for your abuse of authority," Eoghan continued, "and for not putting the welfare of this school or its students above your own agenda. The parents and town of Caisleán stand against you, and we will win."

Everyone sent up a cheer, and Eoghan turned around to the crowd. "Now hold up the signs from your children."

New placards were raised, and Jamie's throat grew thick as he read the signs. All were hand-drawn and some brightly decorated with rainbows and unicorns and sunshine and sayings like *I Love Mr. Fitzgerald; Mr. Fitzgerald for Best Teacher; Mr. Fitzgerald Always Helps.*

Eoghan again faced Margaret Doyle, who yanked on her wool jacket angrily. "Everyone agreed not to bring the children to the protest today because this squabble is among adults, and we don't wish to be sharing any pettiness or mean-spiritedness with the little ones. But these signs were made by the children when their parents asked them what they liked about Jamie Fitzgerald."

Sophie nudged Jamie, and he glanced over to see her holding a sign that said, *Mr. Fitzgerald Listens* decorated with bright yellow sunflowers.

Greta.

Someone patted him on the back, and he turned to see his mother. Tears were shining in her eyes as she patted his chest. "You remember this moment, for it's what the kids say that matters most."

He nodded, looking over his mother's shoulder to see his father gazing at him with pride.

The final webs of shame from Margaret Doyle's assault on him and his character seemed to fall away as he took everything in. The support of his friends, yes, his parents, and the town, but mostly it was the children's support for him that started healing his aching heart.

The smell of oranges flooded his senses as he turned to the crowd and did the only thing he knew to do. He greeted them like he did their children when they came to school every morning. He waved with a welcoming smile.

And in doing so, he started to feel that everything was going to be all right.

CHAPTER TWENTY-NINE

Only in Ireland could Sophie imagine a rainbow appearing at the end of a protest.

"The fairies have done their work today and then some," Eoghan said, doing a few steps of an Irish jig after coming down from the podium and setting aside his megaphone.

"The press is going to have the kind of pictures editors salivate over," Ghislaine said with relish. "Rainbows. Sheep. Handmade children's cards. We're going to make news around the world. Jamie, I have members of the press dying to meet you. Are you finally ready to set the record straight?"

When he nodded, Sophie thought about doing that jig herself. These last few days she'd swung between hope and misery, trusting that their love and that of his friends and those in the community would help him see reason. *Thank you, Sorcha.*

"The ground I'm standing on feels more solid now, as does myself," he said with that honesty she so loved about him. "I wish with all my heart none of this would have happened, but it has, and it's time to talk about it."

Donal clapped him on the back. "Then go with Ghislaine. You're in good hands."

"Will you be here when I finish?" he asked Sophie searchingly. "Or would it be possible for us to stand together while I do my speaking?"

She smiled as she realized he was finished trying to protect her from what he'd seen as his disgrace. "I'd say Ghislaine would love that."

The publicist twined her arm around Donal. "I really would. They say sex sells, but you know what else does? Love."

Yeah, she supposed it did. Ghislaine took Jamie on the rounds, guiding the conversation from the unjust accusations leveled against him to the censorship issue to his relationship with Sophie, which he told every reporter he'd been waiting for his whole life.

"Do I hear wedding bells in the future?" one of the reporters asked.

He turned to her, his mouth lifting, and gestured for her to answer. She made her brow rise but answered with a smile. "Don't you hear them now?"

From there, Ghislaine stepped in and whisked them away. "Always keep them wanting more. This wedding talk is going to make headlines. And the wedding itself! I can already see it."

"Ghislaine—"

"I'm just saying, Sophie," the woman said as they matched her brisk pace back toward their friends. "Of course, we'll have to coordinate dates since Donal and I are hearing wedding bells too."

She stopped short, her mouth dropping. "*What*? I mean I knew—"

Ghislaine cocked her hip and gave a wink. "You're not the only one with a matchmaking ghost helping you. Who do you think told me to drop everything I was doing and come to Ireland? Goodness, Sophie, you'd think after all these years that you'd know I'm a romantic at heart. The Provençal town where I was born was known for its helpful female ghost at the holy well."

Call her thunderstruck. "Really? Does my mother know this?"

She cocked her hip, grinning. "Not yet... I want to see the look on her face when I tell her."

"If it's anything like the look on Sophie's..." Jamie started laughing. "Sorcha is—"

"Yes, let's talk about Sorcha," Sophie said, turning to him and putting her hand on his chest. "Ghislaine, if you could give us a minute."

She kissed them both on the cheeks. "Of course. You two are done! Go. Make up. Sorcha wouldn't have it any other way."

Thank God was all Sophie could think as Ghislaine walked off. "It's a good thing Sorcha finally appeared to me and told me who to call for help. Eoghan has been a godsend, meeting with *every* parent and then some. But if you see Sorcha again, you might tell her to appear to the woman first next time—like she did with Ghislaine. We might have more sense than you men."

Sophie started to smell oranges and wondered if it was Sorcha's way of telling her she agreed.

He scratched the back of his head, fighting a smile. "I haven't proven I have much sense lately, that's for sure, but I love you with all my heart. And I hated being alone and in the quiet, meaning I was wrong about everything. So, if you want to go to Provence and live, I'll go. With an open mind and heart. Because Greta's happiness and yours is as important to me as the sun rising."

She wanted to melt when he said things like that. "Well, we have a new head of the Garda coming, which makes me feel better, and a little bee told me the vandals will soon be coming forward—"

His face blanched. "What? Who?"

"Sorcha," she said with emphasis as he nodded. "And while we may have protests from time to time, I think we can help Greta understand what they mean so she won't be scared of them. I mean, she loves what we did today for you —because no one should get in trouble for something they didn't do. Her words. I was also to give you this when I saw you."

Walking toward him, she kissed his cheek.

His mouth slid into a soft smile. "Give her this back for me when you see her," he said and kissed the delicate line of her brow. "Is she back?"

She pursed her lips. "No. We had her sign rushed here via post. I thought I would give it another day for things to change, although it's killing me to be away from her." She nudged him for effect.

"Hoping I would take an anti-eejit pill, were you?" he asked, his mouth curving.

"It was either that or the shovel," she said dryly. "How could you even *think* to let me go when a matchmaking Irish ghost told you I'm your soulmate?"

He grimaced heartily. "Refer to the eejit pill."

She uttered an uncharacteristic growling sound as she thought about all he'd been willing to give up because of some old-fashioned sense of nobility and sacrifice. "Don't do it again."

He took her hands in his, looking her straight in the eye. "The promise I would give you now is as important as any, and I make it with all my heart. You have my word, *mo chroí*."

Trust bloomed within her, knowing he was a man who honored his promises. "Good!" She touched his chest again, this time with more tenderness. "Now tell me how you really feel after today. Shaving the beard gave me hope."

He winced. "You too, huh? Well, I don't truly know how things will go with the complaint against me, but I am more hopeful today than I've been. And with my complaint against Principal Doyle in the works, I figure there's a strong chance of a new head of the school being appointed. I can't imagine she would be effective after all the parents stood against her. And she has no family to keep her here."

"Eoghan was determined it had to be every single parent, Jamie." She got tears just thinking about how hard he'd worked to make it happen. "He even arranged for the children to be taken care of and called people's bosses to make sure they'd be let off work. He was incredible. Ghislaine said she had trouble keeping up with him."

He glanced away, and Sophie thought he was likely looking for Eoghan, whom Ghislaine had corralled to talk to the press. What an ambassador he was for the center. And to think, he would soon be Ghislaine's father-in-law!

"I owe Eoghan a debt," Jamie said after swallowing thickly. "I owe so many in the village. I'll be buying pints for the rest of my life and quite happily."

She leaned in and finally hugged him. "We both will. Jamie, I couldn't have done this without them. Seeing this kind of support has made me fall even harder for this town. Warts and all."

He caressed her nape. "Me as well. Sophie, I told Bets that I'd like to begin readying for the start of the children's arts program in October."

He scanned the crowd for her. She was among his friends, talking with her hands as Linc smiled winningly beside her. Brady caught his eye and waved dramatically in his direction, miming drinking a whiskey. When Jamie gave him a thumbs-up, Ellie let out a cheer. The pub would be filled to the brim soon, and he couldn't wait to be among them. They had stood for him. And he would remember it all his life.

"Bets says we have so much interest in the children's summer program that we need a whole new strategy," Sophie told him. "She stopped enrollment at two hundred kids—"

"Two hundred!"

"And that doesn't include the adult inquiries." She laughed. "People from around the world want to come to Ireland to learn to paint and draw and all the rest. Some with their children. Jamie, it's incredible."

"We'll need more teachers—"

"And mobile homes," she said with a laugh. "Linc is thinking we might become a premier children's program in a few years if we manage to find the right teachers and physical infrastructure. Your mother has offered to teach, by the way, and is talking to other retired teachers about helping out this summer."

He gave a soft smile. "That does my heart happy. Goodness, we're going to need a bigger shed."

Ireland and their sheds! "Linc is now contemplating having another world-renowned architect design a state-of-the-art school specifically for children. But that's going to take time."

"We have a lot of building ahead," he mused as she took his arm and led him to the corner of the parking lot for more privacy.

They were close to finishing their business talk. Now she planned to do what Ghislaine had said and make up. She twined her arms around his neck as they stopped under a towering sycamore tree. He drew her closer, sighing with her as they felt the homecoming of each other's touch.

"We *do* have a lot of building. Ours. I missed you, Jamie."

He ran his hands up her sides longingly. "And I missed you every moment. With all my heart. I'm sorry I hurt you."

She felt the catch of pain in her throat. He had, but he hadn't meant to, and that made it easier to forgive. "I believe we've covered that. I was trying to steer us toward a reconciliation."

"I thought we'd already— Oh, for the love of— Ah... How much reconciliation do you have in your mind, *mo chroí*?"

He was looking over her shoulder, wincing. When she tried to turn around to see why, he held her firm. "Jamie! What—"

"Were you truly hearing wedding bells earlier, or do you need more time to be knowing the way of things between us?"

His words held an urgency she didn't understand. "With a matchmaking ghost behind us and the love I have in my heart, I'm pretty sure about us."

"One hundred percent sure?" he pressed. "I need an answer now, *mo chroí*."

"Jamie, for heaven's sake, yes, I'm one hundred percent sure."

His breath came out with fervor, and then he kissed her softly but swiftly on the lips. "Then stay here, I beg you, and don't turn around until I tell you."

She narrowed her eyes. "What—"

"Your promise, Sophie."

He waited for her to nod, then kissed her again and left. Behind her, there was a flurry of whispered conversation she couldn't make out and then the tick-tick-tick of something on the pavement.

"You can turn around, *mo chroí*," he called out right as she heard the baying of a sheep.

Spinning around, she pressed her hand to her mouth as wonder and joy swelled within her. Jamie held a rope with four sheep tied together, and with the words painted on them, they asked a simple question.

Will you marry me?

He gestured to Keegan, who was standing off to the right, grinning as if he'd just shot a cow—or sheep—to the moon.

"Keegan says Sorcha told him to do this," Jamie began, "so I can't be taking credit for it. But since you're one hundred percent certain, I'll be asking the question, since I can't have you marrying sheep. In all my days, I never imagined sheep would play a part in my proposal. She's laughing for sure, Sorcha is."

Right then, Sophie could have sworn she heard a trill of female laughter, but she couldn't take her eyes from Jamie to look around for the ghost.

He walked over slowly, leading the sheep until he was standing in front of her. Then he sank onto one knee. The sheep in the front position took this as an opportunity to nuzzle his face, which he deftly tried to avoid by putting his arm around her neck. Then he lifted his gaze to Sophie's, love brightening his cobalt eyes.

"Sophie, my one and only love, will you marry me?"

The sheep bayed and nudged him. "Her, not you," Jamie said, trying not to laugh.

She edged a little closer and then, because she could see the scene in her mind so clearly, she called out to Keegan, "Do you have a sheep with *Yes* on it?"

He pumped the air with a sturdy fist. "Yes! I'll be just a moment."

"Oh, don't be encouraging him," Jamie said with a groan. "He might not even have brought a sheep with the word *Yes* on it. We could be waiting another half hour before he arranges it."

She started to laugh. That was okay to her. They had all the time in the world.

As Keegan darted across the parking lot, he shouted something to the crowd. The cheers started. The whistles sounded. Everyone remaining started to thunderously clap.

Ghislaine hustled to choreograph the remaining reporters closer to the action, which had the sheep growing restless. Jamie held on to two of them, muttering under his breath, trying to keep them from bolting.

That had Sophie laughing harder. In all her life... "Jamie, I believe our engagement is going to make the papers."

He rolled his eyes dramatically. "I'll never understand people's love for sheep. The only people who love them are the ones who don't tend them."

She approached carefully, holding out her hand to the sheep while she helped him to his feet. "I still might want a few of them. Especially now that they will always remind me of you proposing to me."

"I should have taken you to the Eiffel Tower or something." He shook his head. "I'm glad you don't mind it, I suppose. It's part of my life and this community. So I suppose that means you take all of me then?"

She spotted Keegan running with the appropriate sheep sprayed with YES, the animal baying loudly at the urgency of its owner's pace. "I believe my answer is on its way."

He looked back again and laughed with her. "I don't plan on waiting for a sheep to seal it so I can kiss you."

Taking his head with a hand, she pulled him down until he was an inch from her lips and whispered, "Neither do I," as their friends started cheering once again.

CHAPTER THIRTY

Linc wished he could say all's well that ends well as he regarded his friends and fellow townspeople drinking to celebrate the dismissal of the complaint against Jamie Fitzgerald. Not even the joint announcement from the education authority, which had terminated Principal Doyle for an abuse of her authority, could totally cheer him.

Maybe he was getting old but having to fight ignorance and cruelty was a real pain in the balls. Why couldn't some people just get a life and live and let live?

"You're down in the mouth tonight," Bets said, kissing him on said mouth, which made him tug her onto his lap. "As you just told me recently, we need to celebrate our victories."

He kissed her soundly, knowing she was right. But he just couldn't dismiss the uneasiness in his gut. He'd had it before and knew better than to assign it to indigestion. They were still waiting to hear whether the vandals would be caught, although Sophie had shared what Sorcha had told her. Still, he hated being on Malcolm Coveney's clock, knowing it was his decision to make.

"All right, I'll put on my party face and mingle."

She made a little turn in his lap and sent him a flirtatious smile. "I believe we might need the Lucky Charms and company to add to the festivities."

"You do that," he drawled as he watched her saunter off happier than she'd been in weeks. That, at least, was a grace.

When he stood, Donal waved to him from across the room, then tucked his cell phone in his pocket. "I just heard from our new head of the Garda."

"About damn time," he said as they carved out some space in a corner for privacy.

"Yes, the proverbial scapegoats have been served up nice and fine on a platter," Donal nearly spat. "The station received an anonymous tip about three teenage dropouts from Castlebar bragging about being the ones who'd vandalized the house of the female artist who'd made the papers."

Imagine bragging about such a thing. "Innocent little lambs until now?"

He nodded. "First offense, as we expected. They were paid forty euros apiece plus gas money by a man outside the local Centra. They didn't know him. And the camera at the store didn't catch his face when officers investigated. He gave them money and an address along with a spray can and strict instructions about what to paint. He also told them to get away fast. The kids found it daring, it being another boring night around town."

"Jesus." He rubbed his forehead. "Did they charge them?"

"They were fined a fixed charge of €140." Donal swore in Gaelic. "The entry-level rate, if you want to think of it that way. I was told they also got a stern talking to and threatened with a nightly curfew. The incident went into their files, but with their age and all, they said it wasn't worth prosecuting them."

"Like we thought." Linc's jaw locked with tension. "Funny how I don't feel better."

Donal put his meaty hand on his shoulder. "Look at this the Irish way. The fact that Malcolm felt he had to dole out some scapegoats shows he believes our strength is increasing. We can pass the word around tomorrow, as tonight is Jamie's night."

But would others view it as a victory? "I still don't feel like dancing, and I've never once wanted to eat goat, scape or regular."

"Then have a drink and be Irish," Donal told him as he signaled to Brady for two whiskeys. "There's nothing we can do tonight—"

"So enjoy myself among friends," Linc finished for him. "I'm still in the kindergarten class on that Irish lesson."

"You're doing just fine." The whiskeys finally reached them with Brady having them passed through the crowd. "So am I, in fact, seeing as I'm spending my every day with my soulmate. *Sláinte!*"

"*Sláinte.*" He picked up his whiskey and knocked it back, going with the opening Donal had given him. "I heard wedding bells might be in the offing."

His friend gestured heavenward. "She's a downright miracle, my Ghislaine. And I have Sorcha to thank for it."

Linc smiled. He'd heard about the ghost appearing to the publicist. "And here I thought it was Brigitte's mother who put in a good word for us." Although he still planned to thank her when she finally visited Caisleán. They were waiting for things to die down. God love her, but Brigitte didn't know how not to cause a sensation, although Sophie said their relationship had never been stronger.

Donal gave a gusty laugh. "Sorcha's involvement makes for a better story, and I plan to share it with my daughters when they meet Ghislaine next week. I've never been happier, and I say that with thanks for everything that's happened in my life, if you understand my meaning."

They shared a look. He damn well knew what Donal meant. "I feel the same. All our steps led up to where we stand now. Let's toast to our soulmates and to Sorcha for her help. That ghost sure does get around."

He wished he could clone her and put her on a track other than matchmaking. Think of all they could accomplish.

The whiskey helped, as did talk with friends, but then again, the Irish knew their business in those realms. Eoghan suggested he and Sandrine might have a double wedding with Donal and Ghislaine, and Linc bandied back that they might consider having one of Keegan's sheep officiate, which had the older man braying with laughter.

By the time he reached Sophie and Jamie, he was in better spirits. Those two had been taken to the woodshed but were coming out of it stronger. He spied the simple engagement ring on Sophie's finger and smiled at Greta, who was sitting on Jamie's lap. She straightened as soon as she saw him and leapt off to give him a hug. It made his heart happy to be greeted so, and he swung her up into his arms.

"I'd hoped I would see you tonight, Greta," he said, setting her on his hip. "Welcome back from Provence. Why didn't you bring the sun with you?"

Her brow wrinkled. "It's still in the sky even if you can't see it, but it *is* really cold here, isn't it?"

He made a shiver for show, which had her smiling

brightly. "I hear you're the person to talk to about a wedding present for your mom and Jamie."

"You don't need to get us anything," Sophie protested, looking about as happy as he'd ever seen her.

"A good friend is enough of a gift," Jamie said, proving what a stand-up guy he was.

He waved his hand at them. "Y'all are funny. Excuse us a minute. I need to confer with this little one."

When he reached a fairly open corner of the packed bar, he whispered, "How do you feel about some sheep joining your family? I thought I'd buy one for each of you and put your names on them. Carrick has agreed to keep them in his pasture, and you can visit them anytime. What do you think, Greta?"

She clapped her hands in delight. "Oh, that would be wonderful. But we need a friend for January too."

He narrowed his eyes. "Who?"

"My pet sheep." She had a pretty grave expression for a little tyke. "She needs a boy sheep for a friend so they can be a couple too."

He laughed. Little minds. "What about you, Greta? Don't you need a boy?"

That had her giggling. "No! I'm not old enough yet."

"Good thinking. Stay young. In fact, never grow up."

He deposited her back with her mother, her innocence lingering with him. *Never grow up*, he thought. Yeah, he *was* getting old. Still, he made his way over to his baby girl and put his arm around Ellie since Bets was off in the corner with her Lucky Charms, likely conspiring about the music. He didn't have to wait long. Bon Jovi's "Livin' on a Prayer" came on and silenced the bar.

Sophie jumped up immediately. "I love this part! Greta, come dance with Mama."

He nudged Donal in the ribs as Bets snagged Ghislaine by the arm and led her to the front of the bar. "Looks like your woman is being invited to dance with the Lucky Charms. Isn't that wonderful?"

He sat down and kicked back in his chair as Linc did the same. "It's grand, it is, and Ghislaine is going to make a show of it."

That woman had panache, that was for sure. "How are you two going to fix the living situation with her career?"

"She's thinking about assigning a deputy in the Paris office. Like she has in New York. Cutting down on her duties."

"So retiring," Linc summated.

"Yes, but she detests the word so don't use it," Donal said as they watched a very G-rated version of the dance begin.

"Can't talk her into being our full-time media director then, huh?" God knows they needed it with all the requests and queries coming in.

Donal shook his head. "Not a chance. You need someone younger, but it's important they also know and like art."

"I have a few candidates in mind," Linc said, thinking of Sophie's friend, Taylor McGowan. "We have a lot of hiring to do and in a short time. Plus, the building—"

"Time enough for that tomorrow, remember?" Donal slapped him on the back.

"Right. No troubles while drinking whiskey."

His friend met his eyes. "Exactly so."

So he lifted his drink and sipped it, knowing Bets was driving them home. But he still couldn't dismiss the unsettling feeling in his gut.

When Ghislaine returned to Donal and convinced him

to dance with her, Linc decided to give himself some air. It was hot as blazes anyway, and he was sweating a touch under his shirt.

The parking lot was empty of smokers, and he tipped his head up to the sky. My, how he loved the stars in Ireland. Why did no one put that in the tourist brochures? It had one of the best shows out there.

"Hello, Linc."

He jumped and let out a yelp. Sighting Sorcha, he released a relieved breath. "Good heavens, girl, you scared the bejesus out of me."

She chuckled. "I admit, it does amuse me. You seem to need something to lift your mood tonight. I thought I might give you a nudge in the right direction. Seeing as it suits my purpose and interests."

He pursed his lips. "That being?"

"Matchmaking, of course." Her white dress fluttered around her despite the lack of wind. "You're right. The new media director position should go to Taylor."

Now she had his attention. "How did you— Never mind. Stupid question. I'll talk to Bets and the board and make the offer."

"Thank you," she said with a cheeky curtsy. "As for the feeling in your gut, I'm sorry to say, you'll understand the way of it soon enough."

That stopped him cold. "What—"

"Go inside and be among friends, Linc," she said, her face falling. "These are the moments that make everything worth it."

With that, she disappeared. He rubbed the bridge of his nose. His feeling was confirmed. They were going to get another walloping. Sighing heavily, he drew himself up straight and headed back inside.

When he found Bets in the crush of people, she was still flushed from dancing. He put his arms around her and kissed the side of her neck.

"Everything all right, cowboy?"

There was so much to tell her, but he'd do it later, after their own celebration. "Well, we have the name of our new media director in hand. From Sorcha, no less."

Her brows shot to her hairline. "Sorcha! Who—"

"Taylor," he told her and watched as she glanced over her shoulder, a soft smile forming on her mouth.

"*Oh, my,*" she whispered, touching her lips with trembling fingers. "Oh, my, my..."

He leaned closer and followed her gaze. Liam was laughing in the corner at something Kathleen had said. Then he got it. *"Well, I'll be."*

"He's the last one," she whispered and then turned to face him with that beatific mother's smile that had inspired all the Old Masters to paint.

After that, he tried to keep up with Bets. She hugged everyone, practically dancing on air. You'd have thought she'd won the lottery. Then again, maybe to her mind she had. He knew how much she loved Liam, and to know he would soon be with his soulmate... Sorcha's track record was impressive. She never failed.

As he gazed at Liam, the younger man lifted his head and their eyes met. *Your whole life is about to change, son.* Then Liam smiled with just a slight curve of his mouth, and Linc thought, *Aw, shucks, he knows*. The kid wasn't called Yoda for nothing.

Shaking his head, he realized he was no different. He had that feeling, didn't he? Soon he would know what it meant. But Bets needed her night, and he loved seeing her so carefree. So he didn't suggest they slip out a little earlier than the young people. No, they were one of the last couples out of the Brazen Donkey with Brady as he locked up.

As they drove home, his gut seemed to clench all the harder. He looked over to make sure Bets was tucked into her seat belt and her eyes were fixed on the road.

"Drive slow, will you, sugar?"

She glanced over. "I'm not speeding—"

"Just take extra care," he said, all his senses going haywire now.

They were getting closer to it. He could feel it.

When they reached their gate—the one he'd had installed after the event with Sophie—he spotted something resting against it as she clicked it open. "Hang on a sec, Bets."

He jumped out of the car and approached the box slowly. He should probably call their security officer, but by God, he'd be damned if he would wait a moment longer. The slender turquoise box was wrapped in a purple bow. He tore it off and flipped open the top. Inside was an unmistakable dead rose. The varietal that Mary Kincaid had beaten Bets with in the last competition both had participated in. Black Magic.

His stomach clutched.

Then he spotted the card resting under it. Opening it, he turned it toward the light.

Congratulations on your recent victories. Malcolm Coveney and friends

"What is it?" Bets asked, getting out of the car.

"We had a caller," he said, closing the note inside the box with the dead rose for his security officer to see, maybe even the new Garda officer.

"Who?"

"An old friend." He was sure his smile was terrifying with the headlights trained on him. "It seems Malcolm Coveney and Mary Kincaid aren't through with us yet."

She cursed softly.

He did the same. In Gaelic.

The next assault was on its way.

CHAPTER THIRTY-ONE

Ireland!

Taylor stared at the formal offer that had come by special courier.

The Sorcha Fitzgerald Arts Center would like to offer you the position of media director...

She still couldn't take it in. The salary. The benefits. The scope of the position. She'd also be consulting with Ghislaine Monet, one of the biggest and most powerful publicists in the world.

She'd been looking for something new, feeling stuck in her life. Even her own secret way of painting—not like her art teachers had taught her—didn't seem quite enough. She had the burning desire to say and do something truly important. To make a real difference. This was her ticket, given the problems the arts center had faced. Sophie had been encouraged after their recent victories, but she said no one thought they were out of the woods yet. To be a part of that? Well, it was tailor made, she thought, and then laughed at her own pun.

She glanced around her tiny New York apartment.

Man, she wasn't going to miss it. Not one bit. Sure, it had a nice view of the park from its two windows, but she could pretty much brush her teeth and sit on her bed at the same time.

She eyed the letter again. Sophie must have put them up to hiring her. Being selected on her own merit was important to her. Should she ask?

"I wouldn't if I were you."

She screamed. Someone was in her apartment! She dove for her bread knife on the kitchen counter and spun around with it in hand. Only to see a gorgeous brunette in a long white dress standing in front of her gas stove.

"I'm not here to hurt you, Taylor," the woman said gently. "I'm here to help. My name is Sorcha Fitzgerald."

The name struck her mind. *Holy—*

"Sorcha Fitzgerald is dead."

The woman only shrugged and gave a jaunty smile. "Yes, but don't I still look incredible?"

Stars swam in front of her eyes.

"Oh, no, not another fainter," she heard as her knees started to give.

The pungent smell of oranges assaulted her nose. She started coughing.

"I thought the smell might keep you from fainting. Why don't you put the knife down? I'm here on your friend Sophie's advice."

That had her knees going weak again. "This. Isn't. Happening."

"You don't have to speak so slowly. I'm Irish. I understand English quite well. And this *is* happening, so lock your knees and listen to me."

The slap of that command and the assault on her nose had her stiffening her shoulders.

"Good." The woman gave a satisfied smile. "Now... Sophie thought I should change my *modus operandi*, as they say. You see, Taylor, you need to take the job in Caisleán for reasons other than the position itself, although it will serve you quite nicely professionally and personally."

She stared at the woman, a chill breaking out over her arms. "What reason is that?"

Another slow smile broke out over her oval face. "Your soulmate is waiting for you there. You remember him? Sophie sent you a photo after you asked. The one with the green eyes you thought looked like a hot pirate."

His face swam before her eyes, her heart pounding again at the mere thought of him.

She fainted dead away.

Every time you leave a kind review, a rainbow appears in the sky.

Leave a review for Over Verdant Irish Hills and get ready for a splash of color!

More Liam? Yes please! Get Against Ebony Irish Seas, the next Unexpected Prince Charming story!

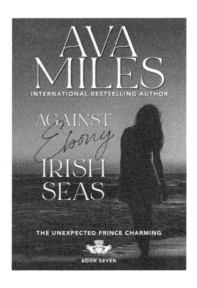

A mystical story about secrets, redemption, and the power of love.

"One word for Ava Miles is WOW."

MY BOOK CRAVINGS

Get Against Ebony Irish Seas!

Available wherever books are sold.

ABOUT THE AUTHOR

Millions of readers have discovered International Bestselling Author Ava Miles and her powerful fiction and non-fiction books about love, happiness, and transformation. Her novels have received praise and accolades from *USA Today, Publisher's Weekly,* and *Women's World Magazine* in addition to being chosen as Best Books of the Year and Top Editor's picks. Translated into multiple languages, Ava's strongest praise comes directly from her readers, who call her books and characters unforgettable.

Visit Ava on social media:

- facebook.com/AuthorAvaMiles
- twitter.com/authoravamiles
- instagram.com/avamiles
- bookbub.com/authors/ava-miles
- pinterest.com/authoravamiles

DON'T FORGET...
SIGN UP FOR AVA'S NEWSLETTER.

More great books? Check.
Fun facts? Check.
Recipes? Check.
General frivolity? DOUBLE CHECK.

https://avamiles.com/newsletter/

Made in the USA
Las Vegas, NV
17 May 2023